Halo

Around the Moon

by
David S. Jones

A CIP catalogue record for this title is available from the British Library.

ISBN 9798620542376

www.david-s-jones.com

I am delighted that you have taken possession of a copy of my novel. It is my greatest desire that you will enjoy the story. This work can be described as a book full of facts into which is woven a fabric of fiction or alternatively a work of fiction that is studded with fact. It is for you to decide which is which. As a novelist, and adult fiction writer, I am intrigued by the possibilities of parallel worlds. Universes, running alongside or in tandem with our own, sharing the same or comparable characters and locations, but with marginally different and distorted events and consequences, which I assume is the fundamental framework for fiction.

Consider `Halo around the Moon/The End of the Ice Age' as a chronicle of an eighteen month period in just such a parallel society. The barrier between our world and the world that I have described may be, just a thin veil and events that I have depicted could easily transcend that veneer and breach the barrier.

My heartfelt hope is that by publishing this work it might cause society to take stock of my predictions and take time to stop this lemming like race to the edge of the abyss.

David S. Jones.

Contents

Acknowledgments

My sincere thanks to Lena Strang for her support and tireless editing. She has tidied up so much of the punctuation mess that I am guilty of leaving when writing. The analogy that comes to mind is that I am a chef who creates a meal and then ducks out of the washing up. She believed in my work, which was a great comfort to me when I had come close to giving up. I am eternally grateful to her.

P.D. Cain (Front cover illustrator, editing, read through and critique) Major Paul Stretton, (Ret) Blues and Royals (technical information). David and Yvonne Whyte (critique). Candice Jones (read through and critique).

Ian Hutchinson Army Air Corp, REME Nuclear Industry (Technical support and continuity).

Ian Thompson, ex Guards Independent Parachute Company, Royal Horse Guards. (Read through and critique).

David Bradley ex Royal Horse Guards (Historical advice).

Susan Morgan-Williams (read through, edit and critique).

"Walk with care upon this earth, for we are no more than temporary privileged tenants."

Matthew 5:5
"Blessed are the meek, for they will inherit the earth."

This is a book with no happy ending; we have yet to write the final chapter. The choice is ours. Think long and hard about what you are about to read. Dear reader, this is a book about you!

Main Story Line

April 2012. The threatened tanker strike drove the population of Britain into a frenzied panic to buy fuel. This highlights something that has been upper- most in my thoughts and in the minds of many others for some years. The dependency on fossil fuels is a disaster of unimaginable proportions, poised and waiting to happen. The tanker drivers' strikes of the last decade pretty much brought the country to its knees within days, and if they had gone on for much longer would have had catastrophic results. Tanker drivers are in reality very small cogs in the overall story of extracting crude oil from the earth to pumping combustibles into our vehicles. We live our lives utterly dependent on a liquid that is invisible to us, hidden within tanks, pipes and hoses that has the magical ability to give life to the engines of our vehicles. Internal Combustion Engine (ICE) dependency must end.

Wheels are spun and deeds are done, and those at the top of the food chain are the only real beneficiaries in this scenario. The great egocentric public are blinkered and see only the carrot being dangled in front of their noses. The riots of 2010 demonstrate the tinderbox volatility of the country.

The catastrophe that I am portraying here will have no beneficiaries once the country has gone into an unstoppable free fall. I am looking at this scenario from a general standpoint centred in England and the consequences involving a specific group of people, but this disaster would reverberate through the world. Are we too blind to see that there are alternatives? It doesn't have to be this way. We just have to pull back the curtains of greed and see the future.

The ICE age of dominance destroyed: Armageddon initiated.

Armageddon (Bible)

The final battle at the end of the world between the forces of good and evil, God against the kings of the earth.

(Revelation 16:16)

Chapter 1

Cassie Richards

Armageddon - 30 days before

When her school contemporaries were spending their teenage years discovering alcohol, sex and the other forbidden delights of growing up in middle England, Cassie Richards was busy studying. Her mantra was that there would be plenty of time for the pursuit of pleasure when her exams were completed and out of the way. Cassie's one goal in life from the age of eight was to be a scientist; nothing else mattered.

There were so many disadvantages in choosing the elected path that Cassie had decided was to be her future. 'Nerd' was a label assigned to her from an early age, which initially hurt and was painful. Many times she considered throwing in the towel and opting for the easy route, coasting through schooling, waiting to see what happened when the time came to take up a career. Then randomly she would watch a TV programme or read a newspaper article with a scientific essence and she became hooked again. A white laboratory coat was not the most glamorous fashion statement, but to Cassie it was all she ever wanted.

Now, here she was, at the age of twenty-five, with a fine degree under her belt, holding down her dream position – a prime job in the biotechnology industry. Her specialty was synthetics.

So, how could it possibly be that after only a year in the post, Cassie, was less than elated with the work that she was doing? Sure, she was part of a cutting edge team investigating the bio-fuel industry. Cassie's lofty teenage dreams of becoming a well-respected scientist, perhaps discovering a breakthrough formula and achieving world status, had not diminished at all, even though her current expectations had been somewhat eroded by the reality of the repetitious nature of everyday scientific

1

research. Something that she had not made allowances for in her dreams.

There was no doubt that it was really interesting work, which could have a huge impact on the petrochemical industry's grip on just about all of the worldwide economies. The team, to which she had been assigned, was dedicated to the research and development of what was considered the critical and somewhat elusive element that gives petrol its explosive capacity. The chemical breakdown of the ingredients of combustible fuels derived from crude oil was well known. They were themselves the product of rotted compressed animal and vegetable matter, laid down millions of years ago and were finite. One ambiguous calculation, by 'Friends of the Earth', stated that a trillion barrels of oil had been extracted from the ground, and estimating that there was something in the region of only one billion barrels left. Replicating this fuel source economically was well within the grasp of today's scientists and biochemists, but the illusive element, which was the specific extra explosive characteristic of petroleum-based fuels under compression, had always been just out of reach.

The newly created bio-fuel was significantly different from petroleum, being the result of an actual living element created by the fermentation and distillation of plants and other organic components. Various base elements could be used, soya beans, sugar cane, corn and even grapes, with varying success, but all this biologically created fuel lacked the vital extra explosive punch inherent in natural oil based fuels. These elements that were the basic ingredients of bio-fuel were considered fundamentally unlimited, in contrast to the finite resource of natural oil.

Infinite they might well be, but the damaging effect that their intense production would impact in other directions, such as deforestation and the utilisation of land, traditionally used to produce food for the ever- increasing world population, would no doubt be harmful to humanity in the long term.

Cassie considered herself environmentally aware. She had examined the argument that there was a looming global population problem and the research that she was involved in could essentially undermine the ever-increasing need for food production. She understood the argument, which reasoned that the planet was moving through a period where food production would not be adequate to feed the ever-burgeoning population. Growing crops for bio-fuels in many instances required utilising land traditionally used for food production, would only intensify the problem. She struggled with this conflict of interests.

As the newest member of the team, Cassie was naturally given the more mundane tasks to perform. This meant hours of cross matching samples, number crunching and a great deal of basic science, which she certainly thought belonged in her past. She was the latest member of a team that had spent several years of scientific research and development in the intensively competitive field of biotechnology. The race to perfect a fuel, which could be retailed through the existing petroleum outlets, was awash with venomous rivalry due to the colossal rewards that would be procured by the first successful company to get their product 'to the pumps'.

Cassie's Company had succeeded in the refinement and production of a synthetic bio-fuel, which could be used to run an internal combustion engine. It worked very well, but frustratingly, lacked the vital extra kick, the explosive punch element inherent in petrol. Decades of experimentation had produced many bio-fuel variants, but they all lacked the volatile component, which the scientists named EA#100 (Explosive Ability).

One of the numerous avenues that had been explored had quite innocently and by chance resulted in the creation of a bio active element, which when added to standard petrol and diesel, bizarrely had the ability to eliminate the elusive, EA#100. Despite this unexpected innovation that the lab had stumbled upon that was exactly the opposite of what the scientists were attempting to achieve, which on occasions was what could happen in experiments of this nature, it was considered that this discovery was nonetheless wholly significant. The element received the name, Combustible Eradication Virus #1 (CEV#1). This was an interesting, unexpected and an exciting innovation. Furthermore, it was reasoned that if this bio enzyme was capable of removing the elusive EA#100, then by subjecting the element to intense reverse bio engineering, manipulation and refinement, thereby isolating its properties, it appeared logically possible that the functions of the element could be inverted and the vital factor could be added rather than subtracted. It was often the case in scientific research that a lateral path could lead to the solution of a problem. Therefore, research into the properties of CEV#1 was sustained.

The two major capabilities of CEV#1, were individually, quite remarkable. The ability to instantly eradicate the flammable capability of petroleum-based fuels after an incubation period was astounding, but in reality, it had little use in the industrial world. There might be some applications within the fire-fighting industry or it might find a use as a fire retardant in fabrics, but it was not the Golden Fleece they were seeking and was not going to earn its discovering bio chemical company, any fortunes. The second property of CEV#1 held a far greater potential. It had the remarkable ability to replicate itself at phenomenal, previously un-encountered speeds and keep on replicating until it filled one hundred per cent of whatever container it might be introduced into, at a far higher rate and speed than any other substance known to man. It was, in fact, a super virus. This was an ability, which did hold enormous promise. What had been overlooked, however, was that CEV#1, in its natural state, appeared benign. But, once added to a fossil fuel, it entered into an incubation period of eight hours during which time the mutation took place. This transformation resulted in a cancerous like super virus.

If this replication ability could be separated from the fire retardant capability, then the uses of CEV#1 could be colossal, as its application potentials were legion.

One solution that all biochemical companies pursued and coveted greatly was the complete extermination of Malaria. This is a disease that is responsible for the death of more human beings throughout the history of mankind than anything else is. The mosquito carries several deadly viral diseases; Malaria, Dengue Fever and Yellow Fever are the most dangerous for humans. Mosquitoes cause more human suffering than any other organism. Over one million people worldwide die from mosquito-borne diseases every year. Killing the mosquito at its waterborne larvae stage was the key, but getting the medium, which has existed in many forms for years and could kill the mosquito larvae in remote locations, was an ostensibly unsolvable problem. If the phenomenal replication ability of CEV#1 could be harnessed as the delivery accelerant and the petroleum nullifying capability could be replaced with a mosquito larvae-eliminating agent, then all rivers, lakes, ponds and streams where the mosquito larvae developed, could be treated with little effort, conceivably from the air. Any scientist working on the team that could rid the planet of the terrible disease would be high in the running for a Nobel Prize and the biotech company that refined and developed it, would reap colossal financial benefits.

The problem that eluded the scientists was discovering how to separate the two independent abilities of CEV#1. As a virus, each molecule had the ability to divide one hundred times in less than a micro or millisecond and create copies of itself at a microscopic level. These one hundred new virus copies then subdivided, again and again, in perpetuity. The super expansion rate of CEV#1 was something, which previously, had been considered unthinkable.

Cassie's Company had made a monumental discovery, but at this stage in development, its lack of an obvious use for it in industry was frustrating and more to the point was generating zero income for them.

Thinly veiled threats and rumours were circulating from the company's senior management, through all levels of employment, that funding could be pulled and redundancies would automatically follow, if a breakthrough was not on the horizon.

Cassie had joined the team late in this endeavour and was given the task of further exploring this phenomenon, which was pretty much considered to have reached a scientific brick wall by that time.

The basic specifics were: CEV#1 consumed EA#100, making it inert. It then continued expanding, consuming all it could find until there was no more explosive capability, resulting in a passive liquid with no flammable properties. Then, after some weeks, with nothing to feed on, CEV#1 became dormant. The tiniest amount

4

of CEV#1 dropped into any sized container of petroleum-based fuel would replicate exponentially and remove 100% of the capability of E A #100.

The incubation period also posed a problem of its own. For the ability of CEV#1 to have a potential future in the fire retardant industry, there could be no incubation period. CEV#1 was subjected to much genetic modification over a period of months. Eventually the incubation period was removed, but only temporarily for a period of one hour, after which it returned to eight hours, altering the basic structure of this remarkable substance was proving to be phenomenally difficult. The new second version required a revision of c l a s s i f i c a t i o n . The original virus with the eight hour incubation period became CEV#1A and the revised incubation version became CEV#1B.

Although working on both versions, CEV#1A and CEV#1B, for Cassie, they each held enormous potential. But, she came to resent the pointless tasks that she had been allotted. Far more experienced biochemists had explored all of the possibilities and given up. What did they expect her to discover? Endless testing, re-testing and number crunching was her regular diet until Cassie sought any diversion from the boring daily ritual of hunting the proverbial needle in a scientific haystack.

A break from the tedious monotony presented itself. Cassie, had been given the task of creating a presentation, combined with a visual demonstration, of CEV#1B's dual ability. Heads of departments from within the company and ancillary amalgamated companies were called to watch the demonstration, in the hope that a marketable use could be found for the substances fire suppressing capabilities. Much money had already been spent in getting to this point, with no profitable application, as yet, suggested. The company was considering reducing funding and even shelving the venture. It was looking as if this was to be a final attempt to put CEV#1B to a lucrative commercial usage.

This was a much-welcomed opportunity that represented a chance for Cassie to break the tedium of life in the laboratory and she leapt at the prospect. She meticulously prepared the experiment, jumping at the chance to showcase her talents, both as an inventive scientist and a talented presenter.

The demonstration consisted of a metre square stainless steel dish, one centimetre deep, and filled with normal standard, low-grade, domestic petrol, from a standard, household petrol container, to a depth of five millimetres, to which a red colorant was added.

Suspended above was a small stainless steel and glass container, from the bottom of which protruded a long slender needle. At the side of the steel dish was a thin tube, which introduced a tiny ignition gas flame to the enclosed interior when activated.

The glass container held a small quantity of CEV#1B, which had been coloured with a blue dye. A fire resistant glass dome, fitted with powerful air extraction, covered the whole apparatus. The experiment was then filmed using an ultra high speed 1,000 plus frames per second camera.

Cassie began the demonstration. Using remote controls, she ignited the petrol. As all of the assembled group could have predicted for themselves, the petrol reacted with violent explosive ferocity, which was contained by the highly engineered, protective glass shield. She immediately quenched the flames by expelling the oxygen from the container. The fire extinguished instantly.

The demonstration had dramatically validated the volatility of the petrol in the tray. Cassie had the attention of the assembled group. After a short interlude during which she explained the explosive power of raw petrol, she continued with the experiment. She allowed a minuscule amount of CEV#1B to flow to the end of the fine needle; so small that it was only just visible. She explained that this was 0.0001 of a millilitre.

At the touch of the remote, the tiny drip of CEV#1B fell into the petrol. It was so small that it hardly broke the surface of the liquid. Immediately, the previously red liquid transformed and became entirely blue. There was not a slow spread of the blue colour; it imperceptibly transformed in a nanosecond. Again, the ignition flame was lit, and extended to 15 millimetres across the surface of the now, blue liquid. It was more than enough to ignite the petrol. There was no ignition. Cassie opened two vents in the sides of the glass dome to indicate that there was a good supply of air and oxygen. The previously highly volatile substance was now completely inert; it had no more combustible ability than water. She then rounded up the presentation by giving a detailed summary, explaining that the CEV#1B that had been mixed with the petrol would only remain active for one hour before entering into the same eight hour incubation period as CEV#1A. The footage from the high speed cameras were able to show the moment when the two liquids collided with each other in extremely slow motion. The flash, when the transformation from red to blue occurred, was barely noticeable, even at such greatly reduced speed. She ended with Q&A acquitting herself admirably. Cassie was delighted that the experiment that she had created had worked well. She was convinced this success would boost her integrity within the section of the laboratory where she was a newcomer. There was much animated chatter and discussion amongst those present and she was hopeful that some positive results would emerge from her presentation.

An internal e-mail informed Cassie that she had a meeting set for ten o'clock that Wednesday morning with the Head of Research and Development, Professor Richard Rodman. This was something of a surprise for Cassie; she had been performing well, or so she thought.

She kept her disappointment to herself, confiding in nobody. Her probationary period had passed, but rumours were furiously circulating that there were to be redundancies within some of the internal sections. As she was the last to join the team, would she to be the first to be given the news that her services were no longer required? Last in, first out, ran through her mind.

Monday and Tuesday passed slowly. The worry of what the meeting might reveal filled Cassie's thoughts, as the anxiety of the possible outcomes took on exaggerated likelihoods. For her to find another position in the biochemical industry would not be simple. There were alternatives that she had considered; working abroad in deprived countries was an option and something that she had investigated, but she knew herself too well and doubted that she could really consider that rather radical alternative. She was a creature who enjoyed the stability of westernised lifestyle far too much. Perhaps a move might have some advantages. She had watched several TV programs, which highlighted the fact that growing crops for bio-fuels was having a massively increasing impact upon the environment. Utilising land previously farmed for food production and the deforestation of primeval jungle and forests, was removing the plants and trees that created oxygen and were effectively the lungs of the planet. Moreover, this land transition was disrupting indigenous tribes of their homelands and robbing the most diverse animal ecosystem of its natural habitat. Cassie had serious doubts about the industry that she was a part of.

Professor Richard Rodman was well known and highly respected, not only as the senior scientist at the biochemical company, but as an international innovator and researcher. He had written several scientific papers that were highly regarded within the scientific community. Generally considered something of a genius, he was someone whose methods were perceived to be slightly unconventional. He was also very much the stereotypical, bumbling, absent-minded Professor, whose attentiveness was all too often involved in resolving some complicated scientific or mathematical problem, and not focused on the day-to-day requirements of life, which, to him, was just an annoying inconvenience. A caring wife steered Richard through the fundamental elements of everyday life, and a super-efficient secretary kept him from slipping on the various corporate banana skins, which were part and parcel of working for a massive organisation.

Cassie arrived at Rodman's office two minutes before the designated time of the meeting, took a seat in the outer office, and chatted somewhat nervously with Professor Rodman's secretary, Emma. Precisely on the dot of ten o'clock, the secretary picked up her internal telephone and called through to the Professor, informing him that he had a meeting booked. She opened the door to his office and said to Cassie with a wry smile, "Professor Rodman will see you now. He is not expecting you."

Cassie entered the room, which was crammed with a bewildering array of equipment. She had heard stories about Rodman's office/lab/ workshop, but the reality was far better than the stories. Much of the equipment was certainly not standard, but rather hand built by Rodman himself, to achieve a specific task from whatever materials were to hand, giving it a definite Heath Robinson appearance.

Professor Rodman was standing at a blackboard, scribbling a bewildering list of equations, completely unaware of Cassie's presence. She coughed several times to make herself known, but Rodman continued scribbling. Finally, the secretary, who was well versed in the idiosyncrasies of her Boss, came back into the room and took charge. "Professor Rodman, Miss Richards is here for her ten o'clock meeting."

Rather like a reluctant child, the Professor drew a line under the equations, snapping the chalk, which fell to the floor, adding to the existing pile of broken chalk and chalk dust. He crunched over the debris, walked to his desk and sat down. The secretary gave him some papers, which he read, and finally spoke. Rodman's fame preceded him, but he was something of a recluse, Cassie had never before actually seen him. Now one-on-one, she was able to scrutinise at close hand, this well known, but slightly elusive, eccentric individual. Her initial thought was that this tall, slender person was, in essence, quite handsome, but further examination revealed a second layer to this man. The preliminary impression was one that he was probably the work of a caring wife who looked after her husband rather like a mother caring for a hyperactive child. Deeper study unveiled the real personality within. His eyebrows were long and bushy giving him a slightly startled expression; they grew not only up, but down, touching his long eye lashes, moving each time that he blinked. The hairs sprouting from his ears were dense and long, making Cassie consider that in time they might meet up with his eyebrows and plait together.

"Ah yes, Miss Richards, one of our more recent colleagues. I have been informed that you acquitted yourself well with your recent assignment to create the demonstration of the dual power of CEV#1B."

As the Professor spoke, his head was constantly turning to look at the blackboard, three quarters of his attention still trying to formulate an answer to the problem that he had been wrestling with and one quarter occupied with the matter at hand. "It's Cassie isn't it?" he added politely.

"Yes, Professor," she replied, slightly disconcerted.

"Cassie," he continued, "the Head of Section has put your name forward for some specific experiments on CEV#1B. This will culminate in you being given a full half day on the electron microscope. This is a rather privileged experience for you as the microscope has an extremely full agenda and is rather costly to operate."

Rodman's head rotated towards the blackboard once again, but he managed to return his thoughts to the matter at hand. "Cassie, it took me years to get a project under the electron microscope, it can magnify an object by ten million times, so I hope that you will make the most of this rare opportunity."

Rodman's feet were visible under his desk and Cassie noted that one of his shoes was black and the other brown. The black shoe was laced and the brown a slip-on style. Evidently, he had left the house before his wife had managed to carry out her early morning inspection on him, and his secretary had also missed the error, or perhaps it was just an everyday occurrence. It was difficult for Cassie not to giggle, particularly now that the spectre of redundancy had passed. Rodman's attitude then seemed to alter, and, for a brief moment, became fully focused on the matter at hand.

"CEV#1B is a most extraordinary phenomenon, Cassie. I have studied it in minute detail myself and its individual abilities are indeed remarkable in its own right. The key lies in being able to separate its capabilities. If this can be achieved, then the uses to which it can be applied are boundless. Of course, the most significant value is in the strength of the CEV#1B, and, like the CEV#1A, its astonishing replication abilities. From the tests that we have carried out, it appears that there is no limit to the replication of both viruses. They simply go on and on, only restricted by the size of the vessel in which contained. I am astounded by this, and I can only speculate to what level this might extend. Nothing like CEV#1A and CEV#1B has ever been discovered, engineered or invented before. Could they, for example, replicate themselves to something the size of a lake or even an ocean? It is my hope that your young brain might approach the problem from a fresh angle. I would suggest that you research the work of Doctor Wood, who is a leader in this field."

That brief, focused interlude had now passed and Rodman's head turned again towards the blackboard and the enigma of the pending equation. It was now evident that the Professor's concentration on the interview had lapsed. He stood up and returned to the blackboard. His last words from the brief and bizarre meeting, he spoke over his shoulder "My secretary will give you all the details."

From anyone other than Professor Richard Rodman, this would have seemed rude and ill mannered, but from him, it was actually quite acceptable.

Now that she had been given the full programme to investigate EA#100, and the perplexing CEV#1A&B, to Cassie it had looked like a dream come true for a fledgling scientist. Her brief from Head of Section was to set up as many experiments, observing the amazing expansion capabilities of both the CEV#1A and CEV#1B virus's, in as many varied conditions as she could think of, in the hope that the replication capability could be isolated. She would be given a precious half day of uninterrupted use of the facility's electron microscope, which was considered quite an achievement for a young scientist.

The clock was now ticking. The decision to allow Cassie to experiment with the CEV#1A and B virus's meant that countdown to Armageddon had begun.

Over a period of the next month, Cassie, devised as many pre-prepared experiments as she could contrive, to observe the rapid expansion of CEV#1A, and B, in such conditions as various temperatures, vacuum, various pressures, nuclear radiation and a dozen more, which could all be viewed through the lenses of the remarkable microscope. She read voraciously all of the available papers written by Doctor Wood, who himself was regarded as a highly admired leader in this field of research.

When the day of her allotted time arrived, she had to work fast in order to set up and test the various experiments within the limited time frame. Each individual experiment was meticulously set within the microscope's viewing zone, and with great expectation, Cassie introduced CEV#1A to the base substance petrol, then a separate experiment with CEV#1B, hoping that she would be the one to detect some anomaly in one of them; a small variance, which would allow the miraculous ability of either virus to be harnessed. Each time, they each flashed for a micro- mini second. The transformation was too rapid for even this expensive piece of technology to detect. By the time Cassie had completed her allocated time, and tested her final experiment, she knew nothing more than she did when the day had started. Her disappointment was palpable. Her initial euphoria at being trusted with this task slowly eroded.

As she chatted over coffee and meal breaks with other scientists, it was obvious that Cassie was not the first to have been set this task. In fact, there had been many other, much accredited, and highly qualified scientists, who had attempted to isolate the virus and failed. Giving the job to Cassie was a shot in the dark, just a wild speculative attempt from the company's bosses, straw clutching. The politics held little interest to her as long as the experiments were interesting and being able to use the electron microscope was a huge bonus to add to her C.V.

Cassie's effort proved fruitless, and the half day of working with such a high-tech piece of equipment passed. She found herself back to the mundane routine of writing up her failed experiments and crunching the inescapable numbers.

Chapter 2

Armageddon

Matthew 24:21

For then shall be great tribulation, such as was not since the beginning of the world to this time, no, nor ever shall be.

Chapter 3

The Genie is Let out of the Bottle

Armageddon - day zero

The day was dragging. It was only Tuesday. Cassie looked at the agenda for the rest of the week. More tests, more graphs and analysis of stuff that had been analysed a dozen, scores, even hundreds of times before. Cassie realised that she had developed a new, sad habit – that of clock watching. She could not have known that she was actually counting down the hours to global catastrophe.

The week had dragged obstinately on, but finally, it was Friday, and the weekend loomed enticingly close. The morning seemed to go on and on; the hands on the clock which she knew she was consulting far too often, sometimes felt as if they were stuck, fused to the clock face. Finally, it was lunchtime and she hurried to the canteen. The conversation over lunch was a break from the monotony, but she found herself remaining on the margins of the discussions. All too soon, the lunch break was over and she was back in the laboratory. She needed to get out of the lab and breathe fresh air. Air not tinged with a mixture of assorted chemicals. She remembered when just the smell of a lab set her heart racing with the expectation of actually being a scientist, and who knows, perhaps being on a team that made some wonderful, life- changing discovery, which actually made a difference to mankind. Now it was all commonplace and mundane. Perhaps she should have taken up hairdressing; at least she would have had plenty of people to chat with.

The almost empty petrol container used to carry the raw material for experiments caught her eye. It had always seemed slightly odd to her that the basis of so much high specification research derived from a substance as commonplace and readily purchased as petrol. Occasionally, it was necessary to go to the local petrol station and buy several litres of petrol. This was to be her excuse for an outing, however briefly away from the lab. Cassie took a stainless steel flask from her workbench and drained the final remains of the container into a flask, put on her coat, and with the petrol container in her hand, she walked over to the lab supervisor.

Laboratory protocols at the bio facility were rigid, but, although they were strict, nobody had paid enough attention to the possibility of what might happen if the CEV#1A or B virus was to escape from the lab.

The primary testing medium was such a base; an everyday substance that could be purchased at thousands of filling stations around the country, meant it was outside the usual stringently monitored bio and chemical material that the lab was used to dealing with.

Tom Saunders was the head of Cassie's section, she was well aware that he had amorous intentions towards her. It was a matter well known within the department. Unbeknown to Tom, he was the butt of many jokes. His strong resemblance to Ricky Gervais did nothing to improve the situation. He was also a stickler for abiding by the labs many rules.

"Tom, just popping out to get some more petrol, won't be long."

Cassie employed a cute, engaging smile, just in case Tom might decide that there was a company rule, which might forbid such behaviour.

Tom held his hands close to his chubby face, palms upwards in a mock display of anguish. He held the cheesy pose for two seconds. "Friday the thirteenth, Cassie."

Did he knowingly mimic Ricky Gervais, or was he just like that naturally? She suppressed a giggle.

"Full moon tonight; better be extra cautious," he advised.

Cassie had become adept at sidestepping his fumbling advances. "Thanks for the advice Tom."

Tom gave her a ten-pound note from the petty cash float. "Don't forget to get a receipt Cassie. You know what these autocrats are like, a piece of paper for everything."

"Don't worry, Tom, I'll be back in an hour." She knew that as she walked away, Tom's eyes would be rigidly focused upon her rear-end, she allowed herself to accentuate her walk, which made her feel a little impish.

It seemed almost abnormal to be driving out through the security gates at anything other than the prescribed hours. Cassie felt a strange sensation, like a naughty child bunking off school. Apart from getting out of the lab, this was an opportunity to kill a couple of birds with the same stone and what's more, on company time. Cassie drove her car to the Pound Lane filling station. It was not the closest to the Lab, but it did have the advantage of a good combined grocery section.

14

She arrived at the pump and filled up her car. She then pumped five litres of low petrol into the laboratory petrol container. Inside the can was a small residue of petrol, contaminated by the highly toxic CEV#1A. It probably weighed no more than a dormouse, but was lethal enough to fundamentally alter the evolutionary path of mankind forever.

Jeff Weldon sat in the office of the Pound Lane filling station where he was the manager. He was a worried man. The petroleum company that he worked for were anal with regards to targets. His promotion two years ago had seemed like a gift, heaven sent at the time. The additional bonus being that the job came with living accommodation for him and his young family, which was a huge added advantage. The convenience store side of the business was just about managing to meet the targets, but fuel sales were substantially down, which was mainly due to mega supermarkets in the area offering tempting discounts on their petrol prices. Now the long overdue tanker delivery was causing Jeff additional anguish. It was Friday afternoon. He had optimistically dipped the fuel storage tanks with the long dipsticks twice that day and knew that the tanks were holding little more than fumes. Frantic phone calls to the head office had not produced the answers that he wanted. A two-week surge in demand had stretched the tanker supply fleet to its limits. He was in a chain and would have to be patient.

He prepared to take the 'No Fuel' signs out onto the forecourt and hang them on the pumps, an action that he had been dreading and one that might have longer-term repercussions. As he walked through the shop with the signs, he was delighted to see a delivery tanker pulling onto the forecourt. He hastily put the signs back in the office and picked up the keys for the holding tanks security locks. As he walked out of the shop, he passed a young woman. It was Cassie, who had just purchased petrol from the final dregs of the Pound Lanes tanks.

They passed in the electrically operated front doors of the shop, oblivious of one another, unaware that they were each significant players in an unfolding drama, the magnitude of which they could never, ever have imagined.

Jeff unlocked the storage tanks security. The driver coupled up the delivery hose and began pumping the much-needed fuel into the depleted tanks. The contaminated fuel in the tanks mixed with the fresh supply. The virus was now set free, instantly expanding and mutating as it travelled back up through the pumps, pipes and hoses, and within a split second reached into the tankers main reservoir. After delivering its consignment, the tanker returned to the depot where it was connected to the huge main holding tanks. From there, the virus was able to expand, unchecked and invisibly into whichever direction it could find fossil fuels, hidden within the labyrinth of hoses, pipes and tanks. The uncontrollable replication ability of CEV#1A knew no boundaries. The virus was now moving at phenomenal speed, hidden within the system.

The seemingly insignificant action of the petrol pump nozzle touching the contaminated petrol can was undoubtedly the most significant action in the history of the human race. Cassie was completely unaware of what had taken place. She had unwittingly released the virus from the stringently controlled confines of the laboratory. The deadly clock was ticking, and countdown for the incubation period had begun. The violent unharnessed Genie was now out of the bottle, and could not be stopped!

As Cassie drove back to the laboratory, she felt contented that she had gained something out of what would otherwise have been another boring day. The added bonus of being able to wander around the Pound Lane station's shop, and purchase all of the weekend items she required, meant she would not have to stop on the way home from work. She was completely oblivious of the momentous event in which she had played the pivotal role.

How was Cassie to know that the simple act of filling a container with petrol would trigger a chain reaction that would have far more significant consequences than the bombing of Hiroshima and Nagasaki in 1945, devastating the modern world? In hindsight, the strict protocol that should have been rigidly implemented when dealing with a virus that had the replication potential of 'The Armageddon Virus' (as it was later to become known), should have been a matter of course, standard practice.

But, hindsight is a wonderful thing. How many times throughout history could a small variation have altered the outcome of so many catastrophic events? The contamination had taken place and now the incubation period was counting down.

Cassie returned to the lab with the petrol and handed in the receipt to Tom. She listened to a couple of his repetitious, rather feeble, jokes, swerved dexterously to avoid his clumsy advances and was grateful when she finally returned to her desk. It was Friday afternoon; only an hour and she would be driving home. Her car was topped up with petrol, she had achieved the weekend shopping, and a welcome relaxing two days away from work was imminent. At five o'clock, her week's work at the laboratory was over. Two of the other younger female members of staff asked Cassie if she would like to go for a drink after work. It seemed like a good idea, until she discovered that Tom, the head of section, would also be there. Cassie politely refused the invite and drove the fifteen minutes back to her flat.

Cassie Richards felt a rather childlike delight. She was pleased with herself as she tidied away her shopping. The weather was unpredictable, sunny one minute and torrential downpours the next. Friday had been a mixture of both, and she was happy to spend the weekend cuddled up in her one bedroom flat watching TV and reading the new novel that she had just downloaded onto her Kindle. She made a sandwich with the ingredients that she had purchased from the Pound Lane filling station shop. Somehow, it tasted better than usual, which was probably due to the pilfered time that she used to make the purchases. She flopped down onto the sofa, grabbed the remote control and switched on the news. She was annoyed to have switched on in the middle of the sports roundup, which, as a non-sporting person, she found irritating. The general news started. It was pretty much the same old twaddle, politicians being asked questions, to which they made no attempt to answer, simply twisting the argument to gain party political points from their screen time. An article, which did grab her attention, was news that the BBC Top Gear team had sold the program concept to China, where a new car driving society was rapidly emerging. It was estimated that 1.5 million new cars were hitting the Chinese roads every month. This was interesting information for anyone involved in the bio-fuel industry and Cassie made a mental note to bring up this point on Monday morning at the first coffee break.

She grabbed the remote control and switched over to the entertainment channels to enjoy an evening of trivia. Cassie settled into a well researched couch potato evening. She dipped into her Kindle several times, but the book that she was reading simply couldn't hold her interest. She watched a little television, but soap operas and cooking programs did little to grab her attention. Then, like a bolt out of the blue, she had an epiphany moment. Why hadn't she thought of this before, actually why had nobody thought along these lines?

Perhaps the supremely disappointing results from attempts to create ground-breaking new products from CEV#1A had overshadowed the scene to such an extent that logical progression and diligence had been swept aside. The inert residue which had been infected with CEV#1A held possibilities of its own. Perhaps, Cassie thought, this could be where her chance to shine as an international renowned scientist might lay. The inherent values which reside in crude oil probably remained in the residue, only the combustible capability had been removed. Were there new plastics and polymers to be extracted from this new base material?

The potentials were stimulating; Cassie's expectations were peaking with the possibilities of what she might discover. But all of this would have to wait until Monday. For now, she decided that a restful weekend would put her in good fettle for what now promised to be an exciting week ahead.

At eleven o'clock, she went to bed, read fifteen minutes of her new novel, and fell into a deep sleep.

Chapter 4

End of ICE (Internal Combustion Engine) age of dominance

Armageddon + 1 day

Cassie was up and out of bed at eight o'clock. She made herself tea and a breakfast of muesli, toast and marmalade. Taking this back to the sofa, balancing a tray on her lap, she ate the muesli and toast before switching on the TV. The usual deluge of Saturday morning cookery programs held her attention briefly for a while whilst she drank the tea. She then turned on the news, which was totally dominated by a series of traffic reports from around the country.

There was a news flash, which caught Cassie's interest.

"We are interrupting this transmission to bring you a news flash that is just coming in to us from Routers News Agency. Apparently, a British Airways aircraft out of Heathrow has just crashed as it was coming into land at Zurich Airport. The pilot sent a brief Mayday message reporting total loss of his engines as the aircraft made its final approach. There appear to be no survivors. We will continue to give you updates as we receive them."

The news continued and another news flash caught Cassie's attention.

"Drivers are recommended to stay clear of the Pound Lane area of West London. Traffic has become severely congested. Police are on the scene."

This was where Cassie had just recently been. Perhaps there had been an accident or a fire? It all seemed to be normal when she was there. The breakfast finished – a little nap was in order. She settled down cosily on the sofa and quickly drifted off to sleep. It was an hour later when she awoke feeling stiff and aching from lying on the cheap sofa. She made herself a cup of tea and switched the TV back on. The news flash concerning the Pound Lane incident had moved up in the coverage priority.

"Police investigating the congestion in the Pound Lane area of West London have discovered that there is an unusually large proportion of abandoned and broken down cars in the area which is causing road chaos. Traffic police have given no explanation for the phenomenon."

This was unusual news for sure, but as Cassie had no pending intentions of driving through the Pound Lane vicinity, and realistically she had no intentions of even getting into her car until Monday morning when this problem, she was convinced, would have doubtlessly been solved.

"The apparent epidemic which is sweeping the nation is growing exponentially by the hour. The government is advising that this is not a human health epidemic, but one that is specifically affecting petrol and diesel supplies. From what our reporters can conclude at this time, the phenomenon is spreading rapidly, just about all of the country's fuel stock appears to be affected. The rampant chemical pollution appears to have begun in the Pound Lane vicinity of West London and has expanded nationwide."

The reality of what had happened hit Cassie like a thunderbolt from hell.

Cassie sank back into the sofa, a strong pain stabbing at her lower abdomen. Quickly she grabbed the remote control and switched off the news, unable to face the reality. She felt queasy and faint. Finally, she rushed to the toilet and managed to reach the sink as she vomited her undigested breakfast. Sweating and nauseated, she staggered back to the sofa and sat with her knees pulled up to her chest, sobbing. An hour passed before she was able to summon up the courage to turn on the TV. The situation escalated hour by hour. News correspondents from around the country were reporting on the fuel disaster, and now a new dimension to the problem was emerging. Supermarkets nationwide were recording a huge surge in customers who were buying whatever they could, in an attempt to stock up, anticipating foreseeable food shortages.

Cassie was unable to watch more than ten minutes of the news before she was completely consumed by dread. She scooped up the remote and killed the transmission, breaking down into uncontrollable sobbing. Finally, when completely emotionally drained, she fell into a deep sleep, filled with nightmares and visions of crowds of people running like lemmings towards a cliff.

When she awoke, it was dark outside; she had slept for more than ten hours. Slowly the reality of what she had seen on her television screen began to creep back into her mind like a deadly, thick, black mist.

Cassie now turned her mind in another direction – denial. Perhaps, upon reflection, she had been too quick in assuming that the guilt for this catastrophe lay entirely on her shoulders. Maybe there was another explanation for what had happened? After all, she was not the only scientist in the lab that had access to CEV#1. With that thought, in her confused mind, she was feeling slightly braver and summoned up the courage to turn on the TV again. A reporter was making a live broadcast from a London suburban shopping centre. Chaos reigned all around him. Looters were everywhere, running in and out of the stores, taking whatever they could, unrestrained. There was a line of riot police, but they were completely overwhelmed, unable to do anything more than stand by and watch. It appeared as if the country had gone mad. The reporter summed up the events of the afternoon.

"Breaking news. The looting began just after midday. The supermarket shelves have been stripped and the first looters started random stealing by running out of stores taking at first, smaller, easy to carry items. These initial looters were perhaps the more predictable varieties, mostly young hoodie types. But, as the hours progressed, more ordinary looking shoppers joined in as there was a complete loss of control and law and order. I suppose the thinking was that if they can do it, so can we. From reports that are coming in from my colleagues, this is not an isolated incident. It appears that looting is taking place in cities all over the country."

This news report was interrupted by a priority news flash.

The Prime Minister made an emergency broadcast in which he stated that, The Joint Terrorism Analysis Centre (JTAC) has upgraded its warning criteria to critical. There was a high potential for a terrorist attack and citizens were to be aware of the imminent danger. They should stay alert, reporting anything that they thought was suspicious. It was suspected that there could be a second wave of violence connected to the unexplained fuel contamination that is sweeping across the country. The PM reiterated that whilst this contamination appeared to pose no direct threat to human health, it was thought that there could be a second level to the incident.

Cassie was unable to watch any more. She turned off the TV and went to the kitchen. She hadn't eaten for a long time, but it wasn't food that she was looking for. There were always a couple of bottles of wine she kept for those occasions when friends turned up unexpectedly.

She chose a bottle of cheap red that she favoured as being just about acceptable for the price, pulled the cork, grabbed a glass and returned to the couch. By midnight she had emptied the bottle, and in addition, several glasses of a cheap Port that she kept for cooking. She fell into a deep alcohol induced sleep but awoke cold and miserable at three in the morning and was relieved to get into her cosy, warm bed. The bed might have been cosy but her sleep was deeply troubled. She had a terrible night and woke up on Sunday morning with a severe hangover. By midday she was feeling slightly better. The news channels were continuing to pump out horror stories from up and down the country, now depicting rioting, uncontrolled looting and unprecedented violence.

Cassie decided that she must face up to what might have been her part in this disaster and report what she knew to the police. She dressed and walked out into the street. The local police station was a ten-minute walk away. What she was confronted with shocked her. Garbage was strewn everywhere. When she reached the local shopping district, the area resembled a disaster zone. Some of the shops had steel roller security blinds, which were intact, but if the shop had more valuable contents, the shutters had been smashed, the doors ripped open and the contents of the shop strewn everywhere. Some stunned looking shop owners were trying to sweep up the broken glass, attempting to salvage what they could from their businesses.

She walked on, distraught at what she was witnessing. When she arrived at the police station, it was a scene of unimaginable chaos. Scores of people were gathered on the front steps shouting, demanding to know what was being done to protect them from this unparalleled, sudden wave of violence. She managed to push her way to the front of the throng and get inside the building. People were everywhere, but there was an unmistakable, obvious lack of police officers present. Cassie

Found her in a long corridor, and when a door at the far end opened, a lone uniformed policeman appeared. The throng of protestors surged towards the solitary policeman. Cassie was swept along with the crowd.

The policeman was holding his hands up in a gesture, which seemed to denote futility, but the crowd continued to press forward until the corridor was a solid mass of bodies.

Cassie was jammed into this stream of human beings. She was next to one of the office doors which led off the main corridor. The throng of protestors now completely filled the corridor, pinning the policeman against his office door. Suddenly, the door to which Cassie's shoulder was forced against, burst open and she was flung into the room falling heavily onto the floor. Several other people fell on top of her. A severe pain sprang through her right arm and she screamed out in agony. Due to the extreme crush in the police station, it took some time for Cassie to extricate herself from other people and drag herself to the corner of the room. Slowly the chaos that had prevailed in the building receded as the protestors realised that there were few police officers to address their grievances. Shocked, Cassie sat on the floor with her back leaning against the wall.

She was frightened to look at her arm because she was quite sure that it was broken, so severe was the pain. Fortunately, there was no blood. She arranged her clothing in such a way as to create a makeshift sling. The local hospital was close by and she could normally walk there in minutes. Perhaps now injured, it would take twenty.

She stood up unsteadily and allowed her head to clear before attempting to move off. Each step was painful and she was aware that she might pass out. Under normal circumstances she could have asked for help, but these were certainly anything but normal circumstances. Everyone who she saw in the street was rushing around. They were almost like hungry jackals, looking for a scavenger treat. Finally, after thirty excruciating minutes, she arrived at the hospital, only to find a scene, which resembled something from a disaster movie. She stood a hundred yards from the entrance to the Accident and Emergency department and her heart sank. The mass of people trying to get in was solid. They were shouting, gesticulating and demanding to be seen, but their cause was useless. The functioning of the hospital had ground to a halt from the sheer weight of patients and lack of staff. There was nothing else to be done. Cassie had only one option open to her, which was to walk home. By the time she reached her apartment it was almost dark. She was exhausted and sat in a chair as the sofa was low and the pain in her arm was so intense that the upright chair seemed the better option. There was another pain that was beginning to gnaw at her stomach. She realised that she had hardly eaten for two days. In the kitchen cupboard she had stored several tins of quick meals spaghetti, beans and soup. She chose spaghetti and struggled to open the tin. This was the first time that she had attempted to do anything with just her left hand. It was hopeless; she would never open the tin by herself with her right arm in its makeshift sling. A thought passed through her mind. On her way into her apartment, she had passed a group of young men who she vaguely knew were neighbours.

She decided to ask them for help. Cassie walked out of her apartment and along the corridor. Yes, the men were still there.

"Excuse me. I'm Cassie from number eleven."

The men looked surprised and slightly amused. "I wonder if you might help me open this tin of spaghetti. I've hurt my arm."

"Yeah, babe. No problem." A tall man in a hoodie, who appeared to be the leader, stepped forward. "Got any more of these tins have you?" he enquired.

"Not many, I'm afraid," she replied, beginning to worry about the circumstances which were now developing. "Don't worry, I'll find myself something else."

But it was too late. Without being instructed by their leader, the men pushed Cassie aside, all walked along the corridor, and blatantly entered her apartment where she had left the door wide open. By the time she dared to go back inside, her home was a mess. The gang of men had ransacked the place, taking what they wanted. She stood in the hallway, pushed against the wall as the gang walked out as if they had been invited in, which in fact in their eyes, they pretty much had.

22

The leader looked down at her as he passed. "Stupid bitch," he hissed, in a pseudo African American accent.

For a brief instant, Cassie linked eyes with the intruder and their minds connected in a symbiotic reaction. She felt that she was looking deep into his distorted soul. A dramatic, highly charged moment filled with a mixture of anger, fear and hatred. It was an emotion Cassie had never experienced before. It opened up dark primeval reactions hidden deep within the recesses of her personality. At this moment he was all powerful; supreme leader of his pack and now living in, what was to him, a dream environment where he could take whatever he wanted with no fear of being apprehended or of facing reprisals. Policing had ceased to exist; this was to him, indeed a paradise.

It was in fact an irrational act. His time as a dominant player in this new anarchist ocean would be sweet to his eyes, but in reality, drastically short lived. Soon, very soon, as food became scarce, the bigger sharks would surface and he would be a minnow crushed without remorse.

The rest of the gang pushed past Cassie, making her stumble into the corridor outside her own home. The young men were invigorated by a new power. This was the supremacy of anarchy, now they could do anything that they liked and there was nobody around to stop them.

Thinking that they had left, she walked inside, shocked by the damage that had been perpetrated in so short a time. As she walked into the living room, she was confronted by two gang members who were still there. They were obviously the youngest of the pack, probably no more than thirteen or fourteen she guessed. To her disgust she could see that they were urinating, spraying the sofa, television with whatever the capacity of their bladders could desecrate. Leaning backwards, thrusting their pelvises, forward they laughed at seeing Cassie enter the room. She shouted at them to stop, screaming 'get out' at the top of her lungs, her anger only tempered by fear that she might be attacked.

When they had finished, they walked towards the doorway where Cassie was standing, effectively blocking their exit. The two boys charged at her, knocking her back into the hallway where she fell heavily to the floor, banging her head on the skirting board. The two young gang apprentices walked over Cassie's prone body with a look of disdain. They were in fact well down the pecking order in gang culture and were unknowingly contributing to their own demise. The pain in her arm was excruciating, but warning bells of a new threat rang in her aching head. Rape! Cassie knew that she was a desirable woman. She had had plenty of offers from a long list of men over the years, but had declined to become involved in any relationship, although she had been seriously tempted on several occasions. Romance and sex was something to be savoured and experienced only when the right man came along and the time was right. At the age of twenty five, Cassie Richards, was a rare specimen of mature womanhood; a virgin.

She laid on the floor, anticipating in terror, the horrific incident which could happen next. She realised that she was wearing jeans, therefore her legs were not exposed, an advantage. With her good arm, she pulled her coat over her breasts. The last thing that she saw before passing out was the two young men bending over her, tugging at her coat.

When she eventually recovered consciousness, she had no idea of how long she had lain on the floor. The realisation of what had happened slowly filtered back into her mind and panic took over. She could see that her coat had been pulled back, her blouse was ripped open and her bra pulled up around her neck exposing her breasts. Her revulsion was overwhelming. It was some time before she regained a resemblance of calm. She dragged herself up onto her good arm and examined the rest of her body. The slim belt around her Jeans was unbuckled, but mercifully she could tell that her jeans had not been undone. There was some clemency in what she had endured. Perhaps the two young boys were interrupted or called away for more lucrative prey, a new shop or warehouse broken into, a rival gang trespassing onto their turf.

By some quirk of fate or good luck, Cassie had narrowly escaped being raped, but the overwhelming feeling of being violated was profound. No man had ever seen her breasts, let alone touched them, now she had been violated by two boys of school age. She struggled to get to her feet, the mixture of dizziness and sheer pain from the injury to her arm, combining to cause her to feel nauseous. Finally, she was able to close and lock the front door, which seemed an almost pointless act considering what had taken place. Cassie never went outside again. She picked up the phone to call the police, but there was no dialling tone. Even if she had managed to get through to a 999 centre, there were no emergency services operating.

Cassie Richards was alone in the world. All the support that she had grown to rely upon throughout her life now ceased to exist. She could do nothing but cry.

A human being can go without food for weeks, but can't survive without water; dehydration is a killer. After five days had elapsed the taps in her kitchen and bathroom emitted only a gurgling sound, but no water. She lay curled up on her bed, unable to fully comprehend all that had so suddenly happened. Day after day, night after night, she lay there; it felt like her sanctuary, the only safe place. She piled all of the bedding that she could find in the apartment onto her bed, in a childlike attempt to protect herself from the collapsing world outside. The sounds reaching her bedroom from the streets frightened her, terrifying screams, angry shouting. She was continually worried that the gang would return to complete the job that they had left unfinished. Her senses focused on the front door, which, although locked, she imagined could easily be smashed open. Worrying about how vulnerable she was, made sleep virtually impossible.

The gang that had so callously vandalized her home never did come back. Their prominence was short lived and they too succumbed to the much greater wave of violence that swept ruthlessly across the country. One recurring thought was about her family, needing to get to her parents' home, but it was too far and any journey would be fraught with danger. Lying in her bed hour after hour, day after day, only sleeping spasmodically, her thoughts constantly churned over the events that had led to this unimaginable tragedy. Was it her that had caused the contamination? Gradually, her mind wandered and hallucinations took over. Finally, like so many others, after sixteen days, death from dehydration released her from her torture.

Chapter 5

MAYDAY

Armageddon + 2

The Virgin Atlantic Airways flight VS001 Gatwick to Newark Airport, New York, was approaching the eastern seaboard within the final two hours of its eight hour, five minutes, Trans Atlantic flight. Captain Ray Ballinger was happy with the way things had gone. In fact, it was pretty much a textbook flight. He had started the day with some apprehension when upon checking the passenger list he had noticed there were some VIPs in first class that were renowned for being extremely difficult passengers and a personality clash was a strong possibility. The inflammatory mix of a high profile politician, notorious for his brash outbursts, plus a reality TV star and his entourage, heralded all of the ingredients for an impending recipe of disaster. Captain Ballinger had complete confidence in the cabin crew with whom he had flown many times, trusting their professionalism and experience. They had kept the potential trouble makers' alcohol consumption to a minimum and the atmosphere in the exclusive section had remained calm. Now most of the passengers were sleeping during the final miles of their journey. The co-pilot, Andrew Connaught, was just finishing his dinner. Conversation in the cabin was cheerful, and each of the men looked forward to a weekend in New York, a flight back to Gatwick and then ten days leave.
"Andy, as soon as you have finished eating, we must start preparing for the landing procedure."
There was a knock at the cabin door, it was the senior stewardess.
She brought coffee and cleared away the dinner plates.
"Good work, Candice, you have done a great job keeping our awkward VIP guests separated and happy. Thought that there might have been some conflict with

the reality TV guy and his buddies, but you seem to have kept a lid on it."

The coffee was drunk and the landing procedures began.

The Airbus 340-600 was flying at 35,000 feet, with an airspeed of 450 knots. The co-pilot started on his check list when suddenly the flight console lit up. The master warning light came on and the warning horn sounded.

"What have you got Andy?" calmly asked Ballinger.

Andy cancelled the horn and as a procedure called: "Engine flame out, port engine number one."

Ray Ballinger made adjustments, re-trimming the aircraft and shutting down the number one port engine, he then re-set the instrumentation engaging the auto pilot. "Do you have any indication as to what might have caused that flameout?" he enquired.

The co-pilot checked his instruments, but could find no obvious explanation. "Everything seems to be functioning correctly; there is no sign of fire or any other malfunction."

"OK Andy, send a Pan Message to ATC (air traffic control), location, speed and altitude reduction, as per protocol."

As the message was being sent the console burst into light. The master warning light and the audible warning horn kicked in again.

"What have you got this time Andy?" Ray Ballinger's voice was beginning to display a little irritation.

"Number two port engine flame out." "What!" he examined, "and the reason?"

"Same as number one, no apparent explanation; it's just shut down." Ray looked puzzled. "Upgrade that Pan message to a Mayday," he ordered whilst he again re-trimmed the aircraft and re-set the instrumentation. The look on the faces of the two men now showed signs of stress. "The passengers will have noticed that there is a problem. I am going to explain the situation to them." He opened the main cabin intercom.

"Ladies and gentlemen, you will have noticed that there is some alteration in the flight parameters. We have experienced engine failure on two of our engines, but I want to assure you that this aircraft is quite capable of continuing the journey to Newark safely on the two remaining engines. We are approximately two hours from the East Coast and although it will take a little longer to reach the airport, the aircraft is completely able to cope with this. Thank you."

Ray Ballinger closed the intercom and turned to Andy. "I have completed this exercise countless times in a simulator and during my training, but never with an aircraft full of passengers."

There was a flurry of radio traffic between the aircraft and air traffic control. His concern was promptly heightened when, for the third time, the emergency warning equipment sprang into life. The two aviators looked at each other in disbelief. Ray didn't need to ask.

Andy's answer was what he was expecting, but dreaded. "Starboard engine, number three, engine flame-out," and then almost in the same breath, "Starboard engine, number four, engine flame out." There was no time for questioning the events; everything had now suddenly turned into fear.

The aircraft was dropping out of the sky. The latest generation of aircraft was flown by wire and required electricity to operate - electricity generated by the engines which were now inoperative.

"Andy, fire up the auxiliary generator, we have to get some power to the controls. We have about eleven miles before we hit the sea, which gives us about three minutes."

His thoughts turned to the passengers. He flicked the intercom button to the flight attendant's location. Candice answered. Trying to sound as calm as he could, he gave the order that all pilots dread. In the background, he could hear screaming, arising from panic of the passengers. The aircraft had now adopted a descending altitude and was losing height rapidly.

"Candice, we are going down and will ditch onto the sea in the next few minutes. You must proceed with the emergency landing on water technique."

There was a brief pause whilst the chief stewardess absorbed the severity of the order. "Right, Captain, we will do what we have been trained to do, Good luck."

Captain Ray Ballinger flicked open the main cabin intercom. "Brace, brace, brace!"

At 16:45, Eastern Time, USA east coast air traffic control reported loss of contact with Virgin Airways Flight VS001.

Chapter 6

Lieutenant Colonel John Jackson

Armageddon + 2 days

Earlier that week, not thirty miles away from Pound Lane in Windsor, a state visit was taking place. Pageantry and ceremony of the highest order that only England can achieve, being acted out in the historic town. The animated crowds waved flags, applauded and cheered. All were excited to see immaculate soldiers riding their huge horses, clattering through its streets, escorting the ornate open top carriages that carried the British Monarch and the President of Italy on a state visit – pageantry, at its best.

The government had decided that, whenever possible, these official visits should take place in Windsor, as opposed to central London, where the traffic confusion caused by the road closures resulted in havoc. Windsor in comparison derived a large part of its income from tourism and the additional living pageantry only served to enhance the appeal of the town.

The Household Cavalry had been rehearsing the event for three days. Reveille on this morning was 05:00 hours. The stables had been cleaned and horses groomed to their usual high standard. The soldiers then had breakfast before saddling up their mounts and donning their splendid ceremonial uniforms. At 09:00 hours, the escort to the monarch, and the Household Cavalry mounted band, rode out of their barracks, through the town to Home Park (the large playing fields which lay to the north of the town), which was skirted by the River Thames, in the imposing shadow of the castle. This was the venue where the President of Italy would officially be met and greeted by the Queen, before being driven in state through the town and on up to the castle.

The monarchs mounted bodyguard is a familiar sight, their scarlet and blue tunics, white and red plumes denoting the two sister regiments, their history and commitment to guarding the sovereign, long and glorious.

Just before the restoration of King Charles II, a Royal mounted bodyguard was formed in Holland, from eighty Royalists who had gone into exile with the King after the Battle of Worcester (1652). In March 1660, the King appointed officers to three Troops of Horse Guards, which formed at the King's return to England in May 1660.

Lt. Colonel John Jackson rode his trusty charge, Rascal, next to the rear wheel of the Queen's carriage. To his side rode his bugler, mounted on a grey mare. TV cameras were everywhere. The flags of the two nations fluttered from tall flag poles, military bands played, and the Colours of Army, Navy and Air force contingents, were lowered solemnly as the sovereign drove past. John Jackson had ridden on many state occasions, but the thrill was always the same.

One doubt that always troubled him was, what if, from his elevated position on horseback, he saw someone with a weapon in the crowd? Would he plough into the cheering mass and skewer the culprit? Suppose he was wrong, and in the frenzy of the moment, what John thought to be a gun, turned out to be nothing more than a camera. His daydreaming turned to the reality of the weekend, having time off with his wife and three daughters, getting away to the isolation of his in-laws home in the New Forest; a place of solitude, away from all the pressures, hustle and bustle of army life was drawing to an end. The vibrant colours of this daydream slowly faded into black and white and gradually dissipated altogether. Such is the way of dreams.

John Jackson shook himself from his day-dreaming, he was sitting back, relaxing into the plastic imitation woven rattan garden chair on the patio of his in-laws' pretty Georgian country house next to their garden centre in the New Forest. Spreading his long legs before him, clasping his hands behind his neck, he looked up into the blue sky. Usually there would be several aeroplanes slashing their silver vapour trails across the magnificent canvas of blue, overlaid with brilliant white fluffy clouds. Doubtless, some of the people on board those planes would have been, or were about to jet-off to warmer climes, but John was more than happy being exactly where he was. Although he was deep in the New Forest, he would normally be able to see at least three aeroplanes cutting their vapour trails across the sky, but today, oddly, there were none. This reminded him of a colleague, who had recently demonstrated to him the Flightradar24, computer program, a live flight tracker which showed all the civil aeroplanes that were in the air in real time, flying between every major city on the globe. The aeroplanes were shown on the screen in yellow, flying in and out of their destinations. The sheer number of circling aeroplanes was quite amazing, resembling a beehive. John had been stunned by the extent of the traffic.

He mused about the fact that he was now viewing the spectacle from a completely different angle – from below rather than above, or actually rather than digitally on a computer screen. Perhaps today's lack of aircraft in the skies above Hampshire where they were usually stacked waiting for a landing slot at Heathrow was due to a strike, air traffic controllers or something, but he had heard nothing because one of the more agreeable advantages of living in such an isolated location was the lack of TV, radio and internet.

In the distance he could hear the laughter and girlish screams of his three young daughters, which was in contrast to the background accompaniment of the New Forest songbirds. Closer to his location, a busy blackbird was intent on letting everyone know exactly where his territory extended. John's thoughts focused on pleasant trivia. "I am a man of multiple labels," he contemplated. To his three daughters, his title was Dad. This was probably his favourite tag. To his close friends and Army colleagues, he was known affectionately as Jacko. Whilst fulfilling his military role as head of a prestigious regiment in the British army, he was addressed as Colonel or Boss, but to his wife and family he was simply, John. John Jackson laughed out loud, he was laughing at the triviality of his thoughts, which, because of the absolute tranquillity of his location, they had allowed calmness to envelope him and de- stress his busy mind. John disengaged his thoughts from this frivolous daydreaming, bringing him back into the present.

The week ahead at the barracks which he headed up, looked to be busier than most. The 'Silly Season' was approaching, which meant that the ceremonial side of the regiment would be requiring space in the barracks for horses as well as men.

There was an Armoured Reconnaissance Squadron preparing to deploy abroad, which required intense training and preparation. The total complement of soldiers within the barracks varied enormously from around five hundred when all four Squadrons were there, to as little as one hundred, when they were deployed to their various commitments. The present number was in the order of three hundred. Also, there were always around seventy horses in the stable block and a recruit troop undergoing the rough riding section of their equitation course in the nearby Great Park. The Household Cavalry was an interesting mixture of traditional ceremonial living antiquity, blended with high-tech modern light reconnaissance, present day soldiering. In addition to this four horses were stabled for the coaching troop.

But all of that worry was for tomorrow. Today he could kick back, relax and enjoy the final hours of the weekend with his family. John's in-laws owned a small family business on the edge of the New Forest in Hampshire. The business was a medium sized garden centre incorporating a farm shop. Sarah's father, Thomas, grew many of the plants that he sold from seed, specialising in orchids. The business wasn't particularly successful, but did give a reasonable, if modest income with which Thomas and his wife had been able to bring up their three children, ensuring that they had a good education and never really wanted for anything. What the business lacked in aggressive marketing and thrusting presentation, was more than compensated by the sheer, quaint beauty of the location and structures. A small trout stream ran through the property, which added the final touch to a superlative location. The value of the property was not enormous as most of the land was agricultural, but it mattered not a jot to Thomas and his wife Annabel.

The pressure was on for Colonel John Jackson, but he was focused and ready to deal with whatever the Ministry of Defence flung at him. Dealing with his three children was an entirely different matter.

Fortunately, his wife, Sarah, was an impeccable mother and coped efficiently with all matters relating to the running of the home.

Weekends at the garden centre were a regular treat for the Jackson family, giving John a break from regimental life, pretty much cut off from the rest of the country, allowing him to be just a regular dad to his three girls, Miranda, Caroline and Alex. The girls all jumped at the chance to work in the farm shop, helping out grandpa and earning a little extra pocket money. There were great country walks and cosy traditional pubs and restaurants within walking distance, which were all explored by the family whenever the opportunity arose.

Sarah walked out into the garden, bringing with her two drinks, the ice in the glasses making the irresistible clinking sound that added to the satisfaction of a cool drink on a warm day. She put the drinks down on the table, walked around to the back of John's chair and laid her chilled hand on his neck. John jumped slightly from the coldness of the wet hand, but then relaxed as Sarah massaged his neck. She was well aware of the pressure he was under at work. John contemplated how lucky he was to have found and fallen in love with Sarah. Seventeen years and three children later she was still as beautiful as ever, and his devotion to her had never faltered.

"OK, Colonel Lazy, time for a walk. The girls need to burn off some energy and I need to stretch my legs." Family-wise Sarah always knew what was best.

"You're right, it's getting towards dusk, a quick half hour walk and then supper should take us nicely up to the time when we will have to leave." John slowly got up from his chair and lazily stretched his arms above his head.

After supper, the three girls helped their grandmother to clear up the dishes. John and Sarah stood on the patio. It was dark now. They were both looking up into the cloudless sky, discussing how many more stars could be seen in this location where there was little in the way of light pollution, and very different from their garden in Windsor.

"Why does the moon look so strange?" inquired Sarah. "It looks as if there is a golden halo around it. It's slightly eerie but really, it is actually quite stunning."

"I've seen it like that before, but never with the halo as vivid and golden as it is tonight," replied John. "There are many Druid and other Pagan myths and legends about the halo around the moon and most of them predict imminent, terrible events. Let's hope that it simply means that the good weather will continue." He put his comforting arm around Sarah's shoulder.

Their goodbyes were said at the front of the garden centre. John thanked his in-laws for a wonderful and as always, restful weekend. The girls were kissing their grandparents goodbye when, back in the house, a telephone could be heard. Sarah's father was aware that John had, as a matter of military protocol, given the garden centre's house phone number as a contact because there was no mobile or internet connection at this location in the forest. Something that Thomas was in no great hurry to change.

"I think that I had better get that." Thomas was ex-military himself and wasn't expecting any calls, he disappeared into the house, returning quickly. "It's for you, John. It's Major Williams."

John walked back into the house and picked up the phone. "Hello, Colonel Jackson."

The voice that replied was his Second-in-Command, Craig Williams. Craig was a competent man who, when on the occasions John left the regiment with him, knew that it was in good hands.

"Sorry to bother you Colonel, I know how much your weekends mean to you and that there is no TV where you are, but there is something brewing that you need to know about."

John's armoured vehicle squadrons were the closest to Heathrow and could get into London fairly quickly causing many possible scenarios to flash through his mind.

"Fire away, Major. What's happening?"

"Difficult to say confidently at this point Colonel, but there appears to be a nationwide contamination of fuel." He paused for a moment, having an afterthought. "Colonel, do you have enough fuel to get you back to Windsor?"

"Yes, a full tank, pretty much. Why?"

"Whatever you do, don't go into any filling stations, it seems to be that the contamination is spreading from there."

"Roger that." This was a strange situation, but not one that seemed to have

33

immediate military connotations. "Is there more?" he asked, wondering where this might go.

"Yes, I'm afraid, much more." The Regiments Second in Command 2i/c, Major Craig William's voice was deadly serious. "Riots are spreading across the country. At the moment they are mainly focused on the major cities, but as the incident progresses, it is predicted that the situation has the potential to worsen. At the moment the police are containing the rioters whose foremost intention appears to be mainly looting. We are constantly being kept in touch with the developments, but it is hoped that after the weekend things will calm down." Craig Williams finished his short summary of the events.

John was thoughtful for a while. "Not a very happy picture that you paint, Craig. Have we actually been put on standby?" This was the all- important question.

"Not at the moment, Colonel, but I have checked our availability and we have 'C' squadron ready to roll immediately if they need us. There is one other thing that you will not be aware of and it isn't known if these events are actually terrorist motivated, but, three passenger aircraft out of the UK have gone missing in the Atlantic. It appears that they simply dropped out of the sky mid-ocean, without warning. The pilots managed to get a Mayday message sent, stating that all of the aircrafts engines had suddenly and inexplicably shut down. A huge rescue flotilla is racing to the locations but nothing else is known at this time."

"OK Craig, I'm on my way back to Windsor right now and will have mobile communication capability in about fifteen minutes, once I am out of the forest. I shall go back to my quarters with the family and stay with them tonight. From there I can be in the barracks within ten minutes if this escalates."

Craig Williams closed the conversation. "OK, Colonel. Given luck this will fizzle out. See you in the morning."

With that, the conversation was ended. John returned to his family. This was serious news, but as a squadron had not been put on standby and he was heading back to Windsor anyway, it was quite possible that the whole problem would be resolved on Monday. There seemed no point in worrying Sarah with the news. "Come on Mrs Jackson, let's load the girls into the car and head back to Windsor. School tomorrow for them, I'm sure that they will all be asleep before we have driven five miles."

Watching television and listening to the news whilst they were at the garden centre was very much a forbidden pleasure that nobody missed or complained about. From late Friday afternoon to Monday morning the Jackson family had no idea what mayhem was befalling the nation. John's only inkling, apart from the Craig Williams phone call that there appeared to be something unusual, was how empty the roads appeared during the drive home, which he mentioned several times to Sarah.

"Are you allowed to tell me what the mysterious phone call was about, John?" Sarah was well aware that there were many aspects of her husband's career that he was unable to discuss with anyone outside the military, including her, but, she was conscious that there was obviously something going on even at a local level.

"There seems to be unrest across the country which appears to be mainly centred in the larger towns. Information at the moment is patchy and it is hoped that whatever the reason for this unrest, it should be resolved early next week." This explanation reduced Sarah's apprehension, but her concern was heightened as they approached the end of their journey.

The next surprise was the number of abandoned cars that were evident when they left the motorway at the Windsor relief road, which now enjoyed the illustrious title of, Royal Windsor Way. Further along the relief road at the Goswell Road roundabout, there was a large group of people milling aimlessly about, and again several stationary cars that appeared to be badly parked but undamaged. There was certainly much that was far from normal, but he decided to play it down and not worry the car's occupants before he knew more.

"Looks as if there may have been an accident," John commented to Sarah as he threaded his way through the cars and people, although there were no police vehicles, ambulances or fire trucks to be seen. "Not much we can do to help. I'm sure that the emergency services will have everything under control."

They continued onwards the couple of miles towards their home in Gratton Drive, St. Leonards Hill, oblivious of the turmoil that was sweeping across the nation. In his mind it looked like something that would be put right in the forthcoming week ahead.

Chapter 7

Reality Strikes

Armageddon + 3 days

It was as hectic as ever in the Jackson household. Sarah was in command, preparing breakfast for the family, hurrying her three lethargic daughters along, trying to get them ready for school on time. Monday morning was always difficult; they needed quite a lot of persuading to become motivated. Time was at a premium if she had to get her girls delivered safely to school. John kissed the family goodbye and drove off on the short journey towards Windsor.

Although globally renowned as a significant world heritage site, Windsor was, in fact, quite a small town, boasting a huge and iconic castle of enormous historical significance. Bounded on the north by the River Thames, there was only access by foot over the river to the distinguished town of Eton. Spreading from the east of the Castle and circling around in a huge arch to a westerly point, the Castle Farm blended into Windsor Great Park, providing another perimeter to the town. Due to its ancient involvement with the British monarchy over centuries, there had been a need for the attendance of soldiers to be readily available. In the past, this presence was of a military importance, but in later years the necessity had been more of a ceremonial requirement. In addition to the long established existence of Combemere Barracks, providing a cavalry military element, there was also Victoria Barracks, which was home to a rotating presence of the Foot Guards Battalions, and who had traditionally provided an infantry responsibility.

In his position as Commanding Officer (CO), Lieutenant Colonel John Jackson

36

would normally have a staff car and driver to collect him, but today he was to take his own car to the barracks as his regular driver/ orderly was away on a course. It was 6:30 am, usually the roads would be reasonably quiet at this time. Today this was not the case. Again, as on the previous night he was aware that there were several cars which appeared abandoned and even at this early hour there were people wandering about rather aimlessly looking bewildered. Half a mile from his house there was a newsagent and convenience store set back from the road behind a lay-by. Outside there was a small group of people. John could see that there was quite a lot of rubbish strewn around in front of the shop. The traffic was sparse and the thought that it might have been a public holiday passed through his mind, although he was certain that this wasn't the case. Upon arriving at the barrack gates there was the usual armed guard, but curiously the gates were closed. The guard saluted and the gates were opened for him to enter. This was unusual, as just inside the gates was a lifting barrier, which was the usual checkpoint during daylight hours. Jacko made a mental note to discover the reason for this change in procedure as soon as he reached his office.

Combemere Barracks was within a mile of Windsor Castle, and it covered an area of over twenty acres. The Barracks dated back to 1804, with some specific buildings, such as the riding school, were from a later date, 1881. In 1953, a redevelopment program had begun, which modernised the accommodation for men, horses and vehicles, and had lasted for about ten years. The vehicle workshop buildings and the Quartermaster (Tech) buildings had been updated in the 1970s. Latterly, in 2006, the gymnasium was completed and the accommodation was brought up to today's standards. John Jackson had spent many years on and off stationed at the Barracks since the time that he had first graduated from Sandhurst Military Academy as a rookie officer, joining his regiment as a young, green 2nd Lieutenant. It had been his first posting. He felt very much at home here and it held a special place in his memory.

John Jackson drove through the gates and on to the Headquarters block where his office was located. As usual, there was much movement. Soldiers that he passed threw up smart salutes, which he acknowledged, but he didn't stop until he reached his parking space. In the short time that he had been in the camp, it was noticeable that there was an unmistakable, but ambiguous air of trepidation, looming over it. However, this was a well ordered, highly disciplined regiment and life carried on normally. As always, the place was a hive of activity. Soldiers going about their various tasks, armoured vehicles manoeuvred, the watering order was returning. This was the daily routine for horses that weren't to be used for specific duties that day but still needed to be exercised. Each Trooper rode a horse and led another. In the outside riding school, a troop of recruits were agonizingly slowly learning the art of military horsemanship. In the indoor riding school a more advanced recruit troop were discovering just how difficult it was to ride one handed with a sword in the other, Cuirasses (breastplates) and heavy state uniforms restricted a lot of movement. Other horses were recruits themselves, being trained by the equitation staff. Combemere was a diverse blend of soldiering, old and new.

From a distant rehearsal room, the strains of music from the regimental band preparing for forthcoming State occasions could be heard. Added to the sights and sounds of army life were the uncommon smells peculiar to this camp. Oil, grease and diesel mingled with the unmistakable aroma of horses.

John loved the vibrancy and vitality of Combemere. It could not be found anywhere else in the world. As he walked from his car to the HQ building, a squad of thirty soldiers passed. They were on a road run which would take them up onto the Castle Long Walk. If they were lucky and the physical training instructors were in a good mood, the turnaround point would be the Copper Horse, a huge bronze statue of George III, situated at the highest point. If they were unlucky, they could be made to run another five miles.

The 2nd Lieutenant in charge of the road run shouted to the PTI's, (physical training instructors.) "Run them to the main gates and back, I need to talk with the Commanding Officer." He veered off from the squad of men and over to Colonel Jackson, throwing him up a smart salute.

"Good morning, Lieutenant, nice morning for a brisk run," replied Colonel Jackson, returning the salute, noticing that the young officer had a worried look on his face.

"Colonel, we have been wondering if it would be wise to take the men on this road run considering what is happening."

It was Jacko's turn to look concerned.

"Lieutenant, I have been away in the country all weekend and out of contact. I have no idea what has been happening. Take the men up to the Copper Horse and back. As soon as I get into my office, I'll be brought up to speed regarding the weekend's activities."

The young officer looked perplexed, saluted, and ran off to join the squad.

Traditionally, early Monday morning, the atmosphere in the regimental office block was positively vibrant with activity; there was much that had to be done to prepare the HQ, 'A' and 'B' squadrons for their forthcoming roles. The adjacent office of the Regimental Corporal Major (RCM) was busier than usual dealing with those errant Troopers who had overstepped the mark in one way or another and were meted out punishment by the RCM. There was an unwritten law within the regiment that if a soldier found himself on Commanding Officers Orders for a misdemeanour, he would have to go before the RCM first. Depending upon the severity of the offence, the RCM would ask the wayward Trooper if he would accept his punishment or go before the Commanding Officer. Most accepted their lot and settled for the RCM's punishment, extra guard duties etc. which was always preferable to the financial option that the CO could hand out.

Colonel Jackson walked into the regimental office block. He noted the action taking place in the RCM's office and felt grateful that the British Army had devised a system that allowed him to deal with the more significant matters, and that luck had given him such a great associate as Warrant Officer Class 1, Dan Buckland.

RCM, Dan Buckland, was a formidable man by any estimation, a larger than life Scotsman. He had risen through the ranks to hold the highest non-commissioned position in the regiment. He was large, not only in stature and personality, but huge in the level of respect in which he was held by all ranks. He had joined the regiment about the same time as Jacko, and served in many locations, both with the regiment, and on secondment to other units.

Jacko walked into the HQ outer office and noticed the uncommon absence of his regimental clerk. Lance Corporal Rogers was the faithful gatekeeper to the CO's inner sanctum. Rogers's job was multi-tasking, filtering the irritating little problems before they were presented to the CO. He served as a military version of a private secretary, knew every soldier in the unit and most of the gossip. He was dedicated to his job and to the smooth running of HQ Squadron. Colonel Jackson was very aware of Rogers's attributes and value. If he was absent from his desk at the time the Colonel arrived, there would be a good reason, but today he would have appreciated a quick up-date from Rogers bringing him up to speed with what had occurred at the camp over the weekend.

Moving on into his office, Jacko sat down behind his desk, looking forlornly at the overflowing in-tray and the highly stacked pending-tray. He tried, but failed, to suppress a small sigh. This was looking to be a busy week. The telephone rang "Hello, Colonel Jackson." "Jacko, its Bill."
"Hi Bill, what's up?"

Colonel William Brand was the Silver Stick-in-Waiting to the Monarch. This was an ancient appointment with an antiquated title, but it required the current holder of the post to be at the forefront of military affairs.

"Jacko, it's not good news I'm afraid. I'm sure that you have been watching the news and you're aware of the crisis that is hitting the country."

Jacko was surprised to hear such a weighty statement. "No Bill, I have been away in the country all weekend, no radio, no TV. What do you mean? You really do have my full attention; tell me more!"

Jacko sat forward in his seat, elbows on the desk, now concentrating. "Jacko, you have to cancel all leave and training. Lock down your barracks and, under no circumstances, let anyone out without explicit orders." His tone was solemn and direct.

"Hell, Bill, what's going on?"

The voice at the other end of the phone was guarded in his explanation. "We're not quite sure at this point John, but it looks like it might be a biological or chemical attack. Just about all of the terrorist groups are claiming responsibility, but the blunt outcome is that there is no petrol or diesel available, and from what we can discover there won't be any in the foreseeable future. All fuel stocks are contaminated.

We are moving from Bikini Black Alpha, to condition Amber. I don't need to tell you that this means issuing personal weapons and ammunition."

There was a palpable pause whilst Bill Brand thought through his next orders. "Ration all of the fuel that you have in barracks, treat it like liquid gold. This looks like it's going to be a long and protracted problem. Don't touch any fuel or any containers that might have been in contact with fuel from outside your location. They are hazardous and believe they might contaminate your fuel stocks."

Bill Brand paused as if not quite believing the statement that he had just made. "Double – no quadruple your regimental police quota. Jacko, you have to make provisions to take in guests."

"Guests? Now you really do have me wondering."

This conversation was taking on surreal proportions and John Jackson was more than just a little intrigued.

"Jacko, the Royal Family will be spending time with you. That's all that I can tell you for the moment, but I'll get back to you as soon as I have more info."

There was a stunned silence lasting some time while both men considered the implications of Bill's words before the phone sprang back into life.

Jacko broke the pause, eager to hear Bill's next words which were totally unexpected. "Anyone but you Bill and I would have thought this was a wind-up."

"This is no duff, I can assure you, Jacko. The predisposed operation of taking the Royal Family to an underground bunker is now deemed unnecessary under the circumstances and considering The Queen's and the Duke of Edinburgh's ages, Combemere Barracks offered the best solution. Get on with what I have told you and I will get back to you ASAP with updates. Jacko, it's still all speculation at this point, but there is a very strong possibility that this could be a diversionary tactic to focus our attention in one place. Jacko, consider this a 'now thing'. Get on it right away. Six armoured vehicles to enter via the Long Walk, as soon as you approach the gates they will be opened for you. All of this might have been anticipated by the attackers and you could be in the sights of hand held anti tank weapons. We can rule nothing out. Get back to me as soon as the mission is completed"

"I'm on it right away," Jacko snapped in reply and the conversation was over.

Jacko could now hear the photocopier in the outer office, denoting that Rogers was back. "Rogers, get me 'A' Squadron Leader."

Major Nick Trevelyan was a well respected and highly competent soldier who had served with distinction in Iraq and Afghanistan. The duty clerk got on with locating the requested man and John Jackson readied his personnel equipment.

One and a half minutes later, Rogers called through the office door, "Major Trevelyan, on the line for you, sir."

Jacko took the call. "Major. Instant mobilization; ready me four Spartans and two Jackals to be ready to roll in thirty minutes, bombed up, but for a very short journey; your best soldiers."

Trevelyan began to ask questions, which Jacko answered in the bare minimum. "Thirty minutes Major, at the main gate."

Those minutes flashed by and Jacko found himself in front of the guardroom surrounded by the formidable troop of armoured vehicle commanders, led by Major Trevelyan briefing them on the action. The engines of the armoured vehicles were loudly idling nearby.

He needed to raise his voice in order to address the men. "The situation is this. We have been ordered to move up to the Castle via the Long Walk, pick up some members of the Royal Family and bring them safely back here. Sounds simple but there is intelligence which suggests that there is a possibility of us being attacked by an unknown terrorist group. I want maximum surveillance on the way in, looking for possible attack locations. They won't attempt to hit us if they are there, until we make the return trip loaded with our cargo."

The plan was simple in the extreme, far simpler than the usual briefings they were used to receiving and also slightly bizarre. There were some frowns, but all nodded their understanding of the mission.

"Mount up!" Jacko gave the command and the men climbed into their vehicles, with Jacko taking the lead Jackal. There was a standard radio check and the troop of six armoured vehicles roared out of the gates and into St Leonard's Road. As they drove the short distance to the interception of Albert Road and the Long Walk, they were all amazed by the transformation that seemed to have taken place so rapidly. Everywhere they looked they saw turmoil. People wandered around having apparently no purpose in the expectation that suddenly there would be an answer to whatever it was that had stricken their lives so abruptly. Some people tried desperately to flag down the troop, seeing them as the only visible entities of authority in a world that had descended into mayhem. Ignoring them and driving past felt like a deplorable action, but the only one available to Jacko under the circumstances. They drove onwards with heavy hearts.

The troop turned left onto the long avenue that led to the southern side of Windsor Castle. Jacko had ridden this impressive entrance several times before on state occasions, alongside the Royal State coach, escorting the Monarch. Then there had been cheering crowds waving flags, military bands and the Regimental Standards lowered, as the Monarch that he was riding next to drove by. Now it was uncharacteristically devoid of people. Previously at any time of the day the Long walk had always been a tranquil scene of tourists, courting couples and dog walkers enjoying the spectacular scenery. The Castle looked truly magnificent from this vantage point. It was slightly more benign than the northern facade with its high walls and craggy rock buttresses. Today was an entirely different occasion. All eyes in the armoured vehicles were alert, on the lookout for potential attackers hidden in the nearby undergrowth.

As the troop roared uphill on the final approached to the Castle perimeter, the huge wrought iron gates swung open and they entered the Castle grounds. The gates were quickly slammed shut behind them. A few hundred meters and they were entering the inner quadrangle. They came to a halt at the Castle's rear entrance next to the saluting dais. The Royal party was there ready and waiting. The Spartans that Jacko had chosen were armoured personnel carriers (APCs). Not the most comfortable mode of transport and certainly not something that the older members of the group would have been used to riding in. Jacko jumped down from his Jackal, walked over to the Queen and threw up a smart salute. He had met the Queen personally before, but only to be introduced and then she had moved on, their conversation being minimal. "Your Majesty, I am to transport you to Combemere Barracks," he announced.

"Yes, Colonel Jackson," the Queen replied, "Most unfortunate, but necessary under the circumstances."

The conversation was brief; and Jacko had no intention of standing around debating the weather. He had a job to do and he meant to do it efficiently. The task of loading the Royal party into the APCs, with a little less than could be described as, a dignified manner, began.

He escorted the Monarch to the back of the first APC and it was then that a new problem presented itself. These vehicles were designed for fit infantry soldiers to jump in and out of. Getting an octogenarian into such a vehicle posed a dilemma. Clearly Elizabeth II was going to require help, a lot of help, but picking up the Monarch and slotting her into the armoured vehicle was fraught with problems. Actually touching the Queen in anything more than a handshake was a definite protocol no-no. The seconds ticked by. Jacko was close to scooping up the Queen and getting the job done, abandoning protocol to deal with the consequences later, when a solution appeared in the personages of Princes William and Harry. They had watched the situation develop and moved forward, taking each of their grandmother's arms, and as gently as could be managed, got her into the vehicle. The rest of the Royal party was loaded into the APCs with as much respect as could be mustered.

Before he closed the rear door of the vehicle, which carried HM the Queen, he stopped to say a few words. "Ma'am, these vehicles are not built for comfort and we will be driving fast to reduce any possibilities of attack, but any discomfort that you might experience will be brief, as the barracks are close by, as you know."

The Queen nodded acceptance of the circumstances. Jacko closed the armoured door and climbed back into his lead Jackal. He gave the order to move out over the troop radio, and the small convoy roared off back through the gates and down the Long Walk. They were back, driving through the gates of Combemere Barracks, within four minutes. There had been no attack. The slightly crumpled Royal party was taken to the Officers' Mess. Jacko took his leave allowing them time to explore their new accommodation. He told all of the soldiers involved in the operation that the presence of the Queen on the camp was, for the time being, to be kept undisclosed, but it was obvious that this would be a short lived secret. Jacko returned to the HQ Regimental block. His first job was to call London and inform them that the mission was completed and successful.

"Rogers, get the RCM, and call a meeting of all officers and senior NCOs for one hour from now in the SNCO's Mess."

The next sixty minutes were hectic. The phone rang continually, apprising Colonel Jackson of the impending fast moving developments.

Rogers returned to the office looking flushed and the worried expression on his face told all. "The Silver Stick on the phone for you, Sir," he advised from the outer office.

"Jacko, this thing is escalating at a pace faster than we could ever have predicted." The tone of his voice portrayed the severity of the circumstances. "What was originally sporadic looting has now become widespread. The police have no control over what is happening. We have deduced that this incident commenced early hours Saturday morning.

We are now seventy-two hours into this debacle and it's only gaining momentum and shows no signs of abating. A lot of aircraft have been reported to just drop out of the sky, like stones, with no apparent reason.

The death toll from these disasters is huge and growing hourly. From what we have learned so far, this appears to be some sort of a biological attack which is rendering all oil based fuels inert. The actual perpetrators have not yet held their hands up, but all sorts of fanatical groups are claiming responsibility. Our scientists think that there is an incubation period before this substance, or whatever it might be, mutates. This has had the effect of aircraft refuelling and taking off, perfectly normally, but then a number of hours into their flight, the engines stop and they are falling out of the sky. Mayday messages are being received by air traffic control from pilots who are reporting that their engines have just shut down without explanation. The best that they can achieve if they are over land is to try to glide the aircraft to a place that is unpopulated when they hit the earth thereby reducing the death toll. Sometimes this has been impossible and some stricken craft has hit highly populated areas. Other aircraft do reach their destination before the incubation period has elapsed but they then refuel; that in turn contaminates the fuel chain in that country, which is making the global spread of this virus even faster. It looks as if there is a complete breakdown in society. Forget the COBRA Committee, that's completely debunked now. There is a radical sea change here in Whitehall. We are on the equivalent of a war footing. An interim government has been set up drawn from all parties, temporary name - National All Party Interim Government or, NAPIG.

The only good to come out of this fiasco so far, is that the party political playground bickering between politicians that we have all witnessed over the past years is now completely swept aside; such is the intensity of the situation. We estimate that electricity will be lost in a day or two; which means that telephones, both land lines and mobiles will crash, this of course includes computers. The government has a team of super eggheads that are constantly monitoring global situations, extrapolating foreseeable outcomes. These are today's version of the types that were at Bletchley Park during WW2. They have worked out a probable chain of events over the next eighteen months. They consider this exercise a no-brainer as there are no complications from political or religious interference. It's a simple case of dominoes, one falling after the other in an easy to determine series of predictable events. I am going to send you a list that the government Think Tank has devised. I suggest that you print it off while you still can and let your men see for themselves what is happening..., and Jacko..., good luck."

For a moment, Colonel John Jackson sat astounded, contemplating the severity of the phone call that he had just listened to. It seemed to be almost too fantastic for words. As the hours passed, the gravity of the fuel disaster sunk deeper and deeper.

In London, an emergency meeting of NAPIG was called, and the combined brains at the Ministry of Defence, Gloucestershire and Chatham HQ and some other obscure, slightly weird and more clandestine groups theorised the outcome of such an incident, and the consequences reached were not at all good.

"Rogers!" He called through the adjoining door. Lance Corporal Rogers was in his office in a flash, eager to know what was going to be the next news from London. "There will be an email from Silver Stick coming through at any moment. I want you to print off two dozen copies of the attachment and take them to the WO's & SNCO's Mess. Stick them on the wall in a place where everyone can see them and keep a dozen copies for the senior ranks."

Closing the door to his office, he called Sarah on his cell phone. The phone rang for a while. "Pick up Sarah, pick up." Finally, she answered. "Listen to me please, darling. This is very important."

Sarah interrupted, "I'm very busy at the moment John. Is this something that can wait until this afternoon?"

"No, Sarah, you must drop everything, go immediately to the supermarket and buy as much non-perishable food as you can carry. You must go immediately. Although this disaster is national, the reverberations are still regional and sporadic, but it will quickly escalate to all parts of the country. I just hope that our local supermarket hasn't been hit and you are able to get supplies. Do you understand?"

The tone of her husband's voice was such that she simply answered, "Yes, John."

"I can't explain any more, but please, do what I have asked. Then go home and stay indoors."

Jacko ended the call, but continued to stare at the mobile phone in his hand for almost a minute, wondering what would be the fate of the people that he loved so dearly.

The hour passed in a flash. The men gathered together in the Mess, all looking apprehensive. Abrupt meetings like these were rare, and tended to predispose bad news.

The venue for this dramatic and unparalleled event was the dining room of the SNCO's Mess, which, a few evenings before, had hosted a dinner, and was still set up for that occasion. In the centre of the room, two large antique, throne like, wooden chairs, which dated back to Victorian times, dominated the top table. These were the traditional seats of the Commanding Officer and the senior Warrant Officer.

The CO of the Household Cavalry Regiment found himself standing in front of the officers and senior NCOs preparing to communicate to them something which was bordering on the absurd. As the Colonel prepared to speak, Rogers was busy with bluetac and sell tape, sticking the A4 sheets of paper to the closed shutters of The bar. The atmosphere in the room was electric, in anticipation of what was about to be imparted to them. The look on John Jackson's face betrayed the anxiety that he was o b v i o u s l y experiencing. He began his speech talking slowly and concisely, there could be no misunderstandings.

"Gentlemen, I have something to inform you and which is of a most dramatic and deeply disturbing nature. Firstly, I will read you the communiqué from the government and then I will break for a recess to allow the significance of this information to sink in. I will then read through some of the salient points of the body of the communiqué." Looking over the heads of the men and women seated before him, he understood the enormity of the task before them. He began reading the first part of the statement wondering how they would react.

"Prime Minister Thomas Matheson. National All Party Interim Government - NAPIG. *It is with great regret that I have to inform you that we are entering a time of grave national and indeed international crisis, which will be of a scale that we could never before have imagined. We are all going to need to find colossal strength and fortitude to take us through the impending apocalyptic event. What you are going to be asked to do goes way past our fundamental core belief, which is loyalty to family. You are going to be asked to temporarily abandon your families so that those who survive this catastrophe may, in time, emerge and create a better life. May God be with you all!*

At this time of national crisis, I have put together a think-tank of the most capable minds in the country to try to predict the forthcoming events and to devise plans as to how we can most resourcefully deal with them.

It is not known if what has happened is actually a concerted attempt to bring down democracy in the civilised world, some random natural occurrence or a scientific catastrophe. Whatever the reason for this adversity, the consequence will be the same. We are still examining the facts to ascertain this, but the outcome is determinable. And, have no doubt; it will be catastrophic beyond anything that mankind has ever encountered before. Fuel stocks around the world are being rapidly contaminated to an estimated 99%. The fuel virus is spreading and appears to be unstoppable. All storage facilities, holding containers, tankers and ancillary equipment are also polluted by this virus. It is not known at this point how long the virus will survive or from where it emanated.

It has been decided that this predominant virus based disaster will be called, The Armageddon Virus.

The interim government considers that the consequences of this dilemma will be as follows:

We shall see strands of collapse in modern civilisation, and disintegration of life in the twenty-first century, as we know it."

Colonel Jackson paused; he looked up from the paper that he was reading from to see faces of men and women.

"Please, take a long look at the second part of the papers that you see on the wall.

They will explain the deeper implications of this disaster, which has been written by a team of the finest minds in the country. They have anticipated the forthcoming apocalyptic events over months and years. I have to tell you that it does not paint a happy scene and you will all be shocked by what you are about to read. We will all have to dig deep to find the inner strength to get us through the horrific experience we are about to endure."

Colonel Jackson paused to allow the gravity of what he was saying to sink into those listening intently, not able to believe what they were hearing; so shocking were the implications of their Colonel's words.

"Surely, this will be nothing more than a storm in a teacup, Colonel," suggested a young lieutenant.

"That maybe so, but for the time being we have to treat this event as high priority and it looks as if it will be on-going. Gentlemen, we will recess for fifteen minutes to allow you to read the communication."

The sheets of white A4 paper that the industrious Rogers was busily fixing to the closed steel shutters of the Mess bar looked iniquitous enough, but the words that were written upon them amounted to nothing less than earth shattering.

There was an obvious air of bewilderment noticeable in the room, added to something akin to anger, as the soldiers began to read the impending projection. Jacko sat down with the Regimental Second- in-Command, Adjutant, MO, (medical officer) senior officers and the RCM. They all had copies of the predicted scenario and read in disbelief, occasionally uttering loud, profound obscenities. After ten minutes, Colonel Jackson reconvened the meeting, calling for quiet. He then read through the second section of the message from NAPIG.

"Mobility.

We are a tremendously mobile society, take away our capability to move around the planet and thus, our privileged section of society, will instantaneously collapse. In addition to contaminating petrol and diesel, aviation fuel is also infected to the same level.

Commuting to the place of work.

Most people in the 'civilised world' commute to work. Without fuel to drive the engines of aeroplanes, boats, trains and road transport, the crucial workers who keep the basic infrastructure of everyday life running, will not be able to get to their place of work. Electricity is generated by various means: coal, renewable, natural gas, hydro and nuclear fission.All of these systems require a work force to operate and maintain them. Even hydro and renewables, which will continue to produce for a while without human intervention, will break down or automatically shut own. In addition, all power generated, flows into a national grid, which has to be administered. A work force not being able to get to their work place will soon cause the grid to stop functioning and the supply of the electricity being generate will cease to be distributed.

Food Distribution.

Practically all the inhabitants of the so-called civilised world rely on their food being delivered. Supermarket shelves will be depleted within two to three days. There will be no more deliveries. Warehouses will be looted. The strongest will take all that they can carry, but without transport, this will be limited to what one person could carry back to their home. Every conceivable type of wheeled vehicle will be utilised such as bicycles and wheelbarrows.

Communication.

Modern society has created, developed and come to be totally reliant upon instant communication, twenty four hours a day, wherever they might find themselves on this planet. This will disappear early in the scenario as the equipment is all electrically powered.

Law and Order.

The inevitable breakdown in law and order will be swift. The majority of police and their civilian counterparts have to commute to work, and they will find it hard to get to their designated posts. Those that do will find a communication breakdown and responding to any call that might be received, even during the initial days of the catastrophe, will be difficult, if not impossible. Within the first days after food supplies disappear, looting will be rampant and anarchy will emerge overnight. It will be impossible to police the situation. The more intelligent folk will see that their only hope lies in the countryside. A smallholding or farm with access to clean water could sustain life for a large family or a small community. Once this has been established, it would be a case of holding on to it and repelling any that might seek to dislodge them.

The Military.

The military currently in barracks could be used to quell rioters in the initial stages of the catastrophe, but this will in essence prove futile. In order for this to be effective, they require fuel to become mobilised, communications to be effective, plus food and water to sustain them. All of this will have disappeared within days, and moving the emergency rations from depots involves transport, which in turn, again requires fuel. Soldiers would fairly soon find themselves in the same situation as the rest of society; hungry, cold, fearful and confused. The combined armed forces would only be able to mount an infantry capability. If the government did decide to mobilise the military, their role would be that of peacekeeping and stability. The competency and effectiveness of these troops would be greatly reduced. These infantry units would not be able to patrol much further than their newly imposed lines of supply allowed. The British Army has enormous warehouses stocked with ration packs designed to last for decades. Moving these supplies to the troops would require logistics that will consume a large percentage of the available soldiers and the remaining meagre fuel reserves. Bringing stability to a nation in anarchy will require soldiers firing upon and killing their own people, who will have formed into feral plundering gangs; people who until recently have been fundamentally, law abiding citizens, now plunged into this turmoil, are only trying to survive.

Hospitals.

Hospitals depend on a steady, almost daily delivery structure of medical supplies, food and other items. They are also dependent on water and electricity. Most hospitals have backup generators which run on diesel and would give some lighting. As soon as the fuel in their generator fuel tanks is depleted, the lights will go out.

Government.

The Government has emergency contingency plans for most incidents, but with no electricity, water, and limited communications, the interim administration has stated that they will be in no position to create and implement special governmental measures to protect democracy. We will be powerless to enforce any measures without a police force and the military. The limited administration capability that they shall be able to operate will be coordinated from the numerous underground bunkers and silos that exist throughout the British Isles. These have the capability to sustain life in the event of a nuclear attack, generating their own power and having a closed air and water supply system. The food stocks are enormous and it would be possible for a government to remain in this situation for years. Communications between the bunkers and strategic locations would be able to continue, due to their internally generated electricity. Preconceived communications to a limited group of locations should be viable. The mobilisation of what forces remained would be very limited.

Water supplies.

It is the NAPIG Think Tank's opinion that, as in the case of the electricity grid, water supplies require people to maintain and administer them. Some of the domestic water supply systems works by gravity, but pumping stations depend on electricity to drive the pumps. This will break down within the first week. Water will not be reaching the majority of domestic outlets very soon into the catastrophe.

Animals.

We think that there will be two schools of thought. Initially, it may be best to let all animals roam free. The alternative could be that as the situation worsens, animals are likely to be considered as a food source.

Banking and wealth.

At the outset of the catastrophe there will be an initial panic run on the banks. Those that can get to the banks by walking, cycling or any other means will be met by locked doors. The majority of bank staff will not be able to get to work. Without electricity and electronic communication, the banking system will not be able to function.

Money and wealth will become immediately valueless. Within a month the negotiable currency is more likely to be a can of beans or corned beef. Valued belongings will become items such as a weapon with which to defend one's self against the marauding gangs who will take what they require by force. Or for the members of such gangs a weapon with which you could impose superiority, enabling you to take what you desired.

Disease.

The population of Great Britain is estimated at sixty seven million. This figure will be reduced to less than five million within two years. The colossal quantity of unburied bodies will bring an epidemic of its own, too appalling to contemplate.

Summary/prognosis

Phase one.

It is estimated that from week one there will be total confusion and havoc – looting, plundering and much wanton destruction. These looters will form into gangs and they will rule for a while. Fortunately, their reign will be short lived.

They will fight amongst themselves and as food supplies dwindle down to nothing, they too will succumb to hunger. Although their reign will be limited, there will be a large amount of mindless damage caused. Policing will be non-existent and martial law is not an option. Fires, which they will have caused, will rage for weeks unchecked. It is assumed that the gangs will stick mostly to the locations of towns and villages. Pharmacies will be ransacked by addicts searching for a fix and other people looking for drugs which they have come to depend upon. Most of the pharmaceutical stock will be destroyed, ending up on the floor and trodden underfoot.

Phase two

Starting one month from The Armageddon Virus, there will be a massive depletion of the population, initially from lack of drinking water and later from hunger. A second wave will develop with even more dire consequences. Disease will spread across the country. Cholera, waterborne diseases and respiratory illnesses will develop due to the rotting corpses. It is the expectancy that most people will actually die in their own beds when thirst, hunger and disease, ravages the country.

Wider Scenario.
Africa and the Middle East

Without the intervention of such agencies as the UN, the tribal feuding will carry on unabated. Additionally, without medical supplies donated by the rich western nations, AIDS will be able to spread even faster and there will be a pandemic. Many of the countries involved have already jumped to the conclusion that this was a concerted attack directed at them, perpetrated by their long-time enemies. The military minds of North Korea, Iran and Israel, have retaliated with rocket attacks. This is predicted to escalate and much of the Middle East will be laid to waste by nuclear missile strikes. It remains unknown at this time how many will perish, and which direction the radiation clouds will pursue. This nuclear warfare would be short lived.

Nuclear waste storage plants.

One of the greatest threats to humanity will come from the many nuclear storage facilities which will go into meltdown. They have been built with consideration made for every conceivable disaster and are housed within bomb proof bunkers. But, as we have witnessed in recent years, these systems are less than fool proof. Chernobyl and the catastrophic meltdown of the nuclear reactor in Fukushima after the Japanese Tsunami are two recent examples. Deaths from cancer are estimated to be in the millions.

There are no definitive figures available concerning the amount of nuclear waste storage depots there are worldwide. The unnerving fact is that all of them require electricity to cool the water which is pumped over the super-heated radioactive spent fuel rods. Everything is fine as long as the rods are cooled for the next 5 to 100 years with refrigerated water. If not cooled, they would stay hot for 1000 years or more. After they are initially cooled sufficiently, they are stored underground in concrete caskets for a minimum of 1000 years. When the electricity fails, the storage facilities backup generators will kick in. They are diesel and will only keep operating for as long as the fuel tanks allow. With no refrigeration and water circulation, the volatile hot fuel rods will quickly evaporate the remaining water. When this is gone, the rods will go into meltdown and finally explode. The ensuing explosions across the planet will have the potential to be at least 500 times that of Hiroshima. This will in turn release a radioactive cloud that will cause cancer in millions. It will depend greatly on wind direction as to how much of the radiation cloud sweeps over Britain. But the deaths from radiation poisoning will be enormous. In addition to the atrocious disasters caused by man, there will still be cataclysms of the natural kind which will go un-monitored or attended by emergency relief teams resulting in much higher death tolls."

The list read like a script from a horror movie, finally he ended the explanation with a footnote which he made a point of explaining that with so much horrific news there was some hope.

"NAPIG. One year on from Armageddon. Those who have survived will have adapted to this new way of life. There will still be some sporadic stealing. Survivors will be of two types. Those survivors, who adapted to the new way of life and created a sustainable way of living off the land, being able to defend themselves against attackers, and those survivors who roam the country stealing whatever they can. Eighteen months from Armageddon the government will start to take back control of the country."

The sense of shock and horror in the room was palpable. Many of Jacko's toughest men looked noticeably traumatised. All were in a stunned state of disbelief at what they had read. They stood in the elaborate Mess, surrounded by memorabilia of soldiers that had preceded them. All of the soldiers in the old photographs and paintings had experienced horrific battles and savagery of warfare throughout the ages and around the world, but none had been asked to face what was about to happen to this current generation of soldiers in their own country, on their own soil. Some men stared vacantly; others studied the small patch of parquet flooring between their boots, not daring to guess what the next episode might be. The atmosphere was highly emotional, and electrically charged.

Colonel Jackson stood up. He took a little time to study the faces before him; faces that were masked in a mixture of disbelief and fear. He continued his address to the shocked soldiers that he would have to lead through what was going to be the most momentous period in human history.

"Gentlemen, now that you have read the communiqué, please allow what you have read to sink in. I will call another meeting to apprise you on any further news as soon as I receive updates. In the meantime, the order has been sent from HQ, London District, that nobody is to leave the barracks. Now it is for you to go back to your men and relate this information to them. I wish you all good luck and may your God be with you."

A large percentage of the soldiers stationed at Combemere Barracks were married. They lived with their families when they were not on duty, in predominately two locations. Directly adjacent to the barracks was army accommodation in an area called Cavalry Crescent, whilst another section of military housing was three miles distant at a locality called Broom Farm. The officers were housed two miles or so away to the west of the town in the far more affluent area of Gratton Drive, St. Leonards Hill. The Jackson family had a regulation four bed detached house on the St. Leonards Hill estate. The implications of what he had said suddenly struck home with a vengeance. "Nobody is to leave the barracks." This order also applied to him!

The Colonel returned to his office feeling physically drained by the meeting in the Mess, knowing that there would be fresh messages from London. Furthermore, the urgent orders sent to Combemere were to be acted upon immediately.

The government had concluded that if this was a terrorist attack, then it gave the impression of being limited exclusively to the deactivation of fuel, which by international reports that were being received, indicated that the incident was now taking on global proportions. There appeared to be no intelligence specifying that there would be a follow up, or second wave, given the total immobility caused which appeared to affect everyone, terrorists included. Therefore, it was becoming increasingly imperative that all the surviving, unaffected fuel was under the strictest level of protection and preservation; not a drop could be wasted. There were good reserves on the camp, but they were not in huge quantities. The scenarios being received from Whitehall were not good. It was expected that within a few days, the electricity grid would go into automatic shutdown. All normal lines of communication would be lost and total panic would be the order of the day. Colonel Jackson was informed that apart from securing rations or providing escort, or high profile personal extraction, he was to lock the gates and sit tight. Whatever fuel he had on the camp was to be used as sparingly as was possible. Any contact with outside contaminated fuel must be avoided at all costs. He called the heads of various sections, such as motor transport and catering; requesting them to give detailed quantities of stocks and expected time scales for rationing.

There were reasonable supplies of emergency and field rations kept in the barracks and a considerable stock of fuel, but nothing that could be considered adequate for this unpredicted longer-term confinement.

Colonel Jackson decided to send a detachment to Aldershot to load up all available transport with as much field rationing as possible. His motor transport officer calculated that eight trucks would have plenty of fuel to easily make the round trip. Permission was received from Whitehall and clearances to Aldershot were given. Tuesday morning at 06:00 hours, the small convoy left through the gates of

Combemere and set off for the short journey to Aldershot. The convoy finally reached the storage facility with difficulty and had been lucky to eventually find a watchman with keys, still on duty. Fortunately, he lived on the premises, but anyone who needed to either drive to work or get there by public transport was unable to do so.

During the day all civilian communication was lost, including cell phones. It was not until later that afternoon that the convoy returned.

They had been successful, but the horror stories they told of what they had seen were hard to believe. Hardly any form of motorised transport was moving on the roads, many of which were blocked by abandoned vehicles. Shops and supermarkets were looted and ransacked, fires blazed unattended. It appeared that law and order had collapsed completely. Bewildered people wandered aimlessly through the streets searching for food, water and answers, questioning why society had so suddenly disintegrated. They were desperate for help, but there was none to be found.

A regular visitor to Jacko's office was the MO (Medical Officer). As the senior medical representative in the barracks it was the MO's duty to ensure the wellbeing and health of all the troops. In Combemere MO at this time was Doctor Sophie Maloney, who held the rank of Major.

Major Maloney was a well respected member of the team. She had been in the army for twelve years, served two tours in Afghanistan and headed up several missions to Africa. At the age of thirty four, her army career had been exemplary. She was married but had no children. Her husband, Jack Maloney, was a GP in the nearby village of Iver, where the couple had their home. There was an additional characteristic to Sophie that made her rather unusual. This attribute was something that had its advantages for the doctor and conversely its disadvantages. Sophie was a willowy beauty who could easily have pursued a career in modelling. She had all of the attributes of a supermodel if she hadn't preferred to dedicate her life to medicine and the assistance of others. She wore little makeup and the dowdy army clothing seemed miraculously transformed when she wore them. Even when she had been working long hours and her hair was pulled severely back in a convenient, practical manner, she still looked striking. Many of the male soldiers would have preferred to have a male MO. They felt uncomfortable explaining their health problems to such a striking woman, whose stunning looks actually intimidated them.

Jacko was always happy to receive visits from Major Maloney, particularly now that revising the camp's medical status was a priority, given the new circumstances.

These were the early days of the catastrophe when it was wondered where this thing would go next. Colonel Jackson sat in his office with the MO, analysing the squadron personnel lists. They were trying to calculate exactly who was in the barracks at this time. Dan Buckland knocked on the door of the CO's office.

"Come in Corporal Major, what have you got?"

"Yesterday, when you got the word from London to go into total lockdown...," Dan paused for a moment.

"Yes, how could I ever forget that phone call?" interjected Jacko, "Nobody in, nobody out."

"Well Boss, we trapped a load of civvies, ten in all."

"Hell! I suppose we must have; didn't think of that with all that's been going on."

"Several Polish cleaners, and the girls who work in the 'all ranks' coffee shop. Two van drivers and the civvie hairdresser. They're kicking up a bit of a fuss. What do you want me to do with them?"

"Let them out, Dan. Now that we know more or less what the threats are, there is no need to keep them here and its more mouths to feed. Have a chat with them, explain the situation thoroughly; send them on their way and wish them good luck, if any want to stay, assign them accommodation"

Major Maloney nodded her agreement.

Dan acknowledged. "OK Boss, I'll get on with that right away."

Chapter 8

A Question of Loyalty

Armageddon + 7 days

Early in the morning, a few days after the fateful day of lock down, the most heartrending episode that John Jackson could ever have imagined in his wildest nightmare unfolded. He was summoned to the guardroom. The NCO guard commander was worried about the large crowd of wives and children that had gathered at the main gate and were demanding to see their husbands. The gates were large, substantial wrought iron structures, currently closed and locked. On the inside of the now enhanced armed barrack, guards stood looking confused and uncomfortable.

On the outside there was a group of about sixty women and children, most of whom John Jackson knew well. The group was mixed with wives of all ranks represented. Some of the mothers were screaming and shouting, demanding to be let in whilst at the back of the crowd others were standing quietly; patiently expecting some form of help to be given. They were now beginning to appreciate the reality caused by lack of available food and a night without electricity. John looked at the crowd and at the rear saw Sarah and his three daughters. Their eyes met and were locked for some time, but there was nothing that he could do, but mouth the words, 'I love you'. He had no option other than to turn his back and walk away, struggling hard not to allow the tears that were in his eyes to be seen by his men. By the time he was back in his office, he had recovered somewhat. He made notes and a long list of options.

Not having contact with their husbands, for a soldier's wife, was not such an unusual event; it was a recognised part of the package of being married to a soldier. The men were often away on various exercises and an assignment, but knowing that they were in the barracks, just the other side of the high walls, was an entirely different matter.

Jacko pitched a plan to RCM, Dan Buckland. "I have an idea and I want your opinion." His eyes were thoughtful, betraying that the plan wasn't fully finalised in his mind. The thought process was still ongoing and he was thinking on his feet. "Fire away, Sir."

"My idea is this. I have decided that we tell the men to write a letter to their families, which are to be placed in the guardroom for collection. The men need to think hard and fast. They have to devise a plan explaining to their families where they think they will have the best chance of surviving this nightmare. My suggestion is a country location. Towns and even villages will be open to vandalism, polluted water and later extreme disease. The strongest will simply take what they want." Jacko rubbed his angular chin between forefinger and thumb, looking pensive. "They must suggest a location to their families in the hope that one day they can reunite. It is a drastic action, so I suggest that that they should first wait a few days and see how the situation develops."

Dan Buckland nodded his approval.

Colonel John Jackson called through his open office door, "Rogers, call a meeting for fourteen hundred hours. All ranks in the cookhouse."

"Yes, sir," came the voice from the other side of the door.

The cookhouse at Combemere dated back to 1953, which was an era when spending on military architecture was less of a priority than the functionality of the structure. This was a bland, grey, miserable, Spartan building, which could accommodate all of the junior ranks at one sitting. The lack of design flair was normally more than compensated by the vibrancy of the soldiers' chatter and banter. No matter how hard the cleaning staff tried; the ever-present smell of cabbage and stale cooking prevailed throughout. This was the venue for Jacko's second address to his soldiers. Today the banter was remarkable in its absence.

There had been many stirring speeches given by stalwart leaders over the course of history and John Jackson knew that what he was about to tell his men would be one of the toughest that any responsible leader ever had to make. Inwardly, he hoped that his strength would not desert him. The cookhouse was filled to capacity. A low murmur of apprehension cloaked the scene. Colonel Jackson stood on a table, looking out across a sea of anxious faces, anticipating what was undoubtedly not going to be good news. A deadly hush spread across the room.

"Gentlemen, what has happened are a global catastrophe of greater magnitude than any biblical, natural or previous man-made disaster. For some unknown reason, a quirk of fate has chosen us to play a significant part in this event. The months ahead will be harder than anything any of us could possibly have imagined physically, mentally and most certainly emotionally. Family is the foremost element in all of our lives and we are being asked to abandon ours to the horrors of, God only knows what might befall them. Many of you have served with the regiment and myself in The Gulf, and later, Afghanistan. You were all asked to write letters to your loved ones when you went into combat zones, telling them of your thoughts, given the possibility that you might not return. I ask you all now to go away and write letters to your family."

As he looked down onto the upturned faces of his soldiers, the look of shock and disbelief was plainly evident on all of them. Ironically, this was a reversal of roles and it was now the families who were the ones facing the imminent danger.

"Please, tell them to prepare themselves to move away. Advise them it would probably be best to go out into the country and find a way of surviving. Collect as much warm clothing as possible and whatever basic tools that they can carry. Anything that is not of use for survival will be an added burden. They must be severe where the children are concerned; nothing unnecessary can be taken. Sleeping bags, tents and rucksacks are a necessity. The best form of transport will possibly be by bicycle, but even something as mundane as a wheelbarrow will be useful. We shall know for certain in the next few days whether this drastic action will be necessary, but it is best that they are prepared to move at a moment's notice. If the worse comes to the worst, and they are indeed forced to leave, ask them to leave a written explanation of what plans they have made at your home. It is the belief of the government that in eighteen months, although this horrific episode will not be over, we will be able to go from this place and look for our wives and family. Finally, tell them that you love them and that you will do whatever is humanly possible for you to be reunited."

Colonel Jackson stood at the door of the cookhouse with the RCM at his side and watched the stunned soldiers file out of the cookhouse. All of their training could never have prepared them for what they were experiencing.

Dan Buckland was the only one to speak.

"I don't think that I remember seeing anything in the Queens Regulations that covered this situation," he muttered banally.

When the cookhouse had cleared, the two men walked silently back to the regimental RHQ office. As they walked through the once animated camp, the picture now was very different. Any soldiers that they passed looked decidedly demoralised. The buzz that had been a constant background backdrop for centuries was conspicuous in its absence. The heart had not quite gone out of the place, but it was certainly missing a beat or two.

Colonel Jackson had begun to realise that his soldiers were tense, and showing signs of stress; and understandably so. He was himself struggling with the life changing tragedy that he had been plunged into so dramatically and the difficult decisions that he had to make. They were locked up in a barracks with supplies of food and water, ostensibly safe whilst all around them civilisation was crumbling into misery – tragedy and devastation never before experienced on such a scale. Electricity had completely collapsed on the third day; water was only available from one tap inside the beleaguered barracks, at the equestrian section, on the wall of the Victorian riding school. This new vital, but previously insignificant water tap was rapidly named by the soldiers, 'The Queen Vic'. Soon a sign was erected stating that, 'The Queen Vic is open licence for business 24/7', and a lowly one hundred year old brass tap became both vital and famous. Without cell phones, the soldiers could not have contact with their families. Even the emergency media were soon non-existent. All TV channels had gone off air from day three. Colonel Jackson felt he needed to do more.

Chapter 9

Family Planning

Armageddon + 11 days

RCM, Dan Buckland entered the office of C o l o n e l Jackson. "You wanted to see me, sir?"

"I have been considering another idea which I want to run by you." "Fire away."

"First things first." Jacko slid the lower right hand drawer of his office desk open and proudly extracted an unopened bottle of Glen Fiddich whisky and two tumblers. "This should improve the thought process," he chuckled. Jacko then relayed his various plans, slowly at first, allowing the separate elements of the idea to formulate in the RCM's mind. Then, he hit Dan with the big one, by first issuing an instruction which he knew would be questioned.

"Dan, I want you to make a tally of how many one and two man tents we have plus sleeping bags, ponchos, medium and small rucksacks.
Talk to the Quarter Master (QM) and find out what he has in his stores." He took another slug of the Glen Fiddich and studied the amber liquid through the glass of the tumbler, waiting for a response.
"For what purpose, sir?" enquired Dan Buckland.

"For the married men whose wives are within five miles of this camp," replied John Jackson, grimacing a little, anticipating the reaction that his next idea would cause, and full knowing that as Commanding Officer he was renowned for radical thinking, well outside the proverbial box.

"I am going to let the men go home to their wives for two hours. Firstly, to say goodbye, but also to give them the kit that might save their lives. In addition, each man will be allowed to take one twenty four hour ration pack for each member of his family."

The look on Dan Buckland's face had to be seen to be believed. But his answer was not what John had expected. "This is one hell of a flyer; you know that some of them won't come back, don't you, Boss?" There was a pause. "The problem is, how many. You're taking a heck of a gamble, but I'm in agreement with you all the way. I suggest that we send them out in groups of ten and keep them apart when they come back. That's if they do. Don't want any of the flaky ones giving the others ideas."

"Good idea, Dan. One other thing that's been worrying me; your home is way up in Scotland; the chances of your wife and boys getting back there are not good."
"I've been thinking that myself," Dan grunted.

"Dan, my wife Sarah's family have a smallholding in Hampshire. It is about as safe as can be expected and could sustain a dozen people easily. I am going to tell Sarah to go there immediately. I would like your wife and boys to go with her. They will stand a far better chance together."

"Thanks John, that's a great offer, and I'm sure Julie will say yes. It's her best option."

There was an uneasy silence. Dan Buckland would have liked to have expressed a suitable reply to show his gratitude, but it just didn't emerge. In reality, such was the high regard in which the two soldiers held each other, there was no need. He broke the tense silence.

"Right, I'm off to organise the stores. I'll get back to you with the numbers."
Dan Buckland left. Jacko sat in his office, which was beginning to feel a very lonely place. He carefully replaced the whisky bottle and tumblers into his desk drawer.

"Rogers," he called through his open office door. The ever-resident Lance Corporal came into his office. "I have decided to call a meeting of all ranks in the cookhouse."
Rogers looked a little dismayed.

"Got a problem with that Rogers?" he enquired. He had learned to listen to his clerk's judgment, as he was far more in touch with the deeper opinions and emotions of the men.

"That's a lot of meetings in a short period of time, sir, and the news just seems to get worse and worse. This is a situation that none of us would have expected and the unease that I can feel from all ranks has moved way past anxiety."

Jacko contemplated this thought for a while. "I hear what you are saying, Corporal and I appreciate your concern, but this is a rapidly moving situation that is progressing hourly. It's only fair that everyone is kept aware of the escalating events. Fate has thrown us together in this set of circumstances and I want to act as objectively as I can for all concerned." He was acutely aware himself that these depressing meetings were becoming all too frequent, but he decided that it was the fairest way to advise everyone of the constantly evolving situation.

An even more depressed group of soldiers assembled in the cookhouse two hours later. They had now had time to digest the implications of what they had been told and were obviously severely shocked. The grim reality was sinking in.

Colonel John Jackson waited for five minutes to allow everyone to find a chair, or somewhere to sit before he started his address. He looked out at the anxious faces before him, and started to deliver his radical address.

"Gentlemen, I have made some preliminary decisions, based upon the scenario that we will be living in extremely close proximity for at least eighteen months. I am revising discipline within the regiment. If we are to live together harmoniously under the dreadful conditions that prevail, then there will have to be many compromises and modifications. I will be starting with rank. The British Army, as we knew it, will shortly cease to exist, along with all of the western armies. We will be no more than an outpost. Basically, we are now just a group of individuals. Other small groups of military will survive, if they were informed in time to take the same drastic measures that we have made. Therefore, I intend to relax much of the discipline that we have all known. If a man is good enough to lead, then he will rise to the top of the stack by his ability and deeds rather than background. For my part, if I cannot lead you without the mechanism of the Army to back me up, then I am not worthy of being your leader. If and when a better leader emerges, then I will happily step down. Some of our number has spent time in Hereford, where 'the no rank, no swank, policy applies' and it works well there."

There was no denying the look of shock and horror on the faces of some of the officers. John Jackson was known for his revolutionary ideas, but this one was a real bombshell.

"We are entering into a new dimension where new rules will have to be devised and new boundaries set. There will be no more saluting and everyone is entitled to call anyone by their first name. Dress code is now at the discretion of each individual. This camp has existed for two centuries, but it is now going to have to take on a new persona. We are going to turn the barracks into as much of a self-sufficient compound as we can achieve. Necessity is the mother of invention and I have no doubt that your ingenuity will know no bounds. When this dreadful situation has passed, and believe me, with your strength and steadfastness it will pass, we will emerge into a new world order and you will be at the forefront of the re-establishment of society. Everyone will have to muck in. Have no doubts there will be no place for drones or passengers. It is going to be tough, very tough. You will be crucial in restoring law and order to what is finally left of the population. There will be a new beginning; from this crucible of fire we will forge a new civilisation."

Jacko paused to allow the weight of his words to sink in. "We are going to have to keep busy, so I have devised some projects that we need to undertake immediately for our survival. Water will be the crucial component for survival. I want two teams of ten men to dig two wells. One on the east side of the camp, on the piece of ground where the demolished squadron block was, and the other behind the managé, on the west side of the camp. There is a strong possibility that the Queen Vic could run dry on us. We require two more teams for gardening. Now you're going to have to come to a compromise on this one as you will see it will become clear as I explain the plan. One group will get wetter than the other. I propose to turn the riding school into a greenhouse and the outside riding school into a market garden. In fact, we are looking at turning any ground, which could be used to plant vegetables, as a growing space. The riding school, being covered, will be the choice winter location and the outside school is where the gardeners' teams will want to be in the summer. We also need communications, so the radio wing will be a priority. I need all the best signallers to get themselves over there from tomorrow, so that we can set up as many links as possible. We are fortunate that our strategic role, as light armoured reconnaissance, has given us a good grounding in radio communication. We have plenty of powerful radios on the armoured vehicles and in the stores. There are limitless supplies of twelve volt batteries lying about in millions of abandoned cars, so there will not immediately be a power supply problem. All information that we receive from this communication source will be posted daily at a news brief in the cookhouse, so that we all know what is happening. We will not be totally isolated. I'm sure that there will be other groups that have dug themselves in as we have and are surviving. There is sure to be a lot of Intel coming from the government bunkers, GCHQ and some other Sneaky Beaky silos that we have never heard about.

Now, for the vehicle wing; I want the best mechanics amongst you to try to devise a form of transport. My thinking is that we find an electric car and somehow drag it back here, take it to pieces and discover the workings. The task that I am setting you is to take a car, strip out the engine and find another means of propulsion. An alternative would be to create our own biodiesel. I know that it's a tall order, but you have plenty of time and we can scavenge whatever you might need. Ingenuity will be the key to our survival.

This brings me to the next group. There will need to be four scavenger teams who will go out, mostly under the cover of darkness to begin with, and bring back whatever the various working teams need. They will compile shopping lists and the scavengers will do the shopping."

Colonel Jackson paused for a reaction.

One voice from the rear lightened the moment. "God, I hate shopping."

"Now, there is a more immediate matter that has to be dealt with. The present dire situation is as such, that it is time for your families to move quickly to whichever safe haven you think they should go."

There was a spontaneous mumble of voices. Colonel Jackson continued, "Now, about sixty percent of you are married with wives and family in quarters locally. I am going to let those men go home to their wives for two hours. Firstly, to say goodbye, but, also to give them the kit that might save their lives."

There was an audible murmur from the men which circulated around the cookhouse like a dark satanic groan. The reality of actually confronting their families and telling them face to face that they would not be there to guide them through this horrendous episode did not bode well. Jacko considered saying something to alleviate the moment, but decided that it was better to forge ahead with his presentation.

"The Quartermaster and his team are sitting across the room. All married soldiers must tell them how many dependents they will need equipment for. We can provide one and two man tents, plus sleeping bags, ponchos, medium and small rucksacks. In addition, each man will be allowed to take one twenty-four hour ration pack for each member of his family. Go back to your families, devise a plan and let them know that you will find them hopefully in eighteen months."

The next segment of his delivery would be hard, he knew. He had given it much deliberation, but could not devise a solution that he thought was acceptable. There was to be much that was not satisfactory, but his concern for the single guys was as genuinely heartfelt as that for the married soldiers.

"To the single men; I know that nearly all of you have families too, and that you would dearly love to be able to do whatever you could to help them, but time for this, like the food outside, is running out, and sadly we cannot send you off to help them. Your best option is to stay here and pray that they are amongst the survivors. The men that will be going to their families will find their names on a list posted on all squadron notice boards. You will be going out in groups of ten. Prepare yourselves. The first group leaves tomorrow at sunset and this will continue throughout the night. Good luck to us all."

The briefing over; Jacko walked over to the Quartermaster sitting at a canteen table, flanked by two corporals. "I'll be your first client Len, put me down for two, two man tents, four sleeping bags, four groundsheets and four ponchos, please."

"OK Boss. I'll be dishing this kit out from the stores as soon as I get the list completed. You won't be expecting these men to sign for this I suppose – will you Boss?" he added with a grin.

"Good work, Len. See you later to pick up my kit."

Satisfied that he had put together a rational plan given the awful circumstances, he walked back to his office to deal with other pressing matters. Sophie Maloney was waiting on the staircase balcony of the HQ block. They exchanged greetings and Jacko led the way into his inner office.

"What's up Major? You look worried."

The usually unflappable doctor did indeed look apprehensive, something he had not seen before.

"John, I just wanted to check with you that the same arrangement applies to me regarding going back to our homes to initiate a survival plan. I'm the only married woman on the camp."

"Of course, Sophie; you have as much right to warn your husband as the rest of us."

Some of the tension left her face and she continued, "I know that Jack will want to stay at his surgery for as long as it's possible, he is a dedicated man."

Jacko had met Jack Maloney on several occasions. He had liked the man but secretly, as were the thoughts of many of the other soldiers, he considered Jack Maloney to be a very lucky man.

"In that case I will go and draw my supplies from the QM." Sophie walked out of the office, looking a little more relieved than when she had arrived.

As she left, Dan Buckland walked into the office and before they got down to the work at hand together; to list the concerns that were immediate, he commented, "How does she do that?"

"How does she do what?" Jacko was confused by the statement. "Make every piece of uninteresting military uniform look as if it were tailor made for her?"

Jacko had to agree, but had no answer.

Rogers knocked on the door. "There's a corporal who says he has something important to speak to you about Sir."

"Please send him in, Rogers." Jacko gave Dan a cautious glance.

The man nervously entered the room. "I wonder if I might have a word with you, Sir."

A corporal from the R.E.M.E. (Royal Electrical & Mechanical Engineers), stood apprehensively in front of the two senior men. Jacko and Dan prided themselves on knowing the names of all the soldiers under their command.

"It's Galston, isn't it?" Jacko's tone was polite; he could see that the young man was apprehensive.

"Yes, sir, I think that I have an idea which might help, regarding the cars which are inside the barracks and are not contaminated."

Galston had made a confident start, but he was now a little flustered. Getting into the Colonel's, new, no rank, scheme, wasn't going to be easy. "David," he replied awkwardly.

Jacko rolled the conversation right along. "David, you have made a very good point. Where are you taking this?" Jacko was intrigued by the young man's reasoning.

David Galston continued to set out his proposal. "The families have to get to a safe location, which will be their individual choice. Getting there is not going to be easy, but if we siphon petrol from the cars on barracks, choose the most appropriate vehicles for the job, top up their tanks and fit them out with as much equipment as can be spared, the families will have a better chance. They are only going to get one go at this, but it's a good option. We aren't going to need the cars in the foreseeable future."

Jacko stood back and took stock of the young man. "Good idea, David. It's not guaranteed that the families will all get to their destinations, but it will improve their chances enormously."

Jacko called Dan Buckland over and explained the plan to him. "Sounds like a goer to me," Dan beamed. "Well done, Galston." "David," Jacko interjected gently.

"Err, yes, David," Dan corrected himself raising an eyebrow. This was going to take a bit of getting to grips with.

"I have taken the liberty of checking out the available cars," David added. "Thought you might," Jacko smiled, "And?"

"There are enough cars available, but some of them belong to the single guys and, well, it might appear a little one sided, as the single folk are going to have to stay put and not get to say goodbye to their families." David considered his latest remark, cleared his throat and made an inspection of his boots.

Dan Buckland intervened smiling. "You're single, aren't you, son?" he enquired.

"Yes, I am, sir, er..., Dan," the young man answered tentatively.

"I think that I have seen you driving quite a nice car, if I'm not mistaken," Dan continued.

Jacko took over the conversation. "David, we are all going to have to adapt to a completely new and unfamiliar way of life from now on. Virtually nothing will be as it was again. We all have to accept that."

Jacko paused for several seconds, allowing his words equally to sink into his own mind, and to that of the young soldier. He continued, placing his hand on the young soldier's shoulder, "Your idea is a good one and we will implement it immediately. Please, go back to the workshop and start the ball rolling on this, and thank you for your much appreciated input."

The young man walked off in the direction of the workshops looking pleased that he had made a strong contribution.

Jacko continued speaking with Dan Buckland. The distraction of talking with him regarding other matters within the barracks was welcome. After talking for twenty minutes, most of the official conversation was complete and the two men could relax slightly.

Jacko took the now much depleted whisky bottle from his drawer, held it up to the light and noted that there was sufficient left for two good drams.

The final precious drops of whisky were drained from the tumbler and Dan Buckland took his leave to make a tour of the camp checking that all was in order. As a senior influence, making his presence felt, he knew from his time as a young trooper had immense value psychologically.

The following day, at sunset, the time had come to implement Jacko's plan for the married soldiers, allowing them to go back to their homes, deliver the vehicle and supplies, and to say their goodbyes.

The workshop had done a great job in selecting the most suitable cars for the wives and families to make their way to the location that they had decided would be the most appropriate to attempt to sit out the worst of what was to come. The vehicles had been checked over and all of the available fuel that had been siphoned from the spare cars was put into the tanks of the chosen vehicles.

Standing outside the guardroom, Jacko and Dan, watched the guard commander tick off the soldiers from his list as they drove off to see their families, for what might be the last time.

"Tell me when you want to go to your family, Dan, it wouldn't be sensible for us both to be out of camp at the same time," suggested the Colonel.

"Yes, I was thinking that after midnight would be as good a time as any. It should be quiet. They will be sleepy and hopefully less emotional."

"I was thinking midnight myself."

"OK, midnight for you, Dan, and as soon as you get back, I'll go."

At 02:00 hours, on the dot, Dan Buckland jogged up to the barrack gates and the guard let him back in. He had a good sweat on from the run. He had measured the distance and knew exactly how long it would take him to run from his quarters on the Broom Farm estate, back to the barracks, thereby allowing him to spend as much precious time from his allotted two hours with his family as possible.

Jacko walked out of his accommodation, loaded with the equipment for his own family. "Everything OK, Dan?" he enquired.

Dan Buckland was only one of five soldiers in the camp to wear the coveted upside down winged dagger of the SAS. He had spent eight years with that elite regiment and was highly respected for it. "Bloody hell, John, I have had to do some pretty tough things in my life, but that was by far the worst." Dan Buckland's face displayed both anger and despair. "Watch how you go out there. It's turned into a jungle and it's full of predators."

Jacko was wearing a Para smock with his own SAS winged dagger on the shoulder. Dan smiled as he noticed it. *"You'll be OK,"* he thought to himself. "I'll see you in the morning. Keep an eye on things whilst I'm away, Dan."

The barrack gates were swung open and Jacko drove off in the car that he hoped would take his family to safety. It was heavily laden with bulky equipment, stowed in rucksacks, with the tents secured across the roof rack on top.

This was the first time that John Jackson had been outside the walls of the barracks and into the adjoining suburban district apart from his rapid trip to the castle since the dreadful episode had begun. He was appalled by what he witnessed. Everywhere was devastation, abandoned cars, burned out buildings. Litter was strewn wherever he looked. Not every day litter, but the contents of people's homes; items that would have been cherished, now useless and abandoned. Smashed windows, looted shops and offices could be seen everywhere.

Above all of this horror, the rancid, sweet smell of death hung in the air like a rank blanket. This was still relatively early into the catastrophe, but the vulnerable folk had already succumbed to rampant violence. The elderly, weak and sick, still lay where they had died; there was not an option of the bodies being buried or disposed of in any manner. This was the next phase of death scything into the population. The following phase would be thirst and hunger, finally disease expedited by contamination that the thousands of unattended corpses would convey. Abandoned dogs roamed about in packs, looking thin and emaciated; noticeable was the lack of street lighting or indeed lights of any description. It was practically pitch black. Only a weak light from a crescent moon gave some visibility when the scudding clouds didn't obscure its weak pale silver light. As he drove past the petrol station on the Windsor Road roundabout, he noticed that abandoned cars were even denser in that location after filling up, having travelled only a few yards before stopping because of the contaminated fuel. He pushed on along Windsor Road. Finally, he arrived at his house and parked the car.

He had lived in the house for two years, but in that time he had never seen it in such complete darkness before, which gave it an eerie appearance as the clouds passed across the moon. He found the front door key in the pocket of his smock and with a pounding heart, opened the door, not knowing what to expect inside.

The house too was in complete and utter darkness. It took a little while for his eyes to become accustomed. Sitting on the bottom step of the stairs, he took off his boots and smock, and then quietly he went upstairs. The door to his bedroom was slightly ajar. He opened the door carefully, hoping not to make any noise and walked quietly to the bed.

Sarah's head was turned away from him, her long hair covering her face. He stood for a minute or two and just looked at the woman that he had shared so much with. Slowly and quietly he undressed and slipped into the warm bed. This wasn't to have been his plan, but he couldn't help himself. Always, when he had devised a plan he stuck to it rigidly, but his military plans had never involved the woman that he loved so dearly; the circumstances had never been so extraordinary.

Gently, he pulled the hair from Sara's face and she awoke. He had been expecting that she would jump with the shock at finding him there but she just opened her eyes and said dreamily, "I knew that you would come for us, John."

A dreadful feeling of guilt swept over him, for he knew that he wasn't here to save them from the hell that they had been going through, but really to explain that they would have to go away and fend for themselves for, at the very minimum, eighteen months. The warmth of their matrimonial bed and the closeness of this beautiful woman were too much for him; he could not resist the temptation of his lovely wife. They fell into passionate lovemaking. When the exquisite moment had passed, they lay in each other's arms, their legs entwined in an all too brief, fleeting moment of pure love. For a brief time, a very short-lived suspended moment, everything seemed to be the way that it had been before. It was obvious that Sarah assumed John's presence meant that the panic had passed and life would be returning to normality. As the passion within him subsided, John came back down to earth and he realised that he would have to break the magic of the moment and explain to Sarah and his girls the real reason for his surprise visit. John kissed Sarah on the forehead and got up from the bed and started to dress himself.

"John, what are you doing?" There was a hint of alarm in her voice. "Darling, please wake the girls and tell them to come down to the living room."

He left the room and went downstairs. This was not what he wanted to do, but there was no other choice left open to him. He wandered about in the dark, looking for whatever items he thought might be useful to his family on the journey that they were about to have explained to them. He unloaded the car to avoid the chance of it attracting looters.

There was a lot of noise coming from upstairs as the girls were woken and screams of delight reached John's ears as their mother told them that their father was home. The living room door burst open and John's daughters rushed in, all eager to put their arms around the man who was their father, head of the family and their saviour. It was some time before the euphoria passed and they were able to sit down and John was ready to explain something that he knew they were not going to like. As their father slowly revealed the terrible truth of the circumstances which now existed, the girls were bordering on hysteria, but when he dropped the final bombshell that he would not be staying with them to guide them through this terrible ordeal, their mood altered immediately to bewilderment and then to anger.

How could he possibly leave them to fend for themselves at such a time as this? They simply couldn't understand his apparent cruelty.

Jacko had been expecting this reaction, but made it no less easy to endure. There was total hysteria in the room. Alex, the youngest, attacked him with flailing fists and even Sarah could not hide the horrified look on her face. Jacko had to be forceful trying to calm the situation, well aware that he needed this precious time period to get as much information to his family, which might make the difference between them surviving or not. He had a very limited opportunity in which to explain many things, his own emotions were running high and he would dearly have preferred to just hug the family whom he loved, beyond belief. It was inconceivable that such an unprecedented chain of events could have driven them to this. His heart was being torn apart; all that he held most dear was in jeopardy. It felt as if the world around them was collapsing.

Getting Sarah and his daughters to understand the gravity of their dilemma wasn't easy, but eventually he was able to get them to see some sense.

Then, all too soon, it was time to say goodbye. The only way that he was able to do this without the super-charged emotions of the moment taking over was to make it as brief as possible. He had brought an extra rucksack and loaded as many useful personal items as he was able to take back to camp. There was a strong possibility that the house would be ransacked as soon as it was abandoned.

John hoisted the heavy rucksack onto his back and began to walk away from his family, not knowing if he would ever see them again. He dared not look back, knowing that he might give in to his emotions and abandon his commitment to the plan that had been devised. His position at the camp, and the responsibilities to his troops, was also a major priority. Was he really doing the right thing?

After turning a corner, out of sight of the family, he broke into a steady jog. The rucksack was bulging but he had carried much heavier loads and the weight didn't worry him unduly. Ahead in the darkness he could make out the figures of what looked like four men standing on the pavement. Jacko was running down the centre of the road; traffic was certainly not an issue. As he approached the group, they moved to block his route. He could have gone around them, but given the burden he was carrying, they would have easily caught him up and brought him down like a pack of wolves. Jacko came to a halt and hoisted the haversack swiftly from his shoulders.

"Oi, soldier boy! What ya got in the bag then, something for us I hope?" Jacko's assessment of the gang was immediate. Four men; two of them, he could see were leaders, two were followers, and all were armed with baseball bats, which they appeared ready to use. They circled Jacko like a pack of hungry hyenas moving in for the kill. Facing him was one heavyset gang member who was undoubtedly the

Alpha goon. "Come and take a look my friend," Jacko offered, making pretence of opening the top of the rucksack. The Alpha gang member advanced to look into the bag, bending forward in the moonlight to get a better view. His haste and greed was his undoing. The alpha aggressor took on a fighting position as he leant forward to inspect the contents of Jacko's rucksack, legs apart in a boxer's stance pivoting on the balls of his feet preparing to attack if necessary. The kick, when it came, was lightning fast and directly on target. Alpha aggressor didn't stand a chance. He slumped to the ground, groaning and clutching his testicles. He wouldn't be going anywhere for a while. The element of surprise was with Jacko who capitalised fully on this advantage. He sprang at the second gang leader with the ferocity of a hungry tiger, punching his fist hard into the second attacker's throat. He could hear and feel the cartilage in the man's gullet crunch beneath the ferocity of the punch. The pent up emotions bottled up in Jacko exploded into violence. The two men lay writhing and screaming on the ground. The element of surprise as an advantage had now passed. Jacko grabbed one of the pickaxe handles that had been dropped by his assailants, weighing it in his hands, feeling the balance and then turned towards the remaining two gang members.

The look on his face was enough for the men, now leaderless, who turned and ran. Releasing the pent up aggression, which the frustration of leaving his family had created within him, was decidedly therapeutic. Standing quietly in the street, Jacko took a moment to compose him. He looked up. The clouds parted dramatically and there was the moon still surrounded by the brilliant golden halo. Perhaps there was some truth in Pagan myths. Quickly, Jacko hoisted the rucksack onto his back and carried on running the last mile to the barracks.

When John Jackson ran up to the barrack gates, he was sweating from the run. He had pushed himself hard on the return slog as a way of blanking out the last wretched hundred and twenty minutes, which as Dan had said, were the worst moments of his life. It was raining hard - something of a blessing as it hid the tears that were running down his face. Dan Buckland was sitting in the museum office, looking out of the window facing the barrack gates. He walked out to greet his friend, knowing full well from his own experience, the stressful episode that he had just experienced. "Everything OK, John?" he enquired knowingly.

"See that you have picked up a little memento."

"You were right, Dan, when you said that was the worst experience of your life. We have both known some dreadful stuff during our careers, but nothing came close to that."

He walked over to the sentry and gave him the baseball bat. "Put that in the armoury, Jonesey; you never know, it might come in handy sometime, if we ever have time for another sports day." The sentry took the makeshift weapon and walked into the guardroom.

John continued the conversation. "Dan, that was a horrific two hours, but I am more determined than ever now that we will hold this place together, and when this shit is over, we shall walk out of here, find our families and try to carve some sort of life from this mayhem."

The two senior men in the barracks grabbed some sleep. When the dawn broke, they walked together to the guardroom to have the conversation with the guard commander, a task they had not been looking forward to. Had their judgement been sound? Was it such a good idea to let the married soldiers go out to their families with the unenviable task of explaining to them that they would not be there to shepherd them through the next horrendous, challenging episode they were facing? Both John and Dan had made the journey, and even with all of the training and experience of hardship and adversity from their involvement with the SAS, they had both found the task the most difficult either had ever endured.

The CO and the RCM walked into the guardroom. The guard commander let them through the door which led to the cells and offices located behind the high counter over which thousands of soldiers for decades had booked in and out of the camp.

"OK, Tomo, give us the news," Dan demanded apprehensively.

"Well, it's not good, but better than I had expected," the guard commander explained in his broad Glaswegian accent. "There are sixteen who are actually adrift - Lloyd from HQ Squadron and a Bradley from the cookhouse. Jenkins, Smith and Talbot from 'A' Squadron are the ones that I have definite knowledge of, but the rest are yet to be verified, although I think that we have seen the last of them. There are a couple of single guys that haven't been seen for a while, they could have gone over the wall, so we won't have a final figure until we have an all ranks parade." Dan Buckland had expected a higher figure and admitted the fact.

"Give me the down side, Tomo," the Colonel said.

"Well, the two hour time limit was pretty much broken by fifty percent, but if you want my opinion, it was a little tight," the guard commander said making his point.

"You might be right, Tomo, but I think that if we had given them longer, the wives would have persuaded even more of them to go AWOL. My feeling is to offer those that decided to take their chances outside my sincere best wishes and hope that one day we will meet again." Dan Buckland added something that the other two men had been contemplating but had not mentioned so far.

"Officially, these men are AWOL, and would be liable to severe punishment under normal conditions." He scratched his stubbly chin and looked at the other two men. "But then again, these aren't normal conditions."

He noticed a rucksack and tents stacked in the corner of the guardroom. "Tomo, have you been out to see your family yet?" he asked. "Thought I'd wait to see the last of the stragglers back and make the official tally before I went," he admitted. "There is one more thing that I think you should know." Tomo shuffled uneasily. "There is one body adrift that I haven't mentioned. I have been waiting until the last minute hoping that she would turn up, but she is way past her time slot. I have to report that Major Maloney is missing."

Dan and Jacko looked at each other uneasily, apart from the fact that she was a friend and great to have around, she was also a crucial member of the team. Survival without the MO would be far more complex.

"Tomo, job well done; now get you off. I'll take over here and good luck; just watch how you go out there."

Dan put his hand on Tomo's shoulder. "Don't stop to talk to any strangers." Dan and Jacko stood alone outside the guardroom. Dan was visibly uneasy.

"Shit, Jacko, how are we going to hold this house of cards together without the MO?"

Jacko didn't answer.

The coming days saw the height of the initial shock period, which had all resulted from the disastrous weekend, when fuel became contaminated and civilisation collapsed. The complete lack of law, order and structured society impacted with vengeance upon everyone, sparing none, shocking the entire population, thrusting them into turmoil. Fires, unattended by fire crews, would burn for weeks. People in a pitiful state came to the main gates of the barracks, begging to be allowed in. The only thing that they could be advised to do was to leave town and seek a suitable location to survive the next eighteen months of dreadfulness. They were told by the interim government that the violent period would pass, and that if they could survive the next one and a half years, there was hope for the future. This was the prediction reasoned from London, but in reality it was not much more than a well researched guess. Nothing of this magnitude had ever happened before.

Jacko sat in his office contemplating the options open to him. A huge sea change had swept across the lives of the men and women in the barracks. Jacko realised that it was vital to absorb as much of the initial impact of what had happened, whilst adapting to the new circumstances that faced them all. He heard Rogers working in the outer office.

"Rogers, can you come in for a moment?" He realised that he hadn't enquired how his clerk had faired when he went back to his family. Rogers came into the room, pen and pad in hand, expecting to be given orders. "I wanted to ask you how your visit to your family went. There was genuine concern in his voice, knowing that

Rogers was a father with two small sons. "Did you find them?"

"Yes, I did, Boss."

"Everything OK?"

"I'd rather not talk about it if you don't mind, it's too painful." Jacko could only respect his request, knowing that each individual deals with sadness in their own way. Jacko saw a new facet in his clerk's character.

Chapter 10

Major Sophie Maloney's Story

Armageddon + 13

Sophie Maloney decided to make the trip to her home in Iver, whilst there was still plenty of light. Just driving had now become a hazardous experience in itself. The roads were littered with all manners of debris and simply by being in a car that was mobile presented its own problem – attack was a strong possibility. She was carrying her sidearm, but wondered if she would be able to use it if such a situation arose.

As she drove, she pondered the words that she would say to Jack. How could she explain to him that she was going to spend the next eighteen months locked up in an army camp, in all probability safe and with food and water, albeit limited whilst he would have to take his chances in a tumultuous world, where savagery reigned and his chances of survival were severely limited? As she approached the small surgery in a side road off the High Street, her worst fears were founded. Devastation and destruction was everywhere. She parked up at the rear of the surgery and apprehensively walked around to the front door. As soon as she passed through the main entrance, the scene inside the building that she knew well was a picture of complete mayhem.

The entire building had been ransacked. She could hear crying and voices coming from inside the pharmacy department. In her life, Sophie, was used to seeing much trauma. It was something that came with the job, but this was personal and hit harder than she had ever before experienced. Inside the room were three people that she knew personally. The senior nurse and the head receptionist were sitting on the floor, clearly in shock. The third person in the room was her husband, Jack. He was lying face up and appeared unconscious. The two women screamed at seeing Sophie, their tears flowing uncontrollably.

Sophie was shocked herself, but automatically checked Jack for vital signs. There were none. She knelt beside Jack's body and held his hand. She was unable to control herself. Her body was racked with uncontrollable sobbing. She had no idea of how long she sat there for, but finally the senior nurse intervened, putting her arms around Sophie's shoulders and led her out of the room. They sat some time in silence, until finally Sophie regained some composure and gathered herself together, enough to be able to ask what had caused this tragedy.

"It is drugs, Sophie," the senior nurse spoke in a gentle tone, aware of Sophie's fragile state of mind. "We have been dispensing Methadone from here for some years as you know, but when the word got around that the supply would dry up, there was a panic. Jack was here trying to avert what was something akin to a stampede by the users, fighting to grab all that they could. He stood his ground, but it was too much for any man. In their frenzy they killed the person who was trying to help them."

Many thoughts passed through Sophie's stunned mind – hopelessness, anger, but predominately the pain of losing someone that she loved. Her marriage to Jack was an unusual relationship, but worked well. Sophie was often away on overseas tours of duty, secondment to various army units and military exercises. The position as MO to The Cavalry in Windsor was a great stroke of luck, which meant that she and Jack could experience something more like a normal relationship for the first time in their ten year marriage. Now that was over, she needed to dig deep into her resilience to find the courage and move forward.

Jack was gone. There was nothing now here for her in Iver. The only solution was to return to Windsor. She had no intention of looking into the house that she and Jack had shared. It was full of memories from happier times and would simply add to her grief. One decision that she did make was to bury Jack. She knew that it would take some time; time that would take her way past the two hour slot that the soldiers had been allotted to go back to their families. Sophie now had no family. She also knew that there was nobody who would bury Jack. It was up to her. She explained the overall situation that had been received in the statement from NAPIG to the nurse and gave her the car and equipment advising her to take her family into the country.

It was eighteen hours later that Major Maloney walked back through the barrack gates and returned to Combemere.

Chapter 11

Sarah's Story

Armageddon + 15 days

The view from the hotel balcony was stunning; a shimmering, and vividly blue sea, edged by a beach of golden sand. The middle distance and horizon was studded with surreal islands rising from the sea like giant cupcakes topped with vibrant green jungle vegetation. The foreground skirting the beach, boasted a dozen sun shades, with woven straw coolie hat design tops. Tables and chairs occupied by diners enjoying the spectacular location and local food; the sea lapped gently onto the golden sand just metres away. Sarah gazed out across the idyllic scene hearing the clatter of knives and forks on crockery, sprinkled with laughter and excited chatter of holidaymakers.

Suddenly the scene changed; the sky darkened, talking stopped and an eerie silence blanketed the beach. Slowly, the water receded, revealing areas of the seabed that were never exposed even at the lowest tides. This continued for a minute, mesmerising all. There was no sound from the people watching, or from the mysterious sea itself. Again, without any sound, the sea began to return, preceded by a four metre high wave. It swept over the previously vacated seabed and up the beach. Now the people on the beach instantly sprang into abject panic. The wave didn't behave like a normal wave; it just kept coming and coming, moving forward at a constant height. The scene, that minutes before had been picture postcard perfect, was transformed into a disaster zone. All was swept aside by the monstrous wall of ocean, which was now carrying with it debris and the struggling bodies of the drowning.

Sarah's eyes sprang open and remained transfixed, staring at the ceiling. She was sweating from the horrific nightmare and lay gazing wide eyed for several minutes until the veracity of the dream slowly faded from her mind.

The new morning light forced itself into Sarah's bedroom. The sun was up and its watery light filtered through the window. It was early, but there was no way of telling the time as the electric alarm clocks and radios were inoperative. Childlike, she wanted only to pull the covers over her head and hope that the world would go away leaving her in peace.

As the dream subsided, one horror was replaced by another. The tsunami nightmare diminished only to be replaced by the reality of actual life that seemed even more cataclysmic than the giant wave event.

She thought back to when this whole atrociousness began, when her husband, John, left for work on what appeared to be a normal Monday, getting the family up and running; fed and off to school and work. But then seeing the disturbing news report that she caught the end of....

"There are conflicting reports of a loss of control concerning law and order, looting is spreading. I suppose the thinking is that if they can do it, so can we. From reports that are coming in from my colleagues, this is not an isolated incident. It appears that sporadic looting is taking place in cities all over the country."

The short text message she received from John's clerk during the afternoon saying that there was some unusual activity occurring and that John might again be detained. Then, the equally peculiar short call on her mobile from John, telling her to be sure to stock up with as much non-perishable food as she could.

She recalled the weekend, before it all kicked off, spent at her parents' home in the New Forest. It had been idyllic.

It was now almost two weeks since she had spent the morning cleaning the house and undertaking the arduous monthly super shopping trip, which required a supermarket shopping assistant to help her get through the checkout and load the two heavily laden trolleys into her car. The supermarket being far busier than usual with people grabbing items from the shelves and loading trolleys, with much more produce than usual. There was the talk of shortages and panic buying. The real gravity of the situation, and its implications, had not yet fully reached this quiet outer suburb.

She returned home and stowed the shopping away, made she a sandwich and a cup of tea, put her feet up and turned on the television. She remembered seeing what appeared to be some breaking news concerning petrol stations, and that her car was practically empty and she needed to fill it up. There was enough fuel in the tank to pick up the girls from school but not much more. It was the first time she noticed that things were, not right, because the afternoon journey to the schools that her daughters attended was strange; an extraordinary atmosphere prevailed. The talk at the school gates was of a petrol tanker strike which was resulting in panic fuel buying. How, at the time, she hurried her girls into the car and drove directly to the closest filling station to fill up her own vehicle's tank, and expected a long queue, resulting from what she had heard at the school gate gossip, but the reality was actually worse.

The first filling station that she went to was closed because there were so many parked cars on the forecourt. She moved on to another garage, but it was the same story. She had no alternative other than to take a chance and drive home. The car was unloaded, but when she attempted to start it later, when it was time to take her girls, the car wouldn't start. It was out of fuel on her drive. She sent a text to John, explaining the situation.

The reply from him was short and to the point. "Forget the car and stay at home."

It was something that didn't go down too well with Sarah's daughters. The girls all had full after school agendas, which to Sarah appeared inconsequential, but to them was of the highest priority – such were the schemes of teenage girls. The complaining was ceaseless until Sarah had to intervene and make them stop, by telling them that they were acting like small, spoiled children by being so negative. Sarah's phone rang continuously. Friends and family were enquiring about any news regarding the tanker strike and other rumours that were now beginning to emerge, ranging from an alien invasion to a terrorist attack. Sarah knew no more than the worried friends who were desperate to discover what was indeed happening to the country, thinking that because of her husband's connections she might be a good source of information.

Confusion reigned. There were conflicting reports from various media pundits, speculating about what was happening. The only factual report that all of the channels appeared to agree on was that little by little, across the country, all combustible fuels, petrol and diesel had been rendered inert. The extent of looting varied from town to town. But it was evident that law and order was deteriorating progressively. Although the finger of guilt was pointed at several potential culprits, nobody really knew who was responsible. Transport had pretty much ground to a halt across the country and from reports this same phenomenon was spreading rapidly.

There was the peculiar phone call from John. "Sarah, I can't tell you too much other than to let you know that this situation is very serious," he said. "You must sit tight, conserve all food and drinking water, and you must be prepared to move at a moment's notice. Did you manage to get the supplies that I asked?" His voice was slow and deadly serious.

"Yes, I bought lots of non-perishable stuff as you suggested, but John, the car has run out of fuel because I couldn't get into any petrol stations. How can I move?"

"Forget about the car, darling."

"Are you serious John?"

"Sarah, I have never been more serious. I'm afraid that I can't tell you anything more at the moment, other than to say that you must prepare yourselves for a hugely difficult ordeal in the forthcoming days, weeks and months." John's voice dropped an octave; there was a discernible tone of compassion, such as she had never heard before in all of their years of marriage. "Remember, darling, that whatever happens next, I love you and the kids, with all my being."

His words stunned her, and it was the moment she finally grasped the situation and knew she must now be positive and find the courage for whatever lay ahead. It was now up to her to be strong for the sake of her daughters. Her anger at her husband was all consuming, not just from her perspective, but as had been more vehemently demonstrated after she told her daughters of the situation. They felt totally abandoned by their father in their extreme hour of need. Whatever adversities they were about to endure, it would all have been overcome with husband and father leading them. However, he had told them that they must survive alone – without him.

Her mind then drifted to the wonderful moment only days earlier, when she woke up to find John lying beside her, and the perfect sensuous intimacy that had passed between them, and for that moment, all that was happening was forgotten.

Sarah, in her heart knew, John Jackson, was without doubt, an excellent father and husband; nobody would deny that. She realised his dilemma was that yes, he was an exceptional father to his three daughters who adored him, and a loving husband to her, but he was also the leader of a regiment where hundreds of men and women looked up to him for guidance. The most difficult decision that he had ever been asked to make had alienated him from his biological family.

She so desperately wanted John to again slide into her bed and cuddle up to her, his strong arms entwining her, making her feel safe, but that was not to be.

Sarah brought herself back into the moment and considered the matter at hand. Lying in bed was no longer an option. This was to be the day that the small group was to set off for Sarah's parents' home in the New Forest. Since the loss of electricity, the days were now regulated by the hours of daylight. Automatically, she set about tidying the room and making the bed before she stopped herself and said out loud to nobody in particular, but ostensibly for her own ears, "What's the bloody point?" knowing full well that she might never again return to that house.

She would have loved to take a shower and carry out the ablutions that had been a lifetime habit. Her bathroom, which had always been immaculate, was now dirty and unhygienic; something that she could never in her wildest dreams have envisaged. However, with no running water, cleaning was impossible and the toilet couldn't be flushed, creating a horror of its own. The advice that John had given his family was to wait a few of days before setting off for the New Forest in the very slim hope that there might be a solution to this disaster. She and Dan's wife, Julie, had met and discussed the plan, but neither actually expected that they would have to go ahead with it. The food that she managed to get, after John had so urgently called her, was beginning to run low, but the more serious need was the lack of clean drinkable water. They were reduced to drinking the water from the rainwater run-off barrel that had previously been used to water the garden. Sharing water with plants was bizarre in itself, but the barrel had become something of a celebrity in its own right. Sarah had realised the value of the water on Tuesday when the taps dried up. She scooped up water in saucepans, filtered it through a muslin cloth, and boiled it on the gas stove, which miraculously was still working. Tuesday, midday, there was a knock at the door and Sarah was surprised to see her neighbours standing on the garden path. Mum, Dad and two small girls. They were all holding an assortment of containers.

"Sarah, I happened to see you taking water from your barrel and wondered if we might have some?" Samantha was an executive level business woman; she was something of a power dresser. She looked anything but powerful now.

"Yes, of course, Sam, please help you."

The word passed, and the water butt was soon empty. Sarah had managed to filter and boil a good store of clean water for her family before the bottom of the barrel was scraped and the gas finally spluttered out.

There was no denying that the situation that her family now found them in was desperate. They had no choice but to implement John's plan. In addition to their own needs, there were stories abounding about neighbours stealing from neighbours, with common decency rapidly spiralling downwards. New disciplines had to be learned and learned quickly. Water conservation being the priority; something so basic yet fundamental to existence, was now a matter of life and death. The stark and austere reality of what was happening to them was impacting with a vengeance upon their lives. Initially, this reality took more time to filter down into the adolescent minds of her daughters who considered that turning on a tap or flushing a toilet was a fundamental right. To begin with they wasted water, using it for less important purposes, but slowly with Sarah's constant chiding, they grasped the severity of their situation and slowly adapted to the new course onto which their lives had been steered. Now they had to relearn the fundamentals of life and disregard the privileged existence that the last generations of modern humanity had inconsiderately and irresponsibly taken for granted. It was to be a tough lesson, hard learned.

She dressed, putting on her most durable and weather resistant clothes. Fashion was now something from the past and functionality was to be the key word from now on. Her long hair was brushed back and tied in a severe bun behind her head. Makeup was not even considered. She looked in the mirror and drew the comparison between herself and the young women who were an integral part of the modern army.

"OK, there's only one way to do this," she decided. "If I am to lead my family to safety, then I have to be tough and my regime will also have to be harsh for all of our sakes." Sarah walked out onto the landing of the house and knocked on the bedroom doors of the rooms where her daughters slept. "Come on Jacksons, today is the first day of the rest of your lives." All a little theatrical and reminiscent of the way that John's NCOs would deal with the situation, but considering what was at stake, it seemed to be the best way to deal with the matter.

Three bleary eyed teenagers slowly emerged from their bedrooms. Sarah could not help but observe that they were all looking far more dishevelled than usual. Several days of not having a functioning bathroom had taken its toll. A reluctance to take on board what was happening was evident. They all appeared to think that these inexplicably horrible events of the last few days had been just a passing discomfort and refused to accept the significance of the reality they were faced with. Sarah would have to make them understand that this was a life and death situation and they must face up to their circumstances. She must do this in such a way that the young, impressionable girls didn't give up hope and descend into abject depression. Without electricity, the technology and gadgetry that they had all become so reliant upon, perhaps even addicted to, it was beginning to appear evident that all were becoming increasingly irritable. Sarah had noticed that she herself had become tetchy, now that she had more time on her hands, resulting from not being able to occupy her mind with the trivia of TV, which even for a motivated person like her, had occupied several hours of her day for much of her life. Cell phones, gaming machines, tablets and computers that had consumed so much of all young persons' waking hours, were now no more than useless pieces of metal and plastic.

The first unpopular decisions had been encountered the afternoon before. The hallway of the house was loaded with all of the useful household items that could be fitted into the car John had delivered. These would be taken with them to the New Forest. Each of the girls had made piles of what they thought would be suitable for life in the forest. This resulted in a very heated and aggressive argument between the women. Sarah had no option but to eject many of the trivial objects the girls thought necessary, which made her supremely unpopular. No electrical equipment, computers, games etc. No clothing which was fashionable and not functional. In short, nothing that didn't have a distinctly useful purpose. The atmosphere in the house was markedly toxic as the four women packed the unfamiliar car that John had delivered with everything that had been selected to go with them.

As the car was being loaded, Dan Buckland's wife and two sons arrived, their own car burdened, close to overflowing. Respect for the law was something resigned to the past. No motorway patrol was going to pull them up and fine them for overloading a vehicle. The Buckland family, led by Dan's wife, Julie, and his sons, Kit and Rory, who were seventeen and fifteen respectively helped with the loading of the Jackson's car. Julie was from Edinburgh. She was a handsome woman, rather than pretty, whose feet were well and truly planted on the ground. Kit and Rory were carbon copies of their father, quiet and considerate, and for their young age, they already projected strong characters. They had all been tossed headlong into this situation, but it was evident that the Buckland boys had grasped the severity of what was happening and were dealing with it in an adult manner, which was far from the denial of the circumstances that the Jackson girls had adopted.

Sarah and Julie moved to one side and made plans. "I have a map of the route to the garden centre which you must take," Sarah explained. "I know the route by heart and there is a possibility that we might get separated."

The two women had met many times in the past and were both involved in social events within the regiment. Their respect for each other was mutual, although they moved generally in different social circles.

"We're only going to get one chance at this," Julie warned. "The fuel is limited and we have no idea of what we might encounter. Dan suggested that we stick to the motorways and larger roads where possible. What do you think, Sarah?"

"John gave me the same advice and it seems good sound logic to me." Sarah was already beginning to appreciate the company of this strong ally.

The convoy of two vehicles, set off. Initially, the roads from the Jackson house to the motorway were littered with debris and abandoned cars around which they had to navigate. Curiously, some of the side roads looked untouched by what was happening, displaying typical British suburbia in all its tranquil normality. What horror was being played out behind the residential façade could only be speculated on. It was impossible to tell whether the houses were occupied or not. There were obviously no lights visible; all doors and windows were closed and curtains and blinds were drawn. The pillaging gangs were on the lookout for anyone who might be hoarding food or surviving by some means or another. If they entered a house, they would ransack the place, searching for hidden cans or food of any description. If the occupants tried to resist, they would be subjected to violence; such was the wretched craving created by abject hunger.

On a roundabout that connected the town to the motorway junction, the tiny convoy encountered a group of perhaps twenty people who were gathered on the central grass reservation. The grass covered hillock lay beneath the elevated section of the motorway on-ramp/exit. The raised grassed circle now resembled a gypsy encampment, strewn with all manner of garbage. There were about half a dozen cars abandoned around the area, their doors wide open, clothes and bedding scattered about them.

Upon seeing two cars that were actually moving, the group ran en- masse towards the vehicles, waving their arms and shouting for them to stop. The people looked dishevelled and desperate. Sarah was confused; these people looked frantic and she slowed thinking that perhaps she might be able to help them in some way. The three girls in the car were now screaming; such was the look of hopelessness, bordering upon aggression on the faces of the people who were rapidly descending upon the car. Sarah's daughters had realised before she did that they were actually being attacked and some of the men were brandishing crudely made weapons. This was obviously a prime location at which to attack and stop cars that were escaping the town and were most likely to be carrying some food.

"Mum, please drive away! These people are desperate, they will take everything and we will just be left stranded as they are!" screamed Miranda, suddenly displaying all of the logic that she must have inherited from her father.

Crunch! Whatever Sarah's thinking had been, it was abruptly brought to a halt by a loud crash which was Julie's car ramming the rear of her car. Perhaps her concentration had been broken by what was happening and no wonder, Sarah thought, but the car behind didn't stop, it kept pushing forward. Looking in the rear view mirror, she could see Julie's determined face. Her right hand was out of the open window motioning for her to move forward. The car wheels were spinning, there was a sound of grinding metal, and smoke was rising from the tyres as the second car pushed the car in front.

"Go mum, just go!" the three girls shouted in unison. Sarah slammed the car into a lower gear and accelerated away from the terrifying scene, checking that Julie's car was following. The tension in the car was electric. There was some subdued crying, but it was controlled. Suddenly, the women had been subjected to the reality of the situation in which they now found themselves. They drove around the roundabout towards the motorway on-ramp, but as they approached it, they saw to their horror, that it had been blocked by several abandoned cars that had been pushed across to form a barricade. Sarah slowed, not knowing what to do. As she did, the mob ran across the central rise of the roundabout and began descending upon the car again. The screaming in the car was hysterical, but above this was the sound of a car horn.

Julie had her hand slammed down hard on her car's horn at the same time she raced her car in front of Sarah's and took the lead. Sparks were flying from the front of Julie's car, caused by metal that had become broken and dislodged by the crash. Sarah followed, desperate to escape from the impending doom.

A man landed stomach down on the bonnet of the car, his filthy face flattened against the windscreen. The car was speeding around the roundabout. The only thing that the attacker could grab hold of was a windscreen wiper. The centrifugal force caused him to slide sideways until the pressure on the wiper was too much and it snapped off, throwing the attacker onto the road. Julie sped around the roundabout. The assaulting hoard regained the high ground in the centre, ready for the next attack. Julie's car frantically screeched around the circuit sparks flying. She drove up the slope which was the lane for traffic exiting the motorway, with Sarah in hot pursuit. The thinking of the gangs on the roundabout was stuck in the past. They obviously expected drivers to obey the law. The two cars drove along the motorway exit road in the direction that would have been against the oncoming traffic, but that time was over and nothing came towards them. Driving carefully to avoid the debris which littered the road, the two cars finally arrived at the deserted M4 motorway. It was eerily desolate. No other vehicle moved on either carriageway. Sarah drove west for a mile and then stopped. She got out of the car and walked to the other vehicle. Julie was standing next to the car and the two women hugged each other. Kit and Rory set about ripping off the damaged front parts of their car, the broken headlight silver reflectors dangling almost comically by their connecting wires. They checked the radiator for damage. Luckily, it was intact and could go onwards.

"Julie, thank you so much. I didn't know what to do. Those people on the roundabout looked so desperate."

Although visibly shocked, Sarah regained some composure. "Can you believe that those people who attacked us and were prepared to take everything from us would have been perfectly ordinary people just days ago?"

"I guess that all of us now know what we are up against, and it puts things slightly more into perspective regarding Dan and John. Better not hang around here too long, we need to get where we are heading before dark. I don't want us to be out here so exposed once the sun has gone down," Julie added.

As they drove into the New Forest, it appeared so tranquil and unspoilt, in direct contrast to the misery that they had left behind. It was hard to comprehend the events that had occurred just that morning, which were now remembered like a horrific nightmare. In some places the road was like a green tunnel burrowing between the overhanging trees. The twists and turns, although appealing, created their own hazard – being an ideal place to set an ambush. All eyes were peeled watching expectantly for any signs of impending attack.

Sarah and her daughters had made the journey to the New Forest countless times and knew the route well but now it was significantly different. Every bend in the road, every obstacle slowing their progress, caused by blockages in the route, brought with it the worry that assailants could descend upon them in the way that they had in Windsor. The atmosphere inside the Jackson car was bordering upon frantic as the family were now aware of the dangers that they faced. During the final miles, the roads were narrower and tree lined, giving an almost claustrophobic sense, where attack could be sudden and potentially lethal. Although the fear of violence was uppermost in their minds, the ancient forest also gave a feeling of protection. It had been unaffected by the anarchistic rage that was enveloping the country. To the occupants of the two cars, they were greatly relieved when they finally reached their destination.

Arriving at the Garden Centre in the tranquillity of the New Forest and finding that it was intact was a huge relief for the two car loads of unpredicted refugees after their harrowing escape from Windsor. There was much to tell Thomas and Annabel when they arrived so unexpectedly, looking drawn, scared and bedraggled. Sarah's parents lived at a fairly remote location. They had never bothered much with TV and the media in general, preferring to live their lives at their own pace and their own terms, more so now that their children had grown and all flown the nest. Thomas and Annabel had hoped that perhaps one of their children would have taken on the family business, but it was not to be. Beautiful as it had been, growing up in the serenity of their parents' home, all of their three children had ventured off into the outside world. Now their tranquillity was to be disturbed by the arrival of two women, three girls, two young boys, and an old cat named Spook, who the girls had managed to stowaway without their mother's knowledge. Finally, the two battered cars drove into the tiny parking area in front of the garden centre. Almost immediately Thomas and Annabel rushed out to greet the new arrivals.

"Oh, God!" Annabel was unable to control her joy at seeing Sarah and her granddaughters. "We have been out of our minds with worry about you all. I have tried calling you on the phone, but the lines are dead. We have had no television or radio for nearly two weeks and before it went dead, the news that we did see was awful."

The three girls hugged their grandparents and tears were much in abundance. Julie Buckland and her sons stood to one side feeling slightly embarrassed at being strangers at such an emotional time. Annabel slowly became calmer, she looked about her. "Sarah, where is John?" she asked nervously.

"Let's go inside Mum," Sarah suggested, "we have a lot to tell you."

On cue, Annabel suggested that a cup of tea might be advisable.

Thomas and Annabel accepted their new circumstances and welcomed the Buckland family with their usual hospitality. The thunderbolt of what the new arrivals had experienced took some days to sink in. But soon..., very soon, the current and shocking reality made itself potently evident.

Chapter 12

Royals

Armageddon + 16 days.

It would be fair to say that the description, 'heroically underwhelming', would be a reasonable portrayal of the Officers' Mess at Combemere. Style, elegance and sophistication had all been sacrificed at the expense of cost efficiency. The building's only redeeming feature was that the interior faithfully resembled the exterior. Grey, boring and featureless, the dejected building stood hidden away in a quiet corner of the barracks. It was suitably garnished by the neglected and rusting hulks of three armoured cars - relics from a bygone era. The austere, unremarkable interior resembled a 1940s council building or tax office. Paintings and regimental silver made a valiant but failed attempt to brighten up the drab, unwelcoming, living space. It was to this building that Colonel Jackson had safely delivered his Royal guests. It was a depleted Royal Family that took up residence; the Queen, Prince Phillip, William and Harry and the Duchess of Cambridge. These were the only Royals that could be brought to Windsor in the short window of opportunity prevailing when The Armageddon Virus struck. The other members of the immediate family were all safely quartered in their country estates where it was decided they would stand a good chance of survival, given their rural location and the fact that they all had livestock and strong facilities for growing produce. It was also decided that all of the royal eggs in one basket would not be a good policy. The main players were housed in Combemere, which had the largest defence contingent. The Officers' Mess was not a revelation to William and Harry, both brothers having started their military careers there, and regardless of the architectural shortcomings, they had enjoyed the time they were stationed at Combemere.

Colonel Jackson made the decision to move all of the officers, himself included, out of the mess. There was no shortage of accommodation, as the barracks were not manned to capacity. He decided that he would take up residence himself in the museum block, adjacent to the guardroom. It had a window which looked out towards the armoury and the front gate. From this vantage point he could see any comings and goings, and it was here, he determined, that if there was going to be action, it would more than likely be from there. He also decided the information that the camp had Royal guests should be passed by word of mouth. It was looking increasingly evident that they were likely to be there for the long haul.

In addition to the Royal party there were eight members of the entourage. Three of the close protection officers who made up this group were well known to the regiment, two being ex-members. The Queen's Personal Secretary, a tall, gaunt looking man, was a familiar figure. The final four, who were female, acted as what would have been historically described as handmaidens (Ladies of the Bedchamber or Ladies In Waiting), but in the age of political correctness, they were simply called Royal Assistants.

Colonel Jackson gave the party a few days to acclimatise themselves to their new surroundings before making his first visit. He was ushered into the ground floor living room which had comfortable seating. He was expecting a lone meeting with Her Majesty, almost along the lines of what the PM would have made in making his weekly summary of the parliamentary events to the Monarch, and was surprised to see all the Royals and the secretary sitting in the room. There was no formality, and apart from the appearance of those present who were almost peculiarly wearing heavy clothing, in what would generally have been a generously heated room, it all appeared quite normal. The Royals looked slightly less than their usual pristine selves as the only water that was getting to the Officers'' Mess had to be carried there in buckets from the Queen Vic. The Queen welcomed Colonel Jackson.

"Colonel Jackson, under normal circumstances we would offer you a drink, but these are anything but normal circumstances, I think we would all agree. So from this point onward we are going to start as we mean to continue and call you, John, which will be a beginning to dispensing of any unnecessary etiquette."

The two younger princes looked pleased with this decision, but the senior prince huffed a little and grunted.

"Perhaps you would allow me to call you Ma'am and the gentlemen, Sir, if that would be acceptable to you, Ma'am," Colonel John smiled. *Your Royal Highness had always seemed a ridiculously pompous title to him and he was relieved to be rid of it.*

"Totally acceptable John – And now, down to business. Please be so kind, as to inform us, to the situation, as you have discovered it to be at this time."

Jacko spent the next ten minutes passing on the information that he had gleaned to date and outlined the plans that he had set in motion, leaving nothing out.

The Royals listened intently, only interrupting briefly to confirm small facts. There was a long pause. Phillip spoke first. "This is indeed, far more serious than we could ever have imagined. If the Think Tank in London has got it right, then this is the end of civilisation as we have known it."

There was another long pause. Jacko broke the silence. "If you will allow me, I think that you have plenty to consider for now and there is a lot to be done in the Barracks'. We are setting up a communications network from the radio wing and I am ambitiously optimistic that we will be able to make contact with anyone around the planet that has survived and has access to a radio transceiver. We have already made contact with government silos and military installations that are in a similar situation to ourselves. We will collate all information and pass it on. The overall situation outside these walls has deteriorated into total anarchy. In the larger towns the scene apparently resembles an extract from Dante's Inferno. It is beyond anything that we could have possibly imagined. Additionally, from what news is being received from the rest of the world, the wider picture has become practically universal. Now, I will take my leave unless you have any more questions."

"No, please go, John," replied the Queen politely, "I'm sure that you must be extremely busy." There was a pause and she asked, "Would you call in as often as possible to keep us informed?"

"Of course, Ma'am."

John stood up and politely took his leave; the two younger princes escorted him to the front door of the Officers Mess. Both men knew Jacko as they had served under him as young lieutenants and were well aware of his leadership skills. Harry was the first to speak. "One hell of a mess, Jacko. I'd like to volunteer to help in whatever capacity you think I might be useful. I know that I'm also speaking for Wills when I say that we want to be part of assisting you in whatever way you may decide." " I knew that I could rely on you both."

"One more thing," Harry added. "Wills and I have been considering our position here and we are both agreed that since we are going to be working shoulder to shoulder with the rest of the guys for some conceivable amount of time we would prefer to be called by more sociable titles; H for me and Wills for my big brother. Could you please pass the word without too much fuss?"

"Can't see that it should be too much of a problem; nearly everyone has known you both for a while and I agree that it would be far more comfortable for all concerned."

The Wales brothers looked at each other and smiled. The meeting over, Jacko said his goodbyes, shook hands with the brothers, and walked out of the mess. He went past the rusting armoured cars and back towards the main barracks, feeling that the meeting, although exceedingly strange, had gone remarkably well, considering the extraordinary state of affairs. Any pre-conceived thoughts he might have had of non- acceptance of the situation by the houseguests taking the stance, 'we'll carry on as usual', were thankfully without foundation. The idea of anybody considering carrying on as usual was fading quickly, and a completely new way of life for everyone, regardless of their previous status, was the reality that they faced. It was now common knowledge on the camp that there was an unusual group of guests occupying the Officers Mess, but with all that was going on around them; the soldiers took little notice of their new neighbours.

As he made his way towards the Guard Room, his thoughts were with Sarah and how she would have loved to hear her husband retell the story of his meeting with HM the Queen in such bizarre circumstances. The obvious descriptions that would spring to mind of most in describing the Queen might be a 'frail old lady', but this octogenarian was anything but frail. Going home at the end of a day in the office was now nothing more than a figment of his imagination; wishful thinking, the reality of what prevailed was almost mind numbing. He could only speculate as to where his family were and how they were coping.

Halo around the Moon

94

Chapter 13

The Garden Centre

Armageddon + 17 days

Even an idealistic, post card location, like the garden centre, which had survived two centuries, had succumbed to modern day living. Piped water, sewage and electricity had all been added to the property over the years. The latest incumbents had taken all of these amenities for granted, but like the house, they had just abandoned, these were now absent services. This was to be a rude awakening.

Thomas was quick to understand the situation and took control. He organised water carrying, food production, fishing in the stream, (which the two Buckland boys were quick to volunteer for). He took each of them, in turn, into the forest and taught them how to forage for edible plants, roots, berries and mushrooms.

Something which took priority was the security of the property. Thomas had two twelve bore and one smaller four-ten shotguns. The ammunition was very limited, so no live firing practice could be undertaken. Nevertheless, he drilled the two boys and also the females in the use of the guns. He knew that their lives could well rely on these tired weapons. Thomas devised a plan. There would always be somebody watching the road, and if intruders arrived, they would take up defensive positions. Thomas and the boys took turns to stand guard outside with a gun ready. Anyone who found their way to the garden centre would be told that there was only scarce food available, barely sufficient to feed the family. They would wish the travellers good luck, making sure they left the premises.

Initially, Dan Buckland's wife and two sons had a quite natural feeling of inferiority as the Colonel's family held a far more important position within the regiment. Sarah was aware of this and quickly levelled the playing field. The inherent strength of the Buckland family was soon in evidence and John's decision to unite the two families had been a good one. Not only did this give Dan's wife and children a strong chance of survival, but their input, as had already been demonstrated, was obvious, which was a factor that would prove to be very positive.

Annabel also played a crucial role in acclimatising her new lodgers. She noticed that, in particular, the youngsters were at a loss of how to occupy their time when they were not working. They had grown up with electrical gadgetry all around them and inventing something to motivate their creativity and ingenuity was a challenge that she relished, her motherly instincts kicking back into action.

Thomas had immediately grasped the severity of the circumstances confronting the group, of which he was, ostensibly now the head. He lectured the group, explaining that there would be gangs roaming the country, taking whatever they could to survive. "These gangs and even individuals will need to be avoided at all costs," he explained one evening, when he thought that the moment was right. "A starving person will do almost anything in order to eat. Even though they may start by just being 'nice' people, they will soon change when they see that we are managing To survive and have some, albeit limited, food."   He drove home his point, "Hunger will drive a human being to the depths of depravity. You must always be on your guard."

Both the Jackson's and the Buckland's had been outdoor families and had done occasional camping trips, but they had a limited amount of survival experience. Even with this restricted knowledge, the rapid transformation that was now their reality required a lot of adaptation, a steep learning curve.

The two vehicles that had brought them there had limited petrol, which was enough for the journey but not much more. It was decided that they should be hidden away. The front of the building, which bordered the road, should be made to look boarded up, even abandoned. Initially, the girls in particular, found it more difficult to adjust. Very quickly the everyday problems of personal hygiene appeared insurmountable to them. The youngest daughter had the added anxiety of starting her periods; this would be a stressful episode for any young girl but was dealt with admirably by Sarah.

During the first weeks of living in the New Forest, there was much resentment from the children against what they considered to be both of their father's selfish actions. This emotion was particularly strong within the younger children, and indeed it even extended to the wives. The feeling of abandonment by their fathers and husbands at this, the most dangerous time in their lives, burned deep. But slowly, as a sense of calm developed, they sat together in the evenings and discussed many topics. Gradually, as they became adjusted to their new environment, they discussed the thorny issue. After some weeks, their resentment turned into an understanding of the two men's actions and the enormous sacrifice that they had made. They were being greatly missed.

Progressively, the group settled into their new environment and way of life. Their smooth adaptation of something so severe was borne out of the strong and dependable support from the senior couple, who, although they had lived all of their lives with the benefits of electricity and running water, had not been as reliant on these amenities as other modern folk. The garden centre was a perfect location to ride out the next months, but the biggest threat was the danger of attacked by outsiders.

Halo around the Moon

Chapter 14

Episodes During Lockdown

Armageddon + 21 days

In every barrel there is always a rotten apple or two, and the Household Cavalry was no exception. When Jacko, walked into the RHQ office, the RCM was waiting for him.

"You look as if you have some news, Dan."

Dan Buckland's face looked almost good-humoured. "How do you want it Boss, good first, or bad?"

Dan, although he had a square jawed, tough, rugged face, took on the look of a mischievous boy, which seemed to be a contradiction in his case, but that was exactly what Jacko was witnessing.

"Let's get the bad over with first, shall we, Dan?"

"OK Boss. Three men have gone missing; over the wall during the night, is my guess."

"And, the good news?"

Dan's face could not hide his amusement. "Your idea about abolishing rank must have got a few people thinking."

"And....?"

"And..., we could pretty much have taken bets on who would be skipping out. Second Lieutenant Good acre. Captain Golding and Corporal Pritchard."

"Bloody hell Dan, that's a bit of a shock!"

"Not really, John, none of them would win prizes for popularity. They all had a lot of grievances stacked up against them. Good riddance is my thinking."

"Yes, Dan, I think you're right. The ship will sail a lot steadier without that trio on board.

A couple of days later, two men were caught stealing from the cookhouse stores. They were locked up in the barracks' cells. Troopers Garratt and Jennings had never been popular; they were always complaining about something or another and some petty thieving had been attributed to them but nothing was ever proven. How to deal with them was a problem. Army discipline has always been strict and punishment categorised, but things were very different now. Stealing food under the previous regime would have been a relatively minor offence, but now that food was such a critical commodity, crucial to the very survival of everyone in the camp, the crime took on a completely different and far more serious complexity.

It was unanimously decided that the punishment that was to be exacted upon the offenders would be a decision taken by all in the camp. A meeting was held and the case for and against the defendants discussed at length. Finally, it was decided that the offenders should be banished from the camp. They would have to take their chances on the outside, with all the ghastliness that went with it. The RCM took the lawbreakers to the front gates and watched them walk away. Dan Buckland was a tough, but fair man; he wondered what dreadfulness might lie in store for the two wrongdoers. It was going to be hard for them, but, Dan knew that these two men were survivors. Their particular felonious skills and mind-set would see them through, he was sure. Even so, he found himself, almost as an involuntary action saying a final "Good luck."

Chapter 15

Culham Science Centre

Armageddon + 32 days

The government had in place, various strategies and preparations, to deal with the advent of numerous national attack possibilities. There were several high priority scenarios that could be triggered by an external attack – physical, biological, chemical or cyber, including internal infectious disease transferral (Black Death, Spanish Flu 1918). In the case of a biological attack, it was estimated that there would be a period when the viral infection would be most virulent, and then a second stage when the aftermath created its own contamination caused by the multitude of unburied bodies. It was estimated that the death toll caused by this cataclysm would be colossal, reducing the population by far higher numbers than the two world wars and the Black Death combined. The best estimates suggested that eighteen months would need to elapse before the country could even begin a recovery process. This was called the Stabilisation Period. The government devised a plan to bring together the pre-registered intelligentsia, which consisted of the best minds in the country. Bletchley Park had highlighted the need for such a group during the Second World War, whose intelligent minds would be paramount in guiding the country through the stabilisation period. Later they would be principal in rebuilding a decimated civilization, and in which Combemere Barracks was to play a significant role.

* Actual reference, Internet source.

"Culham Centre for Fusion Energy (CCFE) the UK's national laboratory for fusion research. CCFE (formerly known as UKAEA, Culham) based at Culham Science Centre in Oxfordshire, forty miles from Combemere and owned and operated by the United

Kingdom Atomic Energy Authority.
In the late 1950's, UKAEA, had identified Culham as a suitable site for the construction of a brand new purpose built laboratory for plasma physics and fusion research.
Culham's status had been further enhanced in recent years by the decision in the late 1970's that the facility would be the site for the Joint European Torus (JET) teams of scientists from our European partners and further afield working together in a combined effort to create clean, sustainable energy sources for future generations.

Culham therefore was comprised of a cosmopolitan community of people. The expertise and campus feel attracted diverse science and technology. It was amongst these academics that some of the intelligentsia selected by the government resided. The restoration of society would require electricity as a power source to revive the devastated economy. Coal fired power stations would require fuel to operate them. Nuclear power stations would go into Automatic Shut Down. Renewables, such as wind and hydroelectric generators, would provide some power initially, but there would be much servicing required getting them back into action.

The National Grid would also be in urgent need of overhauling, but for the positive side of this challenge, there would be a much condensed energy requirement due to the greatly reduced population. The Government therefore decided that the best alternative for the generation of power for the new civilisation should be fusion. Shortly before The Armageddon Virus hitting, CCFE had announced a major breakthrough in fusion research and generators were on the drawing board ready to be built.

Colonel Jackson was called urgently to the radio wing.

"There is a conversation booked for you at 09:00 hours with the Silver Stick, Boss," said the man in charge of the radio section. Jacko wandered around the various classrooms that had previously been used to instruct the soldiers in the techniques of radio communication and had been transformed into the crucial hub, which was the radio centre. He chatted to the operators. Their work was of paramount importance in maintaining contact, coordinating, not only the functioning of Combemere, but monitoring the other surviving locations. At 09:00 hours, on the dot, the connection was made with Government HQ.

"Good morning, John, Bill here." Colonel William Brand, whose title until recent events had been the Silver Stick in Waiting to the Monarch, was a senior military mind.

"And who knows what his title is now," Jacko wondered. There would be no need for radio security given the circumstances. "Morning Bill, what news do you have for me today?"

102

"Got a little mission, which you will have to undertake; nothing too complex."

"Go ahead, Bill."

"OK, the situation is this. The Government has for some time been compiling a list of boffins. We have been rounding them up from various locations across the country and bringing them into secure locations. They are, and will be, crucial to the survival and rejuvenation of the country when this horror story subsides."

"I often wondered what those politicians really got up to," Jacko joked but his interest was roused.

"Yes, I can see the wisdom in their thinking. Anyway, there is a group of them in your zone, eight in number. The Government wants you to go out and bring them back to Combemere for safekeeping."

"Sounds like a search and rescue assignment to me, Bill."

"Yes, you could be right, that's exactly what it is, but that's your mission. Tomorrow at first light is the latest that you can leave as the politicians are worried the boffins might panic and split up, which will make the job of rounding them up even more difficult."

"Give me a location."

"Culham Centre for Fusion Energy, just outside of Oxford, about forty miles from your location."

"OK Bill, I will put together a plan and suggest that we speak again at twelve hundred hours."

"Roger that Jacko. Speak again twelve hundred hours."

At midday, John Jackson, was connected through to Bill Brand in London.

"OK, Jacko, before you give me your plan, I have more info for you which should make the importance of your mission a little clearer." Bill Brand went on to explain exactly why Jacko's mission was of such high priority. "As I explained briefly, when we last spoke, the boffins at Culham are on the cusp of cracking the fusion problem. It's all rather complex, but in basic layman's terms; they can create electrical energy from fusion generators. These generators can be of varying sizes ranging from something that could power a motorcycle or lawn mower to a huge version that could produce enough electricity to power a factory. They can be transportable so that a version, no larger than a briefcase, could, for example, replace the huge bank of batteries and generate the requirements for an electric car. In addition, the unit could be taken from one vehicle to another."

Bill stopped for a moment to allow the significance of what he had explained to sink in. Then he continued, "Jacko do you understand the implication of this?" Pausing, although not expecting an answer, he then ploughed right on with his explanation. "Once we have stabilised the situation, the full-scale manufacture of fusion generators can begin. The country can be rebuilt, only this time it won't be reliant on oil. Every occupied house in the country can have its own generator, meaning that it will not have to rely on sourcing its power from the grid."

"I guess I can see where you are going with this," Jacko replied, "but tell me more. This is heady stuff."

"Jacko, when this nightmare is finally over, we will be looking at an enormous re-building program, both materially and socially. The brains here in London have considered this scenario in very fine detail and a detailed plan has been devised. This will have to be achieved without basic petrol and diesel driven transport. If the boffins at Culham can crack the fusion deal, we will be able to move forward without relying on oil-based fuels. In fact, we will eventually be able to generate all of our electrical needs from fusion generators. The country can be rebuilt, and with a far safer and cleaner energy source. The national grid as we know it will become redundant. It's going to be a long haul. The first generators will be used in transportation by cannibalising existing vehicles and converting them to electric power. Then preliminary rudimentary small factories will produce the first generation of portable fusion generators, and these will in turn spawn advanced, larger and improved versions."

"Wow, Bill, that's quite a phenomenal statement!" Jacko gave himself a brief moment to reflect on the dramatic news. Perhaps there could be some good to come from this horror story after all.

"I will regard the mission to Oxford to be something that cannot be allowed to fail. Bill? Is the information for all ears?" he asked.

"I don't see any reason why not, so what are you thinking?"

"I'd feel a lot better if I can explain to the men going with me tomorrow what you have just told me," Jacko explained.

"Good thinking, it will add to their morale, in fact, it's OK for this to be for general consumption. A good and much needed boost in morale," the senior officer agreed.

"No lack of motivation and commitment from this end, Bill," Jacko proudly announced.

He then went on to explain the plan that he had cobbled together after conferring with the transport officer, and getting an estimate of how much fuel was still available and what vehicles could make the round trip with the carrying capacity for eight passengers. He outlined the plan that he had devised. The best option was to ride to the Culham Centre on horseback with five soldiers accompanying him as it was hard to judge how much hostility they were likely to encounter en-route and at Culham itself. There was no point in sending vehicles that only had fuel for a return trip and nothing more. It might take some time to find all of the boffins; horseback was the far more flexible option. They could maintain radio contact, and when the passenger list was complete, send for the motorised transport. Jacko's plan was relayed through to central government at 18:45 hours and the go ahead was received.

Jacko called a meeting of the five soldiers he had selected. All had held the rank of Corporal of Horse, equivalent to sergeant rank in the remainder of the British Army and were solidly capable men. In addition, he asked the Farrier Major and Regimental Saddler to attend. Jacko stood in front of his men, hands clasped behind his back. He had been entrusted with a mission, giving him the opportunity to get out of the barracks and engage his soldiering skills. This was what he was made for.

"Gentlemen, the plan are this." He carefully considered the faces of the men before him. "We have been tasked by London to round up eight boffin types from a scientific centre just outside Oxford. Six of us will ride there and gather this flock together. When we have them penned and ready for shipment, we will call in motorised transport and get them back to Combemere."

He then went on to explain the significance of the mission relaying all of the information about the fusion generators becoming the salvation for the future. It was, after all, a ray of hope, and he could see from the faces of the men in front of him that they were enthusiastic at both the prospect of the mission and the possibilities that fusion power offered.

He then turned his attention to the Farrier Major, looking directly at him in a measured manner. "The five who will be riding with me can choose their mounts. I will be riding Rascal. Please, check the horses over and make sure that they are one hundred percent fit and up to the job."

Jacko turned to the saddler. "Geoff, I want the saddles for these mounts converted to take saddle bags, plus additional saddle bags made to go over their hindquarters. We will also be carrying swords so there will need to be a facility for them to be strapped to the front of the saddle." He paused, as there was a look of doubt on the faces before him. "The swords might help us to dissuade any aggressors who might fancy their chances. I doubt very much that we will have to use them, but they will be an excellent deterrent. To put your minds at rest we will also be carrying SA80 Assault Rifles."

The saddler was busily scribbling down the ever-growing list of requirements, looking rather perplexed. The other soldiers present were smiling as he turned the page in his notebook and scrawled even more of Jacko's requests.

"Canvas buckets," Jacko suddenly added. Geoff's head snapped up from his notepad as if it were on a spring. "Do we have any? If not can you knock us up six, please?" He thoughtfully stroked his chin. "I think that's about it unless any of you can think of something I might have missed."

The saddler scrutinised the other men with a look clearly saying, "Don't you dare." Jacko paused to allow the saddler time to consider the requirement. His mind was obviously buzzing, planning the mountainous task that he had been given. "All of this to be ready for us to ride out of here by o-six-hundred hours, tomorrow." He turned to the saddler, "I know that this is very short notice. Press gang whatever manpower that you need."

The saddler considered objecting on the time issue, but thought better of it; he could see that Jacko's mind was made up.

"OK, gentlemen, let's get this plan underway," Jacko concluded.

The meeting was brief and the men all walked smartly off to attend to their individual preparations, leaving the saddler scratching his head furiously. The five CoH's had all been in war zones in armoured reconnaissance vehicles and ridden on numerous State occasions, but never did they expect to undertake a mission on horseback.

Colonel John Jackson walked back to his office. His thoughts fully engaged with the matter at hand, the plan continuing to formulate in his mind. He was happy to be involved in a mission that appreciatively broke the monotony of the camp's confinement.

As he walked through the outer office, he spoke with the clerk. "Rogers, two things; just nip out and find Dan Buckland, tell him to get here ASAP. When you get back, make six copies of the list of these names."

Jacko handed the clerk a list of the eight people to be located who were the subject of the mission and went into his office to further plan the impending assignment.

The clerk was also delighted to be given the opportunity to escape from the confinement of his office. He was quick to put on his beret and adjust it in the prescribed manner. He then just as quickly took it off and threw it onto his desk. "That's not the way we do things now," he muttered to himself with a faint smile.

Five minutes later, Dan Buckland, knocked on Jacko's door. "Got something cooking John?" he inquired in a breezy, yet mildly concerned voice.

"Grab yourself a chair Dan, we have something to discuss." Jacko went on to outline the plan and explain its motivation.

Dan Buckland looked pleasantly surprised. "My take on this is that it is actually the first positive news we have received in some time. It gives us something to look forward to. Is this for sharing with the troops?"

"Yes, it is. I want the lads to see that what they are enduring does have a logical motivation. There is some light at the end of this horrendous tunnel."

Dan looked animated by the news. "OK, Boss, so when do we go?" "Ah, that's the next item we have to discuss, Dan. I'm leaving you here to keep things calm. I figure that I will be gone, maybe up to a week. I need you here, Dan. You're the one that the guys trust most." Jacko had anticipated this response and had deliberated for some time on his decision.

"Bit selfish, if you ask me, grabbing all the cream for yourself," Dan replied, his face displaying a look of mock displeasure. Jacko knew that he would have been the best man to have at his side, but he was also well aware that leaving Dan Buckland in charge would reduce a great many of his worries.

As it was likely going to be a while before the two men could get together again, Jacko opened his desk drawer and took out the much- depleted bottle of Glen Fiddich. "Should be just enough for a dram each, and then who knows if, or when, we will get to enjoy this little luxury again."

The whisky was drank in silence by the two men who took slow, measured sips to prolong the enjoyment of something that they might well never get to savour again.

06:00 hours the next morning, six mounted soldiers left the barracks, led by Jacko riding Rascal. The saddler and his staff had been working throughout the night and they had surpassed themselves. The soldiers were well armed, carried walkie-talkies, and equipment for surviving in the field for a week. They created a strange image, a mixture of the old and the new. Horsemen, dressed in a combination of riding gear and combat kit. Uniforms were now simply what the individual soldier felt comfortable in; regimentation was a thing of the past. They carried L85 assault rifles slung across their shoulders and SIG P226 side arms. One of the groups had the HF field radio strapped to his back. Over the years, thousands of cavalrymen had ridden through the gates of Combemere Barracks, but nothing compared with the small troop, which resembled mounted guerrillas, rather than the immaculate pristine Household Cavalry that was known and respected worldwide.

As they rode out of the gates, Jacko went over the plan again, relaying it to all of the men. He had decided that they would stick to the motorways, wherever possible, as he had advised Sarah for her journey.

The horses were lively, happy to be out. Their exercise routine had, from necessity, been reduced and this was a rare treat for them. The men were also feeling relaxed and gratified to be leaving the confines of the barrack walls. The route to the motorway led them to the large roundabout where, even at this early hour, there were a large group of people gathered on the grassy hill waiting for an unsuspecting refugee to leave the volatility of the town. Upon seeing the approaching horsemen, they sensed loot. All were armed with clubs of various dimensions. Jacko called his horsemen to a halt. The distance between the troop and the looters was about one hundred yards.

"One man on horseback is equal to ten men on the ground," he explained. "This is not a problem. I don't want to injure anyone but we have to be allowed to pass. Draw swords."

The six men took the double bridled reins in their left hands and as one, drew their swords from their scabbards.

"Slope swords."

All cavalry trained, they again worked as one. "Advance line abreast, walk march."

The soldiers moved forward slowly. The looters appeared initially not to be intimidated and continued moving forward, shouting abuse and brandishing their weapons, the distance between the two groups diminishing. "Hunger can make a man do strange things," Jacko spoke in a low voice more to himself than to the men with him.

"Trot," the order was spoken rather than shouted.

There was no need for him to shout loud as he might have, had he been leading a full mounted squadron. The men drew their legs back slightly and touched the flanks of their mounts; the six horses broke into a controlled trot. The horses' hooves were now on grass and this enlivened their senses, causing them to toss their heads and whinny loudly. This was too much for the attackers. The huge black horses surmounted by six large men with swords in their hands would frighten most. The looters scrambled for cover, thinking better of an attack, knowing that there would soon be other, unsuspecting victims, making a break for the safety of the countryside. For the looting gang, their craving for food would have to wait for now. The small troop rode on for a further ten minutes towards the motorway.

"Halt!"

The six men brought their horses to a standstill. "Return swords."

Giving orders in the age-old manner was a hard habit to lose and seemed, under the circumstances, to be outmoded, but the men were all thoroughly drilled in these manoeuvres and it was difficult to change their thinking.

Jacko addressed the men, "We will ride for six hours, stop at midday, to feed, water and check the horses, grab some grub for ourselves and move on. Our estimated time of arrival (ETA) will be at about eighteen hundred hours, as long as we don't encounter any more, angry, hungry folk."

The main advantage of riding on motorways was that they skirted the towns, normally the location where the more serious problems lay. A disadvantage was that motorway service stations had become a location where marauding bands congregated due to the shops and cafés that held, or had held, food stocks. Most of these had long been looted out, but with nowhere else to go, many looters stayed on in the hope that something could be gleaned from the premises or unsuspecting

108

passers- by. When Jacko's troop passed a service station, they did so at a trot, to reduce the time that they could be observed and thereby reduce the chances of another confrontation.

The group made good time and reached Henley on Thames at around midday. They remained outside of the town, well away from any housing. There was plenty of countryside and here it looked as if the world was normal, actually rather peaceful and pleasant. Jacko considered the advice he had given to his men and family; escaping to the country was the best policy. The group had attended to their horses and were seeing to their own requirements. John Fisher was one of the Corporals of the Horse in the team.

He was a large rugby playing Geordie, well known for his direct, no nonsense manner and humour. "Did you notice two of our old comrades on that roundabout this morning?" he asked, posing the question to the group as a whole.

"What do you mean, Fish?" enquired Jock Kelly, a three troop, Corporal of Horse, who was also well known as a squadron joker.

"The two low lives's that we expelled from the barracks, Garratt and Jenkins," Fisher practically spat out the names.

"No, can't say I noticed them," Jock replied.

"Well, we might have guessed that they would end up involved in something like that," added Fish.

"Certainly not the type that you would consider breeding stock," Jock commented with an air of knowledgeability. This brought a chuckle from the men.

The short midday break was soon over, the horses made ready to move on and the men mounted up.

"If our luck continues, we should reach Culham well before sunset," Jacko explained as they set off.

They crossed the Thames at Dorchester and headed west towards Abingdon. He gave each of the men a copy of the list that Rogers had made.

"We shall make camp outside the centre, but as close as possible to give us access without drawing attention to ourselves and bed down for the night. We will have to keep guard during the hours of darkness. Fish, will you work out the stags? In the morning, four of us will go into the centre on foot, looking for the boffins, and two will stay with the horses."

The troop arrived at the map coordinates that Jacko had previously decided was an ideal location. It was 18:15 hours. He considered the advantage that it amazingly still functioned, as the satellites power supplies had not been affected.

"OK, now we have to find a place to hide up." Jacko stood up in his stirrups and looked around. "I would rather have the horses inside and we need enough space for the eight buffs. Some of them might take more finding than others." He turned his horse towards his men. "OK, pair off, recce the area and meet back here in 30 minutes. Fish, you are with me."

The men walked their horses away, hoping to discover a safe location. Thirty minutes later they met up again and discussed the possibilities that they had found. "Looks as if the church is the best bet," Jacko decided.

They walked the horses the short distance to the old church, which had something of an abandoned look about it and dismounted. The graveyard made an excellent security perimeter and the Yew trees added to the cover potential. The door was high enough to allow the horses to get inside.

"Any of you religious?" asked Jacko. "Don't want you saying that I have ordered you to desecrate the House of the Lord."

The only reply was from Fish. "Horses are God's creatures too, aren't they?" he reverently pointed out.

The men and horses moved into the church. Some of the back pews were moved around and a small stabling area was formed at the rear of the main isle. The men began to attend to the horses. They took off the saddles and other equipment, rubbed the animals down with a body cloth and picked out their hooves. One of the men, a Welshman, Dai Evans, went to look for water and the others began making sleeping areas for themselves.

"I don't like to be a whinger," said Jock. "But there's an unholy stink in here." He was stating something that they had all been experiencing as soon as they entered the church but hadn't queried. Dai reappeared at the front of the church beside the altar area.

"I might be able to give you an answer to that Boyo," he said quietly, standing looking back across the pews to the rear of the church. "Come down by here." His accent was heavy, his tone, solemn and meaningful.

The other five men walked down the aisle expectantly, and stood next to Dai. There, sitting in the front pew, were an old couple; dead and decaying. These were tough men, but what they saw hit them hard and right to their hearts. The old couple were locked in a death embrace, moulded together in their demise.

Nothing was said for some minutes until Jacko broke the silence in a gentle tone. "OK lads, let's get them outside, and tomorrow, the two men who will be staying with the horses, can bury them."

It was a supremely sad sight. These two old folk must have realised that they would never have been able to compete in the world that had so violently erupted into mayhem and therefore made the decision to come here to die together silently, and with dignity.

Jacko spoke again. "My only hope is that they might have had some tablets which would have reduced the agony and made their passing as quick and painless as possible. They do actually look quite calm."

The men got to work. Dai donated his poncho; gently they wrapped the bodies in it and respectfully carried them out into the graveyard, still intertwined. Night was closing in fast. They went back inside the church to feed and water the horses. The mood was sombre and the episode had hammered home the reality of what was happening all around the nation. The contrast between the unscathed countryside and devastated suburban areas was inconceivable.

"OK guys, before it's too dark, go and check out if there are any candles; should be just the place to find them unless the looting gangs have been here before us."

The men settled down to sleep. They had been in the saddle for around twelve hours and they could all feel the effects. The first night guard was set.

Going outside for the first stag, Fisher made one of his hallmark comments. "Wandering around the grounds of the church on graveyard shift with its new inhabitants will be a definite page in the memoirs," he mused.

That night passed without incident. The church substituted as a good stable and by first light all men and horses were refreshed. Jacko's military mind had been in action during the night. He related his thoughts as the first brew of the day was downed by the team, courtesy of army field rations.

"We could be staying for some days. We aren't going to need the horses, so my plan is to find some good enclosed pasture and let the nags have an unexpected birthday treat. We will still need to guard them, but I don't foresee any problems there." The others agreed that it was a good plan and set about stowing away the saddlery.

The choice of good pasture was limitless; mowing lawns was a pastime long elapsed. A safe enclosed paddock close by was quickly chosen. The horses were led into the field and let go. They instantly loved it, racing around bucking and kicking like naughty children being let out of school for the summer holidays. When they had let off enough steam, they stopped, lay down and rolled on the lush green grass. The six men allowed them ten minutes to watch, what essentially their buddies' was, having a good time. The bond between horse and man was one that had to be experienced.

"Dai, you can take the first stag, watching the nags. Jock, you will also be staying, but you can start looking for tools and begin digging a grave for our two friends in a good position in the graveyard. Also find a good place to stash the rifles. We can't wander around a science centre looking as if we are in a Bruce Willis movie. Keep two out for yourself and Dai, just in case you are visited. We are carrying water purification tablets, find as many clean containers as you can and purify as much water as possible for the guests. They probably haven't had much to drink for some time. We will be leaving the field radio here and keeping in touch with the walkie-talkies. Contact Windsor and tell them that we have arrived and are proceeding with the mission. The rest of us are off to savour the delights of the Culham Science Centre and play Hunt the Boffin." The five men walked back towards the church, leaving Dai Evans to return to observing the equine antics.

"We will only be carrying side arms which I want you to keep concealed. No need to give anyone cause for alarm. Make yourselves look as normal as possible." He allowed his gaze to rest on the huge form of Fisher. "Fish, in your case, just do your best."

In just about every army unit there were guys who didn't fit into the standard clothing and footwear; Fish was just one of the cavalry's versions. His army boots and bed were all custom made.

It was 07:00 hours when the four men set off for the Culham Centre, which was an enormous complex that had been designated high security. As they approached, it was noticeable that the gatehouse was deserted and there was no sign of any security patrols.

Fifteen minutes later they walked through the front entrance of the main office buildings and into a large reception hall, where previously there would have been some form of security, now the reception area was abandoned. The floors were littered with garbage and to one side there were vending machines that had been smashed. Glass and metal littered the floor around them. There were some people walking around, looking very dishevelled and forlorn, almost zombie like. The four new arrivals seemed to draw little attention.

"OK, this is where we split up," Jacko gave the orders in a low voice. All of the team had small field walkie-talkie radios, but the battery life was severely limited, so traffic, it was decided, would be very minimal.

"Fish, you are with me. Morris and Holland, you two start on the first floor. Check your lists. We are looking for Professors James and Gilbert, plus Doctors Hunt, Burgess, Williams, Corrigan and Hann. If you find them first, make contact and we will meet up. Good hunting."

The two groups set off. There was a building plan on the wall of the reception area. Jacko and Fisher checked it, looking for any of the names from the list.

"Fish, ground floor, east wing, room thirty-seven, Professor James's office. Let's start there."

The two men walked towards the sign that pointed to the corridor which was the east wing and into the long passageway. The floor was strewn with papers, books and other material. All of the doors were open and inside it was easy to see the same mayhem. They continued along the corridor until they reached room thirty-seven and walked inside. To their amazement, sitting at a desk with his face buried in his hands, sat a man.

He spoke without looking up seemingly hearing their approach. "I have told you before, there is nothing here to eat or drink."

Jacko and Fish exchanged glances; there was a short period of silence. "Professor James?" softly enquired Jacko, not quite believing his luck.

Could this actually be the man that they were searching for? The man looked up. He was unshaven, his face shallow and deeply furrowed. His whole appearance was one of total despair. He looked utterly broken. It was obvious that he was hungry – very hungry.

"Who are you?" the voice was shaky, bordering on panic.

"I am Colonel Jackson, I have been sent to take you to a place of safety." "Yes, I am Professor James," the man answered almost in disbelief. "And you are here to rescue me?" He then sat back in his chair, staring at the two men, suddenly looking very frightened. Jacko offered him his water flask. The Professor pushed it away; the situation was disturbing him. The very presence of Fisher wasn't doing much to alleviate the situation. The man was huge, although after two minutes in his company, it was obvious that he was not a threat, but standing as he was, towering over the Professor's desk, he must have looked intimidating, added to which the grip of his pistol was visible in his belt.

"Why me?" the defensive stance that the prof had now adopted, was becoming obvious. "There are thousands of good people who need rescuing. Why choose me?"

Jacko continued, "Professor James, please try to relax. We are here to help you. I will explain everything." His tone was reassuring, but forceful. He pushed the water flask across the desk again, took an energy bar from a pocket in his smock and offered it to the Professor. Almost reluctantly the Professor accepted the offer. He ate and drank in silence. Jacko waited until he had finished before he began to relate the reason for his being there.

"But there are so many starving people," the Professor repeated many times, as if not being able to fully take in the bizarre reality of the situation, but slowly he seemed to recover. Fisher took the opportunity to walk back into the corridor and contact the other soldiers on the hand held radio, telling them to meet at his location.

"Fuel contamination you say, and its spread across the entire country," mumbled the Professor. "We have been receiving conflicting reports, but the main concern has been the lack of food and clean water."

"As far as we can tell, the contamination of fuel stocks is 100% throughout the planet."

"My God, now I am beginning to understand the magnitude of this tragedy." He was close to tears.

"Professor, I know that this is all a tremendous shock to you, but we have to locate seven more of your colleagues and we need to move quickly."

Jacko showed his list to Professor James.

"Yes, I know all of these people. They are all colleagues and friends. We were all working on the same project."

The man was beginning to show a little more enthusiasm. "And are they all still in this vicinity?" enquired Jacko.

"Pretty much, nobody knew where they should go. Everyone thought that this would all come to an end and things would return to normality. How could we have known?"

Morris and Holland arrived and were introduced. Within two hours all of the people on the list had been found and were congregated in Professor James's office. Professor Gilbert and Doctor Williams turned out to be women. Finding all of the people on the list so quickly should have been considered something of a result. Jacko had expected them to be spread far and wide, but the reality was there was nowhere for them to go, so as colleagues, they had decided that it was safer to stay together, clinging to the hope that the emergency would soon be resolved, allowing life to slowly return to normality.

Jacko felt relieved, he had achieved the first part of his mission successfully and all would have been well if it wasn't for the fact that some were accompanied by husbands, wives and children. The initial number of eight had now expanded to twenty two!

Jacko looked at the other soldiers with an expression of dismay and utter bewilderment. Nobody had expected this. Now the researchers threw another spanner into the works. They were adamant; all demanded that they went as a group or not at all. Jacko explained that all of his men, himself included, had made the sacrifice to leave their families, but the obstinate academic group refused to accept being divided.

"I knew that this was all going too well, Boss," Fisher added in his usual helpful manner.

The office was crowded and they were generating quite a lot of noise. This was dangerous and could soon attract others to the scene.

Jacko addressed the crowd. "Listen to me. If we stay here, we are in danger of attracting unwanted attention. We must move to a nearby secured location. We cannot walk out of here en-masse. You will be divided up into four groups, led by myself and my men, to the location." Jacko's self-assurance and strength gave the academics confidence and they did as they were asked without argument, understanding that their options were nil. At five minute intervals, the four groups walked out of the Culham Centre and were led by the soldiers to the church. The purified water was greatly appreciated by the new arrivals, but there was little for them to eat.

Jock Kelly was the regiment's top radio operator. Jacko asked him to get through to London where he could explain the situation. He knew that every extra mouth that needed feeding was a burden, but the decision rested with the big boys in government. The situation was relayed to London and the reply was for all the twenty two to be taken to Windsor.

"OK Jock, now get through to Combemere and explain that the transport will have to be for twenty two persons." After the messages were transmitted and a plan was in action, Jacko called his men together.

"The time is ten forty-five hours. It will take at least an hour for the transport to arrive, so the mission here should be wrapped up by thirteen-thirty hours. I don't want to travel with the horses unnecessarily after dark, so we can spend the night here and leave first thing tomorrow. It should be just a gentle ride back to Windsor. How have things progressed with the burial? Dai, Jock, give me an update."

Dai Evens was the first to answer. "No problem finding digging tools, Boss, but the ground, it's bloody hard; we only managed to dig down three feet."

Jock Kelly took up the narrative. "We found a quiet spot and carried the couple there. We thought that we should bury them as they are, intertwined, just as they died. I'm sure that they would have liked that."

Jacko looked pensive. "OK, we have time this afternoon to finish the job and there are six of us now."

The meeting was interrupted by Professor James. "I wonder if I can have a word with you Colonel?" he asked politely.

"Yes, of course," replied Jacko and the two men moved to one side. "I have been thinking about the final development of the fusion engine." He paused as if still considering what he was about to say. "We are leaving here, literally with the clothes that we are standing up in."

"No need to worry about that Professor, we have plenty of clothing stocks at Combemere," Jacko added thoughtfully.

"Well, I wasn't thinking too much about our personal needs, more our academic requirements," he added.

"I think that I need to explain a little more about the fusion generator project that we were working on when this disaster occurred. Yes, it is true that we were approaching a breakthrough in the development of this important technology, but the reality is that it will be an impossibility to move the equipment that we have been

115

building here over the past years. Professor James shuffled his feet, looking perceptibly uncomfortable, what he was about to admit might jeopardise his and his team's chance of being rescued from the hell that their lives had descended into. If he didn't choose his next words carefully his rescuers might just disappear as suddenly as they had appeared leaving them stranded once again.

"Moving the fusion reactor to Windsor would be a task, that even prior to the fuel virus would not have been achievable."

His anxiety was increasing with each sentence that he spoke; he now played the card that he hoped would be his salvation. "Over the years since Nikola Tesla radically altered the scientific community's thinking about energy, there have been countless alternative theories. Many of these have been advanced by eccentric inventors, looking for recognition, the internet was awash with examples, but amongst the crank innovations there have been those that do hold a great deal of potential. It has been the responsibility of our organisation to observe and monitor these maverick innovations, the consequence of this was that we determined that there were several that did indeed work. We monitored the work of scientists such as Dr. Brian O'Leary, who expounded the virtues of free energy from such new technologies as magnetic motors, solid state energy, cold fusion, zero point energy and others. These are the alternative energy sources that have been suppressed by the multi trillion pound oil linked industries. The time was approaching when the internal combustion engine would have been supplanted by a new generation of virtually free, clean energy.

The innovations we selected that warranted further investigation were all low budget projects. We have the data stored and it is these inventions that we will now have to focus our energies on developing, given the limited resources and a new location that will be available to us. Nevertheless the requirement will exist for us to take some paraphernalia with us."

Jacko looked worried; this was a whole different agenda from his original remit.

"Colonel Jackson, in order for us to complete the work that the interim government want us to embark on, we will require our equipment."

Jacko's heart sank. "I thought that I had this wrapped up," he sighed to himself. Almost afraid to ask, he tentatively inquired, "And how much equipment is that?"

"If we reduce to a bare minimum, it might just fit into two of your large army trucks."

This was not what Jacko wanted to hear, fuel was scarce and finding enough to get twenty two people and their hardware back to Windsor was going to be a challenge.

"Leave it with me, Professor," Jacko replied, sounding, but not feeling, overly confident.

He called his team together. "There's been a bit of a hitch," he explained. The boffins now tell me that they can't achieve anything on the fusion deal without their equipment."

He gave the matter some thought whilst his words sunk in to the men.

"Makes sense, I guess, Boss," added Fisher.

"I'm worried that too much movement will attract attention. We're going to have to get the equipment out without the other people in the centre realising what we're up to." All of his men nodded agreement.

"My plan is this. The majority of the boffin group will be sent to Windsor today, as planned. The rest of us will have to stay in the church. I feel that this is the best location as long as everyone remains inside as much as possible. We leave two men there to protect everything, just in case. The other four go back into the centre with half a dozen of the boffins, who know what equipment they will need and prepare for transportation. When the equipment is ready to be moved, and assuming that the transport can be arranged, we take a chance. Get the trucks as close to the centre as possible and load them up in double quick time. When they are loaded, we put the boffins on board and send them straight to Windsor, leaving us to return in our own time."

Jacko scanned the faces of his men, "Any thoughts on that?"

The five men gave it some consideration, and then all nodded agreement. Jacko took Professor James aside and explained his plan. The Professor then went off to pass on the news to his group and decide which of the boffins would be staying.

"Jock, get through to Combemere and explain to them the revised transport requirements, I'm sure they will be delighted. Ask them to send six more twenty-four hour food packs for the boffins that will be staying."

With that, they divided up and went their separate ways to deal with the new plans. By 13:30 hours, the first phase transport had left with sixteen passengers. Jock and Dai, the burial detail, continued digging the grave.

"We will go into the centre at 16:00 hours whilst there is some daylight left. We can then keep working for as long as it takes. I have the transport arranged for 05:00 hours tomorrow morning. God alone knows how they have found the diesel for the trucks, but it looks as if the plan is a goer."

At 15:40 hours, they held the funeral of the old couple. Dai had managed to fashion a rather handsome wooden cross and burned the names of the couple onto it. They had discovered their identities from the contents of the woman's handbag. They were all satisfied with their work and that when the job was finished, they had given the old couple as dignified a funeral as possible.

Jacko said a few words which he thought were wholly inadequate, but he tried his best to find words suitable for the unexpected circumstances. Then it was back to business. "OK guys, same procedure as when we left; five minute intervals between groups. Don't attract unnecessary attention."

Four separate sections moved off, each led by a soldier, and furtively they entered the centre. The equipment was scattered in several locations about the buildings. The men worked throughout the night to get everything into position for the early morning pick up. On the dot of 05:00 hours, two trucks arrived, each with a driver and armed guard. Having four extra men to help with the loading quickened the work, and by 07:00 hours, the two trucks rolled out of the Culham Science Centre filled to the brim with a bewildering assortment of scientific equipment and six tired scientists.

"Job done, it's back to church for us guys," Jacko quipped, feeling satisfied that the job was in fact, well done. "Take the rest of the day off, we won't be moving until o-six-hundred, tomorrow. I'll get the two lads who stayed at the church to round up the nags and take them back inside. They can brush them off and get them ready for the ride home. I think that our mounts have had a long enough mini break in the country."

When the horses were brought back inside, they did indeed look as if they had been enjoying themselves. They were covered in mud and very frisky. It took some time to get them cleaned up.

06:00 hours the following day, after a brew and a breakfast of army rations, the six horsemen set off f o r Windsor. As on the outbound trip, they stopped at the same location to rest, feed and water the horses, grabbing another lunch – ration style. Fisher noticed that there was an apple orchard nearby that had somehow escaped the notice of the looters. He rode over and was filling the now much depleted saddlebags with apples. The others followed him and were also grabbing apples and stuffing them into their saddlebags.

Bang! Shotgun pellets ripped through the apple trees, showering the men with fragments of apples, leaves and branches. The six soldiers were taken completely by surprise. An aging gentleman was standing in the archway of a garden wall, a tiny woman by his side. In an instant six, L85A2, assault rifles were trained on the couple, who were themselves more than just a little surprised.

"What do you think you are doing?" protested the old man. "Those are not your apples, go away!"

Jacko intervened as soon as the initial tension had abated. "Please sir, we don't wish you any harm."

He lowered his rifle and gestured to the others to do the same. The rifles were slung back over the soldiers' shoulders, all of whom were smiling like little boys, because they had been caught in the act of scrumping. Slowly the old man lowered his shotgun.

"If you would like me to explain, I would be most grateful," Jacko offered politely. The old man agreed, and Jacko walked over and shook his hand. He gave a quick explanation of who he and his men were and what they were doing in rural Oxfordshire, on horseback. By this time the man's wife was showing obvious signs of relief. She took over the conversation and invited them all to come to their house for tea.

And so it was that in a country, ravaged by starvation and anarchy that a most unlikely group of eight people sat down to a dignified tea at a farm cottage in middle England. Jacko clarified the overall situation. He thought that these folk were in a stable location and could sustain their existence with the produce that was surrounding them. They were so much luckier that the vast majority of people. The couple agreed that they could never eat all of the apples and were more than happy To allow the soldiers to take all that they wished. A most agreeable interlude passed. Jacko explained that he must get the men and horses back to Windsor before dark and the small troop took their leave, their saddlebags bulging with apples.

At 18:00 hours, the six horsemen arrived at the gates of Combemere Barracks. They were tired and so were their mounts, but all were well satisfied that they had accomplished, a successful mission, however unusual it might have been.

Chapter 16

The Queens Blacks

Armageddon + 38 days

The Regimental Vet and the Farrier Major asked for a meeting with the CO. They met up in the wide expanse of the entrance of the distinctive Victorian building, which was the Riding School. The surroundings were very familiar to all three men. They had all endured the hardships of learning to ride 'cavalry style' in this school and although the training had been hard, they all held the iconic building in high regard. Previously, there would have been an exchange of predictable outmoded salutes, but, to the men now present, this was all redundant.

Tony Sharp, the vet, opened the conversation. "Jacko, there are some things you must take a look at."

Together the three men walked to the hay barn. The barn looked well stacked with good healthy hay.

"There is about two months worth of hay here," the Farrier Major pointed out, "but the problem is in here." He continued his explanation as they walked into the grain store. "We estimate that there are enough oats to feed the nags for about three weeks and the supplements are down to just over a week."

Jacko nodded, indicating that he had absorbed the situation.

"Then there's the matter of water," the vet added. "You know what these big fellows drink daily. We have been extremely fortunate with the tap in the riding school that our Victorian ancestors left us, but we have no idea as to where the water is coming from and how long it will last."

Jacko was beginning to get inkling as to where this conversation might be going.

"We have to make a decision and there are two options, as myself and the Farrier

Major see it." He paused and the CO nodded for him to continue.

"Option One: We systematically slaughter the horses and eat the meat; it would be a great source of protein."

"OK," the CO said, "give me the second option."

The vet took his time to reply. "We take off their shoes, walk them up to the Great Park and let them run wild to fend for themselves." He then expanded the disadvantages of this alternative. "There would be a strong element of risk attached to this. We have heard reports of deer in the Great Park being slaughtered and even swans taken from the Thames for food. These horses have lived amongst humans all of their lives and it wouldn't take much to catch and kill one. The meat would sustain a lot of people, possibly saving them from dying of hunger for a short time until it ran out and they would revert to starvation or the slaughter of another horse."

A decision would have to be made.

The three men walked away from the stable block, past the riding school and the tap, which miraculously was keeping them all alive. There was a queue of eight soldiers of varying rank with buckets; there was always a queue at the tap. The meeting was ended.

John Jackson walked alone back towards the Regimental office block. The responsibility of command was weighing heavily upon his shoulders. The problems were coming thick and fast, and he knew that he was the end of the line, where the buck would finally come to a stop. There was an eerie quietness about the barracks, which was usually filled with the sound of trucks and armoured vehicles in addition to the noise of the traffic from the nearby road. Combemere was also directly under the flight path to Heathrow, but the skies were clear; there was no aircraft noise now.

By the time he had reached his office, he had arrived at a decision. "Rogers, call a meeting, all ranks: Eighteen-hundred hours, cookhouse."

Colonel Jackson stood on the raised dais at the top end of the cookhouse; he was flanked by the Regimental Vet and the Farrier Corporal Major. As always, Dan Buckland stood close by. They watched the forlorn faces of the men that they had served with for many years file in; men who would normally be laughing and joking, but now were looking seriously despondent. Most were experienced soldiers, but now all were wondering what other possible bad news could be heaped upon them.

"Ladies and Gentlemen, there is a decision to be made and I feel that it is not for me alone to decide the fate of seventy of our comrades."

There was a look of bewilderment upon many of the younger men, although the more seasoned had known what was coming, upon seeing the two men who were flanking the Colonel.

"I am talking about the Queens Blacks." A discernible groan was audible.

"We cannot keep them all given the existing situation. Their rations are low and water is scarce, both problems I know you are all acutely aware of. As we see it there are two options available to us unless one of you has an alternative. Please, speak up if you do. The first option is that we systematically slaughter them and butcher the meat which would be a great source of protein. The second option would be to rough them off and set them free in the Great Park to take their chances."

Silence fell over the cookhouse. There was a long deathly hush.

The young trooper, Flint, recently passed out from his equitation course and not known for his intelligence, gingerly stood up. There was a distinct air of anticipation knowing that Flint was bound to say something completely stupid.

"Sir, you know that three troop horse, Rasputin, he has killed two of his riders. The second one was Tommy Thompson, who was in my recruit troop and he was a good lad. Well, couldn't we just eat Rasputin and let the rest go?"

That was enough to break the awful mood of darkness that had prevailed and for a brief, fleeting moment; the smiling faces of his soldiers were as they were meant to be.

Rasputin was well known; he had indeed unseated and thrown two of his riders, and both had died from head injuries received in the fall.

All things equestrian was considered the jurisdiction of the Farrier Major, a huge Geordie, his bite every bit equal to his bark. He shook his huge fist and shouted, "Let the Black Buggers go!"

There was nothing more to be said. A huge cheer erupted throughout the cookhouse.

The final analysis was that they would be keep twelve horses, and the four coach horses; the rest given their freedom. For the next ten days, six horses a day were taken to the forge and their shoes removed. Their feet were trimmed, cleaned and inspected for the last time. Six troopers each rode a horse and led another. The lead horses were the ones selected to be given their freedom. A non-commissioned officer from the riding school led the troop which walked along a designated path incorporating as much grass as possible. These horses' hooves would be fine on grass, but susceptible to injury and damaging wear on tarmac without the protection of their iron shoes. The closest entrance to Windsor Great Park from Combemere could be gained through Stag Meadow, which gave access via a short road that was the entrance to the unlikely neighbours, Windsor Cemetery, which boasted a quaint little gatehouse reminiscent of something from a set of The Hobbit, which was in turn, adjacent to Windsor Football Club.

Each day at 11:00 hours, the troop of thirteen horses went out through the gates of Combemere and a troop of seven returned. Each day there was a large crowd of

122

soldiers seeing them off, wishing them well, shouting out their individual names as you might expect from colleagues saying goodbye to friends that they knew they would more than likely never see again. Each of the horses was a well-known individual and as such, as highly respected soldier as their two legged associates.

The CO was at the stable block when the seven horses returned. They dismounted and the Colonel walked over to the Corporal of Horse. "Everything OK, Mick?"

"Yes, Boss, I took them up to the fields next to the Polo stables at the top of the Great Park. We took off their bridles, slapped them on the arse and they all ran off. We could see that they loved it, most of them rolled on the thick grass. Problem was that as we left, they all followed. We had to turn around and get them into an area where there was a fence between us and them. They were very confused."

Jacko slapped his riding crop against the side of his leg. "What do you think Mick?"

"The place is abandoned; there are no horses and the girls that worked there have all gone. Water will be the biggest problem, but I doubt that anyone will go up there as it's quite isolated."

"Well done, Mick. Keep this going for ten more days? I think that we might keep hold of twelve of the best nags for…" he paused, slapping his leg with his riding crop again before adding, "God only knows what for."

On the day that the final horses were scheduled for release, prepared for their new life of early retirement, Jacko went to the stable yard early. He took his charger, Rascal, from his loose box and tied his head collar to a ring in the yard wall. Jacko and Rascal had teamed up on many state occasions and were good friends. Rascal had carried Jacko impeccably, never missing a beat. Jacko stood back and admired the magnificent animal. His neck was like a carved chess piece, his powerful flanks solid with muscle. Rascal had white socks on all four or his legs; there was a white blaze on his forehead which snipped to his left nostril. Jacko borrowed a grooming kit from a young trooper and set to work on Rascal. An hour later he was content that his horse was looking as good as he could and saddled him up. It had been some time since Jacko had ridden and it felt wonderful to be on top of the faithful Rascal.

Mick had the small troop ready to go and was surprised to see Jacko in the yard.

"You riding with us today, Boss?" he asked in a broad West Country accent.

"Thought I'd come along and see this final bunch off, Mick," Jacko replied.

As had become the habit, there was a large crowd of soldiers at the front gate to say farewell and wish the horses' good luck. The Royals were there every time to say their personal farewell as all were horse lovers. It was not just that these horses were leaving the company of men that had trained, ridden, fed, watered and groomed them, they were somehow symbolic of freedom and hope for the future during this desperate time. Jacko and Mick rode side by side as they walked the troop the short distance to the entrance to the Park.

Jacko contemplated the event. "Over three hundred and fifty years of history, The Household Cavalry and their horses going back to 1660 is ending right here, Mick. Not something that I had expected to be part of," he mused.

Mick didn't have time to answer. He had ridden off and was busy shouting at the troopers, telling them to get a grip of their horses who were all now acting up as their feet touched upon the lush grass of the Great Park. Horses had not evolved to pound the hard streets of London and as soon as they felt the open spaces, smelt the freshness of the countryside and felt grass under their feet they became excited, rather like small children seeing the ocean and walking on a beach for the first time. Mick had chosen the best jockeys who were expecting this reaction and they soon brought the excited steeds under control.

It was a long-standing tradition in the Household Cavalry that the horses ridden by trumpeters were greys. There were two grey mares in the group being taken for release today. Mick pulled his horse around and positioned himself back alongside Jacko.

"Have you thought what might happen to these nags, Mick?" pondered Jacko.

"I think that they will stand a good chance. There are masses of good pasture for grazing; in fact, I would imagine that they will soon be fat and unfit. The biggest problem has to be water."

Jacko contemplated what Mick had said. "Thinking longer term, there is one thing that they can't do and that's breed. All of the males are gelded."

They rode on and up to the Guards Polo Club stables, located at the highest point of the Park. The stables were deserted apart from a couple of horses that were wandering aimlessly about. All of the stalls were empty, the doors all wedged open, it was obvious that the horses had been turned out to fend for themselves. Jacko knew the stables well and was always a little confused by their architectural style. They were built by the Victorians from solemn dark brown brick, and had a sombre appearance, reminding Jacko of a poor house from a Charles Dickens novel. In recent years they had undergone restoration, but still retained an ominous, severe look. The fact that the large building was sitting on high ground surrounded by stunning scenery, made a huge difference. If it had been situated in a city environment, it would have looked dull and satanic.

Mick took the troop to the fields just beyond the stables. "OK, lads, let them go, but sit deep in your saddles and keep a tight rein on your own mounts. They're going to want to join in the fun too."

The troopers unbuckled the bridles of the lead horses and sat deep into their saddles as the six free horses galloped off unknowingly to a new freedom. Their mounts thought that they could do the same and skittered, dancing about and whining as if the ground beneath them had suddenly become red-hot. The six freed horses galloped and bucked for ten minutes, but eventually they calmed, lying down on the soft green paddock and rolled. The depleted team of eight horses turned and walked back to the stables. The horsemen watched what were, in essence, their friends having a great time, but all secretly wondered what would be the fate of these magnificent animals. There were several water troughs in the stables and before they left, they'd filled them all up to their brims.

"Bloody amazing those Victorians," spoke Mick, more from thinking out loud, than in conversation, "Where the hell did they get the water from?"

"I suppose it's a natural instinct for a horse to smell water, but these nags have never needed to do that; guess we have spoiled them. Just hope that the natural instinct will kick in again."

Jacko looked out across the park towards the Thames. "The river isn't too far away, but that will lead them into the territory of humans."

Whenever they passed a gate, they stopped, swung it wide open and wedged it into position. On the track up to the stables from the road, which dissected the park from Ascot to Windsor, there was a large automatic steel gate. With no electricity to open it, the gate was firmly closed.   Jacko told the group to dismount, and together, with some difficulty they manhandled the gate open.

"Well done lads, I don't think that there will be any danger of the nags wandering onto the road and being hit by a car now, which is something in their favour I suppose."

On the way back to barracks there was a chance to give their mounts their heads and gallop across the open parkland. All the riders were shouting and whooping, really letting off steam, Jacko included. He was delighted not only for himself, but grateful to see that some of his soldiers were at least getting a little respite from the horror story that they were now caught up in.

The Great Park was like an island of sanity in a sea of torment, a natural sanctuary. Being away from the town, which was now totally desecrated, allowed the soldiers some relief, but even here the smell of death occasionally prevailed upon the light breeze.

The horses were steaming with sweat when they arrived back in the stable yard. As Jacko dismounted, a trooper came over to take Rascal. It was Flint, the young man who had stood up and suggested eating the infamous, Rasputin. He saluted.

Jacko ignored the lad's automatic gesture. "Don't worry, Flinty, I'll turn him in."

Flint looked momentarily confused. He hung around, obviously wanting to chat with Jacko, which was something that would not necessarily have happened before the fuel contamination.

"Why is it that the officers' horses are called Chargers and everyone else's is just called..., horses?" Flint had a charming naivety, a wonderfully uncomplicated view of the world.

Jacko could not help smiling. "That's something that I don't have an answer to I'm afraid, but it's a good question."

Flint looked disappointed as if expecting that the CO would automatically have an answer for everything. "I've never seen an officer groom his horse," he continued, "it's usually done for them."

"Well, Flinty, not all officers are the same and anyway things are going to be very different from now on." Jacko continued grooming Rascal, But he was quite enjoying the young man's company. "How are you finding the new way of life?"

Flint considered the question. "OK, I suppose, but I would have liked to have ridden on some escorts before all this happened." Jacko knew that the lad had just graduated from the riding school and had never actually taken part in a State occasion.

"Yes, that's bad luck; it was about to be a busy year. And, how about your family? Do you think that they will have coped with what has happened?"

"My mum will be angry because the Bingo must have closed, but I'm sure that they will be Ok."

Jacko could only feel slightly envious of Flint and his child like interpretation of l i f e . With that, ex-Trooper Flint wandered off, mumbling to himself. Jacko released the surcingle and the straps on Rascal's saddle several notches. He unbuckled his bridle, took out the bit from Rascal's mouth and placed the open end of the reins over the magnificent arched neck, then led his horse to the water troughs. Rascal drank copious amounts of water. When Jacko thought that Rascal had drunk enough, he prepared to walk away, but Rascal started drinking again. He shook his muzzle in the cold, clear water, splashing Jacko, who was soaked by the time Rascal had decided that the game was over. He was well named.

They walked back to the loose box that had Rascal's name over the door. Jacko took off the saddle and continued to brush the mud off of the horse's legs, belly and tail. He picked out his hooves and put a warm, New Zealand rug, on the still steaming body. Finally, he filled a hay net and hung it from the brass ring on the back wall of the stall. Satisfied that his charger was comfortably bedded down, he walked over to the Equestrian Wing office where Mick was sitting with his feet on the desk.

126

"What time's feed away, Mick?" he enquired. "Half-an-hour, Boss."

"By the way, I've been thinking," Jacko continued. "Keep an eye on the carriage horses. They might come in useful, could be the only transport in Windsor."

"Been wondering if you had cottoned onto that one, Boss," smiled Mick. "Don't worry about anything down here in the stables. I'll keep a lid on it."

"Right now Mick, a shower would be great, but no chance of that happening any time soon."

With that thought in mind, Jacko, walked back to the RHQ office.

Halo around the Moon

Chapter 17

Dissolution of the Monarchy

Armageddon + 45 days

Jacko made regular visits to the Officers' Mess, updating the Royal group. The Queen asked if there was a medic on the camp and he was happy to be able to tell her that the regiment's medical team, including a doctor, were amongst the group.

Jacko made a point of trying to meet with the Queen at least once a day, even if the meetings were brief due to his workload. He used this time to bring the Monarch up to date with the news, which was now streaming in. Prince William had found a niche for himself in the radio wing and this position enabled him to keep his grandmother aware of the latest news. He was well versed in the use of the technology and fitted in easily. Prince Harry joined the men on the well digging team and appeared to enjoy the physical labour. Both had worked with the men of Combemere before when they were simply called, Mr Wales, so some of the more obvious boundaries had already been overcome.

The Commanding officer called through his office door to his trusty clerk.

"Rogers, can you locate the MO and ask her to be here in fifteen minutes it she is available."

Rogers scampered off, eager to have an official reason to chat with the delicious Doctor Maloney.

Whilst he was waiting, Jacko recalled the profound meeting that had taken place when a totally emotionally and physically drained Sophie Maloney had arrived back at the guardroom. She was a seasoned soldier and was aware that her name was on the missing list. The guard commander was at a loss of how to deal with the situation, and accompanied her to the Commanding Officer's office to allow him to deal with it. Jacko was delighted to see Sophie and listened carefully and sympathetically to her dramatic story. He assured her that as far as he was concerned she was not in breach of any military rules and emphasised the fact that he was delighted to see her again. All of this Jacko dealt with, exhibiting professionalism in the prescribed military fashion, soldier to soldier, but the woman standing in front of him was more than just a comrade who had suffered an enormous loss and was emotionally in need of support. Her eyes were visibly red from crying and her head hung in despair. He was unable to continue with the charade of strict discipline protocol and gave into his human emotional nature. Getting up from behind his desk, he walked around to Sophie and put his arms around her shoulders. She immediately broke down and her face fell sobbing onto Jacko's chest.

Nothing was said for several minutes until Sophie had once again regained her composure and stood back from Jacko. She apologised and the moment passed. Something like a sense of normality returned to the office. Each of the two actors in the short, emotionally charged scene experienced a slight sense of embarrassment.

Jacko cleared his throat with a nervous cough and suggested that she should get to bed and not consider working until she felt well enough, trying to lift the sombre atmosphere with a clumsy joke that seeing the doctor was not an option for her. He was deeply relieved that she had returned, knowing that the reasons for this were not purely confined to her official status on the camp.

This particular episode had played out in the same office almost four weeks earlier. Now, Sophie Maloney was again sitting opposite Jacko in the CO's office. It was evident to Jacko that Doctor Maloney had recovered, superficially at least and had thrown herself into her job. Jacko's thoughts returned to the present.

"What's up John?" she enquired. "Are you feeling unwell?"

"No, nothing so mundane," he smiled. "There is someone who wants to have a chat with you. I think that you might be interested." He leant back in his chair to enjoy the moment.

"Now you have my complete attention, who can that be?" Sophie acted interested, scratching her head in mock confusion. "Has George Clooney dropped by for a coffee or could it be that David Beckham's last tattoo has turned septic?"

Jacko couldn't resist a chuckle and it was good to see that Sophie was returning to her old self after her terrible loss. "None of that dear doctor, none other than the Queen of England wishes to talk with you."

Later that morning, the two officers went to the Mess and Jacko happily introduced Major Maloney to the Queen, who explained that the reason she had asked for the MO was for the doctor to visit her grandson's wife, Kate. Sophie was escorted upstairs to Kate's bedroom and Jacko continued with his regular up-date.

It was at one of these meetings that the Queen asked Jacko to spend a little more time with her as she had something of importance to tell him. It was becoming obvious to Colonel Jackson that there was a fundamental change taking place with the Queen's appearance. Her hair was taking on a more natural look. No longer were there hairdressers and wardrobe specialists to attend to her. It appeared to him that she actually enjoyed walking around in her tartan skirt, brown brogue shoes and green mackintosh. There was always a colourful headscarf to be seen and two of the Corgis were never far away. Prince Phillip took to the new lifestyle, but with a little more difficulty and was still always to be found standing close to his wife.

"Would you mind if I asked you where you went to school, John?" It was apparent that the Queen was taking a personal interest in all of the people in the barracks that this inexplicable element of fate had thrown together.

"Not at all, Ma'am," he replied, wondering where this conversation might progress. "I went to school in Harrow."

"A wonderful school, John, you were indeed lucky. Many of the country's highest achievers began their academic life in that fine establishment."

John had found himself in this situation several times in his life and perversely, he always enjoyed putting the story straight.

"Actually Ma'am, the school I attended was indeed in Harrow, but it was called Harrow County for Boys, or Harrow Grammar School." He wondered what the reaction to this observation might be.

"Nevertheless, I am sure that the educational standards were excellent."

She brushed aside the slight annoyance and continued, "Did you enjoy history whilst you were at school in Harrow, John?"

"Very much, Ma'am and I have continued to pursue that interest." History was indeed one of John Jackson's favourite diversions.

"You may be aware of the works of Juvenal, a Roman writer who lived in the 1st and 2nd centuries A.D. He is the man attributed to writing the sarcastic words 'Panem et Circenses', which is Latin and translates to 'Bread and Circuses'. The declaration becomes more meaningful when you understand that Roman citizens had become increasingly addicted to the free distribution of food, and the frequent spectacle of violent gladiatorial and other contests held in the Coliseum like the chariot races of the Circus Maximus. Juvenal arrived at the decision that Romans had lost the capacity to govern themselves because they had become completely distracted by mindless self-gratification.

"Juvenal's declaration 'Bread and Circuses' is, or was a phrase, that was used to describe a society which is obsessed with trivial entertainment and inconsequential individual pleasures; something that those in power can be attributed responsibility for creating and encouraging. It's a subtle way to control a society, which has lost

131

sight of civic virtues and values, readily submitting to civil authority with unquestioned obedience. Bread and Circuses has also become a general term for government policies that seek short-term solutions to public discontent. Regrettably, Juvenal's words apply quite appropriately to the present day western world and flagrantly to Britain in particular." Jacko was taken slightly unaware by this strong statement that he was certainly not expecting.

The Queen sat thoughtfully for some time, obviously considering the words that she had just spoken. John Jackson, did indeed, know this quote, in both its original context and in today's perspective, but he opted to remain silent, wondering which direction this conversation was about to take. After a while she continued, "John, the news that we are hearing is much worse than any of us could possibly have imagined."

"Yes Ma'am, we are certainly witnessing something more significant than has ever happened to the country before."

"Considering everything that has taken place to date, and all that we can only speculate, will happen. It is plainly obvious that civilisation will never again be as it was. There is no more bread and perhaps it is time for the circus to leave town."

There was a pause. Jacko looked intensely at the woman sitting in front of him. She was small and old, but certainly not frail. The strength of her eyes was a penetrating blue; the eyes of a much younger woman. There was no doubting that behind that gaze there was much intelligence and wisdom.

"John, I have therefore decided to dissolve the Monarchy."

Again a pause while they each looked deeply into one another's eyes. This was a statement that Jacko hadn't expected.

He was caught totally off guard. "Dissolve the Monarchy; Ma'am, are you absolutely sure? This is a monumental step to take!"

The Queen answered his question with the confidence of someone who had obviously given the matter a great deal of thought. "There will be no place for monarchs, titles and privileges in the new world that is emerging. The strong will have to lead and we can only hope that their distinguishing characteristics will not only be those of leadership and strength, but robust morals and a decent sense of justice and duty."

Jacko was still off balance by the totally unexpected radical suggestion. Again a pause whilst he allowed the bombshell to sink in and his equilibrium to return. He allowed some time to pass before he gave his considered reply.

"Ma'am, I admire your decision and think that it is a bold and a sensible way forward for the country, which will be staggering to regain a foothold in reality. The more we can shed any unnecessary obsolete burdens, the greater the chance for success." He paused for a moment. "I think that what you are talking about is meritocracy."

The Monarch looked at Prince Phillip, who was standing in his usual position, a couple of metres to the side of and behind his wife, with his hands clasped behind his back. He nodded his approval. The Royal Secretary stood in the corner of the room and also nodded solemnly. They had obviously spent much time in consultation over the enormously important decision regarding this matter.

"John, this is not a decision that we have arrived at lightly. At a time of crisis like this, there is a strong argument affirming that the country will need something to hold on to, such as the robust symbolism of the monarchy as a unifying force. All of this we have taken into consideration and discussed at great length. The decision at which we arrived is that monarchy is out-dated and would have no place in the world that will emerge from this catastrophe. I have been the Queen for more than six decades and during that time I have undertaken the role with an absolute sense of duty. It would be totally alien for me to abandon the country and my people in its hour of need if we did not think that this was the correct decision."

Prince Phillip moved forward, quietly standing closer to the Queen, allowing his presence and support to be felt but saying nothing. The Queen stood erect, a diminutive woman in her mid-eighties, but with the presence of a sovereign. "Thank you John, I am grateful for your counsel. Please, keep these decisions to yourself for the time being. Furthermore, I would like to address the regiment and inform them myself of my announcement. Would you please be so kind as to arrange a suitable time."

Jacko sensed that there was a huge burden being lifted from this exceptional woman's shoulders. "Ma'am, I will call a meeting of everyone tomorrow at ten hundred hours, if that is suitable to you? However, I think that first it might be prudent to advise the government of your plan."

The Queen looked at Phillip and then the secretary in turn. Phillip, who had been conspicuously quiet, spoke. "Yes of course John. Good idea; we are beginning to feel increasingly isolated here and have to consider that much is still happening with the government in their bunker below London. They are, after all, still theoretically in charge of the country, or so we hope."

The secretary again solemnly nodded his approval.

Phillip added some more of his own, deeply philosophical thoughts. "The fragile house of cards that we have all been living in has now collapsed. A human pyramid, the summit of which we have been privileged to enjoy, will cease to exist. This catastrophe will unpick the fabric of society, unravelling the very threads of humanity which has taken thousands of years to create. This episode will be a global leveller. The words of the final verse from Blake's immortal poem come to mind."

I will not cease from Mental Fight, nor shall my sword sleep in my hand, till we have built Jerusalem, In England's green and pleasant Land."

Phillip's words were dramatic, intense in the extreme, but concise and directly to the point. Everyone present in the room was moved by the statement.

Finally, John broke the silence. "I will arrange for you to visit the radio wing and ensure that only Prince William is in the room to operate the equipment. There you can speak directly to the Prime Minister."

Now, for the first time, the secretary spoke. "That will be fine, John. In recent years, politics has been awash with party political squabbling and bickering. Now that they all have to concentrate their energies on simply surviving, let us hope that Her Majesty's decision will be an inspiration to them, and they too will amend their way of sharing the responsibilities of government, if they can find the courage to rise to the occasion."

With that, a pivotal moment in history was played out in a chilly room in Windsor. The institution of the British Monarchy, whose reign had endured for centuries, was coming to an end.

Jacko took his leave and headed back to the museum. As he walked, he reflected upon his own feelings towards the monarchy that he had grown up with. He had ridden as escort alongside the coach carrying the Monarch many times on state occasions, and from afar, anyone would be convinced that he was a staunch royalist, but secretly this was far from the truth. Few had ever been privy to John Jackson's innermost thoughts. Only those close and most trusted friends knew that John considered that the whole circus was nothing more than a grand charade. *"The best pantomime in town, in fact, on the planet,"* he had said.

Regardless of these thoughts, his admiration for Elizabeth herself was one hundred per cent. She had demonstrated her selfless devotion to duty through decades, which was admirable. He had known William and Harry as soldiers and had found them efficient as well as enjoyable company. Phillip was a surprise. John had expected more intervention and blustering comments, but the old warhorse was remarkably logical and approachable. As he walked alone through the barracks, he had much to contemplate. It was then that he recalled the motto of Harrow County for Boys school, which stood in the shadow of the elite Harrow public school: 'Ability above Nobility'.

Next morning at 10:00 hours, the full complement of the barracks was gathered together in the cookhouse. Jacko noticed with some pride that although he had relaxed discipline and the dress code, all of the assembled soldiers were immaculately turned out. When the Queen arrived, there was a unified scraping of chairs as the assembly stood up as one. The Queen, who was by far the smallest person in the room, walked to the front of the assembled troops, flanked as always by the tall but now slightly stooped figure of P r i n c e Phillip. The feeling in the room was profound, a mixture of bewilderment and trepidation but tinged with expectation.

"My Cavalry, please be seated," she began. "I would like to start by thanking you all for coming here this morning and to tell you how pleased I am to see so many hopeful faces in this time of such adversity. Those of you, who have served for some years, and have been at the presentation of standards and other functions, will know that my predecessors and I have always referred to you as 'My Cavalry'. I have always held a particular attachment; indeed love, for your regiment who have a history of closeness to the monarchy which spans over four hundred and fifty years. We are facing a series of events which none of us could have foreseen or prepared for. The outcome of this transformation of society and culture will be an unimaginable transition. None of us can envisage what form civilisation will take when we emerge from the ashes of this conflagration."

The Queen paused to look at the faces gathered in the drab, functional, altogether stunningly unattractive cookhouse. She did not refer to notes, her bearing and the tone of her voice was somehow different from the woman that all present had grown up knowing.

"My Cavalry, I have decided that in order for the new society which will emerge from this episode to be able to rebuild itself and be given the strongest opportunity to gain a footing in the future so that it can emerge successfully, there has to be monumental change. What is happening in our country and most of the civilised world is cataclysmic. Millions are dying daily and the final toll will be counted in billions. Civilisation is disintegrating. Nothing will ever be the same again. With this in mind, I have come to the decision that I will be dissolving the monarchy."

The gasp from the gathering was audible, all looked around wondering if someone would have a reply but there was none.

"Ladies and gentlemen, it has been my great privilege to have been your Queen for over sixty years, but now that time has come to an end. I hope that you will receive me into your ranks simply as Elizabeth Alexandra Mary Windsor and that I can in some way, with the knowledge that I have acquired over the years, be able to help you with the extraordinarily tough decision making that will have to be undertaken in the forthcoming difficult months and years. My Cavalry, as we enter this new age where there will be no place for royalty and privileges; what this new world needs now, is heroes, and I am indeed honoured to be standing in front of a group of men and women who are all indeed, heroes."

There was then a pause; nobody knew quite how to react. Jacko considered making a speech, thanking the Queen for her years of service, but it all seemed inappropriate. Dan Buckland contemplated leading a rousing three cheers for Her

Majesty, but nothing felt fitting under the circumstances.

The Queen broke the uneasiness. She simply walked forward and started chatting to the soldiers and immediately the whole scene took on a more comfortable feel.

And so it was that Queen Elizabeth the Second, by the Grace of God, Queen of the British Realm and of her other Realms and Territories.
Head of the Commonwealth, Defender of the Faith and Supreme Governor of the Church of England, ended an era of history.

Over the next weeks and months Elizabeth Windsor could be found wandering around the barracks taking a keen interest in all of the activities. Her green Barbour raincoat, wellies and brightly coloured headscarf, soon grew to be a regular feature, so much so that she hardly warranted a second glance. Soon she began to know many of the soldiers by their first names. She remembered what their particular role was in the camp and asked if everything was OK, taking a genuine interest. She was often at the stables spending time with the remaining 'Blacks'. With Kate, together they set up a club for the women in the camp, allowing them to get away from the testosterone charged atmosphere, which of course, dominated. Life in the camp fell into a daily schedule. Lack of electricity dictated that the working day was mostly limited between dawn and dusk. Everyone worked hard on their individual tasks and although there was much quiet anguish and heavy hearts, the continuity of trying to make the most of what they had, offered them a strand of hope to cling to for the future.

Jacko was making one of his regular visits to the Officers' Mess, checking on the progress of the now newly ex-Royals. The main salon had undergone something of a transformation over the weeks. It was the only room in the barracks that was blessed with a fireplace and, as the present incumbents were by far the oldest dwellers in the confines of Combemere, it was only fitting that they should enjoy a little warmth on chilly nights. All of the comfortable furniture had been positioned around the fireplace to enable those present to take advantage of the only heating available. There were several braziers that had been fashioned from 200 litre fuel drums that were scattered around the barracks. These had become popular meeting places where folk gathered on cold nights. The 1950 style Mess building was now taking on a distinct medieval feel. The only occupants in the room when Jacko entered, were Elizabeth, Phillip and the personal secretary, the younger members of the Household were all involved in work of one sort or another. Jacko courteously knocked on the door as he walked in.

"Ah, John, I was hoping to see you." Elizabeth Windsor was reading a book which she put down and carefully removed her glasses. She beckoned Jacko to take a seat next to her. She was wearing her now well-recognized green Wellington boots, a heavy tweed skirt and several layers of Fair Isle sweaters and cardigans. The signature headscarf that usually completed the ensemble was neatly folded and laid across the arm of an adjacent chair. At her feet were the two Corgis that were now regularly seen around the barracks, trotting along behind their owner. The Corgis jumped up as Jacko entered. They scurried across to inspect the new arrival, sniffed his boots and upon deciding that there was nothing of particular interest to them, returned to their position at Elizabeth's feet. Jacko found a suitable chair and sat down, wondering what the reason might be for Elizabeth's need to see him.

"John. We, the family, have been thinking about the Corgis. We realise that many of the people who are in the barracks will have needed to leave their beloved pets behind when they came into the shelter of Combemere. Some of the pets may well have moved on with the families and I can only hope that they have fared well. But we are nonetheless aware that we are the only group that have family pets. Corgis are small dogs, but they too have to eat. We have decided that we are willing, as a group, to forfeit some of our food ration to substitute for what our dogs eat."

This was a slightly unexpected revelation and Jacko was for the moment caught unprepared for such a random request.

"I think that I will have to run that past the catering staff, Ma'am," he replied, looking for an out. "It's something that they will have to decide upon." He made a mental note to continue with his assessment of the overview of life in camp as it was now from his perspective, judging how it was affecting the mix of personnel that he headed up. Previously the title 'under his command' would have been appropriate, but now life was very much altered. Jacko took a brief moment to consider the dilemma that they were experiencing, which was of such horrific proportions and magnitude that none could truly have imagined. They had been asked to walk away from their families and all that they held dear in the anticipation that when this horrific episode abated, they could go out and look for them in the hope that they could start piecing back together the threads of society.

A feeling of utter helplessness had gripped each and every one of the personnel in the camp with a ferocity that way outstretched anything that they had ever experienced. Just metres away, not just outside the walls and across the country, but extending throughout the modern world, people were dying daily in their thousands. There was nothing that they could do to help. Their only salvation was to sit tight and weather the storm in the hope that eventually there would be a new beginning, a reformation, when those who survived could rise like Phoenixes from the ashes of the broken civilisations and ascend again to a better world where society appreciated what the planet had bequeathed them.

The meetings with Elizabeth had become more and more less formal, resulting now in something that resembled a cosy fireside chat. After fifteen minutes he made his excuses and left. He walked out into the light rain and across to the cookhouse kitchens. On his way he could not help but reflect on the selfless request from the diminutive woman who until so recently had lived possibly the most indulged life of anyone from her generation. Jacko arrived at the cookhouse, which was always the busiest location on the camp. He walked around the kitchens which were still spotless, notwithstanding the restriction of water and cleaning materials; a well-appreciated and a credit to the master chef, Toby Walker. He finally saw the imposing figure of the kitchen's boss. "Hey Toby, have you got a minute?"

The big man tossed a greying dishcloth over his shoulder and walked over. His customary immaculate chef's whites were now less than snowy white. The laundry facility, like so many things now, was something from the past.

"What's up Jacko? Have you found me a nice side of beef or ten dozen free range chickens?" Toby's laugh was loud and infectious, the minor miracles that he was achieving with the limited rations and produce that he was allocated was astounding. He was highly respected for the hard work and continual cheerfulness that he radiated.

"Sorry Toby, nothing as exciting as that, just a little matter that needs to be addressed." Jacko went on to explain the request from Elizabeth. "No problem there, Jacko. There are plenty of off cuts etcetera that I can't feed to the troops, more than enough for those little fellas. Tell, herself, not to worry; her rations will be the same as ever."

Jacko was relieved; he had expected this answer, but needed to run it by the Master Chef. There were indeed several times during a month when fresh meat was available, courtesy of the scavenger teams, assisted by the snipers who were sent off into the Great Park to cull the deer population when Toby decided that his clients needed some fresh protein. Jacko thanked the big chef and walked back to his office, contented that he had resolved a problem, no matter how small. His next meeting with Elizabeth and Phillip would contain some happy news.

Chapter 18

Clubs, Committees and Comradeship/Communication

Armageddon + 55

A kibbutz or maybe a commune would not quite be a suitable enough explanation for the astonishing transformation that took place at the vintage army camp behind high walls in a corner of Windsor. Although the basic traditional military regime had superficially disappeared, it had been replaced by a fundamental and equally exacting system of self- discipline and comradeship, giving a strong balance considering the extreme conditions that prevailed. In reality, life inside the walls was certainly not intolerable; the hardest psychological impact on the people within the camp was an acute awareness of the horror that was unfolding only metres away outside the walls throughout the country and across the planet.

Four-man, plain clothes patrols, were regularly sent out to assess the situation. These patrols were alternated between as many soldiers as possible, to let them see for themselves the totality of the humanitarian breakdown that was occurring.

It was reported that deer in the Great Park were largely untouched, apart from some early botched attacks by novice hunters, and the deer were actually thriving. There was evidence of some pursuing and harassing by roving dog packs, but the deer were too big and fast for them to bring down. Humanity had become pampered, used to having their food arrive processed and packaged, so that they were unable to convert a live animal into food. Scavenging was one way of surviving. The bigger and stronger amongst the population simply taking what they wanted from those unable to defend themselves, had become the norm.

The heaviest destruction was in the centre of town. All shops, offices and homes had been ransacked, plundered and looted. Many had been set alight, and with no fire service to deal with the conflagration, had been left to burn for days, the fire spreading to the adjacent buildings unabated. Eventually, the fires had burned themselves out, but not before massive damage had been inflicted. War zone would be a rational description, but that would advocate that there had been fighting between two opposing armies. Fighting had certainly taken place, but only between those taking articles that others had looted. This devastation was caused by the very same people who until quite recently would have strolled through these very streets in an orderly manner, undertaking their weekly shopping expeditions.

It was a foregone conclusion that Sophie Maloney would be voted in as the president of the Household Cavalry Ladies' Club, a post that she took on with her usual drive and enthusiasm. Numerically the group was small, but Sophie made sure that their voice was heard. Due to her commitment in the medical centre, it was not always convenient for her to attend every meeting. It was at one of the meetings of the women's club that met in the cosy surroundings of the WO's and SNCO's Mess, that Elizabeth and Kate raised their game a little. Being a woman and in the minority, marooned in a man's world, could not be described as easy. There were many problems that only another woman could appreciate.

Feminine necessities were obviously the focal topics which were discussed at these meetings. Certain items were essential, and as all of the various groups were entitled to put in their requirement requisition to the scavenger squads, the Ladies' Club was no different in that respect. Colonel Jackson had chosen the toughest of his lads for the scavengers; mostly not the type to mince their words. When asked to bring back such items as sanitary towels, they kicked up. This was just the situation for Elizabeth Windsor to step in and make her point. Upon hearing that the scavenger teams were being difficult, she walked straight into their rest area and confronted them with the women's grievances. Looking rather small amidst the stocky soldiers, it resembled a David and Goliath epic, but within two minutes, she had her way, and the scavengers were all laughing heartily at the thought of the incident. Less than a mere few weeks ago, none of them would ever have expected that they would be arguing with the Queen of Great Britain about tampons!

The Ladies' Club was an immediate success, meeting three times a week. The women all looked forward eagerly to the next gathering. It was at one of these get-togethers that Kate excitedly broke the news to the assembled females that she was pregnant. Everyone was delighted, none more so than the expectant great grandmother, Elizabeth, who had been privy to the information in advance, but kept the news to herself. What a revelation; a child that would have been a future monarch, was now simply to go by the name Young Wales. The news spread around the camp like wildfire, filling everyone with much needed hope, in the expectation that this was surely a symbol of a future. The new baby would not have the title and privileges of its predecessors and indeed, if it were a boy, it would have been third in line in succession to the throne. Now this was just a baby, but symbolically, it heralded a new beginning.

At a meeting of the HC Ladies' Club, it was suggested that in order to help maintain psychological stability and also to enhance the mind- set of those who were trapped, education and artistic groups should be formed. There were no shortage of books that could be brought back to the camp by the scavenging teams and artistic materials could also be sourced. The musicians were involved with anything of a musical nature and a theatrical group could be formed along the lines of the Second World War British concert parties.

A Combemere Think Tank committee was formed, initially from the more experienced soldiers, but it was from the beginning, an open committee, in which anyone could participate and express their views. It was the ideal of the committee that there should be as near to a democratic micro society as possible. There were debating groups created, from which ideas could be brought before the committee and discussed, and if all were in agreement, implemented.

It was agreed that involvement from everyone was crucial. Everyone within the barracks had to have a job and the working hours were for the most part daybreak until sunset.

The days were programmed from breakfast until supper. Food was dispensed for all from the cookhouse using the combined rations, from which the trained army caterers struggled to generate as varied a selection of meals that they could create, given the limited ingredients available to them, and whatever additional elements the scavenger teams could find.

There were meetings of the committee almost every evening, where the camp news from outside was discussed and then relayed to the soldiers at meal times the next day. Typewritten, then carbon copied and posted in the cookhouse entrance.

The radio wing was a particularly active hub of activity. The barracks held a lot of radio equipment. The role of the regiment had been armoured reconnaissance; therefore radios were a crucial part of their basic equipment, many of the men having trained in this discipline with a few good specialists amongst their number. Contact was made with the government and several other army units that were in the same predicament as those in Combemere. In addition, there were some other locations where radio contact was achievable such as radio hams, all of these transmissions helped to build up an overview of what was happening across the country. Slowly, the radio net information spread from survivor radio hams to other beleaguered government and military units. Piece by piece, a jigsaw was assembled, showing the magnitude of catastrophes around the planet.

As predicted, the Middle East used their atomic weaponry to strike against their old enemy neighbours, and the death toll from the initial nuclear attacks was colossal, but no exact figures could be verified; the information being received was patchy at best and could not be relied upon, but it was obvious that the figure was in the many millions. The radiation cloud created in the aftermath of the attacks blew around the regions like an angel of death, reaping its dreadful vengeance on all unfortunate enough to be beneath it.

All cities and civilisations that relied upon motorised transport were devastated by the initial looting and fighting and later disease. Each day, new horror stories were received by the radio wing.

Many sub projects were started. Military vehicles are designed to run on much lower grade fuels and one such venture was a scheme to convert cooking oil into diesel fuel. The scavenger teams were able to discover reasonable amounts of cooking oil at the wrecked supermarkets that hadn't been burned out; as it was not an edible product in that form, it was of little use to the looters. However, this basic ingredient for creating the much-needed fuel was going to be restricted, but nevertheless, it was fuel, no matter how limited, which made it vitally important.

Perfecting the conversion took some time, but time was something that the residents of Combemere had plenty of. The addition of scientists, who had now settled in, and whose knowledge was proving useful to the group, they were valuable in many areas. Their expertise and understanding of chemistry in this case attested to be useful in the task. Finally, after several failed attempts, a useable fuel was manufactured. The process was slow, but by running the conversion unit 24/7, reasonable amounts were produced. Slowly, stocks were accumulated, which gave the beleaguered troops some mobility.

Chapter 19

Death in the Forest

Armageddon + 62

The months passed, summer faded into autumn; the leaves on the trees gave a spectacular display of reds, orange and gold, but this splendid show of nature brought with it hidden dangers. With the trees bare of leaves, the garden centre was far more visible and therefore vulnerable. The cloak of green that had prevailed was now disappearing. In addition, with the passing of summer, the nights were becoming colder, and in a house with no central heating, this could be uncomfortable in the extreme. There were several quite elegant and efficient fireplaces in the house and the location provided an abundance of firewood close at hand. However, the danger of lighting a fire during the day and moonlit nights was too much of a risk with the possibility of attracting the unwanted interest of strangers.

By the time Christmas arrived, they were entirely independent and capable of living within the limits of what resources the plot of land and surrounding forest could supply. The group settled into the lifestyle of living off the land and simply surviving; they were all remarkably healthy. They were aware of the horror that prevailed outside of this, their enclave of relative peace and tranquillity. They constantly worried and wondered how the men back in Windsor were fairing.

The absence of electricity dictated a dawn till dusk existence. The warmest place was in bed. Getting out of bed in the morning was a chilly affair, but everyone had their share of chores to do and staying in bed was not an option. Thomas and Annabel were enjoying those last valuable warm minutes, before leaving the comfort of the bed that they had shared for so many years. This was a time when they discussed their plans for the day.

"I'm worried about the food that we have," Thomas said softly with a hint of concern in his voice. "Everybody is occupied today with their individual chores, so I'm going off into the forest to an area that I haven't foraged for a while to see if I can stock up the empty larder. I remember an old chestnut tree about a mile from here. I'll head for that, and with luck, chestnut soup will be on the menu for tomorrow."

With that the conversation ended, the couple together made their rapid exit from their bed and into the warmest clothes that they could find.

The days passed with routines that had now become the repetitive norm. The major advantage and salvation of the locality was undoubtedly the fact that it had been a garden centre. Even in the cold winter months there was much work to be done, preparing the greenhouses so that food could be grown for the forthcoming spring. Everyone was occupied working on this and other jobs that assured the survival of the group. Thomas had made it an imperative on his part to impart as much knowledge as he could.

At lunchtime the group met up in the farmhouse style kitchen for what was in truth, an inadequate lunch. Annabel could always be relied upon to achieve the best that she could, given the sparse ingredients available to her during the winter months. In reality, soup was pretty much a daily ritual which could have been monotonous, and boring, but Annabel had an amazing ability to create a tasty, thick, nourishing meal from very little. Squirrels and rabbits were a regular supplement.

"Your father went off into the forest this morning, foraging." Annabel spoke to Sarah with a perceptible note of concern in her voice. "I was expecting him back by lunch time."

"Don't worry mum, I'm sure that he will arrive, cold and hungry at any moment."

By three o'clock everyone was getting worried. Thomas often went into the forest to forage alone, but never for more than four hours. It would soon be dark and the weather was bleak, cold and rainy. Julie took control of the prevailing situation. "We must go out into the forest and look for Thomas whilst there is still some light. It would be dangerous for us to go out in the night. The forest floor is treacherous, slippery with fallen leaves, and there could have been an accident."

Julie and the five youngsters put on the warmest and most waterproof clothing that they could find and struck off into the forest. Julie was apprehensive of what they might discover. She had been feeling that Thomas had been taking too much upon himself in recent months and although he was far from frail, he was getting on in age.

It was Kit who discovered the body. Thomas had slipped on the wet leaves and fallen into a ravine. It looked as if he had attempted to crawl out, but the shock and effort seemed to have triggered a massive heart attack. Thomas had died in the forest that he so loved.

"There is nothing that we can do now." Julie did her best to console the distressed granddaughters of a much-loved grandfather. "We will come back tomorrow at first light and take him back home." She led the distraught band back to the house to impart the sad news to his wife and daughter.

During the night, Julie lay awake worrying, as she did most nights, but also devising a plan of how to get Thomas's body back to his home. She knew that the task would be up to her and her boys. Asking his granddaughters to help was also not an option; it was going to be heavy work and up to the Buckland family to do it. Thomas was a big man, about six feet tall and must have weighed about ninety kilos. There was always the possibility of burying him where he lay but this seemed an unsatisfactory solution.

Early next morning, Julie, and her boys, went back into the forest and set about the work of retrieving the body. The ravine that Thomas had fallen into was about twenty metres deep. The sides were quite inclined, but not steep, covered with wet, slippery vegetation, which proved to be both a help and a hindrance. Julie had come prepared, taking with them ropes and spades. She had a balaclava which she placed over Thomas's face in an attempt to make the harrowing task more acceptable. With the rope tied around his chest and under his arms, they began the job of pulling the body up the slippery slope. Each metre that they accomplished was a torturous effort. The boys were strong, but even so, it took most of the day to get the body back. They brought it to the garden centre on a trolley that was used to carry gardening materials. It was decided that digging a grave would have to wait until the next day. During the night they discussed a suitable site for Thomas to be buried. It was not a good idea to leave the body exposed for too long even in the severe cold weather.

In the morning, Kit and Rory set about the task. The ground was extremely hard and progress was slow, taking them all day to dig a grave deep enough. The next evening Thomas was laid to rest in his favourite spot; a grassy knoll overlooking the trout stream.

Annabel was distraught by the loss of her beloved husband, but the strong resilience and strength that resided within this remarkable woman shone through at this time of sadness. She somehow knew that she would outlive Thomas, but now there was some solace in the reality that she was not left to face the future alone. Her task now was to be strong for those around her.

Chapter 20

A Little Seasonal Cheer and Time to Reflect

Armageddon + 169 days

All of the female soldiers were single and in a camp of several hundred men with a very limited choice of partners, they were immensely popular. Gradually, they paired off and as the months passed, they decided that marriage would be a practical option, particularly as three of the women found themselves to be pregnant. There was a regimental Padre at hand and all agreed that it would be good for morale to develop happy events whenever possible. Jacko, the 2i/c, Craig Williams, and Dan, discussed the deeper implications of the matter.

Jacko opened the debate. "Having these pregnant women living amongst us could pose a more complicated problem."

"How come, Jacko?" Dan was missing something.

"Many of the men here, including ourselves, have been asked to leave our families to fend for themselves, for at least eighteen months. I am worried that seeing young children could unbalance them and push them over the edge; they have a lot to contend with."

Craig Williams was less concerned. "The first babies won't be born for many months and when the one and a half year time point has arrived, even the eldest will not be walking so I don't think that there will be a problem, although I do understand your anxiety."

This was indeed a sensible assumption and Jacko's mind was put at rest. "I guess that I am constantly mindful of the strain that we are all under. I am aware that if just one of our numbers goes flaky for us it could bring the rest down like a line of dominoes."

The other two men and the MO were in agreement. Dan thought that it would have been a suitable moment to open a bottle of Scotch, but he had none left.

Dan added another dimension to the dialogue. "And then of course we mustn't forget little baby Wales".

"I think that we can forget about that being an issue. Everyone appears to be delighted with that particular addition to our ranks," Craig added.

All three men found it difficult to disguise a smile, because it was indeed the case. Young George was a welcome addition. Everyone was delighted to have him in the camp and his mother, Kate, became an important personality, bringing another dimension to an extensive mix of people who had been thrown together by this extraordinary series of events.

The scavenger teams had managed to obtain several rather nice buggy, which they rescued from the debris of Daniels, the largest department store in Peascod Street Windsor. They happily donated them to the expectant parents.

Christmas and New Year were approaching. Life within the camp had settled into an established routine. Everyone had a job and worked hard at their individual tasks, and in addition, the overall combined running of the barracks.

The scavenger teams were given requests for such things as wedding dresses, carry cots and other family orientated articles. It was decided that events like these and Christmas should be made as enjoyable as possible.

The regiment had successful sniper sections that were periodically dispatched to the Great Park when an exceptional occasion warranted special food; venison was on the menu that day.   Christmas was celebrated in style with six roasted swans. The first was carved by Phillip with great ceremony before the cookhouse staff took over.

The Musical Director, Peter Greenaway, dropped by the RHQ office to chat with Jacko. Dan and Craig were there at the time. He opened the dialogue.

"The musicians have asked me to come and see you.   They are concerned that playing music at such a time as this might be considered inconsiderate, given all that is going on outside the walls. As you know they are all trained soldiers, but they are all also creative musicians. Music is a strong passion within all of them."

Craig Williams was the first to answer, after which Jacko and Dan added their thoughts, that as long as the musicians fulfilled their role of working within the general requirements of the camp and took their turn supplying personnel for guard duties, their off duty time was their own. But, it was agreed that working together as a combined band and creating loud music was too much under the circumstances.

Agreement was reached. Dan pointed out that it was midday and the four men decided to break for lunch.   Whatever was on the menu for the day would be a sterling effort by the catering staff, but they all knew that it wasn't going to completely satisfy their appetite. Their belts had all been tightened several notches in recent months.

Jacko wandered into Dan Buckland's office in need of a non-official chat. Dan was reading a book as he walked in. When Dan looked up, Jacko noticed that there was something different about his friend. "Hey Dan, never knew that you wore glasses," he commented.

"I was beginning to notice that I was having difficulty reading. My long sight is great, so I took myself down to Boots on Peasecod Street while I was out scavenging and amongst the rubble I found myself a pair of glasses. They do an excellent job," he explained. Then, with a wide grin, he continued, "It's quite amazing what you can discover when you're scavenging around."

He opened the draw to his desk and pulled out a bottle of whisky. "Bloody lovely!" exclaimed Jacko, "I feel that we deserve that."

The two men settled down to enjoy a glass of their much missed beverage. "Gotta make this bottle last," Dan recommended wearily. "Finding this was a fluke, it might never happen again."

The two comrades limited themselves to one glass each, which they took their time savouring. Dan placed the bottle carefully back into his desk drawer, treating it with reverence. They had both witnessed first- hand the wanton destruction that had taken place, everywhere. Shops and offices had been ransacked; many burned and reduced to rubble. During the initial days valuable items were looted, but it soon became apparent that food was the crucial prize. The scavenger groups became adept at sorting through the rubble and discovering useful items that had been overlooked during the primary frenzy, thrown aside and trampled underfoot.

Occasionally, there would be a specifically lucky find and the cookhouse rations were supplemented. Sell by dates had become sensationally redundant.

"I have been thinking," said Jacko, who had slipped into a philosophical mood, helped enormously by the relaxing quality of the whisky. "Have you considered where all of this mayhem will go next Dan?"

"It would be hard not to under the circumstances."

This was a rare moment of calm and Dan's mood was relaxed. He put his feet up onto the desk. Jacko did likewise and the conversation continued.

"It's looking as if the boffins will soon crack the fusion enigma, and they will produce the first production of generators early in the New Year. Professor James has told me that it will be the size of a suitcase but it will only have the capacity to power a vehicle the size of a family car, but from this prototype, they will be able to create more compact forms, and also much larger versions. Finally, these generators will be able to power everything from a small car to a factory."

He paused, considering what he had said. Dan nodded his understanding.

"The latest catch phrase seems to be 'The end of the ice age' – Ice being an abbreviation for Internal Combustion Engine. I rather like that title."

"There will be a new world order, Dan. It will take years, but I am convinced that it will come, and we will have played a crucial part in that happening.
Future generations will reflect on what has transpired and Combemere Barracks will have played a crucial role in its fundamental success."

There was a pause for the significance of Jacko's words to sink in. "John, are you telling me that we will be famous?" Dan injected a little humour into the conversation. "I like the idea of one of those blue plaques with my name on it." He contemplated the idea, interlocking his fingers behind his neck and stretching his spine.

"I have the feeling that we will be very old men by the time that this is anywhere near calming into tolerable existence as we have known it, but even so we are actually privileged to be playing our part in it."

The conversation drifted along. "Whatever happens, this little episode will certainly fill a chapter in both of our memoirs."

The two men discussed their families, their anxiety, anticipation and hope that they had made it to the New Forest garden centre and were surviving.

Chapter 21

Photovoltaic Panels

Armageddon + 180 days

Introducing the radical scheme of 'no rank, no swank' was quite a drastic step to take, but it was now beginning to show signs of success. Individuals who displayed a particular aptitude in a certain field of expertise naturally rose to the top and the benefits were becoming evident. An area that was a good example of this policy in action was the group which became known as 'TT' (The Combemere Think Tank). It consisted of a nucleus of about twenty members, although anyone was allowed to participate and everyone was welcome.

Initially, the Culham group had settled in well. It could be considered that as a generalisation, they were derived from, to some extent a different social background than the majority of the soldiers. They were passionate academics and scientists with a different societal agenda, but as a generality, they settled in well. There was some understandable bitterness from the soldiers who resented the fact that these families had been allowed to stay together. Seeing the young children in the camp was difficult for them to accept and Jacko and Dan needed to use a great deal of diplomacy to keep the situation under control. Those that were not directly involved in the development of the fusion project took on other, quite often mundane tasks, related to running the everyday basic requirements of a group of people faced with the extraordinary predicament they found themselves in. Nobody was allowed to be idle.

By the end of the first month, it was becoming evident that the Culham team were starting to cause major headaches for Jacko. The positive side of the problem was that they were completely enthusiastic about their work and dedicated to solving the alternative energy task that they were engaged in. There was certainly no lack of drive in that area. They could see that the future of Britain, and indeed the world, could be altered for the betterment of mankind if they could achieve their goal. The future was literally in their hands. It was at a Think Tank meeting the new catch phrase was coined and was to first appear. *The end of the ice age* was to become a well-used depiction for the time when oil based fuels became inert, plunging the world into a catastrophic standstill. The internal combustion engine, in its many forms, had given mankind transport on which the economies of the advanced nations had surged relentlessly ahead without considering their total reliability on this finite substance. Its sudden demise plunged the planet into a tragedy of biblical proportions.

The demands that the Culham group were increasingly heaping upon Jacko and in particular, the scavenger teams, was for more material. They needed a vast range of items, which were proving very difficult to source. Jacko doubled the scavenger teams and then added even more, as they had to travel further afield to find the obscure supplies, sometimes being out of the barracks for days.

The scavenging teams did a fine job, but the one elusive requirement that caused the greatest problem was the lack of electricity, a point that Professor James made forcefully at a Think Tank meeting.

"Computers are the tools of our age. We have become totally reliant upon them for so much of what we achieve, and although they are readily available, without electricity they are of less use than a pencil and an A4 notepad. We are sincerely grateful that we have been rescued from, who knows what our fate might have been, and brought here to the security of this camp. There is no doubting all of our commitment to solving the fusion enigma, but in order to achieve this we must have electrical power. At this stage with what is available to us, we can only design scaled down experiments and even if we had limited electricity, create computer generated models. In order to move forward, we need to build hugely powerful lasers and a massive fusion chamber, but for now, our crucial need is electricity."

The assembled Think Tank members were at a loss to come up with a plan to resolve the issue. Several weeks passed and the electricity problem continued to have no viable solutions. Jacko decided that he needed to convene a meeting. He called through the open door of his office to the regimental clerk who was sitting at his desk in the outer office.

"Rogers, please inform the Think Tank members that there will be a meeting at fourteen hundred hours, this afternoon; SNCO's Mess."

Rogers was an uncomplicated soul who had never fully become comfortable with the newly conceived first name system and preferred to remain as just Rogers.

Although he did rather like the idea of calling the Colonel Boss; this was a privilege that had previously been the sole prerogative of senior NCOs who had served with Jacko in war zones. He was quite junior and had hitherto not been privy to that idiosyncrasy and it now gave him an air of importance, which he found most enjoyable.

"OK Boss, consider it done," he cheerfully replied, glad of a break from the necessary, dreary office routine which still prevailed.

At 14:00 hours, the Think Tank convened. Amongst those attending were William, Harry and Phillip, representing the now ex-Royals. Dan Buckland stood at the back with Professor James.

Jacko began the meeting. "Gentlemen, we have a problem, for which I require your input. Our newly arrived companions have come to me with an urgent request I cannot resolve alone. You are all aware of the importance of the work that they are here to do, but they need to have electricity in order to work their computers and other equipment. I am looking for any contribution that you can provide which might help."

Various theories were forwarded; most suggested wiring together banks of batteries.

"That would, I'm afraid, only be a very short term and unsustainable solution," replied the Professor, shaking his head slowly. These batteries will be from vehicles that have now been stationary for six months or more. The majority of these batteries will now be useless because we have no way of recharging.

A silence drifted over the room as everyone present dug deeply into their memories in the hope that they could provide an answer. Some time passed. Jacko was considering calling the meeting to a close when a young man stood up. It was David, from the REME light aid detachment. "Solar panels," he suggested nervously.

"Yes, solar panels would be an excellent solution," implied the Professor in a sharp and dismissive tone. "So would a small nuclear power plant, which is equally unobtainable." David looked embarrassed and started to sit down.

"David, tell us more about your thoughts regarding these panels." Jacko came to the young man's rescue. He thought that there was something about the lad that showed promise; he had acquitted himself well on an earlier occasion. The Professor had been too dismissive and hard on him. He had noticed something else about David. Unusually, the young man had an accent local to Windsor, which was actually quite uncommon as the soldiers in the unit were recruited from all over the country with many varied accents.

David returned to his feet and spoke directly to Jacko as he now saw him as a

152

friend. "I come from this area, my father worked on the Slough Trading Estate in a warehouse which belonged to Suntech, a company which is the biggest producer of these panels."

There was an audible flow of fresh chatter as the possibilities of David's revelation began to sink in.

"I have been there with my father and I have seen thousands of panels boxed and ready for sale. They are the ones that generate electricity, not hot water properly, called Photovoltaic panels," David added.

"David, I apologise for being so short with you," the Professor humbled himself.

Jacko intervened again. "David, that's great news. We won't necessarily be buying these panels, but it looks as if we might avail ourselves of some," he added. The atmosphere in the room altered completely, whilst plans were discussed.

After twenty minutes, Jacko addressed the assembled men again. "OK, it appears that we have the potential ability to generate electricity with resources available to us, but the next obstacle is how do we get the panels from the Slough Trading Estate to Combemere?"

All heads turned to David, but he could only shrug his shoulders. Jacko continued, "There is some fuel left, which might allow us to make some limited trips, but we will need a lot of panels and the trucks won't be able to make many journeys. We have some limited fuel reserves but this must be reserved for priority missions. The distance is actually only a few miles, but without transport this project is a non-starter, we must devise an alternative solution."

Again a hush drew over the room until Mick from the stables stood up.

"The coaching section," he suggested.

Looking around for support, he added, "If we strip out the large coach that's in the coaching section and pare it down to a minimum, it would be able to carry quite a lot of panels."

Heads turned to Phillip, who was well known as an ardent coaching enthusiast.

"Do you mean," he muttered, in a tortured tone, "we tear apart the rare, vintage, Victorian coach, which has been so lovingly restored and cherished by the coaching troop, and turn it into a horse drawn cart?" His head was in his hands in a mocking display of grief. "Then so be it."

The room erupted into laughter. A solution had been reached and all present were delighted with the outcome.

So it was initially decided that a team of ten men in two trucks, led by Dan Buckland and David, accompanied by Professor James, were to complete two round trips to the Suntech warehouse with the precious stock of diesel that could be spared. They broke into the deserted building and loaded the trucks with everything that they thought would be useful. This was a good starting point and work immediately commenced on erecting the panels in the barracks, which soon gave a limited supply of electricity that in turn fired up some of the computers and ancillary equipment. Thereafter, a twice-daily trip was made by the much-reduced coach that was pulled by four of the Queen's coaching horses. It made a truly unusual sight; loaded with large solar panels, the driver and guard sitting on top with two mounted soldiers as escort. The horses had become an important asset.

Chapter 22

A Moment of Doubt

Armageddon + 203 days

The chairs in the Senior Non Commissioned Officers Mess lounge were huge, deep buttoned, ox blood red leather and luxurious in the extreme, but that was where the comfort ended. The usually cosy room was decidedly miserable now, having no heating or lighting. The nearby bar hadn't seen a pint passed over it for months and the cheerful banter of off duty soldiers was eerily noticeable by its absence. The day was dark and morbid, rain thrashed against the windows in squally fits and starts.

Dan Buckland made one of his landmark observations. "Can't make out why the scholars who built this place didn't put in a fireplace, kind of obvious to my mind." He leaned back in the sumptuous chair and focused on an ornate light fitting in the ceiling that was now totally redundant. "Whose round is it anyway?" he inquired dreamily.

The three senior men, Jacko, Craig and Dan, accompanied by the MO, had taken refuge in the mess, as the inclement weather had curtailed all but a few of the outdoor activities. The perimeter guards, who were out patrolling the boundaries of the barracks, were those feeling the most discomfort from what the stormy day produced. Dan had tried to lift the mood, but it was pretty much an impossible task. Even with the company of the lovely Sophie, the men struggled to be anything but gloomy. Depression was plainly obvious from the faces of everyone in the camp; it was palpable that they were all struggling with the epic circumstances in which they found themselves, the confinement was biting hard. The miserable weather was adding immeasurably to the despair that enveloped the camp. Was their commitment to stay within Combemere and await the end of the confinement period the correct decision? Had the brains at government in London got it right? Would there be a need for them to be instrumental in the re-building of society as they had been told, or had they done the unthinkable and abandoned their families for a forlorn and worthless cause? These were the questions that churned around in the tormented minds of all involved, nagging at their consciousness, gnawing like a cancer as the arduous months laboriously advanced. Everyone was searching for the elusive beacon of hope, a light at the end of this abominable tunnel, into which fate had funnelled them.

Craig looked miserable; in a moment of doubt he openly stated what so many were thinking. Jacko, Dan and Sophie threw a quick glance at each other. "What if we have made the wrong call and in reality we are here, simply for our own selfish motives? Perhaps we have abandoned all that we hold precious and dear, just to save our own necks?"

The spectre of doubt understandably loomed large in Craig's mind. The results of what they had done would not be appreciated until the confinement period had concluded and even then, years would have to pass before the final question would be answered. Could peace and tranquillity ever be restored? There was no guarantee that even if the governments plan did work as predicted, their families would be safe. The future looked bleak indeed.

Now Jacko looked a little anxious, hearing a strong man like Craig voice his concern was worrying. He needed his leaders to be resilient. He struggled to think of appropriate words which could motivate.

"Whatever happens next, we have to stay calm and show a positive face to the others. They are looking up to us for leadership and we can't afford to waver. We have made our commitment and there is no going back."

"Don't worry about me, just contemplating the situation, thinking out loud I guess. I'll not be up for wobbling."

Craig shook himself out of his melancholy mood and the conversation moved on to other subjects. The two crucial men that Jacko needed to be solid were Dan and Craig, he knew that he could rely upon them both, but even the strongest were being tested, which included himself.

Sophie made a robust point which helped ease the tension a little. "Much of what has been speculated regarding the predicted outcome of this matter comes from the loftier minds in London and the other locations where the brainy Think Tank boffins are located. We are indeed risking much on the conclusions that they have forecast. But we must remember that these people are without doubt the finest minds in the country, of a far higher intelligence than we can imagine."

There was general agreement from those present. To further make her point, she continued, "We will all have watched University Challenge back in the day when there was such a thing as television broadcasting and although I can see that we are a reasonably educated bunch, I have no doubt that we have all struggled to know what the subject was, let alone the answer to many of the questions. The point that I am making is that these intelligentsia are in a completely different orbit to the rest of us. We have to trust their judgement, making our strategies and decisions from their guidance."

William Wales walked in and joined the quartet. He was wet and looked bedraggled from the incessant rain. He took off his poncho, shook the water from it and slumped into one of the comfortable chairs with a sigh.

"Would you like a pint Will's?" enquired Dan courteously. "You look as if you need one, Jacko is buying."

"I was thinking more of a latte, Dan," William replied.

"Better keep thinking then, hold that thought," Dan suggested.

It was a well acknowledged fact that soldiers dry humour was borne out of adversity.

"We were discussing wobbling," added Jacko, moving the discussion along.

"Ah, I see," William caught up with the conversation. "This weather isn't helping. None of us know for sure what has happened to our families, it's no wonder that some of the guys are feeling flaky. Have you come up with any ideas on how to boost morale?" he enquired with a distinct note of concern in his voice.

Jacko repeated what he had previously said about those within the group of a higher profile showing a strong, positive attitude. The problem of too much time to contemplate their personal demons and difficulties was soon to be resolved. In the coming weeks, they were all to be faced with a menace which had been growing outside the walls and had now reached a serious level; a peril that was to occupy a far greater portion of their time, a threat which would focus their minds upon their own survival.

Jacko added something that had been in his mind for some time. "Whilst we are here in this location, it's a good time to discuss the matter of what we are going to do with the bar and other locations that have alcohol. As you are all aware, we have kept the bars locked since day one. Obviously there was not going to be any more deliveries, but also allowing the guys' access to the alcohol might have caused further problems."

Dan's eyes lit up, it was a well known fact that he enjoyed a tipple. "So what are you suggesting?" enquired Sophie, not quite seeing where this might be leading.

"We open the bar when we have an occasion to celebrate and allow everyone to have a limited drink. This will have to be carefully controlled to make sure that it's fair on everyone. There is only so much stock and if we leave it for too long it will be undrinkable anyway."

All agreed that Jacko's idea was a good one.

"It will have to be run past the TT Committee, but I can't imagine there being any objections," William added.

One by one the group drifted away until only Jacko and Sophie were left. They talked on into the night. Each had been alone for nearly seven months and they were missing their partners. There was little doubt that they had developed a huge affection for each other which had now moved past mutual admiration. It would have been so easy for them to have held each other in their arms, feeling the closeness of another human being in such a time of loneliness. Would that have been so wrong? The temptation was huge and they found it difficult to resist the obvious mutual attraction, but Jacko's wife and family were still out there and he needed to be strong. The moment passed and they said goodnight.

Jacko walked back from the Mess, visions of the gorgeous Sophie still prominent in his mind. He opened the door to his Spartan living accommodation in the museum block. He took off his wet jacket and unbuckled the belt that carried his side arm, and, as he placed the pistol on the bed, he was unable to suppress a sigh. Every day he was in contact with dozens of people, but he was acutely aware that even with the close proximity of so many friends and colleagues, he felt desperately lonely. He missed Sarah and his three daughters; the ever present worry haunted his thoughts. Were they still alive?

Even though he knew that he hadn't used the pistol, his years of training automatically caused him to go through the procedure of making the weapon safe. Checking the safety catch, he pushed the magazine securing button and allowed the magazine to drop onto his palm. He pulled back the cocking mechanism and checked that there was not a round in the breach. Sitting on the regulation army bed, he thumbed the top bullet in the magazine and wondered how this would all end. Outside the night was very dark. Occasionally a watery moon was visible between the ominous black clouds, and, for a brief moment, he had a good view of the moon; the bright golden halo was still there.

Sophie closed the door to her tiny apartment; she knew that she had come close to seducing Jacko, which provoked conflicting judgments in her confused thoughts. She realised that she was becoming obsessed with Jacko, who had now become a permanent fixture in her troubled mind. He was all that she could think about. To Sophie, he had become everything. He was handsome, intelligent honest and brave, but the most important quality about the man was, that he was not hers. They each went to their lonely beds wondering, what if?

Chapter 23

The Nissan Leaf Attack Vehicle

Armageddon + 210 days

A head appeared at the office door. It was Rogers. The reflective mood was broken and normality, such as it was, returned to the office.

"Someone here to see you Boss, can I send him in?"

"Sure Rogers, who is it?"

"David Galston," informed Rogers.

The two friends looked at each other expectantly, and smiled. David Galston entered the room, considered by all of the soldiers to be an inner sanctum. He looked around guardedly.

"Come in, David and grab yourself a chair."

Jacko's offer was genuinely friendly. "Your input has always been remarkably useful so we are anxious to know what you have for us this time," Jacko spoke enthusiastically.

David pulled up a chair and sat gingerly down. "Nissan Leaf," was the singularly odd reply. Dan and Jacko turned to one another, each with a confused look on their faces, both wondering what significant point they must have missed. It was obvious from the expression on David's face that he had expected that the older men would have cottoned on immediately to the implications of the two words, but it was apparent from the lack of any excited reply that it had gone right over their heads.

"Err… David, could you perhaps explain a little more?" Dan encouraged.

"Nissan Leaf," he repeated, slightly agitated. Jacko and Dan were none the wiser. "Give us a little more to work on," Dan coaxed, in a fatherly fashion.

"The Nissan Leaf is an all-electric car..., quite a nice one actually."

Still, no sign of the older men having an inkling of what the young lad was implying. David paused for three seconds and continued, "There is a large Nissan dealership in Slough, on the same estate as the warehouse that we plundered for the photovoltaic panels. They are bound to have these cars in stock and unless there has been a fire, they should be OK. My thinking is; we get these vehicles back here, then we can either use them as transport, because we will be able to charge them from the Photovoltaic capacity, which we now have, or, we could also cannibalise them for their electric motors to power our own military vehicles."

David ended his little explanation and waited for the response.

Jacko answered first, giving a nod of approval, and signalling to David that he was with him thus far. "Bloody hell, David, where do you get these ideas from?"

David looked dejected, obviously thinking that his latest notion was one idea too far. "That's a great idea, what do you think, Dan?"

"Fantastic, David, fantastic!"

Enthusiasm was now in abundance in the room. All three men were equally delighted. It looked as if David was raising his arm for a high five, but thought better of it.

"Rogers, nip out and find Professor James. Ask him to come to this office right now, please."

Rogers scurried off and returned after fifteen minutes with the permanently perplexed looking Professor. Another chair was found and the four men sat in a circle.

"David, please explain your plan to Professor James."

David went over his idea once more for the academic whose speciality subject was indeed electro dynamics.

"David, you have come up with yet another bright idea. The electric car that you have mentioned could be the ideal basis for various options. Mobility will be the key to the next step in returning the nation to its former self." He then qualified the end of that statement. "We actually don't want to return to the way things were. We have to look towards the new future as being cleansed of the greed and waste that we had all thought was our right, and had become complacent with. Let us hope that the new, second chance that we appear to have been given, can be one of enlightenment."

The meeting ended. David went back to his work and the Professor dashed off as time was always of a premium in his life. This left Jacko and Dan.

"Well, who would have thought that an hour ago we would be looking at becoming car thieves," Dan jested, "Guess we had better start putting together a plan to get those Leafs back here."

In the event, car hijacking turned out to be remarkably simple. Dan put together a team of ten men. Five came from the vehicle workshop section and were experienced mechanics. The other five were there as protection just in case the group met others on the outside that might cause trouble.

At 07:00 hours, the team of ten marched out of the barracks. They all carried L85A2s and rucksacks filled with tools that the mechanics thought would be needed, and twenty four hour field ration packs, as it was expected that they might have to spend the night in the Nissan garage. They skirted around the Goswell Way roundabout that had become the scene of so much looting, to avoid unnecessary confrontation, and within an hour they had reached the Trading Estate. The area was deserted. The worry that was uppermost in Dan's thoughts was that the garage could have been ransacked and torched.

The Nissan car dealership was located on Slough Trading Estate. From the Bath Road, the group crossed into Dover Road, over the hump back bridge which crossed the Grand Union canal, past the Honda and Audi dealerships. Nissan's large workshops and showroom were on the left. His worries subsided when he walked over the canal bridge that had obscured his view for the final two hundred yards and saw for the first time that the building was unharmed. It was, in fact, totally intact, and looked as if it had been closed for the weekend and prepared to be opened on Monday morning for business as usual. Bolt croppers were used to snap the padlocks and the team entered the garage with ease.

The men walked into the main showroom and there, just as David had suggested, standing on a raised dais was a shiny white, Leaf, all electric, family saloon.

"OK guys, spread out and look for more of the same, can't be just the one surely."

Dan stayed in the showroom searching for the keys to the Leaf. After fifteen minutes, the men gathered around Dan and reported their findings.

"Well, it looks as if there are eight, Leafs, scattered about the workshops. " Good work." Dan scratched his chin. "Now we have to find the keys and see if these beauties will start up. "Don't worry about log books, we'll come back for them another time," he wisecracked. "The next items that we are going to need will be the charging points. They must be here somewhere and without them the cars aren't much use."

It took longer to find the keys than it did to find the cars, but eventually, all of the vehicles were started and miraculously they were all fully charged. Getting the showroom, Leaf, off its plinth was rather more of a task and the paintwork was less

162

than showroom spec by the time they had it standing outside, lined up with the others. The vehicles were loaded with anything that could be utilised back at the barracks.

Amongst other discoveries in the Nissan building was the spare parts department. This was a huge Aladdin's cave of useful parts for the Nissan range of cars. There were many replacement parts for the Leaf; far too many to be loaded and taken back with them. Dan decided that they were better left in place, where they could be located when they were needed via the spare parts lists. Now that there was transport, they could come back and pick up spares as they required them. The padlocks were put back in position and everything was left as they had found it, minus the pilfered cars and other items.

"So, it's back to Combemere. We are going to have to negotiate the notorious Goswell Way roundabout, but don't expect that to be a problem. The looters are looking to stop cars leaving Windsor not arriving. Keep your speed to below forty until we get to the final two hundred yards before the roundabout and then floor it. The occupants of the roundabout won't know what hit them and we will be gone before they realise what's happened."

Dan gave the matter some more thought. "Eight cars, ten men; I want two men in the two lead cars with your weapons very visible. If you have to fire warning shots, I am sanctioning it, at your discretion, and if you think that you have to shoot somebody, then that's Ok."

The small flotilla of Leafs set off. The return trip was over in less than fifteen minutes. Dan and his men, plus the eight, Nissan Leafs, were back in Barracks before midday. The cars were driven directly to the vehicle workshop. The plan was that one would be stripped and examined and the others were parked up for later use.

Later that afternoon, Jacko and Dan paid a visit to the workshop. The REME, Major Peter Clarke, was standing in front of the shiny line of pristine new cars with a clipboard and pencil in his hand, furiously jotting down notes.

"Afternoon Pete, you look busy?" enquired Jacko as they approached. "Got a lot to do to these shiny steeds before they are ready for what we want them to do. They have been designed for comfortable urban life, taking the kids to school, shopping and that kind of thing. Not exactly what we will be using them for."

"So what are you going to do to them to make them battle ready?" added Dan with a wry smile.

"My first impression was that they might be a little on the flimsy side for our taste, but, I have had a good look at them and actually they are quite well built, and in fact, rather sturdy. The biggest job will be cutting away a section of the roof so that we can mount a light machine gun on top. These things are loaded with electronic gizmos that we will have no need for. I want all of the unnecessary electrical equipment ripped out, even such things as indicators are no good to us. I want to give the batteries the best chance of maximising their charge. Anything chrome and reflective will have to go, and of course, there will have to be a new paint job. Disruptive pattern should look rather nice. There are four versions of this vehicle and we have two of each. The top of the range model has rather smart alloy wheels which we will have to paint black; the others have wheel trims. They will have to go."

"Sounds like you have a lot of work on your hands Pete. We will drop by in a couple of days and check on the progress," Jacko said.

Two days later Jacko and Dan went back to the workshop. Four of the Leafs were ready, their conversion complete. Peter Clarke walked out of his office looking confident. "What do you think?" he enquired.

"Quite a transformation," Jacko admitted.

And, that was indeed the case. The four completed vehicles were still discernible as Nissan Leafs, but they had been professionally transformed into military vehicles. Although they had been heavily chopped about and modified, it had been done with a high degree of skill and workmanship. Strangely, the light machine gun mounted on the family cars roof didn't look as much out of context as they had expected Jacko and Dan both agreed.

"Bloody good job, Pete," Dan enthused. "I would have loved to pick up my boys from school in one of those." And so the Nissan Attack Vehicle was born.
"So, what are we talking about here, Pete?" asked Jacko.

"Carrying capacity. Driver, gunner, and two others. Range, one hundred and fifty miles on a full battery; easily get in and out of London. Plenty of storage for extra ammo and radio equipment. Silent and surprisingly fast. One advantage is that if it does get hit by a round there is no flammable fuel aboard."

He looked pleased with what his workshop team had achieved. "I'll take one, but do you have it in metallic white?" enquired Dan. "Don't be in such a rush to part with your money Dan, there is one, very strong, negativity involved here." Peter Clarke's reply started good humouredly, but then took on a more serious note. "We are an Armoured Reconnaissance Regiment and as the title suggests we are used to just that – armour. I'm afraid that in the case of the Leaf, armour is out of the question. I looked at putting some armoured plate on the vehicles, but it would reduce the range drastically. You are going to have to rely on speed and manoeuvrability. There is also no four-wheel drive capability, but this will be urban warfare, and will, for the most part, take place on tarmac roads. I also looked at the option that the electric motors could be used to power our existing vehicles, but this was also a non-starter as our lightest Jackal vehicle is twice as heavy as a Leaf. We are going to have to wait until the fusion boys and girls come up with an answer."

Jacko and Dan gave Peter's summary some thought. There was going to have to be a serious re-thinks regarding tactics. "It's kind of bizarre," Jacko added. "We are about to engage our adversaries with a Leaf."

"More like Morris Dancing than soldiering," was Dan's interpretation. "But we'll get a bucket load of Brownie points for zero emissions."

Chapter 24

The must have Combemere Fashion Accessory

Armageddon Day + 275

Jacko walked into the medical block on his daily inspection visit to all of the camp's facilities. It was quiet, which was nothing unusual; an advantage from a highly controlled diet, as everyone in the camp was enjoying surprisingly good health. Sophie was in her office reading a book. The morning surgery was over and this was a time for her to relax.

"Hi, Soph, run off your feet again I see. Is everything alright here in the medical nerve centre?"

"Actually, John, you have hit the proverbial nail on the head. I have been helping out in the gardening section to burn off surplus energy. Toby's food is keeping everyone healthy and apart from the occasional emergency, it's pretty much a mundane existence here. Last month's appendicitis caused a bit of a flurry, but mostly it's minor stuff."

She walked over to Jacko, standing perhaps a little too close, looking him squarely in the eyes and asked in a provocative manner. "Would you like me to give you a full medical check-up, Colonel?"

In recent weeks it was obvious that Sophie had begun to flirt with Jacko, which was not only enormously flattering, but a huge temptation that very few men would be able to resist. John dodged the offer and motivated the conversation to move somewhat clumsily along.

Sophie picked up the dialogue and switched to another subject, smiling to herself, guessing that it would only be a matter of time before he succumbed to her advances. She wanted him desperately; his clinging doggedly to the belief that his wife and family had somehow miraculously survived was a very long shot.

"Working in the gardens is very therapeutic, but by the end the day, I am dusty and sweaty, there is only so much you can achieve with a strip wash, I do so miss a shower. I have noticed that some of the soldiers have rigged up ingenious shower solutions. I have been researching this phenomenon." She held her index finger up to the corner of her mouth and pouted like a schoolgirl explaining a solution to a teacher which made her look even more adorable. "I have chosen a design that I want to install in my accommodation."

Jacko agreed that it was a good idea and said that he had been contemplating something along the same lines.

"OK, let's make a deal," she offered, "You help me set up my shower and with my expertise I'll design one for you. I have all the necessary parts in my bathroom. I just need someone to help me put it all together."

"Sounds like a deal, when were you thinking of undertaking this mammoth task?"

"No time like the present. Is your diary full or could you spare ten minutes to help a damsel in distress?"

Jacko did have the rest of the day clear, barring emergencies. They walked off to Sophie's rooms. In recent years the accommodation for soldiers had improved no end and although she was not housed in the Officers' block, she did have what amounted to a tiny studio apartment. The bathroom did, in fact, have a shower, but no water had flowed through the taps for months. Any water that reached the tiny room had to be carried there.

"All that I need now is a strong, tall man, to put this contraption together. Are you up to that, John?"

Sophie had assembled the equipment to create a shower. She had found a good clean bucket, which she took to the workshop, where the men there were delighted to drill holes in the bottom for her. She had two short planks of wood to span the top of the shower, strong enough to take the weight of the bucket filled with water; there was no tap to turn the water on and off. This might be an additional extra that could be added at a later date. It took about ten minutes to assemble the apparatus.

John stood on a chair and had reached the part where he was about to pour water into the bucket. He shouted over his shoulder. "Are you ready Soph? I am about to test this thing."

"Tip in all in, John! Let's give it a good test."

Jacko poured a full bucket of water into the top bucket. "It seems to be working quite well," he called back into the living room.

To his surprise the answer came from the shower. "Yes, it's working very well."

Sophie was standing in the shower tray, naked, her beautiful face turned upwards allowing the water to stream over the curves of her lithe body, the soapy water snaking from her shoulders down her spine and between her exquisite buttocks. She turned and the water now ran between her breasts. She looked up at Jacko looking at her through the stream of water.

"Bloody hell Soph, what are you doing?"

Jacko knew that it was a redundant question, but he could think of nothing else to say considering the circumstances.

"It would be a shame to waste all of that hard earned water, surely. You agree? Get ready with the second bucket. This is so lovely."

Jacko had no option but to wait and pour the second bucket into the makeshift shower. Sophie made no attempt to play the moment coyly. She had made her play, knowing that John's eyes were on her and was enjoying every second. The water continued to cascade down her elegant neck, shoulders and back. The coldness of the water made her nipples erect, making John's blood pressure mount substantially. The second bucket was empty. He then went back into the living room and sat confused on the sofa. It took Sophie, five minutes to finish the shower, before she walked back into the living room. She was wearing a towelling dressing gown and had a large towel on her head.

"Christ Soph, that was a bit unfair." Jacko was actually angry, even though he was, at the same time, captivated by the reckless display.

"You could have joined me, the water actually lasted for longer than I had expected," she taunted.

"Soph, you're not playing fair. Get dressed and let's go for a walk. I need some air!"

Jacko needed to firmly explain to Sophie that his loyalty remained with Sarah, and he had no intention of being unfaithful to her, irrespective of the circumstances that they currently found themselves in.

Chapter 25

The Deer Hunt

Armageddon + 311 days

It was Monday morning again. Many Mondays had passed since the fateful day that Jacko had received the shock order from London to lock down the barracks. Weekends now held no particular significance, the days morphing one into another in the dawn till dusk existence which now prevailed.

One punctuation mark that added a landmark to the week was the Sunday church service. It was interdenominational and well attended, probably by many non-believers who were desperate for something to cling on to.

Jacko walked into his office and offered a cheery good morning to Rogers, who replied with an equally cheery, "Good morning, Boss." Although, truth is known, neither of the men was feeling particularly cheery. It was just the British way.

"Anything significant lined up for today?" enquired Jacko.

Rogers explained that there was a TT meeting scheduled for 10:00 hours, but apart from that, nothing. The camp had settled into a regime where everyone had a job and as the old proverb goes, "An idle mind is the devil's workshop."

One of the more labour intensive and productive chores was the bold attempt at growing, pretty much anything that could be considered edible and was a major occupation for many of the group. Considering their lack of knowledge when they started, the results were quite promising. Tomatoes were easy to grow and were one of the early successes, and there was a readily available supply of manure from the remaining horses. Jacko sat at his desk knowing that when he had a period of inaction, his mind would automatically return to thinking about his family and wondering how they were faring. All sorts of horrible scenarios crossed his anxious mind. The foremost of these being, were they actually alive? He knew all too well that the thoughts that he was enduring were the same thoughts as everyone in Combemere were facing, every hour of every day.

There was a knock at the door and Dan Buckland burst in. Jacko was relieved to see the big man and to have his thought diverted from the all too constant concern regarding his family's fate and survival.

"Good morning, Jacko, what's on the agenda for today?" Dan appeared animated and eager.

"Just a TT meeting at ten hundred hours for me, but what's making you so energised?"

"The medical officer, and Toby, from the cookhouse have decided that we need more protein in our diets and a couple of the deer from the Great Park will fill the bill nicely. I am taking a team to the park for a spot of poaching."

Jacko remembered the matter was mentioned two days ago and he wished that it was him leading the outing. "Who have you lined up for this jolly, Dan? It should only need you and four others."

"One of our best snipers is a lad from 'A' Squadron, David Holland, better known as Dutch, although I don't think that his expertise will be very much tested today. I will be taking big Toby Walker from the cookhouse; his butchery skills will be useful in gutting the carcasses while we are still in the park. No need to carry anything that we can't eat.

I thought that I would give Flint an excursion; he hasn't been outside the gates for a while. And a young lad, Kinch, from the radio wing who has been doing sterling work, he could do with an outing. I will also be taking two horses to carry the carcasses back. Galahad and Falkland are my choice as they are big, but also they have a quiet temperament, which might be a plus as they will have a dead animal slung across their backs."

"Good choice Dan, we must rotate the men when the opportunities arise to get them outside. What weapons will you are carrying? The threat of attack from the marauding gangs is far higher now. There are less of them, but those that have survived have become more devious, and from reports that we are getting, they are now armed and deadly, and will stop at nothing to take what they want."

"I'll stick with side arms, as we will be working on getting the carcass back and don't want to be too encumbered."

"What time are you off, and what entrance to the park have you decided on?" asked Jacko, obviously disappointed that he wasn't going along.

"I was thinking midday and entering the park via Bolton Road onto the Kings

Road entrance. The closer Stag Meadow gate would be easier, but the deer herd mostly graze south west of the Kings Road area."

The conversation moved on to other subjects until it was time to go to the 10:00 hours meeting.

Just after 12:00 hours, the small troop left the confines of the barracks. Dan rode Galahad and led Falkland. They soon covered the short distance to the Great Park, which was less than one and a half kilometres. Moving out into the park it didn't take much more than half an hour before they discovered the herd of deer, about four hundred meters away. The animals were grazing in the early afternoon sunlight. Dan Buckland acted as spotter to Dutch and selected a likely target. The shots were clean and accurate, killing the deer instantly. The group walked over to the carcasses and Toby began his work. Thirty minutes later the carcass was ready for transportation back to Combemere. All went to plan until the group approached the edge of the park where the easterly gate was located. Shots rang out and the thuds of bullets smacked into the ground all around them.

"What do you reckon, Dutch?" shouted Dan.

"Three SA80s at eight hundred meters, not very good shots, but they might get lucky."

The men fired returning shots, but their handguns were not much use at that distance and the attackers were well hidden. The sniper rifle would have been a good option, but they were in open ground with no cover and setting it up would have taken time. The two horses which had been grazing were nervous. Dan took the reins of Galahad and Flint took control of Falkland.

Dan gave the order, "OK lads, we're far too exposed here. Ditch the deer and make for cover in the pink cottage on the town side of the gates."

All five men ran for the cover of the closest building which was the parks western gatehouse. Incoming fire was landing all around them.

As they passed through the park gates there was a horrific thud and a scream. Dan looked around and saw that Flint was down, hit in the back by an attacker's bullet. Falkland was also hit. Big Toby was at the back of the group, his huge frame not as agile as the others. He was the first to reach Flint, and after checking the wound, Toby scooped him up in his huge arms. With incoming fire all around, he carried the young Trooper. Dan Buckland could see that there was nothing more that could be done and they all reached the relative safety of the gatehouse. Dan got there first and threw his huge frame at the front door, which crumbled under the weight. They piled inside, relieved to have some protection from the heavy incoming fire.

Toby lay Flint gently down, then set about applying basic battleground first aid, whilst Dan assisted Dutch to set up the sniper rifle in a first floor window. Once this was operating, the opposition realised that their weapons were no match for the trained sniper and quickly the incoming fire abated.

"OK Dutch, well done, looks as if they have had enough. Kinchy, take over the spotting for Dutch." Dan then turned his attention to Flint. The boy looked bad. He was coughing up blood; the wound was obviously very serious. "We have to get him back to barracks double quick."

Dan had seen many wounded soldiers in his service career and this injury ranked amongst the worst. Flint was fading into shock, which was at least reducing the pain that he was obviously experiencing. He asked Dan if his mother was there, his face looked like a small boys; his eyes scared, as if not fully comprehending what was happening to him.

Dan put his arm on Toby's shoulder. "Toby, we have to get him back to barracks, quickly. He doesn't have long, but there might be a chance if we are quick."

Toby nodded to show that he understood that Flint's chance of survival was slim. "Carry on with the triage, I'll be right back." He then turned his attention to Falkland, who was standing next to Galahad at the rear of the building. His head was bowed and he stood motionless.

Galahad was whinnying softly, obviously nervous. Dan looked at the big horse, he had been hit in the large artery in his neck, blood was flowing from the wound and pooling at his front feet. It was obvious to Dan that the wound was fatal.

He made his decision. He led Galahad to the front of the house and tied his reigns to the fence. When he had returned to Falkland he was not surprised to see that the huge loss of blood had brought the horse to his knees. Dan drew his pistol. "I'm sorry buddy, but this will be quick." Aiming his pistol at the point between Falklands eyes where the fur spirals into a star shape; he pulled the trigger. The magnificent horse slumped and with a last expulsion of breath from his big lungs, Falkland was dead.

Dan stood for a moment, the pistol in his hand hung by his side, emotionally moved by what he had just done. He only allowed himself a brief time to reflect on the event. Flint was now the priority. Dan ran around to the front of the building and back into the cottage. The faces of the three men in the room told all, they had heard the shot and knew exactly what had taken place.

Dan took control. "Galahad is ok, so my plan is for me to ride him, carrying Flint up in front of me. Is he ready to be moved, Toby?"

The answer was less than positive. "As ready as he is ever going to be; he has a pulse, but it's weak," Toby mumbled.

"OK, let's get him outside."

172

Dan pushed the action along. He went out to the front of the cottage and mounted Galahad. The three men carried Flint, and with some difficulty, managed to get him sitting upright in front of Dan, who had the reigns in his left hand, whilst his right arm was around the wounded trooper's chest. They set off walking at first, but when Dan felt comfortable with the situation he pushed the horse into a canter. Time was of an essence. The other three men ran behind. Dan had no idea if Flint was still alive, he couldn't feel him breathing and was unable to check for a pulse in his neck as his hands were fully employed. Blood seeped from Flints back wound, onto Dan's chest.

Twenty minutes later, the sad group reached the barrack gates. Kinch was fast on his feet and had run ahead when they were approaching so that the medical officer and medics were at the gate when Galahad and his passengers arrived. Jacko was there too. Flint was taken into the guardroom but within five minutes the MO made the announcement that sadly, Flint was dead. The men were all attended by Doc Maloney and her medics. Dan pushed them aside, he was angry, eager to go back and search out the gang that had done this thing.

Jacko quickly put together a team of twenty armed men and personally led a scouting party out to look for the aggressors. He returned an hour later, but had been unable to find anything more than the empty cartridge cases that the attackers had ejected from their rifles, which verified that they were indeed using British Army weapons and ammunition. He left a section of six men to guard the deer carcass.

Jacko called an emergency meeting with Dan, Toby, Mick, from the stables, and the MO.

"This attack has shocked us all but we have to look at this realistically. Our priority now is to send out a patrol to bring back the deer and Falkland. Mick, I want you to prepare a wagon from the coaching troop, big enough to carry it." He scratched the stubble on the side of his chin and gave the matter a little more thought. "OK, I have another idea and I want your input on this one."

There was no doubting that he now held the attention of the other four people in the room, his reputation for radical thinking certainly preceded him.

"Toby, I want you to select two of your staff who have butchery skills; we are going to have to utilise the meat from Falkland." There was a deadly silence in the room. Mick was unable to suppress a groan. The horses that shared the barracks with the men of the cavalry were each as much themselves a character in their own right as the soldiers who cared for them. Even Sophie, who wasn't a rider, had become very attached to them. This was going to be a hard call.

"We aren't in a position to pass up the opportunity to get such a large quantity of protein." It was indeed a radical suggestion, but all agreed, even Mick could see grudgingly that it was the only sensible thing to do under the circumstances. "I suggest that when you drive back into the camp you cover the load on the coach with a tarpaulin. I also think that it is best to keep this venture to ourselves and the people directly involved."

All were shocked, but nodded agreement.

Later Jacko was alone with Dan, who gave his account of what had happened. "It came out of nowhere. I wasn't expecting an attack of this type," he admitted.

"We're going to have to pay much more attention to the likelihood of these attacks from now on. Scavenging teams will need armed escorts, more perimeter guards, in fact, a tightening of security in all areas. These guys are now posing a serious threat." Jacko's face was thoughtful. "I think that their policy is to pick us off one by one until we are reduced and weak enough for them to make an all-out attack."

He now moved on to the more pressing matter. "We are going to have to bury Flint in the barracks. Look out for a quiet location. He's the first fatality for us in this development. Who knows how many more there might be?"

The atmosphere in the camp was more sombre than ever with the departure of Flint. His naive character had been infectious. He was a young man who could, on occasions be described as infuriating when trying to explain to him the simplest of tasks, but he was impossible to dislike. His actions could never evoke real anger. The burial service was attended by everyone in the camp, apart from those who were on

Duty, providing the now greatly enhanced perimeter guard. Any outside operations were cancelled for the funeral, which took place in the open by the graveside, in what had formerly been the officers' tennis courts, but was now a thriving vegetable patch.

Flint had spent many happy hours working on this important project and it was a fitting place for him to be put to rest. The Regimental Padre gave a short but dignified service. It seemed to all attending that this one man was to be honoured in the traditional manner. Flint's death had been swift, but it was impossible for all attending to ignore that just outside the walls, countless millions had perished and were still dying, enduring long and painful deaths.

One of the men who had unexpectedly befriended Flint in the early days of the confinement was Harry Windsor/Wales. They had worked together on digging the first well and could often be seen sharing jokes. It was an unlikely friendship, but such was the contagious aura of Flint, that time spent in his company seemed to pass quickly, making the heavy work more tolerable.

Chapter 26

Security Tightened

Armageddon + 313

Jacko and Dan sat in the HQ Squadron office studying a map of the locality surrounding the barracks, in a military fashion akin to urban warfare procedures. They had just returned from scouting a quiet residential housing estate in what had been a sleepy, suburban backwater of Windsor. There was now the worrying potential that they could encounter armed adversaries. Jacko and Dan considered the consequences of the recent attack which had resulted in the death of Flint. The patrol had taken them to the vulnerable areas at the back of the barracks. It was bizarre to be open to attack from armed oppositions or snipers in what had previously been such a tranquil location. The threat had changed substantially now that the gangs had become equipped with military grade weapons. Scavenging teams were now sent out with armed guards, such was the growing threat.

"The three prime infiltration positions will be from the cul-de-sac spurring from Springfield Road." Dan circled the positions on a map that he had in front of him as he spoke.

"They all border on the back of the Officers Mess," Jacko was thoughtful in his reply. "I think that we will have to give these areas priority and perhaps even set up a permanent guard post."

Dan nodded agreement and continued his presentation. "Problem is that this will be a twenty-four-seven event and will tie up a lot of our manpower." He paused. "Under the old regime that would have been the end of the matter, the orders would have been issued and implemented. Things are now very different. OK, these are our findings, but we will have to run this past the Think Tank."

A meeting was arranged and Dan gave a summary of what he and Jacko had discovered and discussed. Dan started the meeting with an overview of the perimeter. "I don't expect that these assailants would attempt a frontal attack on the main gates in St. Leonards Road."

The perimeter wall was constructed from brick. It was two and a half metres high at the lowest point and topped with a metre high spiked steel fence. Behind the barracks was a housing estate running off Springfield Road, where the Alma pub was located. There were three cul-de-sacs leading from Springfield Road to the barrack wall, the most vulnerable of these was Dyson Close, where the wall was lower, and although topped with a substantial rolled barbed wire fence, it could easily be breached. This area backed onto the Officers' Mess.

Dan went on to explain the plans that he and Jacko had devised. The Think Tank was in complete agreement. He moved onto the next subject. "Something else that we need to consider is the security of the scavenger teams." All of the men in the room had at one time or another been on the teams and knew the hazards that they faced. "There is an increasing risk to all of the Combemere personnel both inside and outside the walls.
Our scavengers are obviously armed, but are having to forage further afield as the requirements of the fusion team escalate. We will have to increase the team's personnel to allow for guards to be posted when the teams enter buildings."

There was unanimous agreement and all in the room were aware that these precautionary measures would require a huge increase in man hours and expand what was already a heavy workload. Jacko took over. "There are two more items that we have to discuss before we adjourn this meeting. We want to implement a system whereby each team will leave written addresses of the locations that they intend to visit in the guardroom before they depart. Now that we have the capacity to re- charge our field radios, communications are greatly improved."

That simple, and the obvious additional security measure was readily agreed by all present.

Jacko went on to the last item on the agenda that he and Dan had prepared. "All trained military personnel are to present themselves at the armoury and draw out weapons and ammunition. Up to this point we have followed military regulations and drawn weapons when leaving the camp, returning them to the armoury upon getting back into barracks. The possibility of attack is now stronger than ever."

Dan added one of his inevitable anecdotes, "Rourke's Drift has taught us a valuable lesson." When the meeting ended, it was solidly agreed that the measures discussed would be implemented and that the Camp's protection was to take priority.

David S. Jones

Chapter 27

Trooper Foley

Armageddon + 325 days

The ancient ship's bell that hung in front of the guardroom clanged, but not with the intensity of an attack warning or a stand to arms, more a slow, sad melodious tone. This was a pre-arranged signal for senior members to get themselves quickly to the guardroom. The weather was wet, dark and dismal. The general consciousness of life within the confines of the camp was depressing, like living in a black and white film before the advent of colour.

As usual, Jacko and Dan were the first to arrive, followed by the other senior camp characters. Tomo, the guard commander, walked out of the guardroom looking distinctly troubled.

Dan was the first to speak. "What have you got, Tomo?"

All attention focused on the man who had raised the alarm and summoned the group.

"Bit of a strange one. Trooper Foley, from 'B' Squadron, has taken himself onto the roof of 'B' Squadron block and is threatening to shoot himself."

There was no immediate response from anyone. They had all been dreading a development such as this, hoping against all hope that the beleaguered group inside the camp could 'hold it together'. But the intense physiological pressure was relentless, time was dragging and the weight of the decision that they had made, hung around their necks like an albatross. The stress was difficult for them all to bear.

Jacko broke the silence. "Let's take this gently," he began solicitously. "We have to try to talk him down, and we need to do that by getting as few people involved as possible."

By this time a large crowd had gathered in front of the guardroom, all responding to the alarm. "Stand down everyone. This is a situation that only needs a few of us to resolve. Please, all go back to whatever you were doing."

The crowd, slightly disconcerted, dispersed, as Jacko had asked, leaving him, Dan, Nick and Sophie.

Dan brought the list from the guardroom of activities for the day. He read out the names of those on outside operations. 'B' Squadron leader is out foraging. We need to find the 2 i/c and get all of the information that we can on Foley. OK, let us four walk around to 'B' Squadron, no need to run and get Foley agitated. He will most likely be able to see us coming from where he is."

Nick Trevelyan spoke up. "Foleys 2 i/c is working on the back wall upgrading its defence potential. I'll go and get him." And with that he walked off.

Sophie Maloney added an important point. "His Christian name is Richard. He has been in to see me several times, but only with minor problems."

Slowly they pieced together as much information that they could about the troubled man. Jacko left orders with Tomo to keep folk away from the block and try to maintain as much of a sense of normality as possible.

By the time they had arrived at the 'B' Squadron office block, Nick, and the 2 I/c, Roy Bright, was there to meet them. He filled in more useful information. Foley had a good army record; he was married with two young children, a boy and a girl. He had been in the army for six years and had served in Afghanistan. He wasn't put forward for promotion as he was considered rather quiet and something of a loner, not integrating more than necessary with his colleagues. Given these negative characteristics, he was good at his job and always kept his nose clean. It was well known that Foley was very much a family man.

The 'B' squadron block was three stories high. The roof was flat and there was only one access via wooden steps and a hatch. As they walked up the stairs to the third floor, they discussed their tactics. Sophie Maloney suggested that she would like to be the first negotiator and the others agreed. "Give me four minutes, and if I'm not making any progress, I suggest that, Jacko and Dan, come up and we try a different tack."

Nick added a proposal. "If it comes to the point where Jacko and Dan go onto the roof, I will be at the top of the ladder, out of sight to Foley, with my pistol ready to fire. It's obvious that Foley is unhinged. We can't take chances. It's possible that he might start shooting and you will be the targets. When you move onto the roof spread out, so that you don't block my line of fire." This was agreed by the group.

Sophie was the first to climb up the wooden ladder and onto the windswept roof area. Dan stayed hidden at the top of the ladder where he could hear most of the conversation between Sophie and Richard. Sophie quietly called out to Richard as she slowly climbed the final rungs of the ladder and walked out onto the roof. Richard Foley was crouched down in the far corner about twenty-five meters away from the roof entrance. He looked awful. His hair was long and lank and his beard scruffy and unkempt. He was wearing a black polo shirt, regulation boots and cargo pants, not the best kind of clothing for a cold wet day on an exposed rooftop, but he appeared not to be affected by the inclement weather.

As Sophie approached, he straightened up, kneeling, but upright with his right arm at his side. In his right hand was a nine-millimetre handgun. He looked directly at Sophie. "Don't come any closer, Doc."

At the same time he brought the gun up to his chest and with his left hand he pulled back the cocking mechanism and armed the weapon. Sophie could distinctly hear the bullet slot into the firing chamber. Richard professionally flicked the safety catch to the firing position with his thumb.

"Richard, there is no need for this. We can talk and maybe find a solution for you."

He looked away from Sophie, gazing blankly out across the rooftops into the distance. It was late afternoon and the sun was fading quickly, causing the temperature to drop considerably.

"There is no solution; my family are all dead and I am here. Who knows what hell they have been through, and I wasn't there to protect them."

Sophie tried to think quickly, knowing that Richard was putting into words what most of the soldiers in the camp were thinking. "Richard, have you heard something about your family?" She paused. "Have you received some news?" She knew that there was a remote possibility that he might have somehow received news of his family, but it was doubtful. Any news or gossip spread like wildfire.

"I don't need any confirmation. I just know that they are all dead. I feel it." The last words were spoken louder and with an increasingly angry tone. "They are dead and I abandoned them at a time when they needed me most. It's been more than nine months since I last saw my family and nothing here has become any better." The last sentence was spoken between sobbing. "Is there no end to this horror?"

Sophie searched for soothing, positive words, but was struggling. "Richard, they could all still be fine, waiting for the day when you can be reunited with them. Put the gun down. It isn't the solution."

For a moment it looked as if her words had some effect. Richard appeared to calm down a little, but he continued to stare out across the rooftops. His arm fell slowly to his side, but the gun was still in his hand and his finger remained on the trigger.

Sophie's four minutes were up. Jacko and Dan quietly made their way slowly up through the roof entrance and stood close to Sophie. "This is not the way Richard." Dan spoke in a fatherly tone, which momentarily seemed to be having an effect. "We all know what you are going through and how you feel. We all just have to hang on and see this terrible thing through together; imagine that the boffins have got it right and eighteen months down the line your family arrive here searching for you. What could we tell them, if you do what you are thinking of doing?"

Sophie took a step forward; perhaps a step too far. "Let me have the gun, Richard, and we can all go down and talk about this in a warm, dry, comfortable place."

"I told you to stay where you are." Richards's voice had suddenly become erratic and irrational. He rocked from side to side mumbling to himself. "I left them to die and saved my own skin, what kind of a father am I?"

There was no time for a reply. He raised the barrel of the gun to the underside of his chin and pulled the trigger. The top of his head was blown off, his body slumping into a heap.

Sophie, Dan and Jacko, stood shocked, unable to move, the sound of the gun still ringing loudly in their ears. There was no point in checking the body; it was visibly obvious that life had left the body of Richard Foley. The final rays of a gloomy sun faded over Ascot and Bracknell behind the horizon. Darkness flooded slowly in like a dark grey tide.

"Are you alright Soph?" Nick had emerged from the roof entrance and stood with his three comrades looking at Foley's lifeless body.

"Yes, I'm OK, thanks Nick," she answered somewhat unconvincingly.

It was a sad fact that death was not new to her, an inevitable element of her remit; she had seen men die before, but never while she was actually talking with them. Jacko was the first to shake himself out of the dreadful scene in which they had all been actors; reluctant contributors.

He walked over to the edge of the roof and looked up and down the road below. "OK, we have two options open to us." The others looked on as their minds slowly emerged from the horror of the past minutes.

"Given the vulnerability of everyone in the camp, we could keep this to ourselves and create a story that Foley has jumped ship to look for his family. Tomo has done a good job in keeping everyone away from this area and it could be achieved." He looked directly into the eyes of the three people standing before him; they all displayed the same cynical look.

Sophie was the first to answer, "And the second option?"

He paused. "The second option is to tell the story exactly as it happened and hope that it doesn't entice others into taking the same route." They looked at each other for inspiration.

Dan was the first to reply. "I can understand your thinking, John, but I would find it difficult to live with that lie." The others agreed without hesitation.

"Ok, so that's unanimous," Jacko acknowledged. "But consider what this could mean to others who are struggling with this nightmare. Foley is now out of it and there are others who might follow his example."

Trooper Richard Foley was buried next to Flinty. All wondered how many more lives would be lost before the confinement period ended.

Chapter 28

Mopping Up Operation

Armageddon + 384 days

Outside the walls of Combemere Barracks an eerie and unnerving silence had descended upon the town of Windsor. The streets were now deserted, wind blew rubbish, ash, and in one location, bank notes could be seen scattered amongst the general debris; worthless now, and far less useful than a roll of toilet paper. The only people who had survived in towns throughout the country were those particularly vicious groups who had taken what they needed to survive by force. These gangs were now armed and exceptionally dangerous. The greater percentage of the population was either dead or hiding in more remote locations.

An important communication was received at the radio wing from NAPIG. Jacko considered it was of such great importance that he called a meeting of all personnel. As had become usual the cookhouse was the venue and everyone attended. Jacko studied the assembled crowd as they walked in and filled the large room. This was a conglomeration of not only army personnel but also a composite collection, which now included ex-royalty and scientists. He considered what would be the best-combined title to give the assembled gathering and decided that comrades would be the most fitting.

He began his address. "I have been deliberating on what would be the best way to welcome you all. I have decided that since we are embarking on a new era, the title comrades in the non-Communist vernacular would seem to be the most appropriate. Comrades, I have received a communiqué from National All Party Interim Government that I feel you should all be aware of, as the implications are deep and need to be considered by all of us. As you know, there are other units that are dug in like us around the country. The NAPIG have a superlative Think Tank made up from the finest brains from all over the British Isles. They also have a considerable network of infiltrators, who are embedded throughout the country, reporting back on the continuing circumstances. Their combined situation report for the coming months is as follows. It does not make good reading, although I am sure that you will all have reached a similar conclusion by the time I have read it to you. Jacko began reading from the communiqué.

"*National All Party Interim Government – NAPIG*

The initial scramble for obtainable food supplies resulted in untold deaths; this moved on to millions more dying from starvation once the available food was consumed. Moving out of the towns and villages, into the countryside was perceived to have been the best solution.

Millions did just that. The next chapter in this appalling story was that feral gangs were formed. They were the stronger physical elements of society with lower moral principles and tended to be made up from the localised ethnic groups. Gradually, as the dwindling food supplies became more and more scarce, the gangs fought each other for territories, which further reduced the initial mobs, leaving only the truly desperate and ruthless gangs. The remaining marauding bands have managed to arm themselves, having discovered weapons in police stations and abandoned military bases. These gangs are extremely dangerous.

NAPIG have decided that it will be imperative for the military to eradicate these gangs. They have become well organised. Their reach is now extending out from the towns and into the countryside like a cancer. They are preying on the decent folk, people who will form the nucleus of the emerging new society when the recovery phase is begun. Therefore, like the cancer upon society that they represent, they will have to be surgically removed.

NAPIG have not revised their estimation of eighteen months from the initial contamination, for the recovery period to be reached.

It is their expectation that by this time law and order will have been tentatively resumed and society can start to be rebuilt. As the final food stocks are consumed, stark desperation will be the order of the day. Information is being received from around the country of people resorting to cannibalism. It will fall upon your military group and the soldiers in Victoria Barracks, to firstly eliminate the gang that now controls your local area. When this has been achieved, move on into London, linking up with other military groups to rid the capital of this marauding menace. Similar missions will be taking place around the country. Whilst NAPIG are fully aware of the task, it is asking of its troops, its wish is to make them aware that the alternative would be rule by regional warlords, casting British civilisation backwards over two millennia. Finally, be aware that the threat that you are being asked to eliminate is not going to be easy to defeat. This will be full-on urban warfare. These groups are armed and have set up substantial defences that can be tactically defended and which are booby-trapped. You will be looking at sustaining casualties."

Again, as on the previous occasions when Jacko had been the purveyor of extreme news, there was a deathly silence throughout the cookhouse, which under normal circumstances was always so alive and vibrant with the chatter and laughter of the soldiers.

He continued, "The severity of what we are being asked to undertake here is enormously significant. Not only what we are being tasked with, which is to kill British subjects, but also to shoot people who were, before this terrible disaster encompassed us, for the greater part, law abiding citizens." A hum of realisation swept around the room.

Jacko allowed this last comment time to sink in before he continued. "I have given this much thought myself and it is not something that will rest easy with any of our consciences. I have made a comparison from something that we have witnessed, which is close to where we are now. It helps to put into perspective what we are being asked to undertake. I refer to the looting gang that have formed under the Windsor relief road. They have no compunction in stopping cars that are laden, quite often with families who are attempting to escape from the town, and looting the contents of the vehicles. These are folk trying to escape are the few people with cars that have fuel in their tanks from before the contamination. Extreme violence is perpetrated and many times death has been the outcome for the unfortunate occupants who were simply attempting to defend their families and belongings. The people that I am talking about were given a choice. They could do what their unfortunate victims had attempted to do and go into the countryside to survive – or steal from their fellow men. The feral gangs are decimating the very bloodline of this country's future. I see no other alternative than for us to comply with the orders of the interim government's request and put an end to these gangs."

Jacko waited for the surge of chatter to subside. "I would now like to open a debate in which I want you all to participate."

There was a pause before several people stood up to make their point. William Windsor was the first to speak. "I fully understand the gravity of what the looters on the relief road roundabout have committed, but as we are far more powerful and have superior armed forces, could we not round them up and give them a chance to move on?"

This approach sparked much heated discussion within the room. A second speaker made his point forcefully. A conflicting argument was put forward that rounding up the perpetrators and imprisoning them might be an option. This was immediately quashed by the reality that although there were plenty of empty prisons to take these people, there were no prison officers. The practicality of running them was impossible.

A young trooper stood up and made a valid point adding to the confusion.

"Since we now have no monarchy and rank has been abolished, what are we? We have in reality been abandoned to our own devices. If we are no longer soldiers, then we cannot be ordered to do anything that we don't want to."

This shock revelation caused much deep thinking. Dan Buckland added his thoughts. "I think that the looters have made their choice. It might easily have been one of our families that they attacked. In my consideration they have crossed the red line of civility and should be dealt with accordingly."

This opinion also provoked much input from those present. The debate went on for a further hour; various views were discussed until finally Jacko decided that the time had arrived to put the matter to a vote. The outcome was an overwhelming agreement to eliminate the local looters and all other similar groups as NAPIG had intended.

The snap decision that Jacko made to send the small convoy of eight trucks to the Aldershot military supply depot and stock up with as much non-perishable rations as they could carry and return to Windsor, so early into the contamination period, turned out to be an extremely prudent move. He had taken a huge gamble with the availability of non-replenishable fuel available to him, but it was now proving good foresight. The stock of mostly tinned rations, which the cookhouse ingeniously supplemented with whatever edible items came their way, would hopefully see the camp through the confinement period.

The downside to this forward thinking was that removing the eight truckloads of food from Aldershot was now equivalent to sending eight trucks to Fort Knox and loading them up with gold bars, so precious had storable, edible produce become. Food and water was now the currency and men were prepared to go to any lengths to get their hands on them, including killing.

Combemere Barracks has a main entrance on St Leonards Road, but there was another rear gate which was less obvious and exited into a housing estate. The wall around the barracks was high, but certainly not insurmountable. Jacko decided that as time passed and food was becoming more and more precious there would have to be a 24 hour perimeter guard.

The feral gangs had become experienced and concentrated, gaining in confidence as the law of the jungle prevailed. Ultimately, survival of the fittest and most ruthless triumphed. The gangs had armed themselves with guns and rifles that had been taken from abandoned police stations and army camps that had not gone into the shutdown mode that Combemere had adopted.

Victoria Barracks was given the same directive from London when the Armageddon Virus began. It was significantly smaller than Combemere and less well equipped to sustain a large group of soldiers. The Castle itself had escaped the looting due to the obvious security and the presence of soldiers. The same couldn't be said of the Castle farm which was attacked on various occasions – food being the priority over material loot.

Slough Trading Estate was Europe's largest commercial trading estate; it housed many of the world's most successful companies. Large modern warehouses that had the capacity to store huge quantities of stock, the largest on the estate being a food distribution centre for one of the country's principal supermarket chains. This facility was the major prize in the locality and several severe battles had been fought by the mercenary gangs to gain control of it. These battles had culminated in scores of deaths, but the now dominant gang that had conquered and eliminated all of the opposition had taken up residence and were now known as the Tesco Gang. They had set up a substantial defensive perimeter and booby trapped many of the adjacent buildings. This was to be their target of choice.

There were no hills in Slough, therefore finding a location where observers could be positioned in order to estimate the fighting capability of the entrenched band posed a problem. Finally, when enough intelligence had been collected an action plan was devised. An all out frontal attack was the final decision.

The attack would be led by the Cavalry, followed by the Irish Guards. As experience had proven on so many occasions, a dawn attack was to be the chosen time. Hitting the front gates was favoured, as the perimeter defences mostly faced outwards, and it would take some time for the defenders to turn their weapons inwards. Of course, the element of surprise was another proven advantage. And so the plan was laid and preparations were undertaken. The attack was to be led by two Samson's, followed by a troop of four armoured vehicles. The close proximity of the target area to Combemere was a distinct advantage. The precious diesel that had been so diligently produced was very limited and this was a major factor in the planning. Attacking such a well defended position with Leafs, was not an option, their lack of armour being a major factor. The main assault had to be made by heavily armoured vehicles that could sustain incoming fire. The Leafs would follow, four in number. Being faster and more manoeuvrable, they could drive between the isles of the huge warehouse, weeding out the bandits.

At first light the attack went in. One lone Samson screamed towards the three meter high main gates, reaching 45 mph, as it hit the metal obstructions. There was an almighty crash, followed by the sound of grinding metal, sparks and the screaming of the armoured vehicles engine. Fifty metres inside the perimeter, the Samson ground to a halt, tangled in the debris from the gates and wire fencing. It was stuck in open ground completely without cover and immediately came under a hail of gunfire. Alone inside the compound, the Samson gallantly fought back, returning fire, but was overwhelmed and looked as if it might be destroyed. Then, with a roar of their engines, the armoured troop raced through the gap where the gates had so recently stood, they laid down heavy fire upon the highly defended main entrance positions. A second Samson raced through the entrance gap, and with its bulldozer blade lowered, smashed through the huge shuttered entrance to the larger central warehouse.

Now, the four Leafs arrived; their top gunners firing at anything that moved. The defenders were overwhelmed and pulled back into the protection of the warehouse buildings. This was the first phase of the attack; the breach was successfully made; now the infantry arrived in the form of the Irish Guards. They took over and systematically worked their way through the entire complex. The final tally was one Irish Guard, killed by gunfire, two more by an IED. The two crew members of the first Samson were seriously injured, but the final death toll for the Tesco Gang, was thirty-six dead. The Irish Guards had been given the same remit from London as the Cavalry; no prisoners. They too had discussed the matter thoroughly at length and arrived at their own decision; there could be no prisoners. There were no survivors.

The new style army had now cut its teeth and although any losses were not received lightly, they were relatively low. In future battles the lessons learned in Slough would surely be implemented. There were other warlords in other locations throughout the UK and from this first successful suppression, it was envisaged that the country would be systematically purged from the menace of anarchy. Law and order could be reinstated.

Chapter 29

Eton Attack

Armageddon + 415 days

With security substantially tightened, life continued, but the increasing threat of attacks by the growing armed anarchists was placing a heavy encumbrance upon the soldiers in Combemere. Simply maintaining the everyday requirement of the camp; most of which was without running water and electricity, was burdensome in the extreme.

The day started quite normally. Jacko and Dan made their early morning inspection of the camp and foraging teams had been dispatched. It was decided that Eton had not been explored enough and the Culham team suspected that there might be some useful equipment in the famed school's science classrooms. In the absence of electricity, the large brass ship's bell, which hung outside the guardroom, was the rallying alarm. At 10:27 hours, it was rung. All available personnel went immediately to the guardroom. The senior radio operator, Clive Evans, was there. Jacko and Dan were among the first to arrive and took control.

"What's happened, Clive?" asked Jacko to the serious looking soldier holding a slip of paper which obviously predicted bad news.

Clive relayed the news: "We have just received a 'contact' message from the recognisance team sent to Eton. They went there to see if it was worth a scavenging team taking a visit."

Dan disappeared inside the guardroom and returned immediately with the hand written destination which the team leader had deposited before leaving. He picked out ten men from the assembled group.

"Get your kit together and meet me here in five." Turning to Jacko, he asked,

"Who's taking this, you or me?"

"You go, Dan. I'd better stay here and hold the fort."

With that, Dan was gone, diving into the nearby adjacent museum where he stored his combat kit ready for any conceivable action. Three minutes later the assembled troop was ready to go out of the barracks.

Dan checked his men before addressing them. "OK, this is going to be a matter of getting there soonest, so we are running out of these gates and not stopping for anything until we are in Eton." The usual good-humoured face was deadly serious. "Radio checks Jock," he added, turning to the man that he relied upon for maintaining contact with base.

"Roger that," and Jock gave a thumbs up.

One minute later the eleven men were running as a unit out of the gates. They settled into a steady pace. Dan's consideration, regarding the speed, was determined by his radio operator, who had the heaviest burden.

Pounding on along St. Leonard's Road, they reached the bottom of Peascod Street. The first section was level, but at the end towards the Castle, the road rose quite sharply upwards. The long established shopping area was a distressing depiction of destruction and desecration. Many of the shops being no more than burned out hulks, the surviving shells of shops and offices had smashed windows and doors, the interiors ransacked with goods strewn across the road. There was no human presence apart from more than a dozen, decomposing bodies, with several cats wandered about, seemingly unperturbed by the devastation that lay all around. Upon reaching the top of the shopping street, adjacent to the statue of Queen Victoria, they turned left and headed downhill in the shadow of the northern castle wall, past the Theatre Royal. The squad crossed Datchet Road and entered Thames Street, passing the Bell and Dragon pub, where all of them were likely to have enjoyed a pint in pleasanter times. They approached the pedestrian bridge that crossed the River Thames, linking Windsor with Eton.

Dan's mind was fully focused on the mission at hand, but as he passed the last building on his left, the old Sir Christopher Wren Hotel, his thoughts could not avoid recalling the happy summer afternoons that he had spent walking with his wife and sons, crossing over that same bridge in the company of hundreds of tourists. The ice cream shop on the corner was a favourite with the boys.

The soldiers were accustomed to running, grouped together in the prescribed military manner; old habits die hard. As they reached the middle of the bridge, the first shot came as a complete surprise, totally unsuspected. The man to Dan's right fell to the ground with a sickening thud. The first shot was followed by a flurry of more incoming fire. The rounds were bouncing off of the bridge's road surface and superstructure. The well-trained men took up defensive positions and returned fire. Dan bent down to check the fallen soldier. He made a move to check the man's vital signs, but seeing that half of the top of his head was missing, it was pointless. He looked around. They were horribly exposed, with little shelter from the incoming fire.

"OK, everybody; off the bridge!" he shouted, pointing back in the direction of the Windsor side of the bridge, continuing to fire as they retreated. The remaining men made it safely to the shelter of the hotel shops and offices that were located on the short roads that lead to the bridge.

Dan took stock of the situation. "Have you sent a contact message back to base?" he asked his radio operator.

"Done that, Boss," came the reply.

Dan considered the situation. Most of the incoming fire appeared to be issuing from the plush apartment block that dominated the Eton side of the river.

"Tell base that I want six RPGs (rocket propelled grenades)." He gave the situation a little further thought. "Tell them to send Dutch Holland with that clever rifle of his. We need his help here. I also want a Samson and four Leafs. OK, get that shopping list off right away."

There now entered a period of stalemate; the Eton attackers, secure in the knowledge that nothing could come over the bridge and that for a second force to come around behind them, was impractical, as this was an unusual location. Eton Bridge, being the only access over the Thames for miles, and the western route by road into Eton, would have taken some time to cover, even if the attackers had transport. The exchange of fire went on for fifteen minutes until the reinforcements that Dan had asked for arrived. He sent Dutch to locate a good firing position and prepared the RPGs. "OK, my friends, let's see how you like this." He and two other men aimed the RPGs at three separate locations in the prestige apartment block. "We are going to put two rounds each into their posh hidey-hole and when the rats scurry out, I want you to give them a little farewell present, Dutch."

The luxury des-res were a little less than desirable when the smoke cleared and it looked doubtful that anyone would have survived the onslaught.

When Dan was happy that the threat of snipers was cleared, he went out onto the bridge with two other men to remove the body of the dead soldier, which was sent back to Combemere on the transport that delivered the RPGs. "Our mission here is to locate the recognisance team that reported a contact," he advised his men, motivating them to move on. "This ambush has been a distraction and cost us valuable time, but we are here to do a job. Let's get on with it."

He called up the Sampson to the edge of the bridge and gave orders to the driver. "Your job is to clear the bridge so that we can get the Leafs over. The bridge has been converted to pedestrians only which means that there are some bollards at either end. I want you to cut them off at ground level with the dozer blade."

The Sampson driver gave Dan the thumbs up and the bridge was soon cleared. The group moved on through Eton High Street cautiously, aware that this enclosed street would be an ideal location for a second ambush and create a superb killing ground for the opposition. The top gunners on the Leafs had all of the danger locations covered and were prepared to lay down heavy fire if an attack arose. They reached the end of the High Street and the distinctive Eton College buildings. Dan consulted the paper that had been written and left at the guardroom by the recognisance team leader. Finally, they located the science area of the college. Cautiously, they went inside the building. Oddly, there was less destruction at this end of Eton than they had witnessed elsewhere, possibly due to a school not being an obvious place to look for food, and the school being closed when the Armageddon Virus struck. The scene that they witnessed when they entered the main science classroom was a shock that none had expected. The four men from the recognisance team were all lying dead on the marble floor. They had been dragged into the middle of the room and stripped of any useful items of clothing and weapons.

Dan muttered under his breath, "Now that's six of us they have killed."

Dan organised the securing of the building with his usual military efficiency and quietly came back to the centre of the room to look again at the four dead men, all of whom he knew well. The group's leader was Fisher, the huge man who had achieved so much in keeping the flagging spirits of the soldiers buoyant with his dry humour when the black cloak of depression was lingering so close to everyone.

Dan looked down at the big man and spoke to him, "Jesus Fish, what have you done?"

He knew that what he said was utterly pointless, but he was unable to help himself. Hardened warrior that he was, he knew that men like Fisher were few and far between. Even in death, Fisher appeared to be smiling. Dan shook himself back to reality. "Jock, get me through to base. We need to report this."

Jacko received the sad news and immediately put together a patrol to bring back the four dead bodies. He went to the stables and arranged for Mick to harness up the old coach, which seemed to be the most appropriate form of transport under the circumstances. He selected four Leafs to run as escort, just in case another ambush was on the cards. Later that afternoon, the sad procession returned through the High wrought iron gates of Combemere. The tiny cemetery at the back of the tennis courts now had five more comrades to keep Flint, and Trooper Richard Foley, company.

David S. Jones

Chapter 30

Pindar

Armageddon + 455 days

The next mission was far more complicated. The first obstacle was the distance to London from Windsor. This would have been considered a very minor journey in the past, but now it was crucial and required planning. If the attack unit were to march there, it would have necessitated logistical planning, as the soldiers would have needed to stay there for days. Now, with the Leaf Attack Vehicles, they had fast and highly manoeuvrable transport, although their carrying capacity was restricted and their range was limited. They could only get into central London and back to Windsor with a full battery charge. A fully charged Leaf, loaded with four men, and averaging approximately forty-five miles per hour, could cover over one hundred miles, but even so, there wasn't time for much more than a return journey. What had previously been a modern family saloon was now suddenly transformed into a military attack vehicle. In addition, there was a heavy, Sampson Armoured Vehicle, added to this attack force. This was fuelled by the limited homemade diesel. Previously, two trial trips were made into central London by a troop of four Jackals whose instruction was to clear the roads which had been blocked by either abandoned vehicles or vehicles that had been used as barricades. It necessitated these runs just to clear the path. There was less danger now of encountering the prowling gangs as nothing was moving on any road throughout Britain. The gangs had abandoned their pattern of attacking the fleeing citizens and moved back into the towns. On the second excursion, the armoured troop pushed on as far as Horse Guards Parade, which was the centre of operations.

Dan Buckland walked along the central road which ran through the beleaguered barracks. As he approached the main gates there was noticeable activity of men and vehicles; to his left, stood the guardroom and armoury. It was 07:55 hours, which meant that he was five minutes early. A mantra that he had learned at the beginning of his army career from an old sweat was that a good soldier was always five minutes early for a parade. This was something that he had doggedly adhered to. Parked in front of the guardroom stood, five, newly converted, Nissan Leaf Attack vehicles. He stopped to look at the unusual vehicles that were to be his transport for the day. He pushed his fingers through his thick wavy black hair and scratched the back of his head.

"Bloody Morris dancing, not soldiering," he growled to nobody in particular.

Eight o'clock in the morning was not a normal time to commence a military mission, but now the rule book was being re-written and Dan had to accept that. Dawn attack, element of surprise, and attack at sparrow fart, were largely irrelevant to the mission that they had been assigned.

By eight, the other members of the team had all assembled. Dan addressed his troops. "OK lads, our task today is to drive into London and arrive at Horse Guards Parade for eleven hundred hours. This should take about an hour, so we have plenty of time to sort out our gear. Draw any weapons from the armoury that you have a preference to and a suitable amount of ammo. The reason for this operation is to pick up and bring back the Silver Stick and two other senior officers. There will be one car with driver to carry the brass and the other four cars will provide escort. The car with the brass will have a driver and top gunner. The support vehicles will each have a driver, a gunner and two passengers. If we don't meet any undesirables, I estimate that we will be back here in Combemere by sixteen hundred hours."

Jock Kelly set to work organising the radio communications. He issued call signs and designated one car to carry the heavier radio sets which would keep them in contact with the radio wing at Combemere.

With the advent of the new, limited, electricity supply, courtesy of the photovoltaic panels, the re-chargeable batteries for the personnel radios was now an advantage which had been lost but was now recovered and deemed very useful.

Synchronising watches was something that had altered slightly since the end of the 'ICE' age. Watches that had batteries were more or less redundant as they were useless as soon as the battery ran out; simple wind up was now the preferred choice. There were so many anomalies that had to be considered since electricity had ceased To be available. Time keeping was one of these. A time check was sent from London to all outposts every day at 09:00 hours, and 19:00 hours.

At 10:00 hours, the barrack gates were swung open and the peculiar convoy of five, Leaf Attack Vehicles, and a Samson Armoured Vehicle, turned out onto St. Leonard's Road, not with the usual engine roar that the soldiers were accustomed to, but a barely perceivable whine and whirr from the electric motors.

The journey into London was uneventful. The occupants of the vehicles had become accustomed to witnessing so much of the devastation that was the aftermath of the end of the ice age, but seeing an iconic building such as Harrods completely burned out, leaving nothing more than a shell, was striking in its brutality and somehow emphasised the futility of what had taken place. Many other shops in the road were burned to the ground, giving the appearance of the aftermath of a WW2 Luftwaffe bombing raid, but the cruel fact was that this devastation had been perpetrated by British citizens in their own homeland.

Dan's radio crackled into life. *"Alpha Three Zero, this is Alpha Three Four. STOP-STOP-STOP! Obstruction ahead!"*

"Alpha, Three Zero. Roger, out

Approximately two hundred metres ahead, several vehicles were blocking the road. *"Hello Alpha three-four, this is Alpha Three-Zero, I am coming to your location on foot now, out."*

Dan got out of his Leaf and walked up to the Samson and spoke with the vehicle commander, who enquired, "How do you want this handled, Dan?" A new road block had been set up in the time since the last patrol had cleared the area. Vehicles now blocked the road and the high buildings that remained gave snipers a good vantage point.

"Just blow through," Dan replied. "Roger that. We're on it." No sooner had the words left the driver's lips when incoming rounds ricocheted from the armoured vehicle. Dan ducked down behind the Samson and took stock of the situation. It looked like two shooters firing from the offices above the shops. The Sampson's gunner returned fire. Its guns were of a heavier calibre than those used by the attackers. If they had been trained snipers, Dan would have been killed immediately, but he was in luck that day. He waved the Leafs forward and they laid down additional fire. Their top guns proving to be far more accurate than Dan and Jacko had expected due to the heavy roll cage structure that the REME had installed. Dan climbed back into his Leaf and gave the order to cease fire – incoming fire having abated. The attackers had fled, or were more likely dead, such had been the heavy gunfire from the street. Dan gave the order for the street clearing operation to continue. The bulldozer's blade was lowered on the Sampson. The engine roared and the heavy vehicle impacted the obstructions, pushing them aside, up onto the pavement. With a sound of grinding metal, breaking glass and roaring of the Sampson's big engine, the road was soon cleared. Consideration for pedestrians was not a concern; this high society shopping street was not open for business.

The troop drove on through the Wellington Arch at Hyde Park Corner, down

Constitution Hill along Green Park. When they reached the Victoria Memorial, they did a circuit around the golden statue, known to the Cavalry as the Wedding Cake, taking a good look at Buck House, which appeared miraculously to be intact. The Mall was a mess, but no more than all of the other roads. Dan considered checking out St. James Palace, but time was running out and it wasn't his prime mission. Finally, they turned onto Horse Guards Parade. Half of the soldiers in the group had spent some of their Cavalry service with the mounted side of the regiment and knew the location well. As they drove up the central roadway, the bell in the clock tower rang to announce eleven o'clock.

"Bloody good timing," Dan exclaimed to the other occupants in the car. "Just in time for the Guard change." He couldn't help but wonder who had been winding up the centuries old clock. The eleven o'clock guard change had for many years been one of the major tourist attractions in London. It was the responsibility of the oncoming Guard Commander to get the new Guard there at exactly eleven as the clock struck the hour. There were no tourists this day.

Dan had previously given orders to spread the cars out and not park them together when they arrived, facing outwards, backs to the building, making any attack more difficult. The drivers and gunners stayed in the cars whilst the remaining soldiers took up defensive positions. Dan walked over to the locked gate and waited.

Three minutes later, the sound of the gates being unlocked and swung open was heard and two plain clothed policemen took Dan inside. The unlikely troop of attack vehicles were driven into the inner quadrangle and parked up. Two soldiers were set as guards and the rest of the men went into the accommodation that some knew well.

"Make yourselves comfortable lads; I don't think that this will take too long." And with that, Dan was escorted off into the inner bowels of the Citadel to meet the Silver Stick.

One of the two policemen stayed with the soldiers whilst the other escorted Dan along a labyrinth of passages and corridors, down several sets of stairs. He estimated that he must have walked about two to three hundred metres and guessed that he could be in the vicinity of the Citadel or somewhere under Whitehall, which meant he was about to enter Pindar. He had heard much about the unique building, but only rumours. The final part of the journey was in a lift, which he estimated had descended about three floors. Suddenly, the realisation hit Dan like a ton of bricks. There was electric lighting and of course the lift was driven by an electric motor. The armoured doors of the lift opened onto a corridor where an armed guard sat at a desk. He nodded to the policeman accompanying Dan and smiled. They walked through a door and into a large well lit room.

For a minute, Dan was stunned. The room was populated with about three dozen people. Many were women dressed in the uniforms of Navy Officers.

The scene was reminiscent of a film from WW2 and Churchill's war rooms, but this place was high tech. There were more than fifty TV screens along one wall, most of which were blank. Dan surmised that although Pindar had power, the outlying surveillance cameras didn't. He stood for some time totally in awe of the scene before him. There was a strong humming sound which was produced by the air conditioning, banks of computers and other electrical equipment. The lack of windows added significantly to the atmosphere. A second buzz, which added to the overall sight and sounds of this astounding room, was the murmur generated by the hectic bustle of interactive activity of those present. Several of the people turned to look at the newcomer in the room, they all nodded acknowledgement of his presence and smiled. Dan had the feeling that they knew who he was.

A tall, elegant man stood up from a desk, walked over and introduced himself.

"Good morning Regimental Corporal Major, I'm William Brand. I am what used to be quaintly called, The Silver Stick. Welcome to Pindar."

The distinguished officer wore army fatigues with no rank markings. "I'm sure that you must have plenty of questions, so please, come with me, and we can discuss them over a coffee."

He led Dan to a side room that was comfortable, but showing signs of much use. It was all a little surreal for Dan's taste, but the smell of the coffee seduced him immediately and he sat down to enjoy the first coffee he had tasted in months.

"OK, Colonel, first question. Where are you getting the electricity from?" Dan had always been a forthright character and rank didn't faze him.

Colonel Brand gave a detailed answer. "Below the streets here in London there are several underground rivers and streams. Some that used to run on the surface, but such was the development of the areas, that they were diverted and now run through tunnels. This has been going on for centuries, hence the name Conduit Street and of course Fleet Street. In 1994, when the Pindar project was completed, the engineers took the opportunity to harness this power and install several hydroelectric turbine generators, which have more than enough capacity to supply the electricity, even for this power hungry establishment, and are not susceptible to bombing or espionage."

Dan was visibly impressed and went on to ask more questions.

The interview was interrupted by a third man entering the room. Dan recognised him immediately as the Prime Minister, Thomas Matheson. He shook Dan's hand vigorously, asked him to sit down and helped himself to a coffee before he started his conversation. The man standing before him was no stranger, although he had never actually met him. Thomas Matheson was the country's youngest PM since Pitt and was affectionately called by the media, 'Matheson the Younger', but the man who had just shaken Dan's hand was a much altered version from the one often so previously seen on television. Gone was the thick dark hair which had now thinned and prematurely turned grey. The youthful skin was sallow and pale, and what had previously been an athletic physique was now best described as skinny. A lifestyle, the pressures of which Dan could only assume, and an existence lived almost entirely below ground would have that effect. Given all of these external alterations to this prominent man's features, his handshake was strong and there was a discernible sparkle in his vivid blue eyes.

Dan was a non-political person, but was well aware that Matheson was an Old Etonian, a staunch conservative, whose ideas were known to be right of centre. He had heard that given the severity of the prevailing mayhem, party politics was something that had been put aside, which pleased him immensely.

"Regimental Corporal Major, the success of the way that Combemere has dealt with this terrible tragedy has been an example to all of us.
What we asked of you was beyond what could be reasonably expected of anyone, but you all bit the proverbial bullet, and soldiered on, albeit in your own way."

Dan smiled at the thought of this particular Combemere adaptation to the rules. The Prime Minister went on, "Dan..., may I call you Dan?"

Dan was happy to reply, "Of course, Prime Minister."

The P.M. continued, "The directive that we gave you which was to lock yourselves in, abandon your families and ostensibly, wait until this catastrophe had abated was really more than any man should ask of another. This same directive was given to all of the country's military installations. I have to tell you that only fifty percent of them were able to carry out the plan. This was, in fact, a higher result than we could reasonably have expected. Combemere has fared better than most, part of the reason for this is the location and size of the barracks, but in no small part it is due to the leadership that Colonel Jackson and you have displayed, showing exceptional fortitude. Dan, you have done a truly magnificent job in holding together the frail thread of humanity in truly desperate conditions. I am proud to have shaken your hand."

Dan shuffled his feet a little and hoped that the conversation would move on. He was not a man who was comfortable with or enjoyed flattery. Fortunately, the conversation did rapidly move forward.

The coffee was drunk, and Dan was given a tour of the Pindar installation. "OK, Regimental Corporal Major, almost time for me to go to Windsor in your new mode of transport. I have heard a lot about them and I'm looking forward to the ride," said the Silver Stick. "I have some loose ends to tidy up here so I'll meet you in the quadrangle at fifteen hundred hours. I will get some food sent up to you and your men. The cooks here can work wonders with powdered egg, milk and potatoes."

Colonel William Brand was definitely Old School; he was not going to give up so easily on rank. *"Hope that you like Morris Dancing,"* Dan thought to himself.

The return journey to Windsor went without a hitch. The three officers seemed deeply shocked and moved by what they were now witnessing for the first time. Having been locked inside Pindar since the initiation of this tragic chain of events they had obviously heard of the turmoil that had taken place, but now, witnessing the traumatic devastation for themselves with their own eyes, they were not prepared for the magnitude of the scenes that passed by the windows of their Leaf. They were visibly moved.

Jock Kelly radioed ahead their ETA and as the tiny convoy swept through the barrack gates Jacko accompanied by William and Harry, were there to meet them.

The three visiting officers were first taken on a tour of the now much transformed barracks. Jacko noted that their reaction to what had been done was akin to shock.

They then went into the small conference room which was in the museum building and discussed the plans that William Brand outlined. "The highest priority for the country's future lies here with your teams and the fusion project," he explained. "As soon as the Culham scientists can produce a workable fusion generator and get it into production, then the reintegration program can begin in earnest." He moved on to the next priority. "You are a Cavalry Regiment and you have proved to me today your commitment to manoeuvrability, but the other pressing problem, which has to be dealt with, is that of the warlords and their gangs. They have become a much stronger threat since becoming armed, as you are well aware. In Victoria Barracks here in Windsor, as of course, you know, there is a battalion of Irish Guards. They have fared less well and their numbers are slightly depleted, but my mission here is to assess them and move eighty percent of their number into the Castle. There they can re-establish security on the Royal Farm and from that base, move out to combat and eliminate the dangerous gangs. This will be largely an infantry operation; your remit will be to give support."

Over the next days, the three visiting officers were busy. They spent time at Combemere, Victoria barracks and the castle where the coordinated plan for the next phase in the recovery was put in place. It was late afternoon on their last day in Windsor. Brand and his two associates were in Jacko's office and Dan was in attendance. The purpose of the meeting was to summarise the visit and prepare for the next phase.

Dan had contemplated donating the half bottle of whisky he had left for a farewell drink but thought better of it. The precious liquid would be better appreciated by Jacko and himself in private.

Brand was a slightly pompous individual, but Dan was beginning to discover a more agreeable side to his nature.

William Brand opened the conversation in a surprisingly friendly manner. "There is an element that has been high priority on the agenda of the scientists in Pindar who are monitoring global events. Something that has been an enormous worry to them is the heavily toxic clouds

Of nuclear fallout from firstly the proliferation of strike and counter strike when jittery nuclear states fired off their rockets at what they thought were attacking enemy nations. The second wave of nuclear contaminated clouds came from the meltdown of nuclear waste silos.

These poisonous clouds have been blowing around the planet randomly, taken to where the predominant winds carried them. Humanity has been involved in a no option game of Russian roulette. Millions have been condemned to a horrific, slow, painful death. The figures cannot be verified, but it must be in the tens of millions. It has been impossible to calculate where these clouds would go, but by the grace of god, they did not come to the British Isles. We have been spared that horror and it has been estimated that the toxicity of the clouds will now have mostly dissipated."

He moved on to more agreeable subjects. "A crucial aspect of our visit to Combemere has been the inspection of the work being undertaken in the gymnasium, plus to obtain a person to person update from Professor James and his colleagues. During this conversation it has become evident that the capacity of the gym is inadequate. The Culham team had progressed as far as they could, give their limited resources."

Brand gave the dilemma some thought. "Professor, what is your most significant problem?"

There was no hesitation in his reply. "Even with the photovoltaic panels, the electrical supply is woefully inadequate."

Brand then stated something that had obviously been discussed previously in London. "We have a good electrical supply at Pindar. Do you think that it might be a good idea to move you there?"

"What else do you have at Pindar that might be useful?" the Professor inquired.

"There is a large group of academics working in the governments Central Think Tank. The computers in the installation are powerful. Pindar has plenty of accommodation and an adequate stock of food."

There was no need to ask any further questions. "I think that this would be a good idea, Mr. Brand. And this move would have the advantage of relieving some of the pressure on Combemere."

The decision was agreed. A detailed plan was devised to transport the scientists, their families and their equipment to Pindar at a future date.

Bland then turned his attention to Jacko and Dan. "There can be no denying that the work that you two have achieved here as natural leaders is quite remarkable."

The Colonel was obviously impressed by the transformation that had taken place in Combemere. His two associates added their agreement. "We have been thinking about the significant contribution which has been made by David Galston. Can we perhaps get him in to have a chat?"

Jacko and Dan shot a sideways glance at each other smiling and nodding in agreement.

"Rogers!" The ever-attentive CO's faithful clerk was through the door in a flash. Truth be known, he was more than likely ear wigging the conversation from the privileged location of his desk, which he considered the perk that went with the job.

Life had improved considerably for the clerk after the installation of photovoltaic panels. The supply was limited and the power generated was distributed through a priority system.

Highest on the priority list was the gymnasium and the computers, which together with the equipment to develop the fusion engine, was considered to be the most important task in the barracks. Second, was the radio wing, where communications, were crucial. Powering the Leafs took its place on the priority list, but these three items consumed every watt of electricity generated, leaving the rest of the barracks to continue to be minus electricity. The advantage to Rogers was that he was now able to go to the radio wing and print out orders where he had previously been required to write them out laboriously in longhand.

"Rogers. Could you please locate, David Galston, and ask him to come directly here?"

Rogers considered the assembled company and answered appropriately, in a manner that he felt suitable under the circumstances: "Yes, Colonel."

The senior men continued with their conversation for a further ten minutes until a knock at the door interrupted them. "David Galston, Colonel." Rogers opened the door and the young man entered the room.

"Thank you, Rogers. Please, take a seat, David." Jacko did his best to make the young man feel comfortable in the company of the assembled brass. He introduced the three guests.

Brand opened the conversation. "David, Colonel Jackson and RCM Buckland have related glowing accounts of your innovative contributions to the development of this beleaguered community. You are to be congratulated for your lateral thinking." He allowed a brief moment to consider his next words. "David, we would like you to return to London with us. We are of the combined opinion that your straightforward approach to problem solving would be of great advantage to the Central Think Tank."

David Galston was visibly taken aback, but acquitted himself admirably. "I..., I am sincerely grateful for your offer, but I must decline."

The three official guests in the room looked slightly annoyed, unused to being rejected by someone so much lower in the official ranking system. Jacko and Dan could not hide a cynical smile.

"I feel that my loyalties are here in Windsor with the men and women with who I have experienced so much. We are like a large family and in the absence of our own families that has become something very special."

Jacko broke the pregnant pause which followed. "David, your sentiments are without doubt admirable, but I would like to advise you as a friend and not as your Commanding Officer that your clear, no nonsense thinking is unusually positive and rare. I think that you would be a good addition to the London group of academics who probably need grounding on occasions by a logical thinker."

David's eyes turned towards Dan Buckland, who he admired enormously. Dan made no hesitation in giving his opinion, "Go, David, they need you, and it will advance you in the new society, which you are helping to create."

David looked perplexed as Dan continued, "Remember that when you travel by Leaf, from Windsor to central London, it's only a forty five minute journey. Now, Leafs on the line are perfectly acceptable."

The tension was broken. David agreed to go to London.

The Cavalry had completed their task of escorting Brand and his associates around Windsor. They completed their business and the next day, Dan and his men, made the return journey to Horse Guards Parade. They deposited the Colonel at the gates, having successfully completed their mission.

A plan was devised to expedite the task that NAPIG had assigned to the combined personnel of Combemere and Victoria barracks. The first phase of their mission was to eliminate the looter gang local to Windsor. This was accomplished on foot and took the form of basic urban warfare, infantry style attacks. The soldiers at Combemere were, fundamentally, Cavalry, but all were trained in infantry tactics. In this instance, they were utilised mainly as support to the Irish Guards. The looter band had progressed from nothing more than an undisciplined mob to a dangerous guerrilla force. They put up a strong fight, but were soon efficiently dealt with. No casualties were sustained by the soldiers during the fighting.

Jacko called Nick Trevelyan into his office. "Got a little job for you Nick. How do you feel about a round trip to London?" He knew that Nick was showing signs of cabin fever and could do with a mission, no matter how short.

"What do you have in mind?" asked Nick.

"We need to get the Culham team, their families and equipment to Pindar. This will require three trucks and an armed mobile escort. The workshop has learned all that they can about how the Nissan works and have put it back together, which gives us a troop of eight Leafs."

"I'm up for that Jacko. How many cars do you want for the escort?"

"I was thinking that you take all eight, so that as many of our men can become accustomed to these rather different vehicles."

"Roger that Jacko, I'll put that plan together and let you know when it's ready."

"I need to contact Pindar, round up the scientists and their gang to give them time to prepare for the move. Next Tuesday morning would be a good slot," was Jacko's reply.

Early on the next Tuesday, the convoy left Combemere, and the scientists were transported to their new home.

David S. Jones

Chapter 31

Jacko is Chosen

Armageddon + 557 days

A meeting of the Combemere Think Tank was called rather unexpectedly. Jacko was surprised by the gathering; as far as he knew, everything was moving along steadily. He was also startled to see the meeting had been organised to take place in the SNCO's Mess, as the cookhouse had become the usual venue. The SNCO's Mess was packed and it looked as if just about everyone had turned up. Dan Buckland acted as the chairman and several issues were discussed, none of which Jacko thought were of much importance. He was quite content to stand to one side.

Sitting at the front of the gathering was the group of ex-Royals, and in their centre was Elizabeth Windsor. Dan Buckland rounded up the outstanding matters and then announced that Elizabeth would like to address the assembled group. She walked to the front and began her address.

"Ladies and gentlemen, I don't know how many of you have been keeping diaries, or even taking stock of the days, weeks and months that have passed, since we all came to be here." She paused and turned to face Jacko, "John, to say that this has been a trying time would be a massive understatement."

Jacko was caught off guard now that the conversation was aimed at him; he had not expected to become involved in any of this day's discussions.

Elizabeth repositioned herself to face the audience. "John, please come and stand next to me."

Jacko, somewhat apprehensively, walked across to stand next to the woman who for so many years had been the Head of State and the Commander In Chief of the Armed Forces. He felt rather uncomfortable as at over six feet in height he towered over the diminutive woman.

"John, your leadership throughout this episode has been exemplary. We are all supremely grateful for your strength, determination and fortitude in setting a high standard that has throughout sustained all of us in this dreadful time."

All the assembled people in the room echoed Elizabeth's words. There was a long period of clapping and cheering. Jacko was astounded by the reaction.

"John, not too long ago, I would have been very happy to bestow a royal recognition upon you; at the very least a knighthood would have suited your achievements. But alas, those times have passed and I am no longer able to do this. But, I think that what I have been asked to award you with is, under the circumstances, something far more suited to the times in which we now find ourselves."

There was a hush throughout the cookhouse.

"John, your friends and colleagues have asked me to award you with something which I believe is far more meaningful than a title. You are to be the first to leave the barracks and ride out to find your family."

Again the cookhouse erupted into cheering and clapping. Jacko was a man not accustomed to being caught off guard, but this came as a tremendous shock.

And so the scene was set for the next chapter in this life-changing adventure. Jacko was certainly deserving of the privilege of being first to go out and look for his family, but the significance of the moment had implications far beyond just Jacko. It heralded the beginning of a new phase, when revitalization of society could begin and the horrors of the past months, which could never be forgotten, would start to fade with time.

It was decided that in groups, all of the members in the camp could be allowed to go out and look for their families. It was also decided that the families could be returned and re-housed locally. This looked wonderful on the surface, but each of the soldiers knew in their hearts that what they might discover when they looked for their families, might not be such a happy event.

Chapter 32

Jacko Rides Out

Armageddon + 560 days

As the leader of the beleaguered regiment, clustered within the confines of the transformed barracks in Windsor, Jacko's life had been frenetic. All looked to him for leadership. Now the people that he had led through these challenging times had demonstrated their appreciation and bestowed the honour of allowing him to ride out to look for his family. He was to be the first, and so the event, although it was singularly relevant to Jacko, was also significant to all of the camp population who found themselves taking shelter within the walls of the army camp. This was initially a happy event, but it was also tinged with foreboding and anxiety. None of the camp inhabitants knew for certain how their loved ones had fared during the last horrific year and a half. Even the Royals had received only sparse news, of which amounted to nothing more than scraps of information, gleaned from the few intelligence locations that had radio transmitting ability. All were increasingly worried about the safety of their families.

The night before leaving, Jacko prepared for the trip. He went down to the stables, and, as he did most days, checked on Rascal. Mick was there and they discussed the horses.

"As you know Mick, I'll be taking Rascal out tomorrow. How does he look to you?"

"He's fine, Boss, and more than up to the trip. The outing will do him good."

"Yes, I don't have any doubts that he will get me to the New Forest in good form. He has never let me down"

210

Mick continued with his inspection of the stables, leaving Jacko to finalise checking the saddle and other equipment that he would need. In company with many of the men within the confinement at Combermere, Jacko had from convenience grown a beard. Water was now not such a worry as it had initially been, due to the installation of two wells, but it still required to be carried from a well to the location where it was to be used. There were many variations on the theme of showers. Some were elaborate affairs, but the reality was that a suspended bucket with a series of holes in the bottom was the preferred design; a hot water shower had not yet been achieved. Jacko went to the closest well and carried two buckets of water back to his accommodation. He showered and took a razor to his beard. Feeling much better for being clean-shaven, he checked his weapons and took a final tour of the camp before turning in for the night. Tomorrow was to be a significant occasion.

At 06.00 hours, on a sunny day, with clear blue skies and a sharp chill in the air Jacko saddled up Rascal. His faithful old comrade knew that something exciting was about to happen. As Jacko brushed him down, picked out his hoofs and threw the saddle blanket over his sturdy back, Rascal turned his head to watch his friend with interest. The bond between horse and rider can be strong and this was certainly the case between Rascal and Jacko. A final check and Jacko mounted. He walked through the barracks to the front gate. He was surprised to see that so many had turned out to wish him good luck. There was a strong significance to this event that resonated throughout the camp. He was to be the first, but the event heralded hope for the future. The tall gates swung open, Jacko and Rascal walked through, not to cheering and the clapping of hands, but just softly spoken words of encouragement and wishes of good luck – it was the British way.

Jacko had planned the journey in detail. He knew that on average, a strong, fit horse could cover twenty to twenty five miles in a day. Pushing it, the horse could comfortably go thirty miles with no ill effects. Rascal was a strong, reliable mount at the peak of fitness and Jacko calculated that the journey to the New Forest would take two or perhaps three days. All of this depended on what he might encounter en route. With these factors in mind, Jacko had prepared for at least two nights sleeping out. He also armed himself with an L85A2 and a sidearm. He used the saddlebags that had been made for the trip to Culham Centre and for good measure he had his sword slung from the front of his saddle. He had maps, even though he knew the route thoroughly, but he might need to detour if something unforeseen should happen.

Now alone, with only his horse for company, Jacko had plenty of time to reflect on the past eighteen months. There was now less need to be vigilant as most of the marauding gangs had been eradicated and the smaller groups, having heard of the way in which they were dealt with, had dissipated. The word had passed quickly. There was to be no quarter given to those who were acting as anarchists, most of whom were known. With no resources to imprison the offenders, the only alternative left to them was to fight to the death. This was obviously very brutal justice, but it had the effect of deterring those who were considering the anarchical option. These were exceptional times and called for radical solutions.

Those individuals who had managed to survive were concentrating on exactly that – staying alive. All the same, Jacko was not taking any chances, he was armed as there was always the possibility he could be attacked. The distance, as the crow flies, from Combemere to the New Forest, was about fifty-five miles. This was not a problem for Jacko; his primary concern was that he could find somewhere safe where he could keep an eye on Rascal when it came to the time for them to stop for the night.

Anticipating what he might find when he reached his father-in-law's property, Jacko's mind drifted back over the past eighteen months. Something that was starkly apparent was the evidence that without the intervention of humans, nature was rapidly reclaiming its now virtually undisputed territory. This was unmistakably evident everywhere; plants were growing up through the road surfaces and pavements. Trees overhung paths and on roads away from urbanised districts, the air felt cleaner and sweeter, void of centuries of pollution from vehicles and industry. The skies were free of aircraft and vapour trails.

The massive death toll that had ensued after the first months of the disaster had culminated in tens of millions of dead bodies. The stench of rotting flesh had prevailed everywhere within the built up areas, an atmosphere like a thick, heavy, plagued blanket of death. Nature had performed its cleaning up act and the putrid rotting flesh had mostly disappeared, leaving only the dry skeletal remains of m i l l i o n s . The phenomenon that Jacko found most noticeable of all was the silence. Nothing mechanical could be heard, the constant background noise, something that everyone had become conditioned to and had taken for granted, was gone. Listening to the soothing clip clop of Rascal's hooves on the road surface and the calling of birds in the roadside foliage were the only sounds. No traffic noise or mechanical thump of machinery. No roar of aircraft landing and taking off. Without pesticides, nature was rolling back across towns and countryside alike, and wildlife was re-established in abundance, unhindered by the once dominant presence of humans. There was a small glimmer of hope, which reached Jacko's ears as he rode along. The unmistakably, sweet sounds, of the songbirds, busy reclaiming their rightful territory in the English countryside.

John Jackson felt confident that his family would have reached the location in the

New Forest. Sarah was a resilient woman and Dan Buckland's wife was certainly no wilting flower. His chief concern was that they might have been attacked once they had established themselves at the garden centre. If the attackers were strong enough, they could have been overpowered, and it was a possibility that they might not have been able to defend themselves. He had witnessed so much violence and destruction over the past eighteen months and was well aware to what level of depravity some people could descend when hunger was their driving force.

As before, Jacko decided that the preferable route was predominately on the motorways. He rode through Windsor, along the by-pass, over the Thames and onto the M4. From the high vantage of the river bridge, he could see that there were people, albeit very few, tending small plots of land in the rich soil of the river valley. This was encouraging. He had for some weeks been sending out small groups from the barracks to meet up with just this type of survivor. They were assigned the task of encouraging them and to give them hope for a future. Oddly, this was not a new endeavour for British forces, as the 'Hearts and Minds' policy had previously been adopted in many countries. It was just so extraordinary that this policy was being utilised in middle England. The people in the fields watched Jacko cautiously. They knew that even on horseback, given his location on the bridge, he couldn't get to them before they had time to scatter. So paranoid was their fear of anyone outside of their trusted circles, such had been the agony inflicted upon them by the roving savage gangs. Jacko waved and shouted hello in as friendly a manner as he could.

The initial reaction was cautious, but slowly the survivors responded. Jacko rode on feeling that there was indeed hope for the future.

He continued on the M4, westwards, with the weak summer sun in his eyes. He was enjoying the newfound freedom of leaving the confines of the barracks behind and every mile that passed, he felt as if he were being cleansed of the web of misery that had prevailed like a heavy, dark cloak of doom. As on his previous journey into Oxfordshire, it was noticeable that there were many locations in the countryside where the aftermath of the devastation from the apocalypse, had not spread its sad, destructive, shadow. On occasions, alone in the English landscape, it felt that the previous eighteen months might be nothing more than some terrible nightmare of all nightmares. Rascal too was enjoining the outing; he was frisky and nodded his head, striding out purposefully.

At midday, Jacko veered off from the motorway, found a quiet location and stopped. He loosened Rascal's saddle straps, took off his bridle, hung the reins over his neck and tied him to a sturdy gatepost.

He discovered some clean, clear water and filled the collapsible bucket that Geoff, the saddler, had made for his last trip and Rascal greedily drank two full buckets. This was not to be an opportunity missed when he could play his usual game of getting Jacko wet in the process. The countryside was now horse heaven. The lush grass was everywhere, no gardener had been at work for eighteen months, no lawns had been mowed, and no hedges had been trimmed. Jacko allowed Rascal to graze while he set about making his own lunch. He was aware that too much fresh green feed at one time could be dangerous when a horse had been on dry foods.

"OK buddy, you have had enough. We don't have the farrier and the vet here to sort you out if you get a guppy stomach."

Jacko tidied up his equipment, packed it away and prepared Rascal for the second half of the day. They set off deeper into Surrey and made good time. As the sun was beginning to set to their front, Jacko looked for a suitable place to spend the night.

He came off of the main roads and turned onto country lanes. He rode for five minutes down a narrow lane that was a tunnel of trees and shrubs, allowing only dappled sunlight to penetrate the foliage. The tunnel ended and he rode out onto an open pasture that had previously been a riding school. Jacko investigated the small buildings. The stable doors were all swinging open; there were no horses to be seen. There was also no indication that any people had been there for some time; the place was totally abandoned. He rode around the perimeter, checking for signs of life, but the small complex had no accommodation for people, just stables and a yard. "Looks like a good place to spend the night."

He smiled at the realisation that he was talking more and more to his horse on this trip. Rascal was fed, watered and groomed. When he was comfortably bedded down in a loose box, Jacko fixed himself some food from the field rations. He found a comfortable place to sleep in the stall next to Rascal. He slept well.

The next day, Jacko, set off. He had made good time and calculated that it should be an easy trip barring the unforeseen. By the evening he was very close to his destination. The feelings which abounded in his head were a mixture; a combination of anguish and fear. Anticipation, that given the time that had passed, would his family have forgiven him for leaving them in their hour of need? Would they still be as angry as they were when he made his last fleeting visit in the dead of night? The visit, at which he told them, an option, that amounted to no more than, "you must fend for yourselves." Dread that they might not have even reached the New Forest, given the dangerously chaotic state that persisted at that time. And even if they had reached Sarah's parents' home, would they have been able to defend the place against who knows what threat?

With extreme trepidation he turned the final corner in the heavily wooded forest and faced the front of the garden centre that was the family business belonging to his in-laws. It was immediately obvious that the once brightly decorated façade to the building behind the car park was not open for business. This was usually ablaze with plants of every variety, a kaleidoscope of colour, particularly in spring when the garden centre business was at its peak. Now there wasn't a plant to be seen. All of the windows were boarded up and large tree trunks had been dragged across the exit and entrance to the car park. Jacko reigned in Rascal and they stood hidden by the trees about a hundred metres away from the building. He waited, not knowing what to expect; his anticipation of what he might discover had become clouded by nervousness, due to the many negative scenarios running through his tormented mind. They stood for several minutes before he observed movement to the side of the building.

Jacko could see a young woman; it was his eldest daughter Miranda. His heart was racing. Warrior that he was, this was too much even for him. She was alive, but what about the others?

He noticed that she was carrying something. As his eyes focused in the fading evening light, he could see that it was a baby. Miranda was carrying a baby! So many thoughts flashed through his mind. The one that seemed to have the most validity was the possibility that his eldest daughter and Dan's eldest son who were about the same age and considering the close proximity and the loneliness of their situation, it made sense that they might have become an item and now there was a child. Many more thoughts swam around in his head. Paramount of those was that he was now a grandfather and that Dan and he shared a grandchild.

"There are many things worse in this crazy world," he found himself explaining to Rascal.

He decided to dismount and walk forward across the gravel car park, leading Rascal. He could hear a lot of movement from inside the building.

"Stop right there!"

A tall, lean young man emerged from the corner of the building holding a twelve bore shotgun. "There's nothing here for you, just keep going."

Jacko noticed that the young man had a faint Scottish accent. "Kit, it's me, John Jackson."

Obviously the people in the house had been listening to the confrontation that was taking place in the car park, all ready to defend their position. Screams suddenly erupted from inside, a door burst open and Sarah, his three daughters, Julie Buckland and her other son Rory came running out. They surrounded Jacko, their eagerness to be near to him overwhelming. All of Jacko's darkest premonitions were expelled from his mind in an instant. They were all alive. It took some time before everyone was calm and they were able to actually talk. Rascal was taken into the enclosed garden and the two Buckland boys saw to his needs. Finally, calm was restored and Sarah's mother made tea from a stash of tea bags that she had been hoarding for such an occasion. There were so many questions to be answered, but finally, the baby decided to interrupt the proceedings in the way that babies do. Miranda had been holding the child throughout the commotion. Jacko was now able to have his first look at the infant. He could see that it was a healthy looking boy.

"What is he called?" Jacko asked the question cautiously as this was undoubtedly a delicate moment.

"His name is John," Miranda offered with pride. All eyes were focused intently on Jacko. This was to be a once in a lifetime reaction and not to be missed. "He is your son!" smiled Julie Buckland.

Sarah looked at her husband and nodded confirmation. "Yes, John, he is your son."

She took the infant from her daughter and walked to her husband. "My son but…."

"Think about the night you came to tell us how to survive." She stood with her husband and son. There were tears and even John allowed himself to become emotional.

For a brief moment in time everything seemed idyllic for John Jackson. His family were safe and their future seemed assured. A bonus that he could never have contemplated – a son – was a gift beyond anything that he could ever have wished for. From the crucible of hell that had previously prevailed and against astonishing odds, they had survived. Other thoughts drifted through his mind. How great it would be to pass on the good news to Dan Buckland that his family were not only doing well, but thriving. His wife was well and healthy; his sons were growing into fine young men. There was something else that would close a difficult chapter, which had tormented him over the past months. Now Sophie could move on and hopefully find a partner to live the rest of her life with. She deserved that. There were many good men in the camp. It was a sad but an undeniable fact that few would have fared as well as Jacko when their time came and they would be able to ride out and search for their families. In time, when the pain that was inevitable had receded, Sophie would have her choice of many men. These were thoughts tinged with sadness, but all else that he had discovered hidden in the New Forest was positive beyond any wish that he could have dreamt of. And yet in his heart there was deep sorrow, for he knew that he would soon have to throw the saddle onto Rascals sturdy back and for the second time abandon his beloved family and head back to Windsor, returning to the heavy responsibilities that awaited him there.

The next few precious days spent with his family would be dear to him. They had all endured a great deal, but there was much more to come. What would the future hold in store for them all?

216

Later in the evening John and Sarah wandered out into the garden alone. They looked up at the magnificent sky that was studded with millions of stars. "Perhaps the Pagans knew a little more than we give them credit for," John reflected. He put his arm around Sarah's shoulder and together they looked up and there rising above the tops of the forest trees was the bright silver moon. There was no golden halo.

# # #

Glossary

ATC = Air traffic control. APU = Auxiliary power unit. Awol = Absent without leave.

Corporal of the horse = Household Cavalry rank for Sergeant. Corporal Major = Warrant Officer.

Bergen = Rucksack.

Boss = Term of endearment and respect for a senior.

Bikini Black Alpha to condition Amber and red = Military states of readiness.

Bunk = Bedroom/apartment/living accommodation. Buck House = Buckingham Palace.

"Contact" = made contact with the enemy.

Copper horse. = A huge bronze statue of George III situated at the highest point of the Long Walk Circa 1829.

ETA = Estimated time of arrival.

Elizabeth Windsor = Family name changed 18th of July 1917 Flame out = Complete engine shut down.

Loose box = Stable for one horse. IED = Improvised explosive device. Intel = Intelligence.

RCM = Regimental Corporal Major. By decree of Queen Victoria there are no sergeants (French for servant) in the Household Cavalry. Glen Fiddich. = High quality Scotch whisky.

Mess = Military social location. Nags = Horses.

NCO = Non commissioned officer.

New Zealand rug = Warm rug for covering horses when they have been clipped out.

No-duff = Radio message this is serious and has to be acknowledged. OC = Officer Commanding.

Old sweat = Long serving soldier. PTI = Physical Training Instructor.

Recce = Reconnoitre
Signaller = Trained in radio communications. Sneaky-beaky = Hidden location.
Spotting = Assisting a sniper. Sparrow fart. = Sunrise.
Stag = Period of guard duty.
Silver Stick = The senior cavalry officer next to the Monarch is Gold Stick in waiting. In his absence the second senior officer takes over, he is the Silver Stick.
SNCO's Mess = Senior non-commissioned officers. SA80 = Regulation infantry rifle.
2i/c = Second in command.
The Long walk = The Long Walk runs south from Windsor Castle to the Copper Horse statue of King George III atop Snow Hill It is 2.65 miles (4.26 km)
The Great Park = Windsor Great Park covers 4,800 acres, parts of which are open to the public. Its present area was determined in the 1360s and was popular with Saxon kings as a hunting forest.
Manège = Outside riding school.
Q.M. = Quartermaster.
Quarters = Living accommodation.

Interesting information

The first four stroke internal combustion engine was patented in 1885. German mechanical engineer, Karl Benz designed and built the world's first practical automobile to be powered by an internal-combustion engine. On January 29, 1886, Benz received the first patent (DRP No. 37435) for a gas-fuelled car. It was a three-wheeler; Benz built his first four-wheeled car in 1891. Benz & Cie, the company started by the inventor, became the world's largest manufacturer of automobiles by 1900. Benz was the first inventor to integrate an internal combustion engine with a chassis - designing both together. There were other earlier attempts at creating an engine which worked on the internal combustion principle as far back as 1680 which used gunpowder.

The inventors of the first practical airplane were Orville and Wilbur Wright. On December 17, 1903, the Wright brothers made the first successful experiment in which a machine carrying a man rose by its own power flew naturally and at even speed, and descended without damage. Less than twelve years separates the first motor car from the first aeroplane. Contemplate then the evolution of these two forms of transport. Firstly let us consider the aircraft.

From the early rudimentary configuration of wings, engine, propeller and simple framework to hold these elements together and provide a hazardous location for the pilot, mankind has developed these basic principles to the extraordinary aircraft that we are now used to seeing and using in everyday life. At the time of writing this it is 111 years. The most significant advancement was the jet engine designed and built by
Sir Frank Whittle an English aviation engineer and pilot, he received his first patent on turbojet propulsion in January 1930.

There have been many innovations in the evolution of wheeled road vehicles. The most advanced adaptation of a wheeled vehicle driven by an ICE engine could arguably be considered to be a Formula One racing car. This is a triumph of technology, but still relies upon the original configuration of piston, valves, con-rods, crankshaft, cam-shaft and fly-wheel.

My question therefore is this. If such astounding advancements and innovations have taken place in the one and a quarter centuries since Benz made his first motor car why, has the internal combustion engine only made limited enhancements? Consider the other fantastic discoveries that have been made and the progress that

220

mankind has achieved during that period. The first English electric vehicle reportedly built in the year 1884.

My theory is that oil is the contributory factor in this enigma. The advanced societies on this planet have been coerced into relying upon wheeled transport which is dependent on oil based fuels. Oil is a dominant influence in the modern world, being the underlying factor for much of the conflict that blights today's civilisations. I find it inconceivable that an alternative method of propulsion has not been developed, given all of the fantastic technological discoveries that have been made in recent years. There have been many propulsion substitutions proposed, but funding of these schemes has been minimal. Electric cars are now slowly beginning to be seen but in nowhere the numbers that will make a significant difference as the major obstacle is storing electricity.

There are other options such as Fusion generators and Hydrogen motors, but they are all still, and have been for years 'in development'. If it were not so financially and politically inconvenient for the people who run this planet, our automotive industry would have consigned the internal combustion engine to the realms of history fifty years ago.

The History of the Automobile

The very first self-powered road vehicles were powered by steam engines and by that definition, Nicolas Joseph Cugnot, of France, built the first automobile in 1769 – recognized by the British Royal Automobile Club and the Automobile Club de France as being the first. So why do so many history books say that the automobile was invented by either Gottlieb Daimler or Karl Benz? It is because both Daimler and Benz invented highly successful and practical gasoline-powered vehicles that ushered in the age of modern automobiles. Daimler and Benz invented cars that looked and worked like the cars we use today. However, it is unfair to say that either man invented 'the' automobile.

History of the Internal Combustion Engine - The Heart of the Automobile

An internal combustion engine is any engine that uses the explosive combustion of fuel to push a piston within a cylinder – the piston's movement turns a crankshaft that then turns the car wheels via a chain or a drive shaft. The different types of fuel commonly used for car combustion engines are gasoline (or petrol), diesel, and kerosene.

A brief outline of the history of the internal combustion engine includes the following highlights:

1680 - Dutch physicist, designed (but never built) an internal combustion engine that was to be fuelled with gunpowder.

1807 - Francois Isaac de Rivaz, of Switzerland, invented an internal combustion engine that used a mixture of hydrogen and oxygen for fuel. Rivaz designed a car for his engine – the first internal combustion powered automobile. However, his was a very unsuccessful design.

1824 - English engineer, Samuel Brown adapted an old Newcomen steam engine to burn gas, and he used it to briefly power a vehicle up Shooter's Hill in London.

1858 - Belgian-born engineer, Jean Joseph Étienne Lenoir, invented and patented (1860) a double-acting, electric spark-ignition internal combustion engine fuelled by coal gas.

In 1863, Lenoir attached an improved engine (using petroleum and a primitive carburettor) to a three-wheeled wagon that managed to complete an historic fifty-mile road trip.

1862 - Alphonse Beau de Rochas, a French civil engineer, patented but did not build a four-stroke engine (French patent #52,593, January 16, 1862).

1864 - Austrian engineer, built a one-cylinder engine with a crude carburettor, and

222

attached his engine to a cart for a rocky 500-foot drive.

Several years later, Marcus designed a vehicle that briefly ran at 10 mph that a few historians have considered as the forerunner of the modern automobile by being the world's first gasoline-powered vehicle.

1873 - George Brayton, an American engineer, developed an unsuccessful two-stroke kerosene engine (it used two external pumping cylinders). However, it was considered the first safe and practical oil engine.

1866 - German engineers, Eugen Langen and Nikolaus August Otto, improved on Lenoir's and de Rochas designs and invented a more efficient gas engine.

1876 - Nikolaus August Otto, invented, and later patented, a successful four-stroke engine, known as the 'Otto cycle'.

1876 - The first successful two-stroke engine was invented by Sir Douglas Clerk.

1883 - French engineer, Edouard Delamare-Debouteville, built a single-cylinder four-stroke engine that ran on stove gas. It is not certain if he did indeed build a car, however, Delamare-Debouteville's designs were very advanced for the time – ahead of both Daimler and Benz in some ways, at least on paper.

1885 - Gottlieb Daimler invented what is often recognized as the prototype of the modern gas engine – with a vertical cylinder, and with gasoline injected through a carburettor (patented in 1887). Daimler first built a two-wheeled vehicle, the 'Reitwagen' (Riding Carriage), with this engine, and a year later, built the world's first four-wheeled motor vehicle.

1886 - On January 29, Karl Benz received the first patent (DRP No. 37435) for a gas-fuelled car.

1889 - Daimler built an improved four-stroke engine with mushroom- shaped valves and two V-slant cylinders.

1890 - Wilhelm Maybach built the first four-cylinder, four-stroke engine.

Engine design and car design were integral activities, almost all of the engine designers mentioned above also designed cars, and a few went on to become major manufacturers of automobiles. All of these inventors, and more, made notable improvements in the evolution of the internal combustion vehicles.

The Importance of Nicolaus Otto
One of the most important landmarks in engine design comes from Nicolaus August Otto, who in 1876, invented an effective gas motor engine. Otto built the first practical four-stroke internal combustion engine called the 'Otto Cycle Engine', and as soon as he had completed his engine, he built it into a motorcycle. Otto's contributions were very historically significant, it was his four-stroke engine that was universally adopted for all liquid-fuelled automobiles going forward.

The Importance of Karl Benz
In 1885, German mechanical engineer, Karl Benz designed and built the world's first practical automobile to be powered by an internal- combustion engine. On January 29, 1886, Benz received the first patent (DRP No. 37435) for a gas-fuelled car. It was a three-wheeler; Benz built his first four-wheeled car in 1891. Benz & Cie., the company started by the inventor, became the world's largest manufacturer of automobiles by 1900. Benz was the first inventor to integrate an internal combustion engine with a chassis - designing both together.

The Importance of Gottlieb Daimler
In 1885, Gottlieb Daimler (together with his design partner Wilhelm Maybach) took Otto's internal combustion engine a step further and patented what is generally recognized as the prototype of the modern gas engine. Daimler's connection to Otto was a direct one; Daimler worked as technical director of Deutz Gasmotorenfabrik, which Nikolaus Otto co-owned in 1872. There is some controversy as to who built the first motorcycle, Otto or Daimler.

The 1885, the Daimler-Maybach engine was small, lightweight, fast, used a gasoline-injected carburettor, and had a vertical cylinder. The size, speed, and efficiency of the engine allowed for a revolution in car design. On March 8, 1886, Daimler took a stagecoach and adapted it to hold his engine, thereby designing the world's first four-wheeled automobile. Daimler is considered the first inventor to have invented a practical internal-combustion engine.

In 1889, Daimler invented a V-slanted two cylinder, four-stroke engine with mushroom-shaped valves. Just like Otto's 1876 engine, Daimler's new engine set the basis for all car engines going forward. Also in 1889, Daimler and Maybach, built their first automobile from the ground up. They did not adapt another purpose vehicle as they had always been done previously. The new Daimler automobile had a four-speed transmission and obtained speeds of 10 mph.

Photovoltaic Panels

'Photovoltaic' cells are made of special materials called semiconductors, such as silicon, which is currently used most commonly. Basically, when light strikes the cell, a certain portion of it is absorbed within the semiconductor material. This means that the energy of the absorbed light is transferred to the semiconductor. The energy knocks electrons loose, allowing them to flow freely.

PV cells also all have one or more electric fields that act to force electrons freed by light absorption to flow in a certain direction. This flow of electrons is a current, and by placing metal contacts on the top and bottom of the PV cell, we can draw that current off for external use, say, to power a calculator. This current, together with the cell's voltage (which is a result of its built-in electric field or fields), defines the power (or wattage) that the solar cell can produce.

Armoured Fighting Vehicles

The Jackal, or, MWMIK (pronounced EmWimmick), or Mobility Weapon-Mounted Installation Kit. The primary role of the vehicle in the British Army is deep battlespace reconnaissance, rapid assault and fire support - roles where mobility, endurance and manoeuvrability are important – and it has also been used for convoy protection.

CVR(T) (Combat Vehicle Reconnaissance (Tracked)) comes in a number of variants, like Scorpion.

The FVxxx Scorpion, was originally developed to meet a British Army requirement for the Combat Vehicle Reconnaissance (Tracked). Scorpion was accepted by the British Army in May 1970. Main armament consisted of a low velocity 76mm main gun with a coaxial 7.62 mm GPMG. The first production vehicles were completed in 1972. The first British regiment to be equipped with the Scorpion were the Blues and Royals of the Household Cavalry in 1973.

Striker:-

The FV102 Striker was the Anti-tank guided missile version of the CVR(T). Striker had five missiles ready to fire in a mounting at the rear of the vehicle, with another five stowed inside. Secondary armament consisted of a commander 7.62 mm GPMG. Striker looked very similar to Spartan in appearance and it was only when the missile tubes were raised that identification was easier. Striker is no longer in service, since the Swing fire missile was replaced by the Javelin in mid–2005.

Spartan

The FV103 Spartan is a small armoured personnel carrier (APC). It can carry seven men in all with the crew of three and four others in the rear compartment. In the British Army, it is used to carry small specialized groups such as engineer reconnaissance teams, air defence sections and mortar fire controllers. In mid-2006, the British Army had 478 Spartans in service, which from 2009 were being replaced by the Panther Command and Liaison Vehicle in some roles.

The Coats Mission was a special British army unit established in 1940 for the purpose of evacuating King George VI, Queen Elizabeth and their immediate family in the event of German invasion. It was led by Major James Coats, MC, Coldstream Guards, later Lieutenant-Colonel Sir James Coats, Bt.

The force consisted of:

- A special company of the Coldstream Guards. There were five officers and 124 Guardsmen based at Bushey Hall Golf Club. Every officer and Guardsman was personally interviewed by Major Coats before being assigned to the company.

- A troop of the 12th Lancers based at Wellington Barracks, commanded by Lieutenant W.A. Morris, known as the Morris Detachment. They were equipped two Daimler Armoured Cars and four Guy Armoured Cars. Their role was to evacuate the King and Queen. In addition, the four Rolls-Royce Armoured Cars based at the Royal Mews would be attached to the troop in the event of an evacuation.

- A troop of the 2nd Northamptonshire Yeomanry, based at Windsor Castle, commanded by Lieutenant Michael Tomkin. They were equipped with four Guy Armoured Cars. Their role was to evacuate Princess Elizabeth and Princess Margaret.

- A Royal Army Service Corps section of 12 men, with four Leyland Tiger buses, based at Bushey Hall Golf Club. Their role was to transport the Coldstream Guards Company.

- Military police from the Provost Company of the 1st London Division for escort and traffic control, commanded by Captain Sir Malcolm Campbell. At Campbell's suggestion, they were equipped with fast Norton International Model 30 racing motorcycles, rather than the standard military, Norton WD16H of the era.

226

Initially, two of the Guy Armoured Cars in each troop had their guns removed and additional seats installed to carry members of the Royal Family. These were replaced by four specially built Daimler armoured limousines.

Several country houses in remote locations, reportedly including Newby Hall, North Yorkshire, Pitchford Hall, Shropshire, Madresfield Court (Earl Beauchamp's home in Worcestershire), and a fourth unnamed house (possibly Bevere Manor, Worcestershire), were designated as refuges. Madresfield Court reportedly replaced Croome Court, Worcester (the home of the Earl of Coventry) in 1940. It was also a safe house for King George III in the late eighteenth century, in the event of an invasion by Napoleon.

The mission was disbanded in 1942 and the task of evacuating the Royal Family in an emergency was transferred to a detachment from the Household Cavalry Composite Regiment.

Pindar

The most important military citadel in central London–and arguably in Britain–is Pindar, a bunker built deep beneath the Ministry of Defence on Whitehall. Its construction, which took ten years and reportedly cost £126.3 million, finally came to a conclusion in 1994, but Pindar became operational two years earlier, in 1992. The high cost became the subject of some controversy in the early 1990s. Much of the cost overrun was related to the facility's computer equipment, which proved extremely difficult to install due to the very limited degree of physical access to the site. Pindar's main function is to serve as a crisis management and communications centre, principally between the MOD headquarters and the actual centre of military operations, the Permanent Joint Headquarters in Northwood. It is reported to be connected to Downing Street and the Cabinet Office by a tunnel under Whitehall. In addition, despite rumours, armed Forces Minister, Jeremy Hanley, told the House of Commons on 29th April 1994 that 'the facility' is not connected to any transport system. Although Pindar is not open to the public, it has had some public exposure.

In the 2003 BBC documentary on the Iraq conflict, *Fighting the War,* BBC cameras were allowed into the facility to film a small part of a teleconference between ministers and military commanders. Also, in 2008, the British photographer, David Moore, published his SIG P226 series of photographs, *The Last Things,* widely believed to be an extensive photographic survey of Pindar. The name Pindar is taken from the ancient Greek poet, whose house alone was left standing after his city was razed in 335 BCE.

The Haves
The group of people, who live an exaggerated, self-indulgent, excessive, life style, in contemporary society enjoying all of the comforts and advantages of the privileged minority living in the twenty first century. An enormous consumer of the earth's limited resources, adding massively to global pollution and destruction of the incredible finite balance, which is the mechanism that is best described as Mother Nature. Alternatively, the farming community in the (civilised world), whose technology has been racing forward for the past century, will have to learn to turn the clock backwards.

The Have Nots
The greater percentages of human beings living on the planet are those below the poverty line, enduring a peasant existence at medieval levels. This is by far the larger group who live a hand to mouth existence; subsistence farmers, scraping a living and taking little from the planet other than what is essential for them to survive. This group's habitat and way of life is fast becoming eroded by the continual spread of greed by 'the haves', which necessitates cutting into the natural environment in order to sustain their way of life. The irony of this is that many of those 'without' aspire to what they see as improving their lives and move into the zone of the Haves.

Vignettes Omen

Armageddon -1 day before

Troy Tarantula

As he walked across the tarmac toward the gleaming private jet, Troy Tarantula, felt decidedly smug. He hadn't fallen into the same trap that some of his contemporaries had done and bought his own. He had worked out that this ultimate luxury haemorrhaged money. He was much too bright for that he decided. Troy had seen other rock stars fall for the highly esteemed ultimate toy which had then savagely slashed through their bank accounts like a hot knife through butter. The next step was to sell it off at a greatly reduced price and go back on the road for yet another final farewell tour. It was a bridge too far for Troy. No, whenever he felt the need to take to the air, he hired it. The occasion for this jolly was a highly publicised music concert in Barcelona, which he decided he had to attend, albeit as a guest. In reality, he was thoroughly pissed off by not being included in the star-studded line-up due to petty indifferences between the headliners, agents and record companies. His plan was to go and steal the spotlight with his special brand of charisma. He took with him an entourage of hangers on, numbering a dozen in all. Troy was a generous man, his fortune had come to him effortlessly and part of his contrived persona was to be notorious for splashing the cash as long as the paparazzi were there to catch the event on camera, resulting in significant column inches in the appropriate red top newspapers and musical journals. The group was made up mostly of pop musicians, typically the wannabe's and the also-rans. None had hit the jackpot to anything like the extent that Troy had. Some were still touring and Spider, the drummer, made his living as a plumber. They all clowned around as was expected of them; after all, at this moment, they were all rock stars.

The group was welcomed aboard by the Captain, ably assisted by two attractive female hostesses who had been specially requested by Troy and had introduced some of his previous flight guests to the mile high club. To most folk, the bill for this extravaganza would have appeared enormous, but in Troy's mind, it was well worth the money, as when he walked away after the trip there were no other bills to pay. So smug did he feel that he sat back in the lavish deeply cushioned executive seat and contemplated upgrading his Range Rover, part of his fleet of seven cars, four motorbikes and a fifty foot gin palace; all of which were only to be expected, he mused, by someone of his talent and position in the pop monarchy. The reality was that Troy's charisma level was by most people's judgement on par with an AIDS virus, but, in the world that he inhabited, he was noble and had the trivia bling and a bank balance to prove it.

After causing the planned stir from his bad boy antics at the Barcelona pop concert, and gaining the valuable infamous publicity in the world press, Troy Tarantula flew back to England in the jet he hired, where he had stretch limousines waiting at the airport to take him and his 'friends' to the seventeen bedroom mansion in which he lived. The mansion had originally been constructed in the nineteenth century by an innovator of the industrial revolution whose meteoric rise to wealth allowed him to employ the finest architects and tradesmen to create a strikingly beautiful home in the high Georgian style, full of many innovative features. The land and gardens encompassed over one hundred acres. A highly respected landscape architect of the period was employed and sculpted the Brand farmland to form a tranquil, peaceful retreat. Now, having fallen from the hands of the landed gentry due to heavy death duties, the property had experienced a huge reversal of fate. It was currently owned by Mr. Tarantula, who had brought about his own modifications to the grade one listed building, much to the aversion of the local authorities who were constantly threatening the eccentric owner, but to no avail. The tranquil gardens no longer offered leisurely walks among established exotic, rare trees and shrubs, but rather a track for off road vehicles, quad bikes and trail bikes. The portico facade was now adorned by several zip wires which allowed screaming adults and children to slide across the graceful front courtyard, which had in bygone days, been used to deposit the occupants of elegant horse drawn carriages to the main entrance of the magnificent mansion. A huge, three meter, black, fibre glass spider, was emblazoned above the entrance representing Troy's version of a coat of arms for his pile.

The central heating ran at full blast summer and winter. If it became too hot in the house during the summer, then windows and doors were opened, but it never occurred to Troy to turn off the heating. Troy had seven children. His daughter, Butterfly, the eldest, had grown up like a hothouse plant in the mansion where her father had installed several stepmothers, and six step brothers and sisters, all derived from the selection of second, third and fourth wives.

Troy had been born, Peter Fleming, the son of a long term unemployed pottery worker. His early life had been miserable, but salvation came in the shape of a guitar which Peter purchased from a pawnshop, and which he taught himself to play. It has to be said that he was good. Unable to read a note of music he had a natural talent, and what he lacked in technique, he made up for by turning up the volume on his amplifier. As his career progressed he was able to buy larger, louder and more powerful amps, and so his fame in tandem with the extreme noise he projected, expanded. He added to his stage persona by wearing outrageous costumes and uttering a stream of expletives whenever interviewed. Smashing up the occasional hotel suite and wrecking expensive cars, put the finishing touches to his pop personality. Later that night, sitting in the garden of his much modified home with a group of friends after a heavy afternoon off roading, which was followed by a huge meal, supplied by the local Indian restaurant, Troy smoked a spliff. He was happy, surrounded by his like-minded friends, plus an array of plastic containers left over from the Indian meal. The moon was just rising above the magnificent Cyprus trees recently adorned with a powder blue tongued and grooved clad tree house. The moon's golden halo was bright and clear. Troy glanced at the unfamiliar moon. "Fuck me," he moaned quietly, to nobody in particular. Pursing his lips, he blew a long, slow stream of exhaled breath over the glowing end of his spiff. Studying it intensely, he murmured again, "This really is good shit!"

Lin Foo

Lin Foo, sat in the corner of the rudimentary stable and looked on in wonder as the newly born calf finally managed to stand. It's mother, Moonshine, licked the remains of the afterbirth from the soft fur along her new-born's back and made a low contented motherly sound. This was not the first birth that Lin Foo had witnessed. Ever since he could remember, there had been cattle in the village. Not to the extent that he had seen on the Communist Party centre's television, where in some countries there were herds of cattle. So many cows that Lin Foo could hardly imagine how they could possibly all be looked after. But individual births to neighbours and other small holding farmers' cattle were a common event in this community.

Lin Foo had also been present at the birth of his son at the Party's new hospital. He was allowed to produce a single offspring, so the visit to the maternity hospital would undoubtedly be a once in a lifetime event for this generation. This latest birth was a special occasion because he now owned two cows, which in time would give him a surplus of milk, that could be sold, or if he decided, he could sell the older cow and realise a profit.

The next months would be challenging. The family would have to share the milk with the new calf, but Moonshine had always produced a good quantity of milk, and although it would be difficult, he felt confident that all would be well. There would be big decisions to be made in the coming months. The meagre pasture where Moonshine grazed was barely enough to keep her, so as soon as the new calf was weaned, Lin Foo would have to make his decision. In the harsh life in which Lin Foo existed, happy events were rare, and this one was overshadowed by impending events which had the ability to change Lin Foo's life forever. The Communist Party leader for the village had summoned everyone in the tiny community to weekly meetings over the past eighteen months. Lin Foo had attended more from obligation than desire. What he heard disturbed him greatly and he chose not to accept that the day of reckoning would soon actually arrive. The spread of industrialisation, which was rapidly advancing throughout the Province of Zhejiang like a creeping cancer (for this was how Lin Foo viewed it), was nearing his doorstep. The Party leader had shown the villagers films of high-rise apartment blocks, expounding on the wonderful advantages of electricity, running water, Spartan rooms and piped TV. Lin Foo had only received a rudimentary education but he was intelligent to perceive that the programs shown on the only channel was a diet of unashamed propaganda.

There would be employment for everyone in the new factories, schools for his son and so many advantages that the party leader promised, that his head swam with this temptation of a modern lifestyle. Living in the sky held no illusions for Lin Foo, but having clean, hot and cold running water just by turning on a tap, was tempting. Electricity and all of the gadgets that it could power was also exceedingly seductive. However, in order to have all of these luxuries there must be a hidden agenda. Taps could be disconnected and electricity switched off. Lighting and heating his home sounded wonderful, but it had to be paid for. Living in the sky meant that he was controlled, and would be nothing more than a slave to the Party. He had lived all of his life working from dawn till dusk. Light came from the sky and was free. This was the way that it had always been for him and for his ancestors.

Moonshine was much more than just a cow. She produced milk and had given Lin Foo, three offspring. She pulled the plough and in the harsh days of winter she was brought into the rickety stable adjoining the living accommodation where the heat from her body helped to keep the family warm.

Living in the sky was not what Lin Foo aspired to. Although life was harsh and the harvests unpredictable, he was his own Boss, albeit within the confines imposed by the Party. His feet were on the ground and the ground was his. There was no

232

room in the apartment in the sky for Moonshine.

Lin Foo sat in the tiny yard of his meagre plot of land. Furniture was limited and he was reduced to sitting on the stool which he used when milking Moonshine. His mind was troubled, envisaging the impending changes that were about to impact severely on his life. He looked up and there was the moon, climbing silently above the crest of the distance ancient mountains peaks into a sky filled with ominously dark threatening clouds. It looks strange, so much different from normal. There was a bright golden circle surrounding the silver moon. Lin Foo studied the unusual phenomenon. The ancestors had talked of such a moon and it was said that it was an omen of terrible things to come.

THE END?

It doesn't have to be this way. There is still time if we wake up now!

The Future?

I have endeavoured to write a novel elucidating the catastrophic impact from the scenario that I have created, set in England from the perspective of one group of individuals. But this disaster has more far reaching implications that will spread around the entire globe. There is a multitude of exciting directions that a sequel could take and I look forward to working on that. In addition, I would like to look at this series of consequences and the inevitable outcomes from the viewpoint of other countries. This manuscript is a template for the wider picture. Imagine the ramifications that this disaster would create for example, in the USA? They would vary from the English experience in many ways.

Likewise, how would poorer countries deal with this and what would be the effect resultant of consequences from the consequential nuclear assaults? This is a huge canvas which holds much potential.

Conspiracy theory

All of the major and minor terrorist groups were quick to claim responsibility for the disaster. It was proclaimed to be a sophisticated, well planned, attack by all of these radical factions boasting that they were now using advanced biological warfare. This was a short-lived propaganda endeavour in an amazingly short time the media ceased to exist in the petroleum dependent regions of the world. The ironic truth of this scenario was that there were no winners, only losers. The loss of mobility and the significances of the consequential effects impacted upon all regardless of wealth, race, colour, education or religious belief. Every man, woman and child would be looking out for themselves in a survival situation.

David S. Jones

Epilogue

The era of the marauding gangs would be short lived. They would stay mainly in the towns and live off what was available. This stock would soon be depleted and the gangs would resort to fighting each other until they were in turn exterminated. Tens of millions would die from hunger, water contamination, disease and violence. The survival of the fittest or natural selection in this case, would not mean that the best people would survive. Many of the survivors, who would last the longest, particularly in the towns, would be those who were able to take what they needed from the weakest. Human nature, mankind, can quickly revert to extreme violence where survival is concerned.

Doom and gloom would be a pitiful description for the devastation that I have predicted but stability would eventually return. The greatly depleted population would start to rebuild as civilisations have done throughout history. If this were to happen my only prayer would be to hope that the next generation learn from the past and don't repeat the same mistakes in the future. We are at the end of a failed experiment. A privileged segment of mankind has embarked upon a path of environmental recklessness. The finite resources which allowed us to climb to heights, which were only limited by our own imagination, are now dramatically spiralling downwards.

Mankind still retains the aggressive gene, which has enabled us to survive. This gene, which is within all people, will be the deciding factor of who will survive – The Armageddon Virus/ ICE Virus.

In future we must learn to work with the grain of the Earth not against it. In all of this disaster there were some minor but surprising benefits. Smoking, alcoholism, drug abuse and obesity were all eradicated.

Jacko set his men tasks, in an attempt to take their minds off of what was happening, just the other side of the barrack wall. He was stunned by the ingenuity of his men.

Democratic civilisation in the western world as it had been known would cease to exist. Any enemies that Great Britain may have had would now be neutralised and if any of them could have raised an army … to what end?

Why invade Britain now?   A depleted nation without wealth, and in addition, prone to predominately terrible weather, there would be no advantage. Evolution (or lack of) in motor transport.

The aeroplane preceded the motor car in its present form by approximately only fifteen years, but the evolution of these two revolutionary forms of transport has not evolved at anything like the same pace in the one hundred years plus since their conception. About fifty years after the first flight, jet engines were invented, advancing air transportation phenomenally. This evolutionary process has not been the case for motor transport, which has retained the same configuration of piston, valves, con-rod and crankshaft, continuing to be the basis for a large percentage of land based propulsion. Four wheels driven by an internal combustion engine continues to be the rudimentary layout, although there are now numerous refinements and accessories that have been added. With the huge advance in technology available, fifty years after the first motor vehicles rattled tentatively around our roads it would have been reasonable to assume that, like aircraft a second generation of vehicle propulsion should have evolved.

The steam engine was the power house of the Industrial Revolution. Motorised transport driven by the ICE undoubtedly transformed the world making horse power, for the greater part redundant, changing the beast of burden, that had for millennium been the means by which goods and people were carried across land, to a recreational pet. There were some enclaves where the horse continued to be used.

About sixty years ago in the UK milk was delivered by horse drawn milk carts. This was one of the last bastions of horse drawn transport and was generally replaced by electrically driven milk floats in the 1950's. These electric vehicles were able to function for a full working day, eight hours and are still used in some areas today. The question that has to be asked is why, sixty years ago a vehicle existed that could be powered by electricity and sustain a working day, but has not been significantly technologically advanced?

If research and development had been focused on refining those early electric engines and the storage of electrical current, the transformation from ICE to electric could have been made; what would the world that we are living in today look like? The Western World had been indoctrinated into deviating from the natural evolutionary path that it would have taken and lured into a society of greed and waste. I ask you to imagine a world where the transformation from vehicles driven by a crude oil derivative to a relatively pollution free electricity sixty years ago would look like.

Pollution
Sixty years of pollution from vehicles burning carbon, emitting hazardous carbon dioxide exhaust fumes.

Effects on Global Warming
The rape of Mother Earth in the scramble to discover new deposits of oil, this finite commodity. Oil spillage causing untold damage to wildlife and the environment. The high cost due to transportation of crude oil around the planet.

Health
It would be impossible to even attempt at estimating how much damage has been done to health through extracting crude oil from the ground and transforming it into combustible fuel.

Fire
Fire and the consequence of highly flammable liquid being transported around our towns, villages and even our homes.
Huge storage depots, trains and tankers both at sea and on land, vulnerable to fire and explosion.

War.
And perhaps the most important factor to be considered. Wars that are perpetuated by the mindless scramble to control the production and distribution of crude oil. Countless lives have been lost in the greed that accompanies the wealth derived from oil. Much of the pollution that has proliferated upon the planet in its various guises need not have happened. If we had made the transition from ICE to electrically driven transport more than half a century ago, which I sincerely believe could have been achieved, the planet that we are privileged to live upon would be a significantly different place.

So to summarise who have been the winners and losers in this scenario. Who has benefitted the most?

There are alternative forms of propulsion being made available now, but I have no doubt that these could have been attainable six decades ago.

The course of humanity has to be altered if we are not to bequeath a catastrophic

238

legacy to future generations. We are facing a global disaster that we cannot afford to keep on ignoring. We have been mesmerized into our dependency upon fossil fuels, the majority of which could have been avoided.

This summary is not driven by a political or an ultra green agenda. Just simple logic.

ABOUT THE AUTHOR

David S. Jones was born in London during 'The Blitz'. Upon leaving school at fifteen with nothing more than a cycling proficiency certificate, he tried various jobs. At eighteen he joined the Middlesex Fire Brigade, serving three years, until eventually leaving for Australia on the ten pound assisted passage scheme. Returning some years later, he joined the Household Cavalry and served in Malaya with the Armoured Reconnaissance Squadron. Back home in the UK, after his tour of duty overseas, he became part of the Mounted Ceremonial Squadron, based in Knightsbridge, riding on several prestigious events, including the investiture of Prince Charles at Caernarvon. Having left the Army he worked at various jobs, mostly as a carpenter but also driving trucks.

Eventually, he found unlikely employment as a personal bodyguard to an American millionaire and entrepreneur, travelling throughout Europe. The journey eventually took them to Portugal, he left this employment (he was actually fired!), met and married his Portuguese wife. David has four children from that marriage, two living in Portugal and two in the UK.

He later returned to London and joined the London Fire and Rescue Service, serving for a further eleven years. It was during this time that he had the idea to create the children's character, Fireman Sam, now an international success as a children's TV series. After sustaining a back injury, David had to leave the Fire Service. It then became necessary for him to make a living by doing something, which did not require physical involvement. This led to him developing his writing skills.

Having left the fire service he returned to his beloved Portugal, eventually building and managing a highly successful bar/restaurant complex in the Algarve. He formed a construction company and built some stunning villas. Life then took a sadder path when his marriage failed. Following his divorce and having custody of the children, he concentrated on bringing them up until they had flown the nest. This was a dark and difficult period. Once the children had gone, he decided to raise some money and live his life to the full. After selling his shares in Fireman Sam, he obtained a skipper's licence, bought an ocean going sailing boat, which he named 'Thankusam', and sailed it from the UK to Portugal and later to North Africa.

He has continued to develop as a writer over the past years, and several of his ideas have been considered for TV and film, both in the UK and America.

David is a published fiction author but his latest work 'Halo around the Moon' is a venture into a new genre for him. His style of writing and ability to develop a good story line makes his work hard to put down.

"Halo is much more than just a novel," he says, "It's a wakeup call for humanity to alter course before it's too late."

By Clive Pearson Evans, Welsh poet and sailing buddy.

Read more: http://www.david-s-jones.com

Halo around the Moon

Printed in Great Britain
by Amazon